Playing with Mr. Grant
Elle Nicoll

Rose Hope Publishing Ltd.

Copyright © 2024 By Elle Nicoll

Published by Rose Hope Publishing Ltd.

All rights reserved.

Visit my website at www.ellenicollauthor.com

Cover Design: Abi at Pink Elephant Designs

Formatting: Atticus

Editing: The Blue Couch Edits

No part of this book may be reproduced or transmitted in any form or by any means, electronically or mechanically, including photocopying, recording, or by any information storage and retrieval system without the written permission of the author, except for the use of brief quotations in a book review. It must not be used for any AI training or other means including AI.

This book is a work of fiction, written solely by a human, with a human touch. Names, characters, places, and incidents are either products of the author's imagination or are used fictitiously. Any resemblance to actual persons, living or dead, events, or locales is entirely coincidental.

Note for readers – The eBook of Playing with Mr. Grant is available exclusively to Amazon. If you are reading this anywhere else, then you do not have an original copy.

Content Warnings—This book is intended for adult readers only and contains profanities, detailed sexual acts, reference to family loss, grief, trauma.

To maintain flow with the rest of The Men series, this book is edited in mostly American English, with some British spellings and terminology due to part of the story taking place in the UK with British characters.

Contents

Dedication	VII
Prologue	1
1. Jet	5
2. Ava	11
3. Jet	19
4. Ava	29
5. Jet	37
6. Ava	47
7. Ava	57
8. Jet	71
9. Ava	81
10. Jet	95
11. Ava	107
12. Ava	119
13. Ava	129
14. Jet	147

15.	Ava	155
16.	Jet	171
17.	Ava	183
18.	Jet	195
19.	Ava	203
20.	Jet	219
21.	Ava	225
22.	Jet	235
23.	Ava	249
24.	Ava	255
25.	Jet	265
26.	Jet	279
27.	Ava	293
28.	Jet	309
29.	Ava	321
30.	Ava	335
31.	Ava One month later	345
32.	Jet	363
33.	Ava	371
34.	Ava	379
35.	Jet	389
36.	Ava	401

37.	Ava	407
38.	Jet	425
39.	Ava Two weeks later	435
40.	Jet	441
41.	Jet Six months later	445
42.	Ava Twenty-four hours later	451
43.	Ava	477
Epilogue - Jet		483
Epilogue - Ava		487
Bonus Epilogue - Ava Five Years Later		499
Elle's Books		523
About Elle		525
Acknowledgements		527

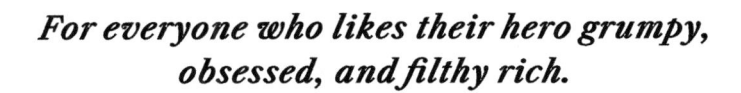

For everyone who likes their hero grumpy, obsessed, and filthy rich.

(Please turn back to copyright page for content warnings)

Prologue

The damp from the mulch seeps through my sock, stones biting into my skin through the thin fabric.

I shift my weight to my other foot, the one in the blood-soaked sneaker. Just then, a fat raindrop splashes my nose like an obnoxious taunt, reminding me I'm still here.

Alone.

Alive. But alone.

My clothes, still damp and musty from yesterday's rain, cling to me. I've been here for one night. I should count them. The more that come, the smaller my chance of being found.

I shiver, pushing away further thoughts. I need to concentrate on walking. One weak step at a time.

A sound makes me squint up through the tree branches. It's a tiny rumble. But it's *something*.

I break into a run, feeding oxygen to my aching muscles. Branches tear at my skin, embedding my flesh with dirt. The trees don't want me to leave. The forest wants to suck me up and swallow me whole.

A branch scrapes across my cheek, the burn and throb in my skin instantaneous. But I ignore it, pushing forward as the sound grows louder.

I want to call out, but they won't hear me.

There's a clearing up ahead.

So close.

They're right above me now, the sound almost deafening. My heartbeat matches the deep vibrations coursing through the previously still air.

So close.

I rush forward, a warm, comforting sensation sparking in my chest at the thought of seeing my grandparents. I imagine helping Gran make lasagna. Reading those adventure stories with my grandfather before bed. The ones I pretend I'm too old for but we read anyway because we both secretly love them. Later, I'll sleep in the bedroom they decorated for me. The one with walls the color of sand and a print of a beach with glowing water.

So close.

The air is punched from my lungs and dirt smashes into my face, reaching inside my mouth as I fall. I tug my foot, but my sneaker is snagged on a root. My ankle stings as I twist it at an unnatural angle to free myself.

Nine of my nails are black as I sink them into the ground to push to my feet. I don't know what happened to the tenth. The tip of my finger is red, caked with dried blood instead.

I stagger, planting a palm against a thick trunk to steady myself.

So close.

I break through the tree line and throw my arms in the air, screaming at the top of my lungs.

Raindrops fall into my eyes, the noise from the downpour muffling the sound I'm craning to hear. It keeps falling, unrelenting, and I struggle to see.

The sound quietens.

Pain shoots up my leg and causes me to drop to my knees.

So I crawl.

I bite my lip to stop the tears as I inch toward the center of the open scrubland.

They *have* to see me.

A deep bellow of thunder rumbles through the air, unnerving my every cell, and leaving them shaking in its wake. The earth groans beneath my hands and knees.

Then it falls quiet.

Relief floods my veins. I won't allow the next clap to catch me off guard. I'll be prepared.

I swipe another raindrop from my cheek as a crack of lightning forks across the ominous gray sky. The storm was forecast to hit Friday—today. *That Friday feeling.* That's what Dad calls it when I'm in a rush for the weekend to start. We're going to the estate this weekend. I can see the lilies. They'll be in full bloom. The thought distracts me for a blissful moment.

Wait. It's quiet.

I crane my neck to search the sky.

They've moved away. The storm's making them leave.

I'm alone.

Again.

So close.

Chapter 1

Jet

"Too close." I drum my fingers against the cool glass of the meeting room table.

My CFO, Hayden, a man who rarely looks flustered, tugs at his tie.

He's rattled, which means we aren't only too close, we're too *fucking* close.

"How long?" I ask, my gut twisting.

"Two, three months, max." He reaches for his glass of water with a trembling hand, draining it quickly before it clatters against the table. "Things have been bad before, Jet, but—"

"It's not over yet." I run my tongue over my teeth as I stare past his head, through the glass wall at the staff working away, oblivious to our crisis meeting.

"It's thirty percent of the fleet."

I bristle, cracking my neck. I've done the fucking math.

"Thirty-one," I mutter. "Thirty-one percent."

Hayden's eyes, red-rimmed from the late nights we've pulled this week, meet mine. Despite all the figures we've crunched, we keep coming back to the same number.

Thirty-one percent.

It's enough to fold the entire operation. What use is an airline if its planes can't fly?

"We made some savings with the fuel hedging, but..."

Hayden refills his glass instead of completing his sentence. He knows that deal means shit if we don't have planes to put the fuel in.

"I'll speak to Rich." Tension tightens my jaw. Going from LA to London seems wrong when my staff need me here.

"Logan Rich?"

"His biofuel engines have already been approved for the aircraft's type rating. If we can get them refitted when they're in for maintenance, we might be able to run a full operation."

His eyes brighten for the first time in days. "I'll speak to the contracts department. Biofuel will mean a lower cost per seat. If we can run at a lower rate, then..." He's already typing on his laptop, his fingers flying over the keys.

"Good." I stand, buttoning my jacket. "I'll get Annabelle to clear my schedule for a few days. I shouldn't be long in London."

I walk through the open-plan office, tipping my chin in terse greeting to the heads that turn my way.

My PA, Annabelle, is frowning at her computer as I approach.

"Mr. Grant?" She looks up with an eager smile.

"I need you to clear my meetings for the next three days. And get me on the next flight to London."

With that, I walk into my office, barely glancing at the skyline of downtown LA through the floor-to-ceiling windows. It's a view I've seen every day since I took over from Atlantic Airways' previous CEO for US operations five years ago.

"The board meeting too?"

"Especially that." I turn to Annabelle as she scurries in behind me, gripping a tablet tightly in one hand while tapping the screen to make notes. "Reschedule everything for when I'm back."

"Consider it done." She lifts her eyes to mine. "Shall I book you in at the Savoy?"

I walk to my desk and pick up the phone. "That won't be necessary... That's all, Annabelle."

Nodding, she hurries from the room, closing the door on her way out. She's timid, but her work is good. I hope she lasts longer than the last one.

I check my watch as the call connects. It's mid-afternoon in London.

"Son?" My father's warm voice filters down the line.

"Dad." I sink into my chair and spin to face the window.

"Everything okay? I wasn't expecting to speak to you until tomorrow's meeting."

I stare at the bright blue sky. Another hot day in California. It matches the rising heat in my blood as I lie to my father with sickening ease. The UK fleet doesn't have the same aircraft as the US. He has no idea.

"Everything's fine. I'm coming over to speak with Logan Rich about his company's biofuel engines. Can I stay at the house? Then I can fill you in on things here."

"Of course you can." The lilt in his voice is unassuming, trusting. We haven't seen one another face-to-face for weeks. I'm overdue a visit.

And this conversation definitely warrants for that.

"I won't be interrupting anything?"

"Hold on." My father's voice muffles as he moves away from the phone, likely speaking to someone else, before returning back to the line. "Just checking."

"Checking?"

"That the playgirl bunnies I have around between your visits can manage without me."

"And can they?" I stretch my fingers out on the arm of my chair in an attempt to loosen the ache caused by hours of typing out figures.

"They said they'll manage." He chuckles.

"That's a relief," I reply dryly. The thought of my father with anyone, let alone someone half his age is ludicrous, yet it's not the first time I've heard the joke.

"I'll tell Margaret to expect you in case I'm not in when you arrive."

Ah, the new housekeeper. He keeps them longer than I keep my PAs. But it's a shame Bella retired. I liked her and her no-nonsense approach to running my father's house.

"Okay, fine," I clip, spinning back to my desk and clicking into a report on my computer I need to go over.

"Bye, Son."

I end the call and lift my head as Annabelle peers around the door.

"You're on the 78 at three p.m."

I nod, and she returns to her desk.

I've got five hours to find a solution before I board that flight.

Otherwise, I need to pray to god I'll find it in London.

Chapter 2

Ava

I STUDY THE KEYPAD. *Main reception. Deliveries. Pool house.*

Did I miss the part where my grandfather told me his old school friend owns a mansion? I figured Magnus Grant would be wealthy, but this is just one of his properties near London. I was expecting a cute cottage with a pretty garden to sit in while I work. Not a beautiful Georgian mansion.

Intricate moldings around the roof peek out from behind a sprawling lawn that's decorated with topiary bushes. One's even shaped like a plane. Grandfather said Magnus was a plane enthusiast, always making those DIY models at boarding school. It makes sense that his family own an airline.

I hover over the intercom before stabbing a guess and pressing the button for main reception. There's an extended pause before a female voice answers, "Yes?"

I angle my face up toward the security camera on the gate's stone pillar.

I flash my best grin, hoping it conveys gratitude for the fact I'm coming to stay rent-free for the next couple of months. I had wanted to contribute, but Magnus wouldn't hear of it. It was a relief, because having just completed my master's degree in business and, with no job lined up yet, money is tight.

"Hi. I'm Ava Roberts. William's grand daug—"

"I know who you are," the voice clips. "Come to the back door. I've just had the entryway stone polished."

"Okay," I say, but the intercom has already shut off.

The giant black metal gates slide open, and I drag my suitcase up the gravel driveway. Gramps lent it to me, not realizing it'd lost one of its wheels until he took it out of the attic. There wasn't time to get a new one, and it wouldn't have been worth it anyway. After all, I won't be using it again.

By the time I find the back door, my arm is aching. I rub my shoulder before raising my fist to knock on the old wooden door. A small woman with pinched features and graying hair pulled back in a tight French twist opens it.

"You're pretty." She purses her lips. "Is your hair naturally that color?"

I tuck a loose auburn strand behind my ear. "Yep, I inherited it from my mother."

She admires it, and I half expect her to reach out to stroke it.

"Very well." Her thin lips stretch into a small smile. "I'm Margaret, the housekeeper. Welcome to Rochwell House."

She stands aside to let me in. I drag my suitcase in and glance at the door as I pass. The wood is solid and thick, closing with a deep thud.

"Follow me. I'll show you to your room."

I follow Margaret up the flagstone hallway, passing an old wooden staircase. We walk into the kitchen, an airy room with cream units and a white stone countertop. It's bigger than the house I was living in at the university.

My eyes bounce around the space as I take in the rows of matching mugs hanging beneath some open shelving, a giant bean to cup machine on the counter beneath them.

"You can help yourself to anything you like. I've stocked this fridge for you." Margaret opens a cupboard to reveal a hidden fridge stuffed full of fresh fruit and snacks. The inside door is lined with cartons of my favorite grapefruit juice. "Mr. Grant asked William what you liked," she adds.

"Wow, thanks," I say, glancing at the eight-seater table set up in front of a large glass door that leads out onto the manicured lawns.

"You can eat breakfast and lunch here, should you wish. I don't come in until the afternoon. Mr. Grant is home around seven, and dinner is served at seven-thirty in the dining room. There's an outdoor heated pool and pool house. He thought you might like to use the pool house to work in."

"That's so kind of him... I can't believe this." I admire the single-story pool house out of the window. "And I love to swim. But I didn't pack a bathing suit, I'll have to order one."

Margaret hitches a brow and her eyes rake over my cropped jeans and T-shirt. "Yes, I suppose you will. Now, there's no bathing suits to be worn wet inside the house. These old floors are a nightmare for slipping on when wet. And I don't like tending to broken bones."

"Noted. No bathing suits in the house."

She nods in approval. She's the housekeeper, and I'm merely a guest in this amazing house. Magnus Grant has saved me from having to move back in with Gramps. As much as I love him, I'll never get the project I'm working on finished. We just keep talking when we're together. I'll agree to every rule Margaret sets in order to make sure I don't abuse Magnus's hospitality.

She shows me around the rest of the ground floor, then we go outside, and I get to appreciate the full expanse of beautiful gardens as we walk to the pool house. It's the perfect base to work. There's a sofa area and a workspace set up, and it has a small bathroom and mini refrigerator.

"David, the landscaper, comes three times a week," Margaret tells me as we head back inside the house and climb the grand staircase in the foyer. "You can invite friends over, but if they're staying for dinner, I require notice."

"My friend, Liv, might come. But she's studying so it would only be for a day or two."

I can picture Liv's face when she sees Magnus's house. She'll be awestruck just like me.

"Very well," she clips as she leads me along the hallway, stopping in front of a closed door. "I'm afraid you'll have to make do with this room. The guest suite is being decorated."

I nod, and she opens the door that leads into a giant, bright room, decorated in cream and white. In the center is a modern four poster bed, minus drapes, and there are doors that lead out onto a small balcony overlooking the garden.

"Oh my goodness." I clap my palms and bounce on the spot, earning myself an amused look from Margaret. She resembles a strict mother. One full of kindness beneath a misleading, rigid exterior. I bet I can have her laughing before my time here is over.

I set my suitcase down at the foot of the bed and take in the vintage airline prints adorning the walls.

"The bathroom is through here." Margaret walks past me, and I follow her through a dressing area, half-filled with men's suits, to the doorway of a marble bathroom with a giant rainfall shower.

"Mr. Grant has beautiful taste," I say as I stare open-mouthed, excitement bubbling through me at the luxurious surroundings.

"He does. He's extremely specific about what he likes." She looks at the dressing room rails. "That side is empty. But if you need more space for your clothes, I can get these suits put into storage."

"No, I don't want to be any bother." I walk over to a giant set of drawers on the empty side of the room and slide the top one open. I bite back my grin at the luxury velvet-lined compartments inside.

Perfect.

"I'll leave you to unpack. Dinner is at—"

"Seven-thirty. Thank you so much." I beam at her, and she nods with a satisfied smile at my obedience.

Once she leaves, I grab my phone from my purse to video call Liv, unable to keep the Cheshire cat grin off my face.

"Hey, Bitch," she answers. "How's the new work retreat?"

"Stunning."

I pan the phone around the room and then go out onto the balcony to show her the grounds.

"Are you fucking kidding me?"

I laugh as she shoves her long black hair out of her eyes and gawks.

"It's official. I'm jealous." She sighs. "I'd get a ton of work done if I was there and not living with a bunch of noisy, overgrown mummies' boys."

I smile at her description. The guys she lives with near campus are a nice, if loud, bunch, especially when it comes to hosting mid-week parties. But she's right.

They're all mummies' boys that take their laundry home every weekend.

Liv still has a year of her marketing degree left. I'm so glad I've already graduated and can have my own space.

"I'm grateful to Gramps for setting this up." I sink into a wicker chair on the balcony and gaze out over the lush green lawn.

"He's a legend," Liv agrees. "And you'll get loads done, being somewhere without distractions. It'll be good for you. *So* good for you."

"You're right."

"I always am." She winks.

She and Gramps have been saying the same thing for years. I need this. It's time I did it.

"Magnus said I can have guests. Why don't you come one weekend?"

"Sounds amazing," Liv hums.

We chat for another twenty minutes, the warm glow of talking about nothing in particular with my friend spreading through my entire body.

"Love you," I say as I wander back inside the room and unzip my suitcase, pulling my laptop out.

Liv blows me a kiss and coos, "Bye, Bitch," before hanging up.

I sit on top of the plush white bedding and fire up my laptop, going straight to the reason I'm here.

The title glares back at me from the open Word document. Two words that bring a barrage of emotions with them.

I hover the cursor over the text, then blow out a ragged breath.

I click on the line below instead and start typing.

Chapter 3

Jet

I LOOSEN MY TIE as I let myself in the front door of my father's house. Atlantic Airways has the most coveted runway slots, yet a strike by London Heathrow baggage handlers means I waited two hours for my suitcase after landing. I guess I should be grateful Logan Rich needed to push today's meeting to tomorrow. It gives me time to go over figures for the rest of the day.

The house is quiet when I set my suitcase on the stone floor of the entryway. My father will still be at work at Atlantic Airways' UK head office until this evening. I plan to freshen up, unpack, then head over there to check on the team.

First things first; a six-and-a-half-hour flight and a baggage delay means one thing... Coffee.

I walk toward the kitchen, alerted to shuffling and the sound of the refrigerator door being opened.

A long pair of legs greets me below the refrigerator door. I study the bright red toenails as one bare foot lifts to rub against the back of one calf.

"You're younger than I expected."

"Jesus! Fuck!"

The carton of juice jerks as she jumps in shock. Light-yellow liquid splashes out of it, soaking her white tank top.

"Were you drinking from the carton?" I grind my molars as I scan her from head to toe, pausing briefly on her red-hued hair.

"No."

Her light blue eyes widen as I arch a brow at the scarlet lipstick ring around the rim of the carton.

"Fuck, okay, yes. You caught me."

"And you cuss openly. Interesting," I mutter.

Her brow furrows before she bends and scoops up the dropped cap from the floor. When she stands, the wet patch on her tank top sticks itself to her chest, revealing a red lace bra underneath.

"Well, I didn't know you were coming today. You scared me." She eyes me curiously, looking at my suit. "Unusual choice of work attire by the way."

It's a struggle to avert my gaze from the red lace as I say, "I could say the same thing about yours."

She narrows her eyes like she's trying to figure me out. "How old are you?"

"Excuse me?"

"You said I'm younger than you expected. How old are you?"

I walk toward her, taking in her bare feet. I need to talk to my father about his recruits. She's clearly unsuitable. What housekeeper walks around barefoot for a start?

"Thirty-three." I extend my hand in greeting.

She eyes it before placing the carton on the counter. The second her wet, juice-covered fingers meet mine in a handshake, my jaw clenches.

"Thirty-three? Wow." She whistles. "I see why you think I'm young. You've got a whole decade on me."

I clench my jaw as her cool fingers coat mine in stickiness.

"It's nice to meet yo—"

"You're twenty-three?" I scoff. "What experience do you have?"

Something akin to defiance flashes in her light irises.

"Enough. What experience do *you* have?"

I suck in a breath through my nose. I might be tired and cranky from the flight, but that doesn't change the fact my father has hired a brat with a bad attitude as his new housekeeper. One who doesn't realize she's doing the equivalent of poking a bear right now.

I take the cap from her other hand and screw it back onto the carton, giving her a pointed look.

"Glasses are in that one." I point at a cupboard, then walk to the sink to wash my hands.

When she snorts, my hands ball into fists beneath the running water, and I glance at her.

"Do the flowers grow better if you wear a tie to water them?" She leans against the counter with her arms folded. The position accentuates the red lace beneath her wet top.

"You think I'm the landscaper?" I dry my hands and turn to face her.

Her plump lips part, and she blinks, confused. "Aren't you?"

Heat fires across the back of my neck as my irritation spikes. "Regardless of who you thought I am, one, next time use a glass. Two, don't cuss while working, and three—"

"Who the fuck are you?"

I stare at her. I should fire her now. Save my father a job.

She inches away from me slowly, her eyes darting to the open doorway.

"Robbers don't let themselves in with a key," I snap, placing my hands onto my hips.

"Then who—?

"Jet."

She looks at me blankly.

"Jet Grant," I snap.

"Oh." She frowns, pausing her creep toward the door. "Magnus said you live in LA?"

The way she calls my father Magnus so easily when she's still in her first week of employment has my shoulders tensing, besides walking around barefoot, wearing a tank and shorts as if she lives here. What's she going to be doing after another week? Registering this address for her personal mail? Walking around nude?

She shivers under my scrutiny.

"I do. But there are these things called planes."

"I'm well aware what a plane is," she snaps.

She continues to watch me as I walk to the coffee machine and flick it on. She's my father's terrible hire. Not mine. He won't be happy if I let her go, despite how tempted I am. Although I'll be making my recommendation the minute I see him.

I roll my neck side to side, cracking it.

"That's bad for your bones."

I repeat the move, forcing another deep crack to ring out in the air.

"And telling me what to do is almost always bad for the other person," I quip, abandoning all sense of civility. I'm tired, under-caffeinated, and have a natural aversion to slackers and freeloaders.

This new housekeeper, young and pretty, or not, is testing my already thin patience.

"Are you always like this?"

"Like what?"

"Rude to guests."

I hover over the coffee machine's button.

"Guests..." I echo before clearing my throat. "You never told me your name."

I don't turn around, unable to see if those pouty lips are wearing a smug smile from uncovering my faux pas. Maybe she hasn't noticed it.

"Ava," she says.

I whirl around. "Ava?"

"Roberts." She raises her chin, holding my eyes.

I narrow mine in response as I regard her. "I see."

"Your father told you I was staying, right?"

I busy myself making my coffee, ignoring her question. To admit that he didn't will be admitting that I thought she was someone else. And that I was wrong.

And I'm never wrong.

"I'll keep out of your way. I'm going to unpack and then head into the office," I say, turning with my coffee in hand.

"Okay. Well, I usually work in the pool house anyway, so..." She shrugs as I blow the steam away from my cup and take a sip.

She looks at me as if she's waiting for me to ask what work she's doing. But I don't care. I don't have time to care.

"Then I guess we'll not see much of each other during my visit." I eye her over the rim of my cup.

"No. I guess not. It was... interesting meeting you." With that, she leaves the room.

The moment she's gone I pull my phone out of my pocket and text dad.

> Me: You didn't mention you had a guest staying?

> Dad: Ava's a friend's granddaughter. You'll love her. Nice girl. She's just graduated and needs somewhere to stay until she finds a job.

I grunt and pocket my phone. A poor, bratty freeloader. Just who my father needs in his house.

I deposit my mug in the dishwasher and grab my suitcase, heading straight to my room. I may not live here anymore, but my father insists I always have a base here, should I need it.

I walk into the dressing room, placing my suitcase down. There's an unfamiliar scent in the air, lemony, but also... aquatic. It must be a new air freshener the real Margaret uses.

I open my suitcase and take out the zip-bag containing my underwear, placing it on the drawers as I slide the top one open. The usually empty velvet interior is filled with meticulously arranged pieces of lace, silk, and pearls.

I hook a crystal strand over one finger and lift it, revealing an intricate lace bodysuit that's light and soft as a feather, swallowing as the unknown scent intensifies, now mixed with something rich and decadent. Like caramel and...

I lean a little closer and inhale.

"What the fuck?"

The material is ripped from my hand in an instant. Blazing blue eyes meet mine.

"Why are you touching my lingerie?"

I jerk back, my eyes dropping over her water-droplet coated skin as she squares up to me wrapped in a white towel.

"This is my room."

"And these are my things." Ava wedges herself in-between me and the drawers like she's protecting them.

"Why are your things in my room?"

"Margaret said this was my room."

I stare at her, wondering where she got such a smart mouth. She's obviously grown up getting away with being a brat. A parent who was poor at discipline, perhaps? One who didn't teach her respect.

"Don't hitch your brows at me like that. Like I'd choose your room if I'd known you were coming back from LA." She spits *LA* out like it tastes sour as she moves to grab an old, battered suitcase and flings it open on the floor.

She huffs as she holds her towel around her and approaches the drawers. Despite the tension radiating from her, her movements soften as the top drawer slides open.

She starts to place the contents of the drawer inside the suitcase. She does it carefully, lovingly, a sereneness washing over her features as she curls her fingers around each item.

"That's expensive lingerie for an unemployed student," I say, spotting a price tag on a deep mocha-colored thong in the drawer.

"I'm a graduate. And what exactly are you implying?" She whirls to face me, dropping the pink panties in her hand on the floor.

Manners make me bend to retrieve them. Her fingers brush mine as she takes them back, a blush creeping up her neck.

"It's merely an observation," I reply coolly, my eyes trained on her as she resumes her packing.

"Yeah, well... I save up, okay?" she huffs. "I like them. They're lucky," she adds, eyeing me warily.

"I don't want to know."

She glares at me. "I mean for exams and things."

"I'm quite sure that I don't know," I reply, wondering why I'm still standing here watching her.

Why I can't take my eyes off her.

"Why? Been that long since you had an exam, you forgot what nerves feel like?" she tuts.

I'm not sure if she's making quips about my age to rile me, or whether she's just plain ignorant about what comes out of her mouth. Someone should teach her some manners.

I clear my throat and push my hands into my pockets.

"I meant I don't know what it's like to have lucky panties. I prefer to wear boxers."

She pins widened eyes on mine. I tip my head to one side, enjoying the way her pulse flutters in her neck.

I like surprising people. Having control. I crave it. I pride myself on my self-control, my restraint. Calmness washes over my gut as her tongue darts out to moisten her lips, unsure what to say.

She might be a brat, but I'm the one with the upper hand. I will always be in control, no matter how much she chooses to push me.

I take the panties from her. She stares at me as I place them back inside the drawer gently, arranging them perfectly, just the way they were. I run the back of my pointer finger down over the fabric, noting the delicate gold waterlily print on the silk.

That's the scent I couldn't place.

Waterlily.

"Despite our initial introduction, I'm a gentleman who knows exactly how to treat *guests*." I slide the drawer shut, enjoying the way she jolts a little as I lean closer. "Enjoy this room. For as long as you're a guest of my father's, it's yours."

She sucks in a small sharp breath but remains silent.

I turn and pick up my suitcase, sensing her eyes on my back as I leave.

Chapter 4

Ava

"Jet sounds like an entitled ass," Liv says.

I hold my phone to my ear as I open the fridge and take out a carton of grapefruit juice. I woke up thirsty after going to bed with a headache. I'm sad I missed dinner with Magnus. I've loved chatting to him since I arrived. He's been telling me stories of him and Gramps and what they got up to together at school.

"He sounds like one because he is one," I grumble.

I place the carton down, then lean against the counter. The silk from my green panties is like a smooth caress against my skin. I love wearing luxurious lingerie beneath a regular outfit of jeans and a T-shirt. It makes me feel powerful and strong.

I can pinpoint the exact moment my addiction began. It was my sixteenth birthday. The day I opened a stunningly beautiful, gift-wrapped box from my mother. Everything about that present was perfect. The champagne silk ribbon tied on the outside. The waft of powdery scent as I lifted the lid. The shimmery cream silk bra and matching panties neatly encased in the tissue paper inside. That set is long gone now, but its memory remains.

The only thing that would have made it better was if my mother had been there to see me open it.

I sigh, looking out at the immaculate green lawn.

"How's it going?" Liv asks.

I know exactly what she's referring to and my spine straightens as something moves outside.

"I've written fifty words."

"That's a start."

"And deleted forty-five of them." I crane my neck to see who's in the garden.

"Five more than you had, though."

I smile at her confidence in me. "True."

"You'll get there. Have faith."

I murmur a response as something flicks past the window.

"I've got to go, I'll call you later," I say as I walk toward the glass to investigate.

"Love you, bitch," Liv sings.

"Love you too," I reply and hang up.

The thing flicks past the door again.

What the hell is that? A whip?

I stop in front of the large doors. An unimpressed groan rumbles in my throat as I spot Jet on the patio. I haven't worked him out. I don't usually have a problem getting along with new people. But there's something about him that winds me up. Maybe it's the self-entitled way he spoke to me yesterday. Arrogant grumpiness flows off him in waves. I've heard about him. Who hasn't?

Jet Grant, billionaire US CEO of Atlantic Airways.

Brilliant, intelligent, *difficult*.

He's known for being ruthless and negotiating deals that have sent Atlantic Airways soaring into position as one of the world's most profitable airlines. He's also known for leaving a trail of broken hearts in his wake.

Smooth in business, turbulent in love.

He lifts his dark blue workout top, pulling the hem of it to his brow and wiping the perspiration away. The move exposes a flash of muscular midriff, and I shift my position to see better.

He picks something off the floor and then straightens.

He starts skipping with alarming speed and precision, the black length of cable circling around over his head and then whipping underneath his sneakers in a fluid motion. His tanned biceps bulge, taut and gleaming with sweat. He's in his own world, unaware he's acquired an audience. I'm enthralled by his every move.

"Beats me why he finds that relaxing."

I jolt away from the glass as Magnus walks in, fixing his tie. His kind eyes meet mine as the morning sunlight highlights the silver strands in his dark hair.

"Would you like one?" he asks, walking over to the coffee machine.

"Oh, no thank you." I smile politely as I walk back to my unopened juice carton and lift it. "I'm all set."

When he nods, I ask, "Does he do that every morning?"

Magnus chuckles, such a contrast to his uptight son. "Yep." He switches the coffee machine on, then turns to me, glancing outside. "Ever since we lost June bug, he's never missed a day."

I press my lips together not knowing what to say. Magnus lost his wife, Jet's mother, five years ago to breast cancer. He's spoken of her often since I arrived, always with a wistful look on his face, a constant companion to the grief. It's obvious he loved her so much.

The back door opens and Jet walks in, his chest heaving.

He greets his father with the closest thing to a smile that I've seen on his face since we met. Then his eyes flick to mine and they darken. I stare back, refusing to be intimidated.

"How's your head this morning, Ava?" Magnus asks, oblivious to the mounting tension in the room as he makes his coffee with his back to us.

Jet walks over to a cupboard and takes two glasses out. He fills one with water at the sink and gulps it down. My eyes fix on the bobbing Adam's apple in his thick neck.

"Much better, thank you. I'm sorry I missed dinner."

Jet finishes his water and walks closer to me. His bare shoulder is millimeters from brushing against my

T-shirt as he places the second glass on the counter. He arches a brow at me and then moves away.

"Don't worry, plenty more of those. You can fill me in tonight on how your work is going," Magnus says.

Jet moves across the room like a moody beast before settling against the counter opposite me. He folds his arms, making his biceps bulge.

I tear my eyes off them. "Oh, not much to tell. I've not gotten very far yet." I smile at Magnus.

"Important matters of the heart take time. Don't rush it. It'll come."

"Thank you," I answer, grateful he's not going to press further. He knows what I'm working on. It's why he's so kindly allowing me to stay here. He agreed with Gramps that this is something I need to do.

He walks toward me, coffee in hand. "Take your time. Do what you need and make yourself at home."

His kindness overwhelms me, making me reach out and lay my palm over his forearm. He gives me a knowing wink as he pats my hand. Then he inclines his head to Jet, whose eyes are drilling a hole into me.

"Speak to you later, Son. Call me after your meeting with Rich."

"Will do," Jet says, the intensity in his glare stepping up a notch as I slide my hand from Magnus's arm, and we're left alone in the kitchen.

The two of us eye one another from opposite sides of the room.

I lift the carton, a frisson of energy darting around inside my stomach as Jet's nostrils flare. I ignore the glass on the counter, instead bringing the carton to my lips. I take a long, deep slug, my eyes fixed on his.

His narrow. That's when I spot the skipping rope in his hands. I've no idea when he picked it up again, but the way he's coiling it around one of his palms, making the veins pop in his forearms as he glares at me has my pulse notching up a gear and an unwelcome heat flaring in my core.

"You're a bit of a brat, aren't you, Miss Roberts?"

I swallow my mouthful of juice before I cough. "Excuse me?"

He stalks closer, looking from the empty glass on the counter to the carton between my fingers.

"You heard me," he clips.

"And you're a bit of an old ass." I scoff without thinking.

"I'm thirty-three."

"So you said."

His wide shoulders still carry a sheen from the layer of fresh sweat on them. And his dark hair has turned into glistening inky strands.

"What if you aren't the only one in this house who likes *grapefruit juice*?" He frowns, reading the carton.

"Margaret said this fridge was for my things. Mag... I mean, your father, said it too."

"My father should know better than to let his hospitality overrule common manners." He transfers the skipping rope to one hand and lifts the unused glass with the other. "Use. The. Glass."

My fingers tingle, ready to take it from him. But I quell the feeling, and instead, lift the carton to my lips, taking another sip as I keep my eyes on his.

My red lipstick leaves a glaring circle around the edge as I lower the carton. Jet's attention zeroes in on it like it's the root of all evil.

"No, thank you. I'm good," I reply, giving him a sweet smile.

A vein in his temple pulses, and he takes a slow, measured breath in as he places the glass back down. He takes the carton from me, his fingers brushing mine and making me jump as an electric shock sparks between our skin. He scowls at the scarlet ring on the spout, and I wait for him to throw it in the trash.

Instead, he brings it to his lips, tilting his head back as he drains the remaining juice from it, then crumples the empty container inside his fist.

"*Your* carton is empty now." He tosses it on the counter. "The next one you open is for everyone, so use a fucking glass."

"You just cursed."

He stares at me.

"You just cursed after telling me off for cursing," I say.

"That was nothing, Ava. You'd know if I was telling you off, believe me."

My thighs clench involuntarily at the deep baritone of his tone. I rest my gaze on the smudge of red lipstick on his lips.

"You have my..." I circle a finger in the air toward the offending mark. It looks wrong on his arrogant lips.

He swipes his thumb over his lower lip, bringing it in front of his face so he can assess it. I wait for him to wipe it on his top, or rush to wash his hands like he did after he shook mine when we met.

"Exactly why you should use a glass."

"You and your glass obsession," I mutter.

He scowls at his thumb, then takes it between his lips and sucks it clean.

My knees buckle, and Jet's eyes land on my throat before they slide up to my face.

"Remember you're here as my father's guest, Miss Roberts. I suggest you watch your mouth."

I don't have time to fire back a response before he strides out of the room, leaving the scent of masculine sweat in the air.

My eyes travel to the crumpled carton on the counter and the unused glass beside it. I pick up the glass and put it back in the cabinet. I won't be needing it. I've no intention of using it now that I know it riles Jet up so much. Because something about the way his blue eyes glimmered with a hint of danger in them has me intrigued. It's a bad idea to push him. Every instinct I have tells me it's a bad idea.

But I know I'll do it again.

And enjoy every second.

Chapter 5

Jet

THE SILVER ESTATE IS magnificent in all its sprawling acres of glory. I shove my hands into my suit pants as I walk alongside Logan Rich through the ornamental gardens.

"Thank you for meeting here," he says. "Things have been pretty busy, it's hard to schedule time away."

I scan the large stately home to the left of us that houses the Silver distillery's main offices. I'd heard Logan was helping run things here while the owner is away serving a jail sentence.

"No problem. Thank you for meeting with me."

"He'll be out soon," Logan says, following my eyes to the main house. "I'll be moving back to the family business with my father full time again. Dax won't need me here anymore."

I admire Logan's loyalty. It's why I was so eager to tie down this meeting. And why I'm meeting with Logan and not his father, Leonard Rich. The two men run their design business together, but I'm told when it comes to any of their biofuel lines, Logan is the one to speak to.

"I'll miss this part, though." Logan tips his head toward the crowd of people spilling over the lawn near the house. "It's fun hosting open days. Some people cannot hold their drinks at the tasting sessions." He chuckles.

"I can imagine." My gaze flits to the activities on the lawn briefly and then come back to rest on his face. "So, the aircraft engines. I'm told the first ones will be ready to be rolled out soon?"

"They will. One hundred percent biofuel. We're the first company to design ones that work. And they can fly more hours than a standard jet engine before needing maintenance."

I hear Hayden's voice inside my head singing with joy over how many hundreds of thousands of dollars this will potentially save Atlantic Airways' US operation.

"So I'm told. And I understand the refit has been going smoothly for the first test aircraft."

"You've done your research, Mr. Grant."

"When it's to do with the future of Atlantic Airways, I'll do anything and everything," I counter, earning myself a chuckle from Logan even though it wasn't supposed to be amusing.

"I'm not sure why you're here, though. No offense."

"I want to buy your engines," I state flatly.

"So does every other airline in the world." Logan shrugs with the easy confidence of a man who knows he has the market eating out of his palm.

"Atlantic Airways isn't every other airline. It's *the* airline," I reply coolly.

Logan faces me, studying me as his lips curl up. "The first batch is tied into a contract. But you strike me as someone who already knows this."

I nod, holding his eyes as he chuckles again.

"Your flights are great; I'll give you that. And your planes..." He whistles with a gleam in his eye that only someone with a true love of engineering and design would get. "They're some of the best in the world. But like I said... The first batch is contracted. I wish I could help."

It's what I expected. He's a man of his word. If I'd walked into this meeting and managed to easily negotiate him into breaking his previous contract to work with me instead, then it would have set alarm bells ringing.

I only work with people I can trust.

"I understand, and I respect that."

He eyes me curiously.

"I'm not asking you to sell them to me."

"Good, because I wouldn't, even if I like your airline better."

"Hm." I tip my head in amusement. "Thank you."

We walk again, following a path past some flowering bushes that leads alongside the edge of a large lake. The surface is covered in waterlilies.

"I know the deal you've signed is with James Callaghan at Skyline."

Logan keeps his mouth closed, neither confirming nor denying.

"I also know that I'm likely to find him in one of three cities over the next few days."

"He keeps a very precise schedule," Logan says.

"He does. His time is precious. As is mine. As is yours."

I pause, holding Logan's eyes.

"I might have an idea where you'll find him. Although talking him out of being the first to get his hands on our engine is not going to be an easy feat," Logan says.

"I can handle Callaghan."

"I'm not one for spilling hints over where my clients like to frequent on their travels, Mr. Grant."

"No, of course not." I shake my head as we continue strolling along the lakeside. "There was another thing I wanted to discuss with you while I'm here, though."

"Go for it."

"The gin we serve onboard and in our first-class lounges... it's *bitter*. We need to replace the entire stock. It's just a question of with what. I've always liked Aunt Iris's blend myself. Nothing compares to it."

His lips twist. "You're right. Nothing does. The Silvers and the family who began it all are the only ones who know the secret recipe. This is the only place that makes it."

"Isn't that interesting now," I muse.

"Indeed," he agrees.

I let the silence stretch on as my offer settles. The next words between the two of us will be figures. I'll let Logan name his price first. He'll come in high, as he should, and we'll meet somewhere lower.

If he knew how desperate I really am, then he'd know I'd happily pay his first figure.

I scan the lake, wondering how many thousands of waterlilies are floating on its surface as I wait.

I don't hear whatever Logan says because my attention is fixed on the bank further ahead of us. Fixed on the auburn hair bent over a notepad as she writes.

She lifts her head, gazing across the water as she drops her pen between the open pages and then wipes beneath both eyes with her fingertips, completely unaware she's no longer alone.

I turn, giving Logan a polite smile. "Maybe we could discuss this over one of those sessions you have running by the house."

"Sure. Let's do that."

We turn and head back in the direction we came from.

"What do we have?" I bark as I open the fridge, scanning the contents.

"The slots into O'Hare?" Hayden offers through the phone.

"Chicago? No way. They took months to get. What else?"

My eyes land on a carton of grapefruit juice. I lift it, gauging its weight. *Full.* I put it back down and grab a bottle of water.

"What about San Jose?"

"We've only just secured Costa Rica," I grumble as I screw off the cap and take a long drink before setting the bottle down.

"It's not going to even get its inaugural flight if we don't get Callaghan to play nice," Hayden says.

"Fuck." I tip my head back and stare at the kitchen ceiling.

"You know he likes things first. He'll not want to share a single one of those engines."

"Leave Callaghan to me," I grit, scrubbing a hand around my jaw.

"Costa Rica?" Hayden leaves the words dangling in the air.

"Fine," I concede. "But it's all he's getting." Even as I say the words, I know they're wrong. James Callaghan might be sweetened with the offer of the slots into San Jose. But there's no way he'll give up some of his new engines in exchange. He's not a fool. He'll be after more. A hell of a lot more.

"What about—?"

"No," I snap.

Hayden exhales heavily. "You know it's about the only thing that might make him consider it."

I walk out of the kitchen and down the rear hallway, all the way to the end until I reach the old wooden staircase the servants would have used years ago.

"That might be the case, but we're not that desperate."

Yet.

"All right. I'll make some calls about San Jose. Leave it with me."

"Fine." I end the call.

I climb halfway up the staircase and sit on the old, weathered wood. It creaks out a familiar welcome that has me rubbing my chest. I tuck my phone away and rest my forearms onto my knees, sinking my head into my hands as I rub at my aching skull.

What a fucking mess.

After the call with Hayden, I changed into my workout gear and hammered my body until it felt as pulverized as my mind at the thought of giving up anything that's mine to James fucking Callaghan. His airline, Skyline, is our biggest rival when it comes to the North American routes. What started as nothing more than healthy competition years ago, turned into me catching private investigators hired by Callaghan rooting through my trash cans searching for dirt on me.

I can picture the smug bastard's face when he realizes he has something I want. As long as he never finds out how much I *need* it, I can stomach the idea of playing whatever little hoop jumping game he'll have me perform in order to discuss the engines. He's always loved theatrics.

Bet he has a tiny dick.

I stop and face the open door out onto the guest room's balcony. There's no furniture on it, and everything inside the room, apart from the bed, is covered in dust sheets. Dad was getting this room decorated before my impromptu visit. Before he invited a certain hotheaded woman to make herself at home in my room. Prickles run along the backs of my arms as I recall seeing her lingerie hanging up to dry in the laundry room this morning. She's making herself comfortable, that's for sure.

I walk out onto the balcony and crane my neck to see the pool house at the other end of the gardens. I haven't seen Ava since I came home, so I assume she's still holed up doing whatever it is she's doing in there.

She's probably stirring up potions to share with her coven. Ones that place men like my father under a spell that allows them to command supply of their own fridge in a house that isn't theirs.

A tinkle of laughter accompanied by a low voice carry from around the side of the house. I step closer to the stone railing to peer below. A shimmering flash of copper moves beneath me as Ava strolls along chatting animatedly with my father's landscaper, David. She lifts a hand and tucks a strand of hair behind her ear, but it promptly falls forward again. David's arm moves, and I lean over the railing, my teeth grinding as he reaches for Ava's hair. She beats him to it and tucks it back again.

I can't hear what they're talking about, but whatever he just said must be fucking hilarious because Ava throws her head back and laughs, clasping a hand over her mouth. They continue walking along the side of the house before disappearing around the corner.

"Fuck." I suck in a sharp hiss as my palms sting. I pull them back from where I've been gripping the railings with enough force that the old, rough stone has scratched and made small beads of blood gather on my skin.

I walk inside my room and grab a tissue, just as the sound of crunching gravel from the driveway announces my father's return.

I stride straight to my bedroom door. It's time to talk about James Callaghan, and just how far up his ass my head is about to go to save our airline.

Chapter 6

Ava

"Go on. I can finish these."

I take another of Magnus's freshly ironed shirts from Margaret and slide it onto a hanger.

"I like to help," I say, ignoring the pointed look she's giving me.

"You like to procrastinate." She chuckles as she takes the hanger from me and places the shirt on a rail beside others.

"No." I try and reach for another shirt, but she moves it before my fingers graze the cotton.

"Your work won't do itself. Besides, you'll be running me out of a job," she says.

I lean against the laundry room counter as she continues ironing. This has become our routine. I follow her around, helping with whatever jobs I can. Today was a huge grocery shop that had us out for the majority of the afternoon. She's right, maybe I am avoiding the reason I'm really here. But I'm enjoying spending time with her. I knew she'd be softer under that stern exterior. She's traveled so much with her husband. I love hearing about where they've gone and what they've seen.

"Go," Margaret presses. "You've got some time before dinner. Get out to that pool house and start typing."

I glance at my watch. I can probably get some words down before Magnus comes home.

"Go on." She lifts a brow, and with a sigh, I leave before she forces me out.

I head out the back door and walk along the path that runs around the perimeter of the house. A guy with sandy-colored hair is digging in one of the flower beds.

"Hello." I raise a hand in greeting.

He stops and his brown eyes connect with mine.

"Hey." He sticks his shovel into the earth and walks over. He brushes his soiled hands against his cargo pants, then holds one out. "You must be Ava. Margaret said you were visiting."

"That's me." I return his smile as I shake his hand. "And I'm guessing you're David."

"That's me."

He's younger than I expected. Late twenties, maybe. And he's solid. Built like a bear. His sandy hair is long over his collar, and he has a ruggedness about him that seems so natural and easy. I can't imagine him wearing a suit.

I can't believe I mistook Jet for him.

"It's nice to meet you." My eyes drop to the Def Leppard T-shirt he's wearing. "'When Love & Hate Collide', amazing song." I grin.

"Yeah? You like them?" His eyes light up as he bends to pick up a drinks bottle. "Ah," he tuts, seeing it empty.

"They're amazing." He wipes his brow with the back of his arm. He must be roasting digging out here like this. "I was just headed to the pool house. You can come get a soda if you like? I have some in there."

"Yeah?" He hitches his brows. "Sounds great, thanks."

We fall into an easy chat as we walk around the house. David tells me he's worked for Magnus since before June passed away. Magnus hired him to plant flowers all around the house so that no matter which window June looked out of, she would see color.

"That's beautiful... romantic," I say.

His eyes twinkle as he sees me checking his left hand for a ring.

"No girlfriend," he says, answering my silent question. "No boyfriend, either."

"Was it that obvious?" I laugh as we turn the corner of the house. I tuck a strand of hair behind my ear and the breeze immediately blows it across my cheek again. I tuck it behind my ear again. "It's just, you have this Charlie Hunnam thing going on. My best friend, Liv, is kind of obsessed."

"Really? Tell me more about Liv. She sounds very interesting." He grins, and I throw my head back with a laugh.

"She's going to come visit. You can ask her whatever you want to know."

The two of us continue chatting about the house and the gardens, and David tells me about his older brother who he runs his landscaping business with. By the time he's done drinking his soda and gone back to tidy up his tools, it's almost time for dinner, so I decide to head back into the main house to freshen up.

A loud voice hits me the moment I step inside. It's coming from Magnus's office. In order to reach the bottom of the main staircase, I need to walk right past. My feet pause on the stone tiles as the voice scoffs.

"She drinks it straight from the carton like an uncivilized delinquent."

"Can't stand the stuff," another voice I recognize as Magnus's chuckles.

"It's poor manners. Someone else might want to drink it. She leaves her berry-flavored lipstick all over the rim."

Berry flavored.

"Who else would want to drink it?" Magnus asks.

"Me!" Jet's voice pitches and goosebumps scatter up my spine at how incensed he sounds over a little bit of juice.

"You hate the stuff, said it makes you feel sick," Magnus replies.

I lean a little closer, straining to hear Jet's response, but it's a deep mutter of something I can't make out.

"She should use a glass," he grits, his voice gaining power again. "Even if no one else likes it, it's not the point."

"Then what is the point, Son? Because as far as I can tell, you've come stomping in here like your ass is on fire, and so far, all you've talked about is juice. I thought you'd come to fill me in on your talk with Hayden?"

"I just don't see why you're so enamored with her. You know nothing about her."

"I know exactly who she is. She's William's granddaughter."

The breezy tone of Magnus's response, like it explains everything, seems to rile Jet up further and there's a thud that sounds like a hand slamming down against a desk.

"Are you screwing her?"

The venom in Jet's tone makes me flinch.

"What?"

"Is that why she's here making herself comfortable? Turning the pool house into her home office?"

"Of course not!" Magnus mirrors Jet's volume for the first time.

I should leave. This isn't for me to hear. But to get upstairs, I run the risk of them seeing me as I pass the door.

I hover, scanning the hallway for another route but come up empty.

"How dare you even suggest that... There's not been anyone since..." Magnus chokes on a sob before clearing his throat. The sound is weighted with something that makes my heart clench.

"I'm sorry, Dad. I didn't mean..." The remorse in Jet's voice is just as tough to listen to. It sinks into my skin and scrapes over my bones. "I shouldn't have said that. I'm sorry."

"Jesus Christ," Magnus mutters. "Listen, Son. We're all feeling this. We're all fucking stressed. We can't go firing off at each other at the first sign of trouble. We're in this together. You might be across the pond, but Atlantic Airways is one family, always has been."

Heavy silence stretches out before Jet says, "This is all my fault. I need to be the one who fixes it."

"You couldn't have seen it coming. We'll deal with it together. Now... what do you need?"

"Time with Callaghan," Jet says. "Time to work on him."

Magnus huffs. "He's an ass, it won't be easy convincing him."

"That's why I need a big carrot," Jet grits.

"Hayden's handling things in LA. I've got Callaghan's schedule for the next couple of weeks."

"I don't trust him," Magnus clips.

"Neither do I. But our legal team is the best in the industry. We get an agreement with him, and they'll make it airtight."

"Regardless, you should take one of the team with you. Have someone else watching him, too."

"That's not necessary."

"I disagree, Son. Callaghan can be a snake."

Their voices lower to a hush. I take a step closer to the open door. If I make a bolt for it, maybe they won't see me. So I take a deep breath and go for it.

Bad idea.

I collide with Jet's solid chest so hard the air is knocked from my lungs.

"Shit, sorry."

He stares at me, his fingers curled around my upper arms where he's steadied me.

"What are you doing here?" he snaps.

"Ah, Ava." Magnus smiles behind him as he exits his office.

The genuine warmth in his voice makes me want to run into his arms. How Jet came from his genes, I'll never understand.

"How long have you been here?" Jet's eyes return to mine, burning with accusation.

"I just came in," I lie.

His jaw clenches as though he sees right through me. He lets go, leaving my skin tingling.

"Good day? Get much done." Magnus asks, ignoring the icy glare aimed at me from his son. He's probably used to Jet's social setting being one degree below Arctic.

"I did, thank you."

"Lie number two," Jet murmurs, loud enough for only me to hear.

I slide my eyes to his, and he arches a brow.

"You haven't been here all afternoon. And when you did get back, you spent your time flirting with David instead of working on whatever little project you have going on," he says.

The way he says 'little project' with such disregard, as though I'm a silly girl working on something meaningless enrages me more than anything else that's come out of his arrogant mouth since we've met.

"I went grocery shopping with Margaret."

"Why? She's paid to do that. You aren't."

I rake my gaze over his face in disgust. "Sometimes, it's nice to spend time with people without expecting anything in return. And David and I were just talking."

He grunts.

I tear my eyes away from his and look at Magnus. His attention bounces between the two of us and he narrows his eyes like he's contemplating something.

"Ava. Do you find working in different places and getting out of the pool house helps the words flow?"

My mind flicks to the waterlily lake and all the notes I managed to get down while I was there. "Absolutely."

"Your master's degree is in business, isn't it?"

"It is."

"Well then. Maybe you can go with Jet to a meeting he's got coming up. Lend an extra set of ears to it."

Jet stiffens immediately, a muscle ticking in his cheek. "Absolutely not."

The excuse on my tongue slides away as the hairs on my arms prickle up in annoyance. *Does he think I can't manage to take notes for his stupid meeting?*

"I graduated with a first in my degree." I fold my arms as I hold his stare.

"And?"

"And I'm more than capable of whatever it is you'll require me to do."

His eyes flick up and down my body, and I feel like a science project being scrutinized. "I'll be the judge of that."

The urge to prove him wrong has my palms itching. I'd also like to slap the disdainful look off his face. But this will have to do.

"I can go with you to this meeting. In fact, I'll give you my expertise for the entire day, be your personal *ass*istant." I smile sweetly, making sure I emphasize the ass.

"There's no need. I'm sure you're far too busy working on your—"

"My *little project* will be okay without me for a day."

He stares at me, unblinking, and the way his jaw works as he grinds his teeth has a pop of perverse victory firing in my stomach. He thinks he's so much better than me. He'll not expect me to be able to keep up with him.

It'll be fun showing him what I can do.

"Great." Magnus pats Jet's shoulder with a wide grin. "Take Ava with you to meet Callaghan tomorrow. He's a slimy bastard, though. Watch him," Magnus directs to me.

"I will," I answer before he walks down the hall, leaving us alone.

"What time are we leaving in the morning?"

Jet narrows his eyes like he expected me to retract my offer the moment Magnus was out of earshot.

"Seven-thirty."

"Great." I flash him an obnoxious smile. "I'm so excited I might pee myself."

His lip curls in disgust like I've actually done it.

I turn and walk off with a spring in my step.

Pissing Jet Grant off is fun.

And the idea of seeing his arrogant face eat his own words when I show him what I'm capable of is positively exhilarating.

Chapter 7

Ava

"What do you mean you don't have a passport?"

Jet's dark gaze bores into mine like an interrogation as I stand in the hallway, dressed in a pencil skirt and blouse that belongs to Margaret's daughter. After the reality sunk in about what I agreed to, I realized I hadn't packed anything suitable to wear. I was supposed to be working in the pool house, not trailing Jet Grant around London while he chases some guy around.

"Exactly as it sounds. I don't have one."

"Did you lose it?" Jet frowns.

"No, it expired."

He sighs, rubbing at his temples like I'm the biggest blot on an otherwise perfectly white sheet of paper.

"Fine. Fetch your old one. It'll make the process faster."

He lifts his eyes to mine when I don't move.

"It ran out ten years ago. I threw it away."

The disbelief on his face would be priceless, and something I'd take delight in, if my stomach wasn't in painful knots at the way this conversation is skating so close to memories I'd prefer not to think about right now.

"You haven't left the country in ten years?" he balks like I've told him the world is about to ban all drinking glasses so that everyone has to drink straight from the carton now or die of thirst.

When I say nothing, he shakes his head, blowing out a breath. "Marvelous," he mutters, pulling his phone out of his navy suit pants and tapping out a message.

"Do I need it, just for one meeting?"

"It won't be just one. There will be several. Like my father said, Callaghan is a snake. But I understand if one is all you can squeeze in."

Boredom creeps into his tone. He's giving me an easy out. He wants us working together as much as I do.

Like a punch in the nose.

"I can work on my laptop in the car if I need to catch up. And I prefer working in the evenings anyway." I shrug, not wanting to give him the satisfaction of being the one who backs out. Besides, I still haven't managed to write more than one page since coming here. Writer's block sucks. "I'll come for as many meetings as it takes to get what you need from him," I add, and he grimaces.

"Fine," he grits.

"Can't you use my driver's license?"

"No." His gaze is set on his phone, his lips pressed into a firm line as he continues to type on it.

He's being difficult on purpose. Surely, I can have a company ID issued with my license. It's not like I'll be going anywhere unescorted. I doubt Jet will let me out of his sight, probably worried I'll act like an *uncivilized delinquent* as he so kindly called me.

"Why not? It has my photo. I've got a library card, too."

He pockets his phone. "You can't leave the country with a library card."

A tide of nausea curls up my windpipe and wrings the air from it, until I feel like I'm choking.

"Leave the country?" I must have misheard him. "Jet?" I press when he doesn't respond.

I will my pulse to slow down. It's beating so loud he'll probably hear it and get excited thinking I'm having a heart attack.

Maybe I am.

"That a problem?" His gaze narrows on me like a predator, sensing weakness.

"Of course not." I fidget with my skirt, wiping my sweaty palms on it.

"Then let's stop wasting time." He strides to the front door, holding it open for me. "Callaghan left London a day earlier than expected. We'll have to go to him."

I force myself to relax. "Where is he? Are we getting the Euro-tunnel, or a ferry?"

"New York."

"New York?" I freeze in the doorway and gawk at him. "As in, East Coast of America?"

"Where else?"

My heart rattles against its cage.

"You're making us late." He looks down his nose at me until I move. He closes the door and I stumble in my heels as I try to keep up with the long strides he takes across the driveway toward a sleek black town car.

A driver opens the rear door as we approach, and I give him a bewildered smile, before sliding into the leather interior. Jet climbs in beside me and the door is shut behind him.

"Where are we going?"

I perch on the edge of my seat as the driver climbs in and starts the engine.

"Fasten your belt," Jet instructs.

"I can't go to New York. I don't have a passport," I say, so close to the edge of my seat that one small move of the car and I'll end up on my ass in the footwell.

"Fasten your belt," he repeats.

My heart hammers as I stare at him. New York?

A fresh masculine aftershave mixed with mint assaults me as Jet leans over me, making me fall back into the seat. His left cheek is so close I can see every single one of his thick, dark eyelashes. He clears his throat, the vibration rolling through me as he pulls my seat belt over my chest and clicks it, before moving back to his own seat.

"You told me yesterday that your meeting was in London," I say as he signals the driver to go.

"No, I didn't."

"Yes, you did."

He pulls a laptop out from a compartment by his seat and opens it.

"I said I was meeting Callaghan today. I didn't say where. Although, plans change in business. We don't all get to work from someone else's pool house every day."

My blood boils at the way his face remains calm, like insinuating I'm abusing his father's hospitality is just small talk and not rude and insulting.

Arrogant jerk.

"So, Callaghan's in New York?"

"Yes." He begins typing on his laptop.

"And you're going there to meet him?"

"No."

Thank god. I exhale and sink back into the seat. It must be a video meeting. My mind must have been playing tricks on me earlier when I thought Jet said we were leaving the country. That'll teach me for staying up late trying to write.

"*We're* going there to meet him."

I swing to face him so fast my brain rattles.

"But I don't have a passport."

"An inconvenience, I must say." He scowls at me like I planned the entire thing to piss him off. "If you can't handle lending me your *expertise* for these meetings, Ava, just say it and save us both the time. It makes no difference to me." His focus returns to his laptop screen.

I gnaw my bottom lip as I stare down at my skirt, running my palms over it.

"Make your mind up. Your walk back to the house is getting longer." He sighs, sounding bored as the car pulls onto the road.

His eyes slide to mine, and I swear the cold bastard's lips curl up as I pull in a shaky breath that echoes around the interior.

I settle into the seat, clasping my hands in my lap to hide their trembling.

"I prefer not to talk on car journeys, don't you?" I turn toward the window and stare out.

"Something we can both agree on," he murmurs.

For the rest of the drive, the car is silent except for the tapping of the keys on his laptop. Each one is like a nail being hammered into my skin, making me wince.

But I don't have a passport.

So Jet can be as much of a jerk as he likes because I'm not going anywhere.

"The car will be here when you're done."

Jet's words pull me to my senses, and I turn away from the window for the first time since we left Rochwell house.

"Excuse me?"

"The car will be here when you're done," he repeats, closing his laptop.

"I heard you the first time."

"Then why are you still here?"

His blue eyes connect with mine as my door is opened by his driver.

I lean closer to him so I can look out of his window and up at the building we've pulled up in front of. I can feel the heat of his disapproving eyes on my face as I realize where we are.

"The passport office?" I swallow around the thick lump in my throat.

"They're expecting you for your interview."

"Interview?" I reach for my blouse and undo the top button. It's stifling with the door open and London's city air flowing into the car.

"It starts in five minutes."

I gather up my purse when he doesn't say anything else. Maybe I can run and he won't notice. Or I can tell him the passport printer ran out of ink.

I take a deep breath and climb out, thanking the driver as I walk toward the building, staring up at it.

I glance back at the car. Jet's watching me with dark eyes. He flicks his fingers at me in a shooing motion. *Asshole*. His eyes narrow like he heard me, and I look away.

At least this way, I can escape being confined in a vehicle with him. I continue walking toward the building. My legs threaten to buckle.

I take a deep breath and stride through the doors.

Thirty minutes later, I join him with my shiny new passport burning a hole inside my purse.

Jet barely glances at me as I thank his driver for opening the door and slide inside.

"Did you get it?"

"Yes."

"Good."

I side eye him. He's reading something on his phone screen.

"The signs in there said the fastest appointment you can get is in two days. And that you need your old passport to get an immediate replacement."

I keep staring at him, and when he finally looks up, he lifts a single, dark brow.

"That was a statement, not a question. If you have a question, Ava, then ask it."

"Did you... how did...?"

"You can get a lot of things when you know the right people." He looks back at his phone.

I refuse to ask what exactly that means. But I expect it's exactly as it sounds—when you're a billionaire, you can get anything you want.

Jet Grant's probably never been told 'no' his entire life.

"So where are we going now? Has Callaghan's schedule changed?"

"No. He's still in New York," Jet tsks as he brings his phone up to his ear.

"Hayden?" he barks. "Talk to me."

He curses, then nods, before murmuring some sounds of agreement. He ends the call and tosses his phone onto the seat.

"Fucking brilliant."

He pushes his thumb and finger into his eye sockets, tension radiating from him in waves.

"We need to make this quick," he says to the driver. "Take us to Knightsbridge. Harrods will have what we need."

"This whole day has been insane."

I walk around the side of the house with my laptop cradled in my free arm as I hold my phone in front of me and talk to Liv on video call.

"Are you really going to go?" Her eyes widen as I blow a strand of hair out of my eyes.

"I don't know."

I nod a greeting at David, who's across the lawn, sitting on a ride-on mower. He waves back before I turn the corner. Liv was supposed to be coming to visit this weekend, but that might be on hold now.

It depends how long we're in New York.

If I get on the plane.

"Why don't you tell him?"

I jerk my head. "No. It's none of his damn business."

"Ava," Liv insists, "he'll understand."

I snort. This is Jet. I'm pretty sure he only understands how to act like a pretentious pig. He didn't even let me choose my own luggage when we went to the store after my passport interview. I wanted this nice red suitcase with wheels. It would have saved him money, instead of the extortionate price he paid for the silver suitcase and matching carry-on he selected. But I guess he cared little for the cost judging by the way he didn't look at the tags before handing over his black Amex to the sales assistant.

"I've got sleeping tablets. I'll have a couple before take-off."

The false confidence in my voice doesn't fool Liv, she's known me too long.

"I'm not saying you can't. In fact, I think it's amazing. You'll finally be able to visit your mum."

"Yeah." My response comes out choked as I juggle my laptop so I can open the old, wooden back door. Margaret's just polished the main hallway, and I'd hate to leave a mark on it.

"What time's your flight?"

"Eight."

I don't have to look at my watch to know that I have approximately forty minutes to pack and be ready to leave. Jet was adamant we leave on time. He stormed off the minute we stepped inside the house earlier, and the only evidence of him since was the whipping sound of his skipping rope coming from outside.

"Will you call me at the airport? I'll be here if you need anything, okay?"

I manage a weak smile and lean back against the door. "Thank you."

"You can do this."

I tip my head back and blow out a breath.

"The idea of it is making me feel sick if I'm honest. But I told Jet I would, so—"

"So you want to keep your word?"

"No! I want to show the asshole I'm not a freeloader. He thinks I'm incapable of doing anything. He's so far up his own ass, Liv. Honestly, wait until you meet him. You'll see what I mean."

"You make him sound delightful."

"Jet's as delightful as a yeast infection on a hot day."

"Eww."

Peals of laughter echo down the phone, and I grin, feeling a little better about the mess I'm in.

"He's got a stick so far up his ass you could fly a flag out of his mouth."

Liv's cackles grow louder.

"And he accused Magnus of screwing me. He's son of the fucking year," I say as I push away from the door and walk down the hallway.

The hairs on the back of my neck prick up as I reach the old wooden staircase, the feeling of being watched overwhelming.

My throat goes dry as I lock eyes with him, sitting halfway up.

"I'll call you back, Liv." I end the call.

His eyes are bloodshot and he's in his workout shorts, his shoulders slumped forward like he's lost the will to move. The skipping rope is coiled around one of his hands, turning his knuckles white.

"Don't stop on my account." His lips flatten into a grim line.

My eyes drop down his naked chest, over the scattering of hair there, and then lower to the dark trail leading beneath his waistband. The outline of a dick as thick as my wrist presses against the thin fabric of his shorts as he stands. He's all man in the most intense way.

Somehow, it makes me dislike him even more.

He walks down the steps, stopping in front of me. Beads of sweat pepper his collarbone and run down his chest. The heat from his body overtakes the hallway as he stares down at me.

"Your luggage has been put in your room. I suggest you pack. We leave in thirty-six minutes."

He walks away, leaving me with the sight of his broad, muscular back, shining in sweat, and a firm ass that would make every man want to immediately take up skipping.

I head up the old staircase to get to my room—Jet's room.

I place my phone and laptop on the bed before going into the dressing area. My new luggage is here, just like he said. I open it and come across a champagne-colored object. It's made of the smoothest silk I've ever felt. I hold it up, studying the zip on the side, and the delicate embroidered seams in gold-colored thread.

A lingerie bag.

I didn't see these when Jet paid for the luggage. But he must have bought them today because they have a Harrods tag on.

I walk over to the drawers, sliding the top one open, and lift out the pale pink panties with the gold waterlilies on. My lucky pair.

Tracing the delicate fabric, I take a deep breath and start filling the first silk bag.

New York, here I come.

Chapter 8

Jet

AVA SUCKS IN A sharp breath as a call button illuminates across the aisle, accompanied by a soft *ding*.

"Just a call bell," she murmurs, pressing her back into her seat.

Her fingers drum up and down on the armrests of her first-class seat beside me, stealing my attention away from the report I'm reading on my phone that Hayden's sent through.

"Are you going to talk to yourself the whole flight?"

She glares at me. But the force fades immediately, and she looks away, her eyes darting after the flight attendant who's walking past with a package in her hands.

"What's she carrying?"

"An infant life jacket," I say, resuming my reading.

"Why does she need that? That's for water, isn't it?"

"It's for if we ditch."

"Ditch?"

"Land on water," I confirm.

These new figures Hayden has sent through are concerning to say the least. Callaghan better be ready to make a deal because there's no way I can leave him alone until he does. I'll follow him when he goes to take a dump if that's what it takes.

"Planes don't land on water. They crash."

I look up into Ava's rounded eyes.

"Correct."

I rub a hand around my jaw as I signal the flight attendant. She comes over with a silver tray and I take two champagne flutes off, placing them onto the small table between the seats.

"So nice to have you onboard again, Mr. Grant." She gives me a sexy smile before she moves away.

I know the rumors that circulate Atlantic Airways. That I fuck my flight attendants, then gift them luxury holidays to keep it out of the press. But I'm smarter than to shit on my own doorstep. And recently I've been too busy trying to save their jobs to have time to give my dick any action.

Ava rummages around in her purse and produces a bottle of pills. Her hands shake as she tips two out into her palm. She picks up one to place it back inside, then changes her mind and throws both into her mouth, knocking them back with half of her champagne.

"What are those?"

"Nothing."

"Ava?"

She ignores me, so I reach down and swipe the bottle from her hand before she drops it inside her purse.

"Jet! Those are mine."

Her cheeks flush as she tries to grab the bottle back from me. I hold them out of her reach as I read the label.

"Sleeping tablets?"

"They're herbal. I've used them before, it's fine."

She drains the rest of her champagne.

"Did you take more before those two?" She ignores me and I snap, "How many have you taken in total?"

"Enough that you won't have to worry about making conversation with me until New York." She snorts.

"Ava," I growl.

Her eyes flick to mine. "Four." She shrugs.

"Jesus Christ." I pinch the bridge of my nose. "And you're mixing them with alcohol when we're about to take off."

As if to prove my point, the flight manager announces over the PA system for all ground personnel to leave the aircraft before the final door is closed.

The flight attendant retrieves Ava's empty glass and reaches for my untouched one.

"Not thirsty, Mr. Grant?"

"Sorry, no."

Ava grabs it and downs it, before handing it over with a wobbly smile. "Thanks."

The flight attendant raises an eyebrow, grabs both the flutes, and walks away. Ava tips her head back, exhaling loudly.

"It's fine, Jet. The pills are herbal."

"So is cannabis. Are you going to whip a joint out next and smoke that?"

"Maybe... I can share it with you, loosen you up a bit."

Her gaze darts around the cabin, her chest rising and falling in quickening breaths.

"Then where would the flags get flown?" I grumble, placing the pill bottle down onto the table.

She turns to me, her eyes raking over my stony expression. Then she laughs, clapping her hand over her mouth.

The aircraft jerks as it's pushed back from its parking stand.

Ava's laugh stops and she grips both the armrests again.

"Have you ever been on a plane before?"

"Yes. Plenty of times." She's staring out of the window at the pushback coordinator walking alongside the plane and talking to the pilots through his headset. Once we're fully pushed back and lined up on the taxiway the pushback vehicle detaches from the front of the plane, and we begin to move forward.

I scroll through the document Hayden sent as we taxi to the runway and wait in line for take-off. A muttering breaks my train of thought. Ava's eyes are screwed shut and she's pressing her thumbs to the tip of each of her fingers one by one, counting from one to five over and over.

I abandon Hayden's email and slide my phone into my pocket.

"I didn't know you were scared of flying."

"Because I never told you."

"Don't you think you should have?"

"Why? You can't do anything." She takes a deep breath, then blows it out slowly.

"We have courses for nervous flyers. You could have taken one."

"Oh yeah, while Callaghan waits for us, you mean?" She peels an eye open and gives me a pointed look. "Exactly... Anyway, I'm fine. The pills are starting to kick in. You don't need to worry about me."

"I'm not."

"Nice. Thanks," she scoffs.

We turn onto the runway and full power is applied to the engines. Ava's eyes fly open, and she makes a high-pitched whining sound. She stares out of the window as we tear down the runway.

"Oh fuck, fuck, fuck." She closes her eyes again, then they pop open like she doesn't know whether to look or not. Her knuckles turn a ghostly white on the armrests.

"Can I do anything?"

"Shut up, Jet," she snaps.

I ease back into my seat as we lift off the ground. My stomach lurches with the pull. I love the feeling. There's nothing like it, knowing you're about to climb through the clouds until you're literally on top of the world.

"Oh god." Ava grabs my hand, clutching it so hard her nails bite into my flesh.

I clear my throat. "It's okay. You're safe."

She shakes her head side to side, tears filling her eyes. "It's not okay, it's not—"

We climb through the clouds and the plane bumps.

"Jet!" She throws her arms around my neck, catching me off guard, and buries her face into my neck.

I pat her back awkwardly. "I'm here. You're fine."

"Talk to me. Tell me something to distract me."

I think for a second. "My record is eight hundred skips in a row."

She sniffs. "You're so weird for finding that fun."

"I never said I find it fun."

"Then why do it?"

Her arms tighten around my neck as the plane shakes with light turbulence.

"It clears my mind. And sweating helps me when I'm stressed."

I pause mid-pat on her back as she trembles, clutching my collar. I switch to rubbing gently up and down her spine. "Is this okay?"

"Yeah," she breathes out shakily. "Keep doing it."

I lift my chin a little, resting it on top of her hair. The copper strands smell like the caramel and waterlily I noticed in her room.

"Why are you called Jet?" Her lips dust my neck as she speaks.

"My father likes planes."

She chuckles against my skin. "I thought it might be that."

"Original, huh?"

"My father liked them too."

Liked.

"When did you lose him?"

She stiffens in my arms. "Ten years ago."

"I'm sorry. Losing a parent is hard." My chest squeezes in empathy.

"I'm sorry about your mother. Your dad talks about her so much. She sounds like an amazing woman."

"She was." I dip my nose into her hair and inhale. "She really was. What's yours like? I've not heard you mention her."

The seat belt sign chimes off, indicating we can move around the cabin. Ava stays glued to me, her breathing slowing.

"She lives in LA. She's an actress. She moved there after Dad died."

My arm tightens around her, and I draw her closer.

"You chose to stay with your grandfather?"

"It was for the best. Mum wasn't coping well with her grief." Her voice wavers, loosening like she's getting drowsy.

Jesus. The image of a young Ava losing her father and then her mother in a short space of time makes me take a deep breath.

"You'll know her. Zena Hamilton." Pride fills her voice as she inches herself away from me.

I've no idea who she's talking about. She blinks, looking around the cabin with glassy eyes.

"How long do we have?"

"Another seven hours and forty-two minutes."

"Oh." Her lips part as she wipes a hand over her forehead. "I think the tablets are working. I feel calmer." She gives me a woozy grin. "Like I just got off the teacups at the fair."

I grab the bottle of water beside my seat and hold it out to her. "Drink this. And no more alcohol."

She giggles. "No glass?"

I unscrew the lid and hold it out to her again. "I'll make an exception. Now drink."

Her glazed eyes try to focus on mine as she drinks until she's finished the bottle.

"Good girl."

I take it from her as she wipes her lips with the back of her hand.

"You feeling okay?"

She gives me a goofy grin. "I feel gooood. Relaxed." She sways a little in her seat like she's dancing to an invisible tune. "I told you, Jet. Herbal pills... they're the way to go. I've never taken them with champagne before. It works."

"Uh-huh."

She sinks back into her seat with a deep sigh. When I'm satisfied she isn't going to move anytime soon, I get my laptop out and open it up. I'm five minutes into making notes in the document when she starts giggling beside me.

"Flags..." She snorts. "Can you really skip eight hundred times in a row?"

"Yes."

I feel the heat of her gaze on the side of my face where she's turned toward me in her seat.

"I'm setting Liv up with David. I think they'll really hit it off."

I drop my hand away from my laptop and turn toward her. "David?"

"I wasn't flirting with him," she whispers theatrically, looking increasingly out of it as her brows fly up her forehead. "I don't want to have sex with him."

"I see."

"But Liv will. She'll want to climb him like a tree."

I turn my attention back to my work. "Okay."

"Do you know what guys ask me the most?"

I sigh and turn to face her again.

"They ask if my hair down there matches my head."

My gaze falls to the apex of her thighs.

"It kind of does when I have some. But it's bare at the moment. Completely naked. Sometimes, I have a strip there, you know, in the middle. Right here." She draws a line over the seam of her leggings.

I swallow as her pale pink fingernail slides up and down over herself.

"A landing strip.... Oh my god, like planes, get it?"

She laughs loudly, attracting the attention of the flight attendant.

"Everything okay, Mr. Grant. Does your companion need anything?"

"She's fine," I grumble as Ava hums to herself, twirling her fingers in the air.

"Okay," the flight attendant says, not sounding convinced.

Ava leans over and grabs the flight attendant's wrist, her voice serious. "I've never orgasmed from penetrative sex. Have you? Please tell me it's possible."

Jesus Christ.

"Maybe another water," I say, extracting her hand and holding it in mine so she doesn't grab the flight attendant again.

"Of course, Mr. Grant."

Ava looks at me with a dopey expression, her eyes hooded. "I love grapefruit juice."

"I know."

She rests her head against my shoulder.

"You don't like it."

"No, I don't."

"But you drank mine." She yawns, nuzzling into my bicep.

"I did."

"You had my lipstick on your mouth. Berry flavored..." she murmurs, before falling into a loud snore and dribbling on my shirt.

My arm is dead by the time we start our descent into JFK.

Chapter 9

Ava

"Welcome to The Songbird," the receptionist beams as we approach the check-in desk. "So nice to see you again, Mr. Grant. How was your flight?"

"Good, thank you," Jet says.

"It was better than I expected." I glance around the opulent white and cream marble lobby. "I slept from take-off until landing."

I turn back and grin at the receptionist. My nerves have been easing since the moment I woke up as we pulled up to the gate at JFK airport. The flight is little more than a hazy memory. Now I can enjoy being here. I've never been to New York before. We're staying in Manhattan, so hopefully I'll get a chance to explore.

"You're in our newly designed penthouse, the Oriole." The receptionist taps away into her computer.

I look at Jet. "We're in the same room?"

"It's a duplex, twin floor," the receptionist says. "Five and a half thousand square feet. But I can change—"

"No, it's fine. We live together in London..." I crane my neck to look at the giant crystal chandelier. This hotel is stunning; I can't believe I'm actually here.

Jet continues talking to the receptionist as a bellman comes over and loads our suitcases onto a cart.

"These will be waiting for you in your room, Mr. Grant," he comments as he places my silver suitcase beside Jet's matching black one.

"My suitcase is the same as yours," I say.

We look like we're on honeymoon with *his* and *hers* luggage.

Jet inclines his head toward me, a muscle in his jaw tightening. "They're the best. You want your things inside protected, don't you?"

I watch the bellman disappear with my suitcase that's filled with my lingerie. Except my waterlily panties. I needed to wear those on the flight. I'll hand-wash them for the way home. It's silly, but they're my lucky ones.

"Yes, I do. Thank you."

Jet motions to me to place my hands on the device the receptionist is holding out.

"We use your fingerprint to access the penthouses," she explains, scanning my finger. "Okay. You're all set. Would you like me to show you to your room?"

Jet shakes his head. "That won't be necessary, thank you."

He leads me away from the desk and toward the elevators. We ride up in one alone, then step out into a beautiful hallway, the walls covered in gilt-framed oil paintings.

"I need to make some calls," Jet says as he scans us into our room.

I step inside as he holds the door open for me and fight not to let my mouth hit the floor.

It's like walking onto the set of *Bridgerton*. The walls are painted cream, with ornate gold cornicing adorning them. And the decor is luxurious—velvet chairs, shining gilded side tables, Parisian rugs, thick drapes at the floor-to-ceiling windows. It's an opulent renaissance-styled heaven.

"Callaghan is staying here too. He'll be dining downstairs this evening. You'll need an evening gown."

Jet walks past me, taking his suit jacket off and folding it over the back of a velvet chair.

"Is it a dinner meeting?"

He walks back over to me, taking out his wallet.

"It will be."

"Hold on. Will be? Do we actually have a meeting scheduled with him?"

Jet's jaw tightens as he meets my gaze. "I'll be talking with him tonight."

"We've come all the way to New York, and he isn't even expecting us?" I gawk at him. "That's ridiculous.

"What's ridiculous is that I have to chase a man I abhor around the world because he has something I want." His blue eyes flash. "But I always get what I want in the end, Ava."

I look at his outstretched hand and the matte black card between his fingers.

"Buy whatever you need. Take a nap when you get back from shopping if you like. Just be ready for dinner at seven."

"I don't need your money. You already bought me suitcases."

He sighs impatiently. "I have a driver waiting in the lobby for you. He'll take you to the stores that will have what you need. Now, please, I have work to do."

"I can buy my own dress."

"This is a business trip; therefore, your expenses are mine. Take the card, Ava... and use it." His eyes hold mine with a look that tells me not to contradict him again.

My fingers tingle with the desire to push him. But I also really want to get out and see some of the city.

"Okay."

He nods once like I've pleased him, then turns and strides across the room, pulling out his phone as he goes.

"Take a drink. You need to hydrate after a flight," he clips before he disappears down a hallway.

I look around the room and locate the kitchen through some double doors at one end. I open and close the cupboards before finding a concealed refrigerator inside one.

It's stocked with mini bottles of water and grapefruit juice.

I grab a juice, then head out of the door with a smile.

"If that's him, why aren't we going over there? They've almost finished eating."

Jet's eyes darken as he looks at the man dining with an attractive younger brunette across the room.

"He's with his daughter."

"And? Maybe she works with him."

"She doesn't. Francesca is a model."

I look at the beautiful woman again. A perfect, wide smile lights up her face as she talks with Callaghan. She's stunning.

I straighten the sweetheart neckline of the cobalt blue dress I bought from Fifth Avenue. It was fun shopping with Jet's card. I picked up matching lingerie for underneath too, and some business outfits.

"Don't fidget," Jet clips.

I scowl at him. He's been a moody jerk ever since I came back to the penthouse. I hope he packed his skipping rope because he has serious stress to work out judging by the pulsing vein in his temple.

"The dress is perfect. Leave it," he adds, sipping his wine.

I look down at my dress and smile. It *is* perfect. The sales assistant at the store looked at me strangely when I handed her Jet's card to pay for it. His driver called him to appease her, and I didn't need the speakerphone to hear his annoyed response at being interrupted while he worked.

"Ava Roberts can buy whatever she wants to. Charge it to my card."

I mean, if that isn't an invitation to go a little wild, then what is?

I shuffle in my seat, a frisson of energy dancing up my spine at the feel of my new lace G-string. New lingerie always makes me happier. And after braving my first flight in ten years, I deserve a treat.

"So, what's the plan?" I ask as I finish the last spoonful of my dessert.

Jet's attention is on Callaghan as he rises from his table.

"You stay here. I'll be right back." He tosses his napkin onto the table as he follows Callaghan across the restaurant in the direction of the restrooms.

I sit back in my seat, soaking in my surroundings. The restaurant is busy, and I spot the mayor of New York and his partner dining with another couple in a far corner.

"We're leaving," Jet snaps.

I look up to where he's appeared beside the table. He's tense and the vein in his temple looks close to bursting. I flick my gaze to Callaghan's table. It's empty.

"Did you speak to him?"

"Now, Ava," he grits, taking my elbow so he can steer me from my seat.

He places his palm against my lower back and leads me from the restaurant. It's like having a hot poker against me, his fury seeping into my skin.

"Where are we going?"

"I need a fucking drink," he hisses.

I keep my mouth shut as he hails us a cab. We drive for less than ten minutes before pulling up alongside a deep emerald awning in front of a non-descript building.

"Where are we?"

Jet hands the driver some folded notes and climbs out. He comes around to my door and opens it.

"Somewhere Callaghan won't be."

He waits for me to climb out.

"No way... Is this Seasons?" I look up at the green awning. There's no name on it. But I've heard rumors about this place. You have to be *someone* to be accepted as a member here. Royalty, The President... CEO of a globally celebrated airline.

Jet places his hand on my lower back as we approach the entrance. The two suited security guards nod at us, opening the doors and granting us entrance.

"Have you been here before?"

"Yes. But mostly their LA premises."

"Oh." I walk alongside him down the dimly lit hallway. Another security guard opens a doorway at the end, and we walk into a giant, lavish bar bustling with people.

I take in the intimate tables and long bar along one wall. At the far side is a stage with a giant grand piano on it. A woman in a long sequined dress is sitting on top of it, singing a low, sultry song as a man plays.

We take a seat at one of the tables and Jet orders for us, the server returning moments later with two tumblers of clear liquid on ice.

"Are you going to tell me what happened?" I lift the glass and sniff. *Gin.*

"Nothing happened. Callaghan's still the same bastard he's always been," Jet clips.

"Where's he going to be tomorrow? Are you going to try to speak to him again?"

He takes a long drink then leans back in his seat, spreading his arms over the sides. The half-empty glass dangles between his fingertips as he holds it by the rim.

"No. He knows I want to speak with him now. That's the first step. His curiosity will win out. But not before he's had us follow him around like dogs first. It's a power game. He'll cave, though... eventually."

"So we're just going to keep showing up until he'll have a proper meeting with you?"

"Something like that." Jet grimaces as he drains his glass. "I hate him for having the upper hand. But he won't for long. Like I said, Ava. I always get what I want. I play to win."

The grit in his voice piques my interest. I enjoy winding him up. Seeing the dangerous flicker in his eyes has heat rushing in my veins. With me, it's a game, I know that. But this? This is deadly serious.

And there's something captivating about Jet Grant when he looks like he's willing to burn anyone who stands in the way of him getting what he wants.

"Miss Roberts?"

I look up into the male flight attendant's eyes.

"Yes?"

"I'm Connor. This way, please. We have a different seat for you for takeoff."

"Oh?"

My heartrate kicks up a notch as I grab my bottle of herbal pills and shove them into my purse. I haven't taken any yet. I was just about to do it but held off, wondering where Jet is. I haven't seen him since the departure gate. He pulled aside one of the airline's ground staff as I boarded our flight back to London and told me to go ahead.

I managed the flight here, but I'd be much calmer if the grumpy ass was sitting beside me again. Just knowing I'm not alone is all I need.

Sweat prickles along my hairline. *I don't want to feel alone.*

I follow the flight attendant to the front of the first-class cabin and into the plane's galley.

"Is Mr. Grant sitting where I'm moving to?" I ask, trying to conceal the anxious tremor in my voice.

"He is." Connor gives me a warm smile, then walks to the open cockpit door and says something to the pilots.

I glance around nervously as a member of ground staff exits the cockpit with a tablet in his hand and says something to the flight attendant standing by the open door where the last few passengers are boarding. I don't see Jet among them.

I wipe my clammy hands on my skirt as Connor calls me.

"Miss Roberts. You can come and take your seat now."

I inch closer to him, stepping inside the cockpit and spying the controls. There are buttons, levers, and lights everywhere, stretching up and over the ceiling.

"I don't understand."

"Take this one here." Connor points to a seat on the left-hand side behind the pilots.

I drop into it.

"See you in the air," he calls to the back of the pilot's heads.

The one on the right lifts a hand in response and then looks at me.

"I'm Brock. Nice to meet you."

I take his offered hand in a daze and shake it.

"Ava," I say.

The pilot on the left—in the Captain's seat—turns, pinning his blue gaze on me.

"We need to make our runway slot. Fasten your harness."

I stare back at Jet, my eyes dropping over the uniform he's changed into. There are four gold stripes on his shirt's epaulets.

"Y-you're flying us?"

"We both are." He motions to Brock. "One of the pilots got sick. We'd have had to cancel the flight otherwise."

My eyes ping-pong between them as my breathing quickens.

"You'll see everything that happens in here," Jet says with a measured, calmness to his tone. "Nothing to worry about. If we don't look worried, you don't need to be, okay?"

I nod, taking a slow breath in as I look into his clear, confident eyes. I might not like him, but I know he's capable.

"Okay... I trust you."

He presses his lips together, his jaw hardening. "Fasten your harness."

I look at the straps hanging from the seat. My hands shake as I reach for them. They aren't like the cabin seat belts. There are four, and they all clip into a central buckle.

"Need a hand?" Brock offers, rising from his seat.

"She's my passenger." Jet unclips his belt and gets out of his seat before Brock does.

He leans over me, his face serious as he does the first strap up. I move to help him with the second, but I catch my skirt as I fumble. It hitches up my thighs, exposing gold waterlilies on pink silk.

"They're my lucky ones," I explain as my cheeks heat.

Jet's eyes bore into the delicate strip of fabric between my thighs. He clears his throat, then smooths my skirt back down over my thighs with a brusque brush of his palm.

"You don't need luck when I'm flying you, Ava." His breath dusts over my neck as he fastens the shoulders straps for me and pulls them tight.

My gaze skates over his angular jaw and down his broad chest. His pilot uniform fits him like a glove. Like he was born in it.

"I should have guessed you'd be a pilot," I mumble as he straps back into his seat and puts his headset on.

"Been flying since before I was born," he says, before slipping into full concentration.

I'm enthralled as he and Brock go through their pre-take-off checks together. He's right, being up here has made it easier. Seeing how in control he is, knowing he's got the power in his hands for everyone's safety makes me calmer in a way I'd never have expected.

The cockpit falls into silence as we hurtle down the runway. The only thing I hear is blood rushing in my ears and a faint acknowledgment of something called 'V1' and 'V2' between the two men.

Once we're in the air and cruising gently, Brock turns to me with a grin.

"First time up front for takeoff?"

"In a plane this size," I answer, glancing out of the window at the clouds below us. I push away the rising memory. I can't think about it now. Not up here.

Jet looks at me curiously but says nothing.

I chat a little more with Brock about what I thought of New York, despite only seeing a little of it. Jet is on the radio talking to air traffic, and checking readings on the controls, the thick veins in his forearms pulsing each time he reaches to one of the switches overhead. His face is a picture of calm as he slides a pair of aviators on and looks out of the window. The sight brings reassurance to me.

There's a chime from the cockpit door and Jet checks a camera screen, then presses a button, unlocking it.

Connor comes in and checks if everyone is okay and offers us coffee.

"Why don't you go and get some sleep, Ava." Jet finally turns to me. "Without any herbal aids this time."

He looks at Connor who smiles at me. "I'll take you to your seat."

"Okay. Thanks."

I look at Jet, but I can't tell where he's looking behind his sunglasses. I unfasten my harness carefully so I don't flash my panties at him again.

I follow Connor into the cabin, and he shows me to a first-class seat at the front, near the galley.

"Can I get you anything, Miss Roberts?"

"I'm good. Thank you."

I slide into the seat and take a deep breath. My anxiety isn't as bad now that we're in the air. As long as it isn't turbulent, I can trick my mind into thinking I'm on the ground. Or riding in a train. I look around the cabin and at the fresh flowers on top of the inflight bar. *A really fancy train.*

"Grant insisted. He wanted to take this one."

My ears prick up at the conversation floating out from behind the galley curtain.

There's a chuckle that sounds like Connor. *"When the boss asks, you say yes."*

A man opens the curtain and steps out. His eyes meet mine and he gives me a friendly smile as he passes. I turn and look at the pilot uniform he's wearing. It's exactly the same as Jet's.

Including the four stripes on his epaulets.

Chapter 10

Jet

"He shot you straight down?" Hayden asks, sucking in a breath.

I lean back in the chair in my father's office as I eye him on the laptop screen. "As I expected him to."

Callaghan's reaction to my surprise appearance in New York is enough for now. He'll be scratching his head wondering if it was mere coincidence that I was there when he was. But the smug glint in his eyes when he asked if I was there to finally give in, is what set my pulse racing enough that I needed a drink to calm down afterward.

He's never getting *that* from me, not unless he pries it from my dead hands. A fact I shared with him outside the men's restrooms in The Songbird. He'll be questioning what my true motives are now. He's exactly where I want him to be.

"I'll leave you to schmooze dinner with two of our shareholders tonight, then." Hayden chuckles at my responding curse.

I hate this part of our business. Dad and I are the majority shareholders. But we have a small handful of investors who have clung on since September 11th when my father had to sell shares to raise capital and keep us going. They're onto a good thing. We've made them millions. All they need to do is sit back, enjoy it, and let us get on with it. But they like to meet with me when I'm in London. It's a way of making themselves feel important and getting their dicks hard with an all-expenses paid night to the strip clubs we end up in.

I've probably funded a brand-new house for every Destiny, Chardonnay, and Crystal over the past five years I've been US CEO.

"Wasting time is the last thing I need. Callaghan is my priority."

"Take Ava," Hayden suggests. "They won't expect you to spend the night getting lap dances then. Unless she's into watching other women?" He raises his brows.

"I've no idea what she's into."

I rub my thumb over my lips. If Ava comes, I won't lose an entire evening with two chumps who like young women grinding on their married balls.

"Callaghan's in London for two more days. What's the next move?"

"We wait," I tell Hayden. "He'll be sweating. The next time he sees me, he'll be tripping over himself to find out what it is we want."

"Okay. You're the boss." He runs a hand back through his hair, his eyes darting to someone behind the screen as they hand him a coffee.

"Don't fuck my PA while I'm gone," I hiss once she's had a chance to move away. "I don't have time to get a new one."

He chuckles. "The last one left because you made her cry."

"I meant the one before her."

"Mindy." His eyes light up. "If you'd been on the receiving end of her lip skills, you wouldn't be saying that." He leans back in his chair with a wistful sigh. "Fuck, she was a hard worker."

"Goodbye, Hayden." I hang up, cutting off his laughter.

Footsteps approaching signal my father's early arrival from work. He walks into his office and smiles as he sees me sitting at his desk.

"Good trip back, Son? Crewing told me you took the flight."

He walks over to the sideboard, lifting a crystal decanter of whiskey, tipping it to me.

I shake my head. He pours one for himself and then sinks into the seat opposite the desk with a sigh.

"I did. Thought it was a good idea to keep my hours up."

"How was Ava on the flight?"

"Did you know she was a nervous flyer?" *And that she's never orgasmed through penetrative sex?* I grind my teeth, recalling the confessions that spilled from her lips like confetti.

"I suspect it's because that's how her father died... in a plane crash."

Fuck! I lean over the desk toward him.

"Her father?"

Dad blows out a breath. "William wasn't sure she'd get on the flight."

"Why didn't you tell me?" *Why didn't she tell me?* "Jesus." I run a hand around my jaw. It makes sense why she was swallowing those herbal pills like candy now.

"I didn't know you were going to be flying to New York after I suggested she help you." My father's eyes meet mine. "When I found out, I spoke with William. He said if she hadn't mentioned anything, then not to. Ava's a strong girl, Jet. It was time she did it, but on her terms." Leaning back on his seat, he adds, "She's been through a lot. She'll tell you what she wants you to know."

I nod. That's my father's code for, he knows more, but it isn't his place to tell me. He's a man of his word, and a vault when it comes to the secrets of those he cares about.

"So, Callaghan...?"

I grunt. "Still the same smug bastard."

"I expected nothing less."

"But he's curious now. He's where I need him to be."

He takes another sip from his glass, studying me. "You've got this, Son. This airline has survived ever since your great grandfather started it. We aren't going to fail now."

"We *can't* fail." My shoulders tie up into knots as I pick up a framed photograph on my father's desk. He smiles as he looks at it.

"She'll help us." His eyes shine as I place the picture of my mother and me as a child standing beside the Boeing Stearer Bi plane back down.

My throat dries up.

"I've got dinner with Jones and Carmichael tonight."

My father snorts. "A late one for you, then."

"Not if I can help it. I'm inviting Ava."

I rise and walk around the desk, put a hand on my father's shoulder, and he places his palm over the back of it, patting it.

"Good idea, Son. She'll keep you out of trouble."

"Doubtful," I grumble. "The woman is—"

"A spitfire." He chuckles, his gaze falling back onto the photograph and my mother's long auburn hair.

I swallow the lump in my throat as he gazes at the picture.

"She's something," I mutter as I walk out.

"Oh, I'll use the main stairs."

I look behind me to where Ava is cautiously hovering at the top step of the house's old rear staircase.

"I wouldn't. Margaret washed the front hallway floor earlier; it's still drying."

"You don't want to get on the wrong side of Margaret," she says with fondness.

"You don't," I agree with a grunt. I liked our old housekeeper who retired. I didn't think anyone would run the house as well as her. But I like Margaret, and so does my father. He's more than capable of taking care of himself, but since we lost Mum and I moved to LA to take over as CEO, I've felt better knowing he isn't in this house alone all the time.

And my father's always liked strong women with a *don't-mess-with-me* attitude.

Spitfires. Like my mother.

"Do you sit here a lot," Ava asks as she inches down the stairs toward the one I'm sitting on. She's changed out of the skirt she flew home in and is in a white T-shirt and tiny denim shorts that hug her hips.

"Sometimes."

Her bare thigh brushes my leg as she sits beside me. I stiffen as waterlily and caramel wafts in my nostrils.

"Weren't you on your way downstairs?" I side-eye her.

"Don't worry, I'm not staying." Her lips twitch. "I know how you moody CEOs like your space."

How many other CEOs does she know? Has she dated any? Have any asked her if her hair matches her... Fuck, I must be jet-lagged.

I sigh, and she turns her body toward mine.

"I wanted to say thank you."

I meet her eyes, breathing through my mouth so I don't have to inhale her scent.

"For what?"

"Not treating me like a freak on the plane." Her lashes fan over her cheeks as she looks at her feet.

"You're not a freak. I used to throw up every time I got near a plane as a kid."

Her eyes are round as she brings them back to meet mine. "But you said you've been flying since before you were born?"

"I have. But my first memory of being on a plane is screaming the whole time because I hated it. But when your great grandfather starts an airline that becomes the family business, you have to get over it."

Ava laughs.

We sit in companiable silence for a while until she asks, "This deal with Callaghan, is it serious?"

"It's important I get what I need from him. The airline is everything to me and I'll do whatever it takes to ensure its success. Nothing and no-one, even an ass like Callaghan, will stop me doing what's best for it."

"Hm." She smiles softly. "I love that it's your family business. It must have brought you all closer, working on the same goal over the years."

She makes no attempt to move from her place beside me. Instead, she lets out a contented sigh.

"You know, they say that if you like sitting on the stairs, it means you had a good childhood."

"Who's they?"

"I don't know." She shrugs, her lips twisting into a smile as she glances at me. "Some people with a lot of time on their hands to think these things up."

"Figures," I grumble.

"I'm guessing it's true though, right?"

Maybe it's the hint of something in her voice that sounds like she's desperate for a distraction, or maybe it's what my father told me in his office, knowing that she lost her father so cruelly, and then her own mother left her behind and moved away.

Whatever it is, it has my fingers curling around the edge of the next wooden step down and tugging.

Ava leans forward with interest as I pull the top loose and slide it forward, revealing the small space beneath.

"This was my hiding place," I explain, looking into the gap. "My father still doesn't know about it. But my mother did. She used to leave me secret notes here. And gifts."

I reach inside and lift out a toy airplane that's covered in a layer of fine dust.

"That's so sweet," Ava breathes, as I turn it over.

"I guess that answers your question." I drop the plane back inside and fix the step into place, swallowing the unexpected lump in my throat.

"It must be hard... missing her. I know what that's like."

"It is." My eyes slide to hers. "I'm sorry that knowing the pain of losing a parent is the one thing we have in common."

"The *only* thing we have in common." Her lips twitch in a ghost of smile. Ava's gaze drops to my hand and the fading red nail marks on my skin. "I'm sorry I clawed you on the plane."

I look into her pinched eyes. "Don't be. It's fine."

"Maybe I can make it up to you? Untangle your skipping rope if it gets knotted or something."

The sound that comes from the back of my throat almost sounds like a laugh.

"Sure. You can do that." I pause for a moment. "Actually, I have a dinner with two investors tonight. They're boring, leery bastards. But if you come with me, it'll save me from a late night, entertaining them alone."

Her brows shoot up her forehead.

"Forget it. I shouldn't have asked. It's not Callaghan. It's not what you agreed to—"

"Okay. I mean, sure, if you want me to? I don't mind."

We stare at one another as something shifts in the air. Her teeth sink into her plump lower lip as she blinks at me.

"Jet?" she breathes, leaning a little closer.

I inhale through my nose, my senses assaulted by sweet caramel and fresh flowers.

"Ava?"

"Umm." She looks at my mouth, then up into my eyes. If she comes any closer, I'll be able to taste each exhale passing through her berry lips.

A loud thump in the hallway makes her jump back like she's been branded.

"Stupid thing," someone mutters.

Ava rushes down the stairs, picking up a grapefruit that's rolled along the floor. Margaret appears, huffing, a grocery bag with a broken handle held between her hands.

"Thanks, Ava, love," she says, taking the fruit and stuffing it back inside.

Margaret sees me and nods in greeting. "Your father said you don't need dinner tonight?"

"No, thank you. I'm eating out."

"So am I." Ava's eyes meet mine for a spilt second.

"Okay, that's fine. As long as I know." Margaret looks between the two of us and then continues down the hall. Ava goes with her, and the sound of their easy chatter grows quieter.

I pinch the bridge of my nose, my shoulders tight with tension over whatever the fuck just happened.

Whatever that moment was.

Asking her to dinner was a bad idea.

I should have taken my chance with Jones, Carmichael, and the strippers.

Chapter 11

Ava

I TAKE IN THE red crescent-shaped marks on the back of Jet's hand as he places his wine glass down and nods, feigning interest in Jones's conversation.

Carmichael, his slimmer but pervier companion leans into me, his hot breath fanning my cheek. "Jet doesn't usually bring such beautiful company with him."

"Oh?" I smile politely.

"He always comes alone." His eyes move over my hair and down to my cleavage. "This is a nice change. Tell me, there's always something I've been curious about with redheads..."

Jet's darkened gaze bores into Carmichael, making me shudder.

"Is your hair that beautiful color everywh—?"

I tip my wine glass over, decanting my merlot into his lap.

"Oops. I am so sorry. I'm so clumsy." I fake an apologetic smile as I grab my napkin, passing it to him. As he looks down, I use the opportunity to inch my chair away. We're sitting at a small round table, so my movement makes me brush up against Jet.

He stands quickly. "Take my seat, Ava."

"There's none on her seat," Carmichael says. "It's all on me."

Jet holds my eyes. "My seat," he clips.

I slide across onto it and he steps around and lowers into mine.

"How's your wife?" he asks as Carmichael blots his wet pants. "You told me she'd taken up painting last time we saw each other."

Carmichael's jaw tenses and he drops the napkin back to the table. "She's enjoying it. She has a talent for it."

"I'm pleased to hear it."

I settle into Jet's chair and the server brings over a fresh glass of wine. The men begin talking about Atlantic Airways and new route announcements. The majority of the evening has been Jet answering their nitpicky questions about things. He's right, they are boring. I stifle a yawn, hiding it behind my hand.

"Lost a lot of money, I bet."

My attention piques as Jet stiffens at Jones's words.

"We've heard rumors that if you don't get these engine issues fixed, then the whole airline is at risk," Jones continues.

"Your US operation could drag the UK one down with it. Ruin both sides," Carmichael adds, his eyes wandering to me and dipping to my cleavage again.

"You should know better than to listen to rumors, gentlemen," Jet says with a sharp edge to his voice. "Atlantic has been in our family for generations. We aren't about to change that."

"Maybe it's time for something new." Carmichael leers at me. "I always like trying out something different. Maybe a new CFO would—"

"Hayden Marks is the best there is," Jet snaps. "You have nothing to worry about. Your *minority* shares will continue to bring you healthy dividends."

Carmichael visibly shrinks in his seat. Dinner just got more interesting at least.

The conversation continues with Jones grilling Jet, while Jet deflects every question easily without actually answering any. The two men have had enough wine that they don't even realize he's not told them anything new for the past twenty minutes.

"Where's that pretty young waitress?" Carmichael swings his head around. "I need a refill."

I catch Jet looking at me from beneath his dark brows, his eyes traveling over my face and narrowing like he's worked something out.

A spark ignites low in my core, traveling up my spine until my whole body feels like it's tingling.

I got closer to him than ever before on the staircase earlier. I don't know what came over me. Relief at having finally stepped onto a plane again, maybe? Or the comedown from all of the memories and emotions it dredged up? After we got back, I went straight to the pool house to work. I wrote more in a couple of hours than I have since the day I arrived at Rochwell house. It's like the lid was finally lifted off and things started to flow. I can only attribute that to the fact that for the first time in a decade, I took a flight. Something I once loved but has been the source of indescribable pain to me for so many reasons.

Jet's softer eyes are still on me as I sip my wine.

This isn't right. We can't suddenly start getting on. He might think he understands me better since that flight, but he doesn't. No one knows everything. Not even Gramps.

The thawing in his gaze makes me yearn for him to look at me with disdain again. I don't want him to feel sorry for me. I'd rather he reprimands me for not using a glass and calls me a delinquent than feel sorry for me.

This isn't right. Everything about the neutral position of his lips is wrong. He's lacking the signature scowl I'm used to. It's unnerving, and it makes my throat scratchy.

An idea hits me that's sure to piss him off and provoke a reaction. I make my excuses and head to the ladies' room.

When I slide back into the seat beside Jet, I reach into his lap beneath the table and lean in close.

"All these tough questions being fired at you, and you're doing so well, but I thought you still might appreciate a talisman. They aren't my luckiest pair, but maybe they'll work for you."

He freezes, a muscle in his jaw tightening as my breath dusts his ear.

His fingers curl around mine beneath the table as I deposit the tiny scrap of lace into them.

I sit back in my seat and lift my wine glass to my lips with a smug smile. Jet's listening to Jones as he talks, but the miniscule roll of his jaw tells me he's grinding his teeth. A vein bulges in his temple, and he nods swiftly, pushing his chair back from the table.

"I'm sorry to cut this short, gentlemen." He signals the server and passes over his card. "Ava and I flew in this morning. The missed sleep is catching up on us."

The men's faces fall as Jet pays and stands, pulling my chair out for me.

"But it's still so early," Jones complains.

"And there's a cab waiting outside to take you for a nightcap and some entertainment," he says smoothly. "All with compliments from myself and my father, of course."

Carmichael's brows hitch. "Well, then. We should go if it's all organized."

Jones nods in agreement, and Carmichael manages a final, parting leer of my breasts as we say goodbye.

Jet marches me to the exit of the restaurant with one arm around me, his hand gripping my elbow.

"What the fuck are you doing?" he snaps, taking me around the corner of the restaurant into a small alleyway.

"What do you mean?"

"These!"

He yanks my cream lace panties from his pocket and brandishes them in front of my face. I step backward into the wall as he moves closer, pinning me between his body and the brick.

"Oh, those. Pretty, aren't they? I bought them in New York." I admire the tiny strip of lace dangling from his finger. The golden flecks woven into the fabric glint in the moonlight.

His eyes bug before he closes his fist around them.

"Why the fuck are you handing me your panties beneath the table at a business dinner?"

I smile internally. The incensed glint is back in his eyes as he towers over me.

"They're lucky." I shrug.

He sucks a deep breath in through his nose and slams the fist holding my panties against the wall by my head.

"I should spank your ass so hard that you can't sit for a week after pulling a stunt like that." His chest heaves as he leans in closer to me. "We work together, what the fuck?"

Excitement bursts in my core as he struggles to rein in his anger. His choice of reprimand is... intriguing, a rare glimpse into Mr. Always-in-control's psyche. So he's into spanking? It's probably just talk, but still... *interesting*.

I lick my lips trying not to let my smirk show. "I'm not sure spanking employees is an acceptable form of management. Besides, you're not even paying me."

His fingers flex against the wall as the delicate lace dangles from them. I want to demand he be careful, so they don't get snagged by the rough bricks.

"What the hell are you playing at?" Heat radiates from his body while his blue eyes spark like flames.

"Relax, Jet. It was just a bit of fun." I pat him playfully on his solid chest.

His nostrils flare. "A bit of fun? You think handing me your panties is fun?"

"Jesus, calm down." I roll my eyes even though I'm loving every second of his reaction.

A vein throbs in his temple, almost as if on the verge of being ruptured.

"Come on, we both know you're not actually going to spank me." I roll my eyes. "So shall we go?"

I try to move past him, but he blocks me. I sink my teeth into my lower lip, energy racing through my veins as he slowly rakes his eyes up, pausing briefly on my breasts, before he glowers at me.

"You won't do it. You're too scared of losing control," I whisper.

"Ava," he growls, sending a shiver hurtling up my spine.

"Go on." I lean closer until my lips almost touch his. *"I dare you."*

His pupils blow wide. Then he spins me, knocking the air from my lungs as he pins me against the wall with his chest to my back and his mouth lowered to my ear.

"You think I won't make this sweet ass bright red. Leave my handprint on you... mark you as *mine*." His words are like gravel grating over my soul and making me shudder.

I incline my face over my shoulder as I try to bring my breathing under control. My panties are at eye-level beside me, clenched firmly inside his white-knuckled fist.

"I know you won't. You don't have it in you to be so reckless," I taunt. "You're all about control... You wouldn't lose it for a delinquent who doesn't use a glass."

His eyes burn into mine as my chest vibrates with a quiet laugh.

"I knew it." I smirk.

Cold air whips around the back of my thighs as my dress is shoved up roughly.

I gasp with a mixture of surprise and satisfaction that I've made him crack. Butterflies rage in my core as his warm breath dusts my ear.

"One thing you should learn about me," he murmurs, "is that I'm *always* the one who has control."

He presses his torso against me, forcing my nipples to graze the rough wall. Then he slides his hand over my naked ass cheek and squeezes with enough pressure to make me whimper.

"You're going to regret ever playing with me, Ava... I always win."

The first strike makes me cry out. "Fuck!"

"Count to three," he hisses.

I clamp my thighs together as he slaps my ass again. Without thinking, I arch back, chasing his hand as he moves it away.

"Count!"

"One," I cry as he spanks me again, sending a rush of hot blood between my thighs.

"Two," I yelp as he strikes me again.

"Another," he grunts.

"Three!" I curse as the final one lands harder than the others, setting off a deep thrumming that travels through my body before culminating in my aching clit.

His warm palm flattens over my skin, massaging it until the stinging fades. "You took that so well."

Holy fuck.

I mumble incoherently, the warmth of his praise rendering me speechless. All I can feel is a delicious energy in my skin where he struck me. I push back into his hand, wetness coating my inner thighs.

"Please," I whimper.

"Such a brat," he mutters as he slips his fingers between my legs from behind. He swipes them over my swollen clit and tuts as I mewl shamelessly and try to grind onto his hand. "Getting wet from being spanked, then begging for more."

"Jet..." I breathe. He stays still, as I wriggle and writhe until I manage to position myself so that I can slide down onto his fingertips. I moan, clenching around them as I get the tips inside me.

Then they're gone.

"Huh?" I spin around.

He takes a step away from me. "The fuck am I doing?" he hisses. His eyes darken to deep blue pools as he scowls. "Cover yourself up, for fuck's sake" he barks at me.

"But—?" I yank my dress down, my cheeks burning as humiliation courses through me.

He slides the fist holding my panties into his pocket, then reaches forward, placing his other hand on my lower back.

"Let's go. I have an early start tomorrow."

I shove his hand away. "Don't fucking touch me!"

I march ahead of him to where he parked his car. My pussy throbs with unmet need as I listen to his steady steps behind me.

I can't believe he did it. It's been so long since anyone touched me. The last time was a drunken night at university that I barely remember. But despite how close I was to getting off on his fingers, the fact I begged him before he ruthlessly shot me down has shame burning through my gut like acid.

I sense him behind me a moment before he leans forward, opening the car door for me.

"I told you that you wouldn't want to play with me, Ava." His breath touches the shell of my ear, and I hate that my clit throbs in response.

"Fuck you. And fuck your games." I seethe as I drop into the seat. "You're a fucking asshole."

He waits until I've finished hurling insults before he closes my door gently and walks around the front of the car. He's a picture of controlled calm in his dark gray suit and cobalt tie.

I can't stand him. In fact, I hate him.

He opens the driver's door and slides into his seat.

"Fasten your belt," he instructs.

I do it, not to obey him, but because he'll lean over and do it himself if I don't. And the thought of having him close to me again makes me shake with rage.

We drive back in silence. He doesn't even put the radio on. I hear every measured, relaxed intake of breath the bastard makes. Meanwhile my pulse races, and the back of my neck is on fire.

Jet might have won tonight's little game I started. But if he thinks he's in control just because I moaned his name in a moment of unexpected arousal, then he's wrong.

So wrong.

Chapter 12

Ava

I DON'T SEE JET the following day since he skips dinner with Magnus and I. I work on my story, managing to get a lot written. But it comes at a cost bringing it all back up. I spend most of the night crying, and wake with puffy eyes.

I walk into the kitchen for breakfast and the familiar whipping sound coming from outside slaps me in the face. I open the fridge, grabbing a carton as fast as I can.

I have my back to the garden doors when the sound of one opening makes me slam the fridge shut with force.

Tension creeps up my spine, making me take in a slow, purposeful breath as I keep my back to the looming presence behind me.

I haven't looked into Jet's eyes since the moment he pulled his fingers from inside me and told me to cover myself up. Shame makes my lungs burn. I wanted to mess with him, make him scowl at me like he usually does.

I didn't expect to walk away feeling like shit after.

"You need to be ready to leave in thirty minutes."

I stiffen as the words hit my back.

"Did you hear me?"

I turn slowly, steeling myself to meet his gaze. He looks back at me, the blue of his eyes cool and unwavering.

There's nothing in them. No recognition. Nothing.

"Thirty minutes?" I hate that my voice comes out hoarse from my restless night. I clear my throat, but even that sounds like an animal crooning in pain.

He takes a step closer, and his eyes pinch at the corners.

"Why?" I ask, turning my back on him.

"I need to go into head office. There are some people I need to speak to about a new supplier contract I'm setting up."

"Doesn't sound like a meeting with Callaghan." I busy myself with fetching a packet of bagels from the cupboard.

"It isn't. But it's connected."

His voice moves closer, and my back grows warm with his nearing heat.

"Fine. I can be ready."

"Turn around." His deep voice cuts through me, and I halt my movements, dragging in a breath.

"I'm busy." I force my hands to work and open the bag, taking out a bagel that I have no appetite for.

"Ava?"

The way he barks my name has tingles running through me.

Tingles of regret.

Large hands bracket my upper arms, and he turns me. His eyes sweep over my face, settling on my eyes.

"You've been crying."

I drop my gaze to the side before I see anything that might resemble pity, or fake concern in his eyes.

"I didn't sleep well, that's all."

He lets go of my arms but stays close to me. He's shirtless. Beads of sweat have gathered over his perfectly defined torso, collecting in the small dusting of dark hair that covers his pecs. They look so soft. Like the perfect place to rest your head and be held. To be safe. To be protected.

You'd never feel alone lying on a chest like Jet's.

"Cover yourself up, for fuck's sake."

I force my feet to move and push past him, abandoning my bagel and juice.

"I'll be ready in twenty-five," I snap as I stride out of the room.

The head office of Atlantic Airways is truly something. Jet left me in their large café area while he went off to speak to people. But once my latte is finished and he still isn't back, I begin to wander.

There are training drills for the flight attendant's going on behind a giant glass wall. They're all dressed in boiler suits and sliding down a large evacuation slide that's rigged up to some industrial looking stairs. I watch them for a while, fascinated, before following a wide corridor adorned with photographs from the airline's history on the walls.

I stop at one of a younger Magnus with a much older man with familiar striking blue eyes. The plaque beneath reads, *Magnus Grant and his grandfather, Atlantic Airways' founder, Cedric Grant.*

I carry on walking and the corridor opens up into a double-height foyer with small trees in giant pots scattered about. In the center is a vintage-looking plane with two large flat wings on either side of the fuselage. It must be a life-sized replica or something. I've never seen anything like it.

I glance around as I walk over to it, but the space is deserted.

The metal is cool as I place my hand on it. I stroke my palm along the side as I look at it in awe. I've seen a few types of small aircraft. But never one with two wings on top of the other before.

"It's a wing-walker."

I jump at Jet's deep voice and pull my hand away.

"It's fine. You can touch it." He walks over to join me, standing beside me as he looks over the plane with a tight-lipped expression.

"Is it a replica?"

He shoves his hands into his pant pockets. "No."

"You have an actual plane in the office?" I admire it again, running my hand over its faded blue paintwork.

"We are an airline," he clips.

I meet his eyes and there's a glint of amusement in his, but it's gone in a flash.

"Besides, it probably wouldn't fly now. It's the last undamaged one of its kind. Most were destroyed when newer models were designed."

"It's amazing." I smile. "Have you always had it in here?" It's a small plane, but it's still a huge thing to have on display like this.

"For the last thirty-three years. My father bought it just before I was born."

"Oh."

Jet's phone rings in his pocket, and he pulls it out, frowning at the screen.

"I need to take this. Then we'll leave."

Before I can ask where we're going next, he brings the phone to his ear.

"Francesca?" Her name rolls off his tongue like warm honey.

Something twists my gut as he wanders off, chuckling softly. I stare at his retreating back until he disappears through a door.

I walk around the space to pass the time until he comes back. I stop at another photograph on the wall in black and white. It's of the plane that's on display. It's flying high up in the sky and there's a figure standing in the center of the top set of wings.

'June's Blue Bird.'

I look at the plane, then to the photograph again. I step closer, squinting to make out the image. It's not clear enough to see much detail of the figure standing on the wings with their arms in the air. But from the curve of their hips in the boiler-style suit they're wearing, and the locks of hair flying out from beneath their goggles, I'd say they're female.

"June," I murmur. Magnus always calls his late wife June Bug when he talks about her. I'd bet money that this is her in the photograph.

I grow restless as I amble around the space some more. How long does it take Jet to talk to Francesca? Why is James Callaghan's daughter calling him anyway? Maybe she's acting as a go-between for her father and Jet. Perhaps they're about to strike a deal on these new engines Jet needs. Then I'll no longer need to follow him around like a pathetic puppy. The thought perks me up. He doesn't even need me. So far, I haven't taken a single note down in any meetings. Instead, I've shopped in New York, been out for two fancy meals, and been spanked.

The only reason I'm still here is because I refuse to back down. Jet will make out he's won something over me if I try and get out of my promise to be at his side until this deal is sorted.

What was I thinking? Stupid.

I fiddle with the strap of my purse, irritation spreading through me. If Francesca's call is about the deal, then he should have placed her on speakerphone so I could hear. Then I could offer assistance, which is the whole reason I'm here.

Maybe it wasn't about the deal? He seemed rather familiar when we saw Francesca dining with Callaghan in New York. He told me she was a model, so he knows that much about her, if not more.

I pull my phone out of my purse and type Francesca Callaghan into Google. The screen immediately fills with perfect image after perfect image. I click on one of her on a runway wearing lingerie and a pair of giant feathered wings. *Wow.* Her legs would reach up to my chin. I click out and scroll down the page.

A picture of her with her hand on Jet's cheek as he gazes at her at some red-carpet event steals the air from my lungs. It's a punch to the gut, even though the moment I heard the way he spoke her name when he took her call made me suspicious.

That bastard. The photo is dated a few years ago, but he could have told me. We're supposed to be working together on this deal. Surely the fact that he dated the daughter of the man he wants to negotiate a deal with is a fact he should have divulged to me.

I shove my phone back into my purse and stomp through the door that Jet disappeared through, muttering the word *asshole* under my breath as I stalk down the corridor.

I round a corner and am met with a staircase. Jet's sitting a couple of steps up, his head in his hands.

"Oh." My angered advance falters at the defeated slump of his shoulders. He lifts his head and there's something in his gaze that makes my chest tight. Then he blinks, and it's gone.

"Everything okay?" I ask tentatively.

"Of course." A deep V forms between his brows. He stands and descends the stairs, stopping directly in front of me. His eyes penetrate mine with an intensity that makes me swallow. "Nothing for you to worry about."

"Was it about the deal?"

"No."

I search his eyes for a thread of dishonesty, but there's nothing but a hint of annoyance in his dark gaze.

"Fine." I cross my arms. "Then I definitely won't worry about it."

He nods once, a muscle ticking in his cheek. "Let's go. I want to catch Rich while he's at the estate. He won't be there this afternoon."

"Rich?" I fall into a hurried step beside him as I try to keep up with his determined strides.

We walk back down the corridor, and he produces an ID card from his pocket, tapping it to a sensor beside a door.

"Logan Rich." He holds the door open for me to exit. I step outside. We've come through an unmarked exit door and are in the car park where Jet left his car earlier.

"He's at the Silver Distillery. We're going to be serving their gin on all our flights and in all airport lounges from now on."

"We're going to the Silver Estate?" I puff as he marches toward his car, and it unlocks automatically.

He opens the door for me and looks at me over the top of it as I climb in. "It won't take long."

He shuts the door and is sinking into the driver's seat moments later. I'm stifling a yawn as he starts the engine.

"Why don't you get some sleep on the way? You clearly need it," he mutters, indicating he finds it highly inappropriate that anyone dare yawn during the workday.

"I'm fine," I cut back harshly. I might have stayed up all night writing and crying, but there's no way I'm sleeping in his fancy-pants car. Even if the seats *are* heated and feel like toasty hugs.

We drive without talking, but he at least has the radio on this time. It's some instrumental piano music. Gentle, soothing, melodic notes drift around the comfortable leather interior and I turn my face toward the window, hiding another yawn in my shoulder.

Damn it, why didn't I get three espressos instead of a latte?

The music continues, washing over me like a gentle wave as the lanes of motorway traffic give way to green hedgerows and stretches of rolling fields.

My breathing begins to match Jet's calm, rhythmic inhales from beside me.

"I'm not tired," I say, my eyes fixed outside the window.

"If you say so," he replies.

"Not tired at all." I yawn.

Chapter 13

Ava

I WAKE WITH A start. We aren't moving anymore. Everything's quiet.

Jet's gone.

I stretch, straightening in my seat. A logoed Atlantic Airways blanket slips from my chest and pools in my lap. I lift the soft fabric and a hint of Jet's aftershave drifts toward me. My core thrums to life.

I shove the blanket off and onto the driver's seat with a scoff.

We're parked in front of the main offices of the Silver Estate. It's a beautiful, period stone mansion that sits at the center of the sprawling country estate and gardens. I knew every inch of the grounds here like the back of my hand once. I haven't been here for years. Not until the other week when I saw an event advertised.

I wasn't sure how it would feel coming back here alone. But I did it, anyway. And I filled a few pages of my notepad with memories. Pages that were the reason I never slept last night, and then fell asleep in Jet's car.

I crunch over the gravel in my heels, making my way to the front door to press the bell. It takes a few moments before a young woman answers.

"Hi." She smiles. "Are you here with Mr. Grant?"

"I am. I'm Ava."

"Nice to meet you. I'm Jasmin."

Realization dawns as I look over her face and long, dark hair. *Jasmin Silver*, one half of the brother-sister duo who inherited the estate from their grandparents.

"Is he inside?" I smooth the back of my hair down with one hand, conscious that it could be mussed up from my impromptu nap.

"He and Logan headed over to the warehouse." She points to a large building in the distance. "One second, I'll grab my car keys and take you there."

"There's no need." I smile at her gratefully. "I'll walk, I could use the air."

She looks at me with uncertainty.

"Honestly, I love the grounds here. It'll be nice to walk."

I worry that she'll offer to come with me and ask more about how I know the estate.

"They're beautiful. We're really lucky. The waterlilies are in bloom if you head that way."

Relief makes me match her smile as I thank her, then walk across the gravel driveway. I step off it and onto a smooth stone path that weaves its way through manicured gardens in the direction of the warehouse. I'm going to miss the lake. It's over to my right, the other side of the tree line. I rub a hand over my chest knowing it's so close.

A few lilies blooming last time I came. But knowing they're all blossoming now... I can't miss it.

I head off the path and over the grass, slipping through the line of leafy trees, stepping onto the path at the other side that runs around the perimeter of the lake.

Tears prick at my eyes without warning, and I slam to a halt.

The surface of the water is barely visible beneath the blanket of pink and white. The flowers' fresh scent hangs delicately in the air. *Just like it did that day.*

Inhaling, I walk closer to the water, soaking it in. Time has no hold here. If I close my eyes, I can hear my mother's delighted giggle.... Gramps' deep voice... my father's laugh as I splashed him at the edge of the water.

"You're awake."

I snap my eyes open, the memory fading. Jet appears beside me, hands thrust into his pockets as he surveys the surface of the lake.

"Did you discuss what you needed to with Mr. Rich?"

His eyes stay on the waterlilies. "Yes. Everything's sorted. We can leave now." He clears his throat. "Unless you'd like to stay a little longer?"

"No, I'm good." My eyes return to the lilies, but I can't make my feet move.

He rolls his shoulders and there's a large crack. "Actually... I think I need another minute before I get back in the car."

I side-eye him, but he's not looking at me.

"Sure. Let's stay." My chest softens in relief. It's too beautiful to leave just yet.

He rolls his neck this time, and it cracks too.

"That's bad for your joints."

"So you tell me. Must be my ancient thirty-three-year-old bones." He turns toward me, and I feel the heat of his gaze on my cheek. "No age-related jokes? You must still be tired," he mutters.

"He was thirty-three when he died." I swallow the lump in my throat.

"Your father?"

I glance at Jet, then away again. I focus on a flower instead, allowing my eyes to trace over every dip and curve of its perfect petals.

"He was too young to die," I whisper. "I think about what could have been if... It was caused by pilot error. The press reported on it a lot at the time."

"I'm sorry, Ava."

I'm grateful that there's only a tinge of empathy in his voice. I got used to the sympathetic looks and words cooed over me when I was younger. Hearing them again resurfaces all that pain. I'd rather keep it submerged, blanketed in happy memories of lilies instead. Hidden in the depths where it doesn't burn my lungs and sear my heart thinking about it.

"Did you find the flight back from New York easier?"

"Yes," I answer without hesitation.

"I can only imagine the flight there was the hardest. Your first one since."

I wrap my arms around myself, pushing away more memories before they can flourish into another sleepless, tear-filled night. "The way home was better... knowing you were the one flying me."

Seeing any other pilot in that captain's seat wouldn't have helped me. But for whatever reason, seeing Jet sitting there did.

"I knew you'd be in control. I knew you wouldn't make a mistake." I hide my wavering voice with a quiet laugh. "Because you always win. Just like you told me after dinner with Jones and Carmichael."

"Ava..."

His soft voice has my chest burning. I turn toward him and finally inch my eyes back up to his face.

"That was..." He inhales through his nose as his eyes roam over my face, settling on my lips. "It was wrong. I shouldn't have touched you."

I clamp my mouth shut so that I don't blurt out that the touching didn't bother me one bit. It's the way he acted afterward. Like he was disgusted.

He drags in a ragged breath, then blows out slowly. "I had no right to."

"Yet you did it anyway. *Five* times."

His eyes darken, and his jaw clenches.

I sigh and turn back to the water.

"I used to come here with my parents and Gramps. The last time we were all here together, the lilies were in bloom like this."

"Do you miss your mother?"

His question catches me off guard.

"Of course, I do."

"You said she's an actress in LA?"

Pride swells in my chest. "She is. She's played some good roles. Like Bonnie in *The Hidden Paths*."

Jet looks at me blankly.

"The sitcom? It was picked up by Netflix."

There isn't even a flash of recognition. He probably doesn't even watch TV, probably thinks it's beneath him or something.

"She left when you were a child?" It's delivered like a question, but I don't miss the judgmental undercurrent.

"She didn't deal with her grief well after Dad died."

"When did you last see her? I'm assuming she visits you often seeing as you told me New York was your first flight in years?"

My torso tightens as I pin him with a scorching glare.

"She's busy. But she's always sending gifts. She paid for my private schooling. She did everything she could to make sure I had what I needed."

"I see." He purses his lips.

"You see, do you?"

His nostrils flare and his lips thin as he looks down his nose at me.

"I've had enough of people 'seeing' things they know nothing about. Yes, I miss my mum. No, we're not together. But she's still my mum. I thought you'd understand what it's like not seeing them every day. It doesn't mean you stop loving each other. It doesn't mean—"

"My mother died, Ava. She didn't *choose* to leave me behind. She was taken. And I was an adult." His gaze bores into mine, cold and unyielding.

My chest caves. I blink, struggling to breathe.

"You're such an asshole..." I turn away from him, screwing my burning eyes shut. "Such an entitled, cold-hearted asshole!" I fire before I stride away.

"Ava!"

His continued shouts of my name are drowned out by blood rushing in my ears as I break into a run. I pump my arms harder as my feet slam heavily on the path. I don't even know where I'm going. I just keep running, needing to be away from him. Be as far away as possible from his accusations and his self-righteous bullshit. Jet knows nothing about my family. Nothing about me. Yet he thinks he can cast judgment on my life like he's superior to everyone around him.

Asshole.

My mother loves me. She's invited me to LA to live with her countless times. I'm the one who's stopped us seeing one another much over the years by not being able to get on a plane. I tried so many times. Made it as far as the boarding gate once. But then the tightness in my chest would start, followed by the spots in my vision. The last time I tried was when I was eighteen. I'm still amazed I finally did it with Jet. I should have tried herbal pills and the need to get one up on an arrogant asshole as an incentive years ago.

My legs burn. Running in heels is hard. I slow a little, hoping I've put enough distance between me and Jet.

Mum's work keeps her in LA. If she could have survived after Dad died by staying in England, she would have. I was the one who didn't want to move to the US with her. I wanted to stay near Dad's memories. Near Gramps.

I was too scared that starting over somewhere alien to me would make me feel alone.

I drag in a splintered breath that sounds like a sob.

I didn't want to feel alone.

"Ava!"

I'm spun around, large hands bracketing my upper arms as Jet's wild eyes search out mine. His chest is heaving, and his tie has been thrown back over his shoulder.

"Get. Off. Me." I struggle, but it only makes his hands curl tighter.

"I'm sorry."

His eyes are murderous, he looks anything but sorry.

"Fuck you!"

I expect him to flinch, to react to the venom in my voice. But he doesn't. His cool blue eyes just delve into mine like he can see all my secrets.

"I'm sorry," he repeats. "You're right. I'm an asshole."

"One thing we agree on." I struggle some more.

"Stop." He walks us backward until I'm pinned between his body and a large birch tree.

"If you let me go, I'm going to smack your stupid face!"

He drops his hands. "Be my guest."

My hand flies up like a rocket, but Jet's faster. He grabs my wrist, then pulls my arm out, gripping my wrist tightly. He brings my palm back sharply against his cheekbone with a satisfying *whack*, making his head snap to the side and forcing a hiss to spill from his lips.

My hand throbs immediately before he encases it in his, rubbing the hot flesh with his thumbs.

"What the hell is wrong with you?" I gape at the growing red handprint on his cheek.

"Didn't want you going easy on me."

He looks into my eyes and my breath stutters as I realize my heart is no longer hammering at the sight of him all pent-up. My pulse has moved lower... and now, it's thrumming a deep rhythm between my legs.

"I wouldn't have."

"In that case, next time you can slap me yourself."

"How about you stop being an asshole and no one gets slapped?"

We stare at each other like two angry bulls.

I tear my hand from his grasp and glance at my palm.

"I am sorry." He tilts my chin back up, so I meet his eyes. "*Truly.*"

The regret in his voice makes me screw my eyes closed, and I try to turn away. But he turns my face back to his.

"I let my feelings get away with me, and I spoke out of turn."

"You have feelings?" I snort.

He doesn't blink as he studies me. "You have so much fight in you, so much spirit. Yet, you keep yourself here in your safe little box."

"I—"

"Tell me you don't crave adventure, Ava. Tell me you don't feel alive with possibilities when you think about all the things you haven't seen in the world yet."

He's right. I always wanted those things. *I craved them.*

Until the thought of them gave me nightmares.

"I saw the way you looked when you came back from sightseeing in Manhattan. You were *glowing*. And it makes me mad knowing you were left behind. That you could have been seeing the world all these years."

"I couldn't," I croak around the dryness in my throat as he tears my fears wide open. "Not wanting to fly, it's—"

"—because flying stole your father from you. And made it too hard for your mother to be able to stay… I know how hard grief can be, Ava."

I grimace as he leans closer.

"And I'm an asshole for even implying anything else. I'm sorry."

I've lost count of how many times he's said sorry. But each one has been sincere. Each one has made the coiled muscles in my body ease a little more.

Warm breath fans over my skin as he presses a gentle kiss to my forehead.

My heart stalls.

He lowers his face, his eyes boring into mine. "I'm sorry."

I don't know how my hands travel to his chest, only that they're fisting the fabric as I cling to him.

"I don't forgive you." My gaze drops to his lips.

"Good. I don't deserve you to."

I wet my lips, unable to look away from the glimpse of his perfect teeth as he breathes in slowly.

"I don't even like you," I say.

"Not many people do."

He's staring at me in a way that has me forgetting to breathe.

"You're a stuffy suit with an unhealthy addiction to skipping."

He leans closer until his lips almost brush mine. "What else?"

"I've never seen you smile properly. I bet you're incapable. Emotionally stunted."

"And?" His breath falls onto my lips, making them part so I can taste him.

"And you sweat a lot when you're working out. It's kind of gross."

I'm lying, it's totally hot.

"You use glasses," I continue. "As if you're too good to drink out of a carton."

"I drank out of yours."

I stall. "And how was that for you?"

A deep rumble vibrates in his chest, making my stomach flutter.

I twist his shirt inside my fists. He's refusing to move any closer. It's like he's adamant he won't be the one to take us past this line.

But ever since I met him, I've been unable to resist pushing Jet Grant. The flare in his blue eyes when I do is a thrill I doubt I'll ever grow tired of. There's something dangerously addictive about it.

"I bet you're a terrible kisser because you can't ever let go."

One of his thick dark brows arches, but he remains rooted to the spot, making no move to prove me wrong.

"It'll be like kissing a dead fish." I lean closer. "Absolutely terrible…"

I slam my lips against his, expecting him to stiffen and push me away. Or to be uptight and awkward.

He's none of those things.

He groans, and my knees buckle as he pins me against the tree. He sinks both of his hands into my hair and kisses me back. Feverishly.

I swallow back every word.

Jet kisses with a ferocity that floors me. But I refuse to let him win. So I match him. Stroke for stroke.

Groan for groan. Desperate, groping hand for groping hand.

Jet Grant's kiss could launch rockets, end famine, *destroy* hearts.

It has every nerve in my body firing out in confusion, energy buzzing through me in every direction it can go, then slamming back on itself and making my stomach flip and my head light.

"Jesus," he groans, drawing back enough to nip my lower lip before he pushes forward again, turning me inside out with pleasure with the way his tongue commands my mouth.

His curse is the only thing that alerts me to how deep my nails are digging into the back of his neck as I kiss him. He looks at me with hooded lids as I grab his tie with my other hand and yank it loose. My hands fly to his shirt, fingers fumbling with the buttons.

He kisses me again, and I tear at his shirt, ripping it. He groans as I slide my hands over his chest, running them through the short smattering of hair. It's soft and silky, just like I thought it would be. I scrunch my fingers, tugging on it.

"Fuck," he hisses, grabbing one of my thighs and hooking it around his waist. My skirt is forced up, bunching around my hips.

He follows my eyes to his exposed chest.

"You ruined my shirt."

"You can afford a new one." My glossy red nails weave through his chest hair, vibrant against the dark strands.

"I liked this one."

I tug at his hair in response.

His eyes flash. "You're such a brat."

"What you going to do? *Spank* me?" I bite my bottom lip to hide my smirk. But it's ripped from my face as Jet yanks my soaked panties to one side.

A whimper escapes me, causing an arrogant glint to flare in his eyes.

He hasn't even touched me, yet my body is a quivering wreck because of him.

And he knows it.

"No... but I will make you come on my fingers. The way you were so desperate to when I spanked you."

I jerk my head back at the way he delivers the words in a deep husk.

"I wasn't desperate," I snap.

He spears me with two fingers, and I gasp. *Greedy, traitorous body.*

"No?"

"No." I shake my head in defiance as he holds my eyes and crooks his fingers inside me, making me shudder.

"Okay." He lifts his chin like he's only agreeing to appease me. "So you weren't desperate for this..." He pumps his fingers, and I fight not to give him any further reaction that would indicate how amazing it feels. "You're a brat, Ava. You won't convince me otherwise."

I swallow a moan as my wetness coats his fingers. "You say that like you're some sort of good boy who's better than me."

He curls his fingertips over my G-spot. His eyes are laser focused on mine as he finger-fucks me with precision. My hands tremble against his chest as my heart rate picks up.

"There's nothing good about the things I'm thinking of doing to you."

His thumb slides over my clit. A twitch of his lips is his only emotion as I whimper, on the verge of coming already.

"Do you know why I call you a brat, Ava?"

"Because you have unresolved Daddy issues?" I tease.

His pupils dilate, and he grasps my throat with his free hand, curling his fingers around my windpipe.

"Because you are one."

Pump, pump.

"Because you like to push me."

Pump, pump.

"Because you secretly want me to punish you and keep you in line."

Swirl, pump.

"Fuck off," I moan.

Grunting, he rubs his thumb over and over my clit, using my arousal to slide over it effortlessly.

"And because you secretly crave to see what it feels like to come on my cock so hard that you forget your own name... but scream out mine."

"God!" I come hard without warning, clamping down on Jet's fingers as stars burst behind my eyelids.

My head falls against his chest, and I breathe in his aftershave that's lingering on his torn shirt.

He slides his hand from my neck, cradling the back of my head as I shatter in his arms.

"Shh," he coos. "That's it. Let it go."

"Fuck." Another wave tears through me as he continues massaging my clit.

I cling onto him to keep myself standing as my orgasm ravages through me, making my breath stutter.

He keeps his pace going, until another orgasm is coaxed from me.

"Jet," I whimper as I come again, melting into his arms.

"Good girl. Say my name." His deep voice flows over me, warming my chest as he slows his pace, wringing out every last drop of pleasure from my body.

I lift my head, my chest heaving as I catch my breath. He lifts his fingers between us—obscenely wet... covered in me.

"Open."

"What—?"

He shoves his fingers past my lips.

"Suck," he growls.

My eyes water, my throat full as he pulls his fingers back achingly slow so I can suck them clean. The sweetness of my arousal floods my tongue as I run it along his skin.

He slides them out and inspects them, then runs his thumb over my lower lip.

"Now swallow."

I do as he says, his eyes burning into mine.

"I can't afford to get distracted, Ava." His jaw tightens. "And knowing what you taste like when you come for me would be a big distraction. My head needs to be on securing a deal with Callaghan. You understand, don't you?"

I nod in shock.

"Good." He uncurls my leg from around his waist and lowers it to the ground, then smooths down my skirt. "Let's go."

He places his hand on my lower back and steers me through the tree line and back onto the path leading back to the main house.

The weight of his hand scorches the base of my spine as we head back to his car. He's straightened his shirt, hiding the rip beneath his tie.

What the hell was that? How did I make the same mistake with him again? I love to push him. The way he makes my blood heat makes me feel alive in a way I haven't in years, but still... The rebuttal afterward wasn't as sharp this time, but the message was the same.

This is nothing more than a game to him.

I hear him loud and clear.

I climb into the car without looking at him when he opens the door for me. He lifts the blanket from where I dropped it on his seat, and folds it neatly, placing it inside the back of the car before getting in.

Neither of us says a word on the drive back to Rochwell.

His words ring in my head. But not the lust-fueled ones. Those sinfully hot ones are marred, tainted by the ones he said before the two toe-curling orgasms he wrung from me.

"Because flying stole your father from you. And made it too hard for your mother to be able to stay... I know how hard grief can be, Ava."

Maybe he does. We both have lost a parent.

But that's not what makes it so hard.

It's the things I didn't tell him about that were also stolen from me.

All gone in a single day where I lost everything.

Including myself.

Chapter 14

Jet

"Are you listening?"

"Of course, I'm fucking listening," I snap at Hayden on the phone, my eyes glued to the pool area.

"So where to next?"

"I'm not sure. Callaghan's changed his schedule. Bastard's been off grid the past two days. He'll have seen the announcement about us changing suppliers to stock Aunt Iris's gin. He's doing it on purpose because he knows I want to speak with him."

"He's slipperier than a dick on a porn set," Hayden quips.

I grunt in response.

Ava gets up from her sun lounger and stretches. Her love of expensive lingerie must extend to swimwear, because she's wearing a barely-there white bikini with a ruffled trim. The back of it cuts high up over her ass cheeks. Cheeks that were bright red with my handprint only days ago.

"I've already got the team on it. They'll sniff him out in no time. Callaghan's not one to miss a moment to gloat about whatever fancy place he's visiting."

"Good."

Ava's talking to her friend, Liv, who's visiting for a couple of days. She spent the morning in the garden typing on her laptop and wiping her eyes. She's not spoken a word to me since leaving the estate yesterday. I saw her scowling at me through the window when I was skipping this morning, but since the moment Liv arrived, she's been beaming. Their laughter's echoing around the house.

It's the happiest she's been since I arrived.

"Oh, and the kid signed the non-disclosure," Hayden says, bringing my attention back to him.

"He knew what was good for him, then?"

"His father ripped him a new one when we told him you were serious about banning all employees of their company from flying with us again."

"It's the least he should have expected. No one takes videos of our passengers and tries to sell them to the press for a quick buck." I follow Ava with my eyes as she walks along the poolside, smiling and waving to someone.

"She wasn't even that drunk. I've seen way worse," Hayden says.

"She wasn't drunk. She'd taken a herbal remedy that she didn't react well to. She said things she doesn't remember."

"Whatever it was, the video's gone now."

"Thank you."

My shoulders tense as David and another man join Ava and Liv. The four of them begin chatting and laughing like it's a fucking party. "I've got to go. Call me the second you find Callaghan," I say, hanging up.

I toss my phone onto the desk and stand with my hands on my hips surveying the scene outside. David's chatting to Liv. And Ava's got her hand up, shielding her eyes from the sun as the other guy stands far too close to her.

I turn back to the desk and throw myself into the chair. This has got to fucking stop. She's already occupied my thoughts more than I should allow. This deal with Callaghan must be my sole focus. I can't lose my head over a feisty brat who likes to push me. The only reason she's getting under my skin at all is because I haven't had sex since I left New York.

It's blue balls. That's all it is. They make it hard to focus.

I clench and unclench my hands a couple of times, then open up the emails on my laptop.

A guffaw, followed by female laughter outside, makes my fingers jolt on the keys. That's fucking it! Some of us have businesses to run. I abandon my laptop and storm through the house, leaving the door wide open as I march across the grass to the pool.

Ava's back is to me. But David sees me, and his eyes widen.

"All right, Mr. Grant? This is my brother, Ed. He runs the landscaping business with me."

I nod a curt greeting at the other man.

"They were telling me about the new club we're going to tonight," Liv announces.

"Sounds fun." I breeze past without glancing her way. "Ava?" I snap.

Her spine straightens before she turns slowly.

"I need to speak with you."

She frowns. "Sure."

"In private," I add, when she doesn't move.

She sighs. "Fine. I'll be back in a bit, guys."

I catch the way she smiles at Ed, and I bite my tongue to prevent myself from firing David on the spot so he and his brother never step foot here again.

I gesture through the door, and she walks in first. My attention drops to her ass, my palm twitching with the urge to spank it hard for flirting with another man in front of me.

"What do you want?" She whirls to face me.

I close the door, keeping my voice low. "Why are you distracting David from his work?"

She laughs. "You're unbelievable. I wanted to introduce Liv to him. I saw him drive in with Ed. They were picking up the ride-on mower. David needed Ed's help."

"Fuck the mower, we can get some sheep to cut the grass if it means Ed won't be coming around again."

Ava looks at me like I've sprouted wings and taken off.

"Since when were club recommendations part of David's job description?" I grit.

Ava scoffs, crossing her arms tightly. It pushes her breasts higher in her bikini, and I run my tongue over my teeth.

"Liv wants to go out. Ed offered to drive us all."

"They're going *with* you?" I take a step closer. She tilts her chin up, glaring at me.

"So what if they are? I'm working with you. You don't get to dictate what I do in my free time. You haven't even given me any real work to do!" She throws her arms wide. "You're chasing some guy around, who's gone AWOL. So until you find out where he is and tell me where we're going next, I can do whatever the hell I like."

"You're a guest in this house, in case you forgot," I snap, stepping closer. She holds her ground, remaining rooted to the spot.

"Yes. For which I am eternally grateful to *your father* for." She drops her arms, shaking her head as she goes to barge past me. "You're such an asshole."

I catch her opposite hip and hold her in place.

"Are you going to sleep with him?"

"What?"

"The older brother who needs a haircut. Are you going to fuck him?"

"Oh my god. Would you listen to yourself?"

I am listening. I'm listening to my blood pounding in my ears at the thought of a man's hands on her.

"Don't," I growl.

"Don't what? Tell you how ridiculous you're being? Tell you how inappropriate this conversation is?"

"Don't have sex with him." My hand flexes on her hip, and my gut settles a little as she allows it to stay there.

"We're going out to have some drinks and a dance. *To have fun*. Not that you'd understand that."

She's so close I could claim her mouth if I lean in.

"Those things lead to sex, Ava."

"Not always," she snaps.

"I'm not a gambling man."

"Let me guess." She snorts. "Because you always have to win."

I look into her eyes, keeping my voice calm. "I don't want you with other men while you're living here. This might be my father's house. But don't forget, you're my guest too. You're sleeping in my room. In my bed."

"Fine." She pouts, and the tightness in my chest eases. "If we're going to have sex, we'll go to Ed's place."

"Ava!" The force of my shout doesn't make her jump. It makes her smile coyly.

The brat's pushing me on purpose... Again.

I move forward, caging her in between my arms against the wall. My rapidly rising chest brushes against the thin fabric of her bikini top as I lean over her.

Her eyes drop to my tie, and she reaches up, running a fingernail down it. I bat away the urge to grab her hand and place it on my hard dick.

"What about Liv? She's a guest, too."

My eyes fall to her mouth. "Liv can do what she wants."

"Ah, so you're an asshole and a hypocrite." She smirks.

"I don't care who Liv fucks."

"But you care who I do?" She lifts her eyes to mine as she waits for me to say something.

My jaw tenses. Nothing comes out. We shouldn't be having this discussion. I have one focus. And it's not her.

I step back.

"You know what? Fuck you, Jet," she whispers, pushing past me.

She turns to me as she reaches the door, giving me a sarcastic smile. "And don't wait up."

Chapter 15

Ava

"There's nothing better than looking at a guy and catching him already staring at you."

I follow Liv's gaze to David and Ed, who are getting another round of drinks at the bar. David's focus is set on Liv, a smile tilting his lips.

"You should go for it." I knock shoulders with her gently. "Enjoy yourself."

Her eyes roam all over him. "Oh, I intend to."

I laugh and lean into her side. I've had the best time since she arrived. It's exactly what I needed after all the heaviness of the last couple of days.

"You could, too, you know?"

I wrinkle my nose as I look at Ed, who's been flirting with me all evening. "He's nice, but not my type."

"He's not a certain dark-haired, blue-eyed storm in a suit, you mean?"

Heat floods my cheeks. "Stop. I wish I'd never told you."

"Shut up. We're best friends. Like you could ever *not* tell me about your boss spanking you and then getting you off in public."

"They were moments of insanity. Nothing like that is ever going to happen again."

"Sure." Liv gives me a knowing smile. "Whatever you say."

"Shh." I elbow her as David and Ed pick up our drinks and turn away from the bar.

"Fine. But at least admit that Jet's been good for your writer's block."

"Getting on a plane again was good for my writer's block." I lean back into the leather booth seat and blow out a breath. "Although I'm questioning why I decided to write it in the first place."

"You need this. Your therapist suggested it years ago."

"I know." I scrub a hand over my forehead. "And it feels good to finally do it. It's just dredging up old feelings, that's all."

"The nightmares?" Concern fills Liv's eyes.

"A couple. Nothing major."

I smile gratefully at Ed as he reaches our booth and hands me a drink. David drops beside Liv, and the four of us break into easy chatter. I laugh at their jokes, relishing the feeling of being carefree for an evening.

"Thanks," I whisper, closing the car door as quietly as I can before waving Ed off.

I creep in the back door, removing my heels, and walk barefoot down the dark hallway, past the old staircase, and into the kitchen. I grab a juice from the fridge, pulling the lid off to take a deep gulp as I swing the door shut.

"Fuck!"

Jet is standing behind it like something from a slasher movie.

"Where the hell did you come from?"

"I was sitting on the back stairs." He walks over to the sink, tipping the remnants of his water away, before turning to me. He's wearing a pair of sleep shorts low on his hips... and nothing else.

"I walked right past you. You could have said something." I put the juice back into the fridge. "It's 2AM. Why are you even up?"

"You're alone," he states, staring me down as the moonlight illuminates him from behind through the window.

"Liv's staying at David's. Ed dropped me off."

He looks to the side, sniffing and running a hand over his stubbled jaw. "Straight from the club?" Stiffness bunches up his huge shoulders.

"Yeah."

"How many men did you talk to tonight?" He pins me under his piercing gaze. A bolt of excitement fires in my gut.

"At least twenty," I lie.

The air he sucks in through his nose makes a sound that cuts through the room, and I soak it in, reveling in the way his brows channel into a deep V.

"Did any of them buy you a drink?"

"Some." I shrug. "I lost count." I lean back against the counter.

"Did you like any of them?"

"Yeah, I did. They were all hot." I level my eyes with his as he walks toward me.

"Did you picture yourself sucking their dicks?" he hisses, stopping in front of me.

I bite the inside of my cheek, keeping my expression neutral. "I did better than that. I had an orgy, right in the middle of the dancefloor. Ed started it off, and then four other guys joined in. I ran out of places to take them all at the same time."

A shot of adrenaline explodes up my spine as Jet pounces, sliding his hand around my throat and pushing me back into the counter.

"What?" he spits with wide eyes.

I'm glad he's angry. Because he's made me fucking angry with the way he's been treating me.

I squeeze my thighs as heat pools between them in response to his body pressing into mine. The scent of him, all warm and masculine, surrounds me.

Being close to him does something to me physically. I hate it, but I still want more.

His thumb curves around my windpipe, running up and down it slowly. "Ava?" he grits.

"You heard me. I fucked every single one of them," I say sweetly before pressing the lightest of kisses to his lips with a smirk.

"Lie to me again and I'll silence you with my dick. You'll be too busy choking on it to be such a fucking brat."

My breath hitches as the flare in his eyes grows.

"You're really talking yourself up here. You sure it measures up?"

His nostrils flare. Then he pulls me to him by my neck, bringing his mouth down onto mine. Jet steals every drop of breath from my lungs, kissing me until I gasp.

"I told myself nothing more was going to happen between us," he says as his lips slide to my neck and he nips it roughly, his stubble grazing my throat. He grabs my waist and hoists me onto the counter.

"Then what are you doing?" I moan as he kisses a path down my neck and across my collarbones.

"I'm taking what we both want," he grits, pushing his hands up my sequined miniskirt until his fingers graze the lace of my panties.

"You don't know what I want." I throw my head back as his mouth covers my breast through my silk top, and he sucks hard enough that I feel the heat of his tongue around my nipple.

"You won't be satisfied fucking guys like Ed, Ava. A brat like you needs taking care of in a certain way."

"Let me guess, you know what that way is?" I snort.

But he's right. Jet has got me hotter than any other guy ever has. I was soaking for him in the alleyway when he spanked me. And never in my life have I come as hard as I did by the lake.

I hate that he's right.

He straightens, claiming my mouth again until I'm moaning around his tongue. His hands dig into the flesh of my ass as he lifts me against him.

"You're catching on. No one does it like me."

"You're such an arrogant bastard," I huff as I wrap my legs around his waist and grip on to his neck.

He strides across the kitchen and sets me down on the oak dining table.

"I always get what I want, Ava." He places his palm over my chest and eases me back until I'm lying down. He lifts my legs, placing my feet up on the edge of the table.

"And what *do* you want, Jet?"

My eyes roam over his broad torso and inky black hair. The front of his shorts are tented with the outline of something far too big to be real. I blink. The darkness of the room is playing tricks on me.

"I want you. Every piece of you." He slides his hands up over my ribs, making me shudder. "I want these." He engulfs my breasts with his heavy palms, rolling his thumbs over my nipples. "This." He grabs my chin, squeezing until my lips pout. "And this." He cups my pussy, and I arch off the table. "And you're going to give it all to me, aren't you?"

He holds my eyes, watching me pant as he eases my panties to the side and painstakingly slowly circles my clit until I'm shaking with the need for more friction.

I grab the back of his wrist, urging him to speed up.

He halts his movements altogether.

"You're an asshole." My spine drops against the table as I fight the urge to cry with how badly I want to come.

"So I've been told."

He pushes my top up, freeing both breasts. He pulls one tight nipple into his mouth while teasing the other with his fingertips, making me arch into his touch.

"That's good," I whimper.

He stops the moment I speak, and I cry out in frustration.

"Let's try again, Ava," he says, his deep voice washing over me and sending goosebumps prickling up on my skin.

He sucks my nipple back into his mouth, his fingers sliding over my swollen clit.

"Jet," I whimper.

"Better," he rumbles. But he stops what he's doing again, and I wilt back against the table, frustration oozing from every pore.

"Keep being a good girl, and you'll get rewarded."

He's placed his hands on either side of my legs and is bracing his weight as he lowers his head. The thick, corded muscles in his shoulders and forearms bulge.

"Again," he instructs with the same authority as when he made his Captain announcements on the flight from New York.

His mouth hovers over me as he looks up and arches a dark brow. I clamp my lips together, but he just watches me, his eyes hardening. My pussy throbs, and I huff out a frustrated sigh.

"Ava, I can play this game all night. The sooner you accept that I make the rules, the sooner you will get what you want."

I glare at him. I should go upstairs and finish myself off. But I know it won't be enough. It'll barely take the edge off. And then I'll be here, playing this game with him again until one of us gives in.

And I *really* want to come.

I wriggle, parting my thighs wider.

"Please, Jet."

A flash of satisfaction crosses his face before he lowers his mouth and seals it over my clit through the lace of my panties. He grunts, and I buck off the table, pushing myself against him.

"Good girl, rub it on me. I can smell how much you want me." He licks the soaking fabric, the tip of his tongue dragging over me. "I can taste how desperately you want my cock."

"Fuck off," I bite back, regretting it immediately when he stops.

He pushes away from me, and I want to scream with disappointment. But then his hands slide up my thighs, and he hooks his thumbs beneath the lace, dragging my panties all the way down my legs.

"Ava," he tuts. "Admit it. You want my cock as much as I want to feel how tight you squeeze me when you come all over it."

I gulp as he lets out a satisfied grunt, lifting his chin.

"Please, Jet," I whisper, looking into his eyes. I don't care if I'm begging. I'm past the point of self-respect. I just want to come. I can't even think straight.

He lowers himself down again.

And I'm a goner.

I sink my hands into his hair, grinding against his face as he eats me out in a way that makes me feel like I'm going to explode at any moment.

"Yes! I'm so close."

"You know what I want to hear." His voice vibrates against my skin, making arousal rush from me.

"Jet," I moan.

He sucks my clit as a reward, and I arch my back, screwing my eyes shut as I come. Everything in the room disappears as I come apart on his mouth. I'm lost inside myself, consumed by deep waves of pleasure commanding my body as I writhe and cry out. Nothing else exists except for white-hot heat searing my veins and altering my brain chemistry.

Everything's muffled as if I'm underwater. Every cell in my body is alive with energy.

"Take it out."

I force my eyes open. Jet's outline is a silhouette as I blink to bring my focus back. A strong hand lands on my hip and squeezes. I shiver at the contact.

"Be a good girl and take my cock out, Ava."

I inhale, my senses returning as Jet's eyes hold mine. I lift up from the table, moving to sit on the edge. He watches me, his giant frame still and quiet as I reach for the waistband of his shorts. His jaw tightens as I pull them down slowly, letting them drop to the floor.

I suck in a breath as his dick springs free.

The darkness wasn't playing tricks on me.

"Now spit on it."

I lift my eyes, meeting his.

"Spit on my cock, Ava," he growls.

I lower my head and do as he instructs.

"Good girl," he rumbles, slicking himself up, mixing it with the pre-cum beading on the broad head.

He grabs the back of my neck, pulling me to him for a bruising kiss as his other hand finds my hip, pushing it wide.

He presses the head of his cock against me.

"Are you on birth control?"

"I—"

He moves back, our contact broken.

"Wait." I curl my hand around the base of his cock and pump up to the tip. A hiss leaves through his gritted teeth as he looks at my mouth. I slide my hand back down until my fingers hit his balls.

"I'm on the pill."

"Would you like me to wear a condom?" he asks seriously, like we're negotiating contract terms.

I shake my head.

"Words," he snaps, his torso remaining rigid as I stroke his cock, rubbing the head of it against my clit.

"No condom," I whisper.

"Fine."

My mouth is engulfed by his as he takes my hand from his dick and impales me with one deep thrust.

"Fuckkkk!"

"Ava," he rasps against my lips, holding himself deep inside me. It's the sexiest sound I've ever heard.

I roll my hips, and he grasps my neck and kisses me again, his body remaining still.

"Jet," I moan.

"Wait," he growls.

I sink into his kiss, pushing my hands through his hair and wrapping my legs around his waist. My clit pulses as I try to rub it against him.

"Fuck," he breathes, looking down at where I'm stretched around him. His jaw tightens and he pulls back, then drives forward again.

I throw my head back. "More."

"Lie back."

He grasps my hips and I lean onto my elbows, planting my feet back onto the table.

"All the way," he snaps.

I lie down, and he lifts my hips, dragging me to the edge of the table beneath him. He plants one hand by my head, which pushes my knees up against my chest. His broad body crowds over mine as he sucks in a breath.

"Good girl. Open for me. Let me in."

I part my legs wider, allowing him to sink deeper with a rough curse.

Then he holds my eyes and fucks me.

His hips piston, hard and deep, thrust after thrust. His eyes bore into mine until my cheeks heat.

He drives deeper each time, his heavy balls hitting my skin.

I can't look away.

I don't want to look away.

"I know you won't come like this," he rasps.

"What?" I gasp.

He spits on his fingertips, then snakes his hand between our bodies.

"But you *will* come on my cock. Your pleasure is mine now."

His fingers connect with my clit and it's embarrassing how loud I cry out his name.

"Now," he growls.

The deep timbre of his voice is my undoing. I come, and he picks his pace back up and fucks me right through my orgasm.

His eyes never leave mine. He drinks me up, watching the way I shudder beneath him and pant for air.

My orgasm washes over me as I stare back.

He takes all that he can, before his fingers slide away from my sensitive clit and he grabs a handful of my ass. He lifts it, angling me how he wants me.

His pupils blow wide and the arm bracing himself above me goes rigid.

"Fuuuuckkkk."

His lids hood, but he keeps his eyes on mine as he comes, spilling deep inside me. The base of his cock stretches me wider as his whole body expands above me.

His nostrils flare, his perfect teeth sinking into his lower lip.

"Fuck, yes," he groans.

I feel fucked. Utterly fucked, lying in a ragged heap beneath a hulk of a man whose body is burning like an inferno above me.

"Jet," I breathe, blissed out.

He breaks eye contact for the first time since he pushed inside me. A deep breath expands his chest, then he blows it out, his taut shoulders relaxing.

"Jesus, you feel so fucking good." He flexes inside me, and I whimper.

"I've never come so hard," I admit, not caring what he thinks. I'm in a beautiful post-orgasmic haze. He shifts inside me, then pulls out. The alien feeling of being filled with hot cum makes me bite my lip. Some of it trails toward my ass.

I like it.

"I'll even use a glass for you one time after an orgasm like that," I tease, closing my eyes and tilting my head back as I blow out a relaxed breath.

"Really?" Jet's gravelly voice sounds faraway. I don't care if he fucks off to bed and leaves me here. I'm sated and blissfully boneless.

"Mmm..."

"In that case, you can do it now."

Something cold touches my inner thighs and his large palm slides over my lower stomach, pushing down gently.

"Good girl. Squeeze it out."

"What are you doing?" I open my eyes and push up onto my elbows.

"You're full of my cum." His gaze is fixed between my legs. "Squeeze for me." He presses his palm into my stomach, making my pussy clench. "Good girl." He bites his lower lip. "So fucking beautiful."

He lifts his hand, assessing the glass between his fingers. There's at least an inch of white liquid in the bottom of it. I stare at it as he moves closer, his hand sliding around the back of my neck and easing me up into a sitting position.

"You know what to do."

He arches a dark brow.

My core tightens. He's challenging me, I know he is. It's another game to him, a demonstration that he's the one in control.

He doesn't think I'll do it.

I part my lips in invitation, keeping my eyes fixed on his. He brings the glass to my lips, his breath stalling before breaking into a sharp hiss.

He tips the glass, and I drink.

His pupils blow wide as my throat contracts with each gulp. The mix of us tastes like sin. I smile as I drain the last remnants from the glass.

"Good girl." He places the glass down on the table and lowers his mouth to kiss me. It's slow and lingering. I trace a finger along his jaw.

"Ava," he groans, "you taste like—"

"You?" I murmur.

"Us," he rasps, sliding his tongue over mine.

I sigh into his kiss. "I like it."

He kisses me slowly, savoring it, before finally easing back. His thumb traces my cheek as his eyes roam my face. His lips curl a fraction in one corner.

"It's time you went to bed."

Chapter 16

Jet

Ava fidgets, closing her thighs. I part them again with a firm palm against her soft skin.

"I'll leave you alone once I'm finished." I press the warm washcloth between her legs and groan as more of my cum seeps from inside her.

She needs this. She tried to fight it. But I carried her to her room and told her to lie on the bed so I could take care of her. It's what she deserves after being such a good girl. She loves to push me, and I went hard on her. But after the playing comes the aftercare.

"You'll leave me alone?" she muses. "I doubt that. You don't seem to be able to keep away from me."

I grunt as I finish up my task and rise from the bed to go to the en-suite. When I come back, Ava's stripped off her clothes and is lying on her side beneath the covers with her phone.

"Good night, Jet. Don't trip on your way out," she hums, satiated and smirking as she scrolls through social media.

Brat.

I climb in behind her. She stiffens, glancing at me.

"What are you doing?"

"Staying until you sleep." I pluck the phone from her hand and toss it onto the carpet. "You don't need that. You need sleep."

"Because you know everything about me and what I need, don't you?" she huffs.

"I know you better than you think, Ava. And right now, you're mine to take care of."

She scowls and turns away. "You couldn't have just left it at the orgasms, could you? Had to go and ruin it by opening your mouth."

"Shut up and sleep."

"This doesn't have to get weird. It was just sex."

"Ava..."

"God, you're so bossy," she tuts.

"And you're so difficult. Now go to sleep."

I pull her toward me, so her back is against my chest and my arms are encasing her. I expect an argument. A bratty protest. But she must be worn out, because within a few minutes, her body softens and her breathing levels out.

"Good girl." I kiss her shoulder. "Sleep."

I watch her for a while to make sure she won't wake up. Then I slide my arms away and climb out of the bed.

"No!" she cries suddenly. "I'm here!"

I lean over and stroke her auburn hair away from her cheek. Her forehead is wrinkled, a troubled expression on her face as her lower lip trembles and she mutters something unintelligible.

"Just a dream, Ava." I tell her, my lips dusting the shell of her ear.

I walk to the door, opening it quietly.

A whimper leaves the back of her throat as she sobs in her sleep.

I stare at my hand on the doorknob, flexing my fingers as something cold radiates up my spine.

She continues crying. It's quiet; I can barely hear it. But it's there.

I make my way to my room. I climb into bed and lie on my back, staring up into darkness.

Sleep evades me.

"Damn it." I fling the sheets back and jump out.

I stalk down the hallway and peer around the door into Ava's room. Everything is peaceful. She's no longer crying. I start to close the door to head back to my room.

A whimper, almost inaudible, comes from the bed. It's so slight it might have just been a sound outside.

Or it could have been her.

Closing her door, I join her in the bed. I don't pull her to me. I just lie beside her, listening to her breathing, making sure she sleeps.

"What have you found?" I drop my skipping rope onto the low stone wall that edges the terrace and swipe up my towel, wiping the sweat from my bare chest.

"He's in Thailand," Hayden says.

"That's where we're going, then." I gather up my rope and head toward the back door, walking the long way around the house.

"We? Ava going with you again?"

"That a problem?"

There's nothing for her to do. She knows it. I know it. But she won't back down. And I'm not about to leave her at Rochwell when Ed might decide to come over. I saw the way he looked at her.

"No problem." Hayden chuckles before asking, "Do you think Callaghan will listen now that he's been offered the San Jose slots?"

"I'm counting on it," I grumble as I enter the house through the back door.

"You know there's still—?"

"No."

My mind wanders to Ava's serene face when I woke this morning. She'd ended up in my arms with her head on my chest.

"That's still not on offer," I say.

"Just making sure nothing has changed."

"It hasn't." I walk up the hallway toward the kitchen.

"All right. Well, I'll send you the flight details." Hayden yawns. "You know it's the middle of the fucking night here and I'm still in the office."

"You help us get this deal and I'll give you a raise."

"Twenty percent?"

"Ten."

"Fifteen," he counters.

Silence blankets us, before he laughs. "Okay, you tight bastard. Ten percent. And the promise not to kill me when I tell you that you need to look for a new PA when you come back."

"Jesus. Can't you keep your dick separate from business?" I clear my throat as the events of last night come into full vivid technicolor in my mind. Ava beneath me on the table. Ava crying out my name. Ava's eyes holding mine as she came for me.

"I've never come so hard."

She was right to call me a hypocrite. I had no right to blur that line between us.

"I mean, I could... for twenty percent."

Hayden breaks into laughter as I curse him and hang up. He knows I'm not really pissed. I'd have needed a new PA when I got back anyway. Annabelle shook like a leaf in a breeze whenever I walked into the office.

"Come on, how was it? Did you at least get a kiss from Ed?"

Liv's voice carries from the kitchen, and I slow my steps.

"You're the one who's just rolled in wearing last night's clothes, and you want to know how my night went?" Ava giggles.

Liv responds with something I can't hear as I walk into the room.

"Oh." Her eyes widen as she looks at me in my shorts.

"Morning," I say, walking past the table where they're both sitting.

Ava's eyes flick to mine, then away again just as fast.

"Morning," she replies.

My father walks into the room and smiles brightly at the two women.

"Morning, ladies. Have fun last night?"

Liv chats with him, and Ava walks over to the coffee machine.

"Ava?" I move closer to her and lower my voice so only she can hear.

She continues preparing the coffee without looking at me. "Yes?"

"What's wrong?"

She glances at me. "I don't know what you mean."

I rake my eyes over her furrowed brow and tense jaw while she grabs a spoon and drops it into the cup. If she stirs any harder, she'll break it.

She hands the cup to my father, a smile spreading over her face as he takes it gratefully.

"Thank you, sweetheart." He takes a sip. She's made it exactly how he likes it and realization dawns on me that this isn't the first time. How did I miss the fact she's become so at ease around my father, like they're friends?

"No problem." She crosses her arms and leans against the counter.

"Back to the studies later, then?" he says to Liv.

She rolls her eyes. "My train's at ten. Although I'd much rather stay here."

"I bet you would." My father chuckles as Liv's attention is piqued by the sound of the lawnmower starting up outside. "Well, sweetheart, you're welcome anytime you like. Come and give this one some company." He tips his head toward Ava. "She only sees Margaret and my old face."

I clear my throat.

"And Jet, of course." My father smiles into his coffee. "Spend most of your time writing, don't you?" he says to Ava.

"I'm trying." Her eyes soften as he winks at her.

"You're doing your father proud."

Ava's eyes mist at his words and she nods before busying herself with wiping down the counter.

My father drinks some more before setting his cup down. Liv bounces over to him, throwing her arms around his neck as she kisses his cheek. "Thank you for having me. You're amazing. If you were into younger women, I'd totally sleep with you."

He laughs, then steps back. "I think the young man in the garden might have something to say about that. Safe travels back." He smiles at the girls and then nods at me before he leaves the room.

"Your dad's so nice," Liv sings as she pours some juice in a glass.

"He's not into younger women," I bark.

She smirks into her juice. "That's a shame. But I was only teasing. Your dad's fun." She gives me a pointed look like she thinks I'm anything but fun. I've heard what Ava's said about me when they've been on the phone with each other. Liv thinks I don't know how to take a joke.

Ava yawns and I turn my attention to her.

"Did you sleep okay?"

She doesn't meet my eyes as she shrugs. "I guess."

"It was a late one. Ed dropped her home. I slept over at David's," Liv says, an easy smile on her face.

"I'm aware," I clip, placing my phone and the rope on the counter so I can fetch a glass of water.

Liv looks between the two of us, before settling her gaze on me with interest.

"How do you know?"

"Excuse me?" I lean back against the counter as I chug the water down.

"How do you know?" Liv looks at me.

"How do I know that you fucked the landscaper? You just shared it with everyone."

She doesn't blush, just narrows her eyes at me. "I mean, how do you know Ed dropped Ava home?"

"Liv," Ava mutters. "Leave it."

"I know because I was up when Ava got home," I say, placing my glass down and pushing off the counter. "And I carried her to bed."

Liv frowns at Ava. "You weren't that drunk that you needed help."

Ava chews her bottom lip. "I—"

"No, she wasn't drunk at all."

The way Liv's eyes light up as she ping-pongs them between us has me smiling internally.

I know how to have fun.

Liv's frantic whispers erupt the second I leave the room.

"I'm so proud of you. What you've done so far... It's amazing."

"It's flowing, finally." Ava smiles.

"You'll be done before you know it," Liv says, pulling her into another hug and eyeing me knowingly over her shoulder.

The two of them have been hugging and saying goodbye for the past ten minutes in the train station car park.

"You'll miss your train," I remind her.

Liv grins. "I get it. You want her all to yourself."

I lean against the car, folding my arms as Ava ignores Liv's comment and squeezes her again.

"Call me when you get back."

"I will, Bitch. Love you."

"Love you too." Ava smiles.

Liv walks onto the small country station's platform just as the train pulls in.

"Thank you for giving her a lift."

"No problem."

Ava climbs into the car without looking at me. I close her door and walk around it, sliding into the driver's seat, but I don't start the engine.

"Something's bothering you. Tell me what it is," I say, breaking the silence.

She presses her lips tightly together and looks out of her window.

"Was it the nightmare you had?"

"What? No, of course not. I don't even remember having one." Her shoulders bunch up as she keeps her attention away from me.

"Fine," I clip. "Then, was it me? What we did?"

Her brow furrows as she glances at me. "I, um..."

Something heavy settles in my gut.

"Okay." I start the engine. "Then let's deal with it."

"What do you mean?"

"It won't take long," I reply.
"What won't? Jet?"
My eyes drop to her mouth as I clear my throat.
"You'll see."

Chapter 17

Ava

"WHAT IS THIS PLACE?" I stare out of the window at the modern glass-fronted building. There were signs for oncology and maternity as we drove into the grounds.

"It's a private medical facility."

He gets out of the car and comes around to open my door.

"What are we doing here?"

I step out and he closes my door, his aftershave washing over me as he leans closer and places his hand on my lower back, steering me toward the main entrance.

"You need to trust me, Ava."

"What are you talking about?"

He leads us into a waiting area that looks more like a luxury hotel than a medical practice.

"Jet Grant," he says to the receptionist. "I usually see Doctor Kingston, but I'll see whoever you have available since I don't have an appointment."

"No problem, Mr. Grant," she replies with a smile as though she's used to people walking in and demanding to be seen straight away. "What's the nature of your visit, so that I can place you with the right specialist?"

"Sexual health screening," he replies, his fingers flexing against my lower spine. "I want to be tested for everything."

I glare at him. "What are you doing?"

"What's necessary," he clips, thanking the receptionist.

I sink into a plush white sofa beside Jet in the waiting area.

"I can't believe you," I whisper.

"It won't take long." He checks his watch and then pulls his phone out of his suit pocket and starts tapping away on it.

I put my hand over the screen, earning myself a dark arched brow. "Are you serious right now?"

"Deadly." His blue eyes fix on mine.

"I don't have anything." I seethe. "But if it makes you feel better, then by all means, get a stick shoved up your dick to tell you that. It'll match the one up your ass."

I yank my hand back, enraged. Does he think I make a habit of sleeping around without protection? Getting fucked on kitchen tables in the middle of the night?

He slides his phone into his pocket and rises from his seat. He walks back over to the reception desk and then turns and points me out to the receptionist.

"Make sure my results go to Miss Roberts, please."

The receptionist nods, smiling at me, and he walks back over, sitting calmly. He pulls his phone back out and begins tapping again.

"Why do I want them?"

A muscle in his jaw ticks, and he sighs and pockets his phone once more. "We're here to reassure *you*, Ava."

"Reassure me of what?"

"That you're safe. I don't make a habit of not using a condom. But last night was..." He purses his lips, his eyes pinching at the corners. "... unexpected."

"You're getting tested to reassure me?"

"Why else?" He frowns. "I know I don't have anything."

"So it's not because you think I gave you something?"

His eyes snap to mine. "Is there something you're not telling me?"

"No!" I hiss. "I've never had a guy"—I glance around the waiting room—"*come* inside me before."

"Never?" Jet arches that brow of his again and I want to rip it off his face.

"Never."

"Hm." The corners of his lips lift into the closest thing resembling a smile I've ever seen on him. "What about in your mouth?"

I shift in my seat. "Maybe a couple of times."

His lips flatten into a grimace.

"Oh, come on." I scoff, sitting forward in my seat. "You can't slut shame me for a couple of blow jobs. It was either spit it out or get it over my face. Liv said it stings like fuck if you get it in your eye."

"You spat it out?"

"Yes."

"Hm."

I huff and sit back in the seat knowing I'm not going to get anything else out of the cold bastard. We sit in silence for a couple of minutes before I shoot to my feet.

"Ava?" he warns. "Where are you going?"

"Shut up," I snap at him as I stride over to the reception desk.

"Ava Roberts." I smile politely at the receptionist. "I'm with him." I jerk my thumb over my shoulder at Jet who's watching with darkened eyes. "I'd also like a full sexual health screening, please. And you can give my results to Mr. Grant."

I thank her and spin on my heels, taking my seat beside him again.

"Problem?" I ask, feeling his eyes on me.

"No." His voice is a deep rumble as he rests his hands on his legs, close enough that his pinky almost brushes my thigh. "No problem."

Rochwell is empty when we arrive back. Margaret hasn't arrived yet, and Magnus is still at work.

"You need to pack," Jet says as we walk in through the front door.

"Why? Where's Callaghan?" I put my purse on the floor and reach down to take my heels off, enjoying the coolness of the flagstone beneath my bare soles.

"Thailand," he clips before heading upstairs.

"Thailand?" I follow him as he walks into the guest bedroom and takes the envelope containing my test results out of his jacket pocket and drops it onto the bed.

"That's what I said."

He takes his jacket off and places it neatly on the bottom of the bed before removing his tie.

"Are you even going to open it?" I pick up the envelope and wave it in the air.

Jet's fancy pants medical center got the results ready for us before we even left. I tore his open the second we got back into his car, expecting him to do the same.

"I didn't ask you to get tested." He starts unbuttoning his shirt.

"But I did." I push the envelope against his chest. He curls his hand over mine, holding it in place.

"The purpose of that visit was for you to trust me, Ava. Not the other way around."

I glare at him. "In case you haven't realized, getting tested isn't a relaxing activity I'd choose to take part in daily. I did it, the least you can do is read it."

"Fine." He sighs as if I'm a misbehaving child that's worn his patience out. "Read it to me."

He lets go of my hand and pulls his shirt off his shoulders. I ignore the dark hair covering his broad chest and rip the envelope open, scanning through the results.

"All clear," I announce, tossing the paper onto the bed.

"Feel better now?" His condescending tone makes me snap my eyes to him. He's ridded himself of the rest of his clothes and is standing naked with his hands on his hips. His fingers are resting at the top of the deep V muscles on his lower abdomen.

"No, I feel…"

I can't help focusing on his dick. It's soft, but Jesus, that fit inside me?

"Go and pack," he says, walking into his bathroom.

He's turning the giant rainfall shower on as I stalk in behind him. My step falters as I eye his thick muscular thighs and firm ass.

"Why do you have to look like that?" I mutter in disgust.

He steps underneath the spray and groans, rolling his neck side to side with his eyes closed.

"You still staring?" he asks as he tips his head back and soaks his dark hair. He peels an eye open and looks at me. "Either go and pack or take off your clothes and get in."

The blood in my veins heats. Whatever I do, it'll look like I'm following his orders.

"Five... four..."

"What's with the counting?" I demand as I unzip my skirt. My movements are jerky, fueled by anger that once again, Jet has control. I should have chosen the packing option.

I glance down at his hardening dick and my pussy throbs in response.

Or not.

He pushes the water through his hair, his biceps bulging. "If I get to one and your lips aren't wrapped around my cock, then you'll find out."

"Asshole," I snap.

"Three... two..."

I shove my skirt down and tear my blouse off over my head. Jet frowns as the water obscures his vision. He moves out from under the spray, his attention fixed on me in my cobalt blue lace bodysuit.

"You like it?" I reach around and unhook the top section. "You bought it when we were in New York."

"You paid for that with my money?" He leans against the tiles, running his hand around his jaw as he forgets to count.

"Yep. Check your card statement."

His eyes flare with desire as I peel the lace down, freeing my breasts. I push it over my hips, stepping out of it as it hits the floor. "There'll be an entry on it that says, 'Ava won this one'."

He lunges forward and grabs my wrist. "I don't think so." His eyes drop over my body, making me shiver. "I always win, Ava." He pulls me under the water, his lips dusting my ear. "*One*," he whispers.

I gasp as he pushes me to my knees.

He grabs the base of his cock and taps the head against my lips. I blink up at him. The water's falling behind him, flowing down over his shoulders, the tiny droplets gleaming in the light. He looks like sin. And after last night, I know he tastes like it, too.

"Open."

He rubs the crown across my lips, smearing pre-cum over them, then pulls my hair, jerking my head back.

"Open your mouth, Ava, so I can fuck your throat."

I hold his eyes and part my lips. He pushes the fat head past them, sliding all the way in, making me gag.

"Fucking beautiful," he rasps as his other hand slides into my hair.

My eyes water as he picks up his pace, fucking my mouth with deep, guttural groans. The sight of him has heat flooding my core, and I put my hand between my thighs to give myself some relief.

"You ready to swallow my cum again?"

I whimper around his dick.

"I knew you were a good girl beneath all that brattiness." He strokes a tear from my cheek, his gaze softening.

I gurgle in defiance, but he picks up the pace again, his hips thrusting hard.

"Fuck!" he roars.

Fiery heat hits the back of my throat.

"Swallow it, Ava." He fists my hair tighter. "You might have spat other guys' out, but you'll swallow every drop of mine like it's your goddamn favorite taste in the world."

I swallow the first load greedily, sucking in a breath through my nose. More spills into my mouth as Jet curses above me. I splutter and it spills from my lips along with my spit, spraying back down the base of his cock and onto his balls.

He keeps thrusting, groaning my name in a way that has butterflies taking flight in my stomach. I swallow again, and he slows his movements, before stopping completely. He gazes at me, stroking my lower lip as he takes his cock out of my mouth.

"You made a mess," he tuts. "Clean it up."

He watches me raptly as I stick out my tongue and run it over his balls and then up his dick, gathering up everything that I spat out. He strokes my hair the entire time, tipping his chin in satisfaction once I'm done.

"Good girl."

He pulls me to my feet, caging me in-between his arms and the tiles. His eyes rake over my face before he lowers his head and kisses me slowly, leisurely sliding his tongue over mine. It's tender. A direct contrast to the lust-fueled urgency that he fucked my mouth with.

"You didn't make the count," he rasps.

"So?" I slide my hands up over his chest, threading my fingers into the hair.

"So, there are consequences, Ava." He takes my face between his hands and kisses me deeply until my head spins.

If this is Jet's idea of punishment, then I'm going to be a brat every single second I'm with him.

"Do your worst," I whisper against his lips.

He growls and spins me. "Hands on the seat."

I place my hands on the tiled ledge that acts as a seat inside the shower. It's low and forces my ass up in the air. I don't get time to brace before Jet's palm lands on my wet skin.

"Jet!" I fly forward, my ass cheek throbbing.

"Straighten up," he barks.

I fix my arms into place, wetness pooling between my thighs at the delicious burn lancing across my skin. I cry out as a shot of pleasure rolls through me when the second spank comes.

"Sounds like you're enjoying this a little too much," Jet clips, planting his large palms over my ass cheeks and kneading them both gently. "Such a fucking brat."

I don't have time to reply before his cock is pushing into me.

"Jesus, Ava. The way you squeeze me," he hisses as he bottoms out, before retreating and slamming back inside me.

I moan, unable to move as my toes dance on the floor. Jet hitches up one of my thighs, placing my knee onto the seat, then pulls me back onto his cock. The depth makes my breath hitch.

"Fuck, that's good," I moan.

"It's not enough," he grits.

I look at the tiles beneath my hands as he places his foot up on to the step next to my knee. His hands engulf my waist, and he holds me in place as he drives back into me at the new angle.

My eyes roll in my head.

"That's better," he groans.

He's deeper than I've ever felt before, and I struggle to form a clear thought as he fucks more and more pleasure into every cell of my body with each drive of his hips.

"God," I cry. "Please... I'm so close."

His solid chest is like a slab of hot granite against my back as he leans over me and reaches between my thighs, circling his fingers over my clit.

"Mine," he rasps in my ear, making me shudder. "Your pleasure belongs to me. And one day, I'll make you come with just my cock. Mark my words, Ava."

I shatter just from his voice, coming in deep, breath-stealing waves around him.

"Like that. Just like that," he urges, playing with my clit.

My muscles spasm and grip him hard as I cry out.

"Fuck." He sucks in a breath, his grip on my hip tightening as he spills inside me. I squeeze my eyes shut, riding out the rest of my orgasm, as he thrusts into me with deep, husky praises.

This time, I don't fight him when he lifts me into his arms to take care of me.

Chapter 18

Jet

"You're still doing that in this heat?" Ava eyes my skipping rope as I walk back into our air-conditioned overwater villa.

"I skip every morning. You know that."

I close the sliding glass door that leads out onto the private decked terrace with jacuzzi and loungers and place the rope down onto the top of some wicker drawers. I turn to face her, but her attention is glued back on her laptop screen. Her pouty lower lip is sucked into her mouth as she types.

"You never did tell me what you're working on."

I walk toward the table she's sitting at, but her shoulders tighten, and she closes the lid before I get close enough to read anything.

"Nothing I care to share." Her nose wrinkles as she slides her eyes away from mine.

"Noted." I walk past her to the giant glass wall. The sheer drapes are open, so I can see right along the length of the coastline and to the scattering of other private villas like this one that extend out into the crystal blue ocean.

"Callaghan hasn't checked in early if that's what you're worried about."

"How would you know?" I narrow my eyes as I study a person walking along the beach. "You've been working on your non-sharing project for the past two hours."

She retrieves a bottle of fresh grapefruit juice from the fridge and breaks the seal.

"Since when were you so interested in what I'm working on? I've been staying at your father's house for weeks now and you've never shown an interest."

I turn, lifting the towel that's slung over my shoulder to dry my chest. Even at 6AM, Krabi feels as hot as the devil's ball sack.

"Never said I was interested."

She scowls as I walk over to her and pluck the bottle from her hand. "Want me to fetch you a glass?"

I neck half the juice, then hand it back to her. The bite of citrus hits my tastebuds and I savor the tang it leaves on my tongue. Grapefruit juice is growing on me.

"Ha-the-fuck-ha." She frowns before drinking the rest of the bottle.

She's barely said two words to me since we fucked in my shower. I cleaned her up after, kissing her bratty lips. Then she went to her own room to pack. We caught the flight over here, switching onto a private seaplane transfer for the final part of our journey. That's the one that rattled her. She managed the take-off out of London with little more than some heavy breathing and tense armrest gripping. But when we took off in that tiny seaplane that bounced around on the breeze, she grabbed my hand like her life depended on it. And I can't lie; the way she murmured my name as I held her against me and told her she was safe, had my chest swelling with something primal.

I took control, and it calmed her.

I cross my feet at the ankle and curl my hands around the edge of the counter. Ava settles beside me, following my gaze across our luxury two-story villa and out over the beach. I rented the largest, most private villa because its location means we can see as much of the luxury resort as possible from this position.

"What's the plan, then?" She pulls her hair tie free and re-does the messy bun on top of her head. My eyes drop over her white bikini top and frayed denim shorts. We arrived late last night. Too late to look around the resort properly. Ava headed straight into her room with a cursory good night flung in my direction.

My palm itched to spank her ass bright red for it. But the entire reason I'm here is for Callaghan. I can't get distracted now. I've already allowed our games to taint my focus. I'm running out of time.

"He checks in this morning. I'm going to make sure I'm in reception when he does."

Ava rolls her eyes. "Let me guess, you don't need me to do anything."

"Good girl, you're a fast learner."

The pulse in her neck flutters at my words, but she avoids my eyes.

"Fine. In that case, I'm going to go and work on the deck. I might as well get my work done, seeing as you won't let me help you with yours."

She pushes away from the counter, but I grab her wrist. Her eyes drop to my fingers circling around it.

"Why do you tell my father what you're writing about, but you won't tell me?"

I curse myself the second the pathetic tone carries the words from my mouth. I drop her wrist and fold my arms.

Her eyes narrow, sweeping over my face. "What happened to, *'I never said I was interested?'*"

"I never said I wasn't, either."

She holds my gaze, the two of us locked into one of our silent battles.

The corners of her lips lift.

My palm twitches as I picture bringing it down onto her ass.

"You answer me a question, and I'll answer you one. A truth for a truth." She steps closer, looking at me from beneath her lashes.

I allow my gaze to soak in her breasts beneath the thin fabric of her bikini. Her nipples are tight little peaks, straining against it.

"Fine. You first."

Her eyes light up. "Why are you the way you are? Why all the games, all the control? Don't you ever just... Have you ever had a relationship where things were equal? Have you ever been in love?"

"That was four questions."

A deep groove etches between her eyebrows as she huffs. "Suit yourself. I knew you'd never answer anyway—"

"I'm like this because I want to be. I have to have control because I hate feeling like I have none. All relationships I've had have been a mutually beneficial arrangement for both parties, and I won't ever allow myself to fall in love."

"Mutually beneficial?" She snorts. "Sounds more like a business contract than a relationship."

"I suppose it is."

"What?"

"I like things a certain way, Ava. When people want more, things get complicated. I make sure they know what they're getting, and what they're not, before we start anything."

"That's so..." she screws her face up, "... clinical."

"It's necessary."

She shakes her head. "And you never want to fall in love? Ever?"

"No one has control in love. I refuse to play that game." I roll my neck, cracking it.

"That's bad for—"

"My bones, I know."

"—your heart, Jet." She looks at me sadly. "Don't you ever want to throw caution to the wind and give up control for once?"

"No."

She waits for me to say something else, searching my eyes with an eagerness to understand that is like a vise grabbing onto my lungs and forcing the air out.

"When control is lost, it all goes to shit. The doctors lost control of my mother's cancer, and my father and I were forced to stand by in some soulless hospital and watch as it stole her from us in a way that no one should ever have to suffer through," I spit.

"Jet," she whispers.

I hate the pity in her eyes, hate the way it scrapes at my insides, leaving giant welts there.

"Don't you ever—?"

"No, I don't."

"But—"

"But nothing."

"Jet, listen to me. What about—?"

"Stop!" I yell so loud it echoes off the walls.

The memory of my mother's dying body is too much to bear. The way her hands that once pulled me into a hug were too weak to lift from the mattress when I held them those final days. So thin and fragile, withering away as even talking became a source of exhaustion to her.

"You're a good man, Jet. I'm so proud of you. And I love you more than anything."

Ava's eyes widen as I step forward, crowding over her.

"Stop talking. Don't lecture me about control." Blood rushes in my ears, zeroing my vision in onto her blue eyes and nothing else. "Don't try and fucking psycho-analyze me with bullshit theories."

"I wasn't," she snaps, squaring up to me.

She isn't frightened of me in the slightest. But she should be. I could ruin her before she even realizes it.

I lower my voice to a menacing growl, putting everything into making sure my words wound her, make her keep her distance. "You might be a great fuck, Ava. But don't mistake my short-lived addiction to your cunt for knowing anything about me."

Whack.

My head snaps to the side as her slap makes my eyes bug out.

"Was that one hard enough? Or did I go too easy on you?" she snarls.

I bring my eyes back to hers and am met with a fire burning so brightly that it reaches into my gut and brands me.

"Careful, baby, you'll make me hard," I spit. "You know I like it when you fight back."

"What the hell has gotten into you?" She glares at me. "You're being an even bigger asshole than usual."

"You're the one with the attitude that I should fuck right out of you."

"I'm not making that mistake again," she hisses. "Besides, we never talked terms." She gives me a condescending smile as she flicks her fingers back and forth between us. "So whatever this was, it's over now."

"Suits me," I snap, something gnawing at my gut. I never did lay down any rules with her. I just thought with my dick. Too fucking keen to get a taste of her. I should know better. I *do* know better. This deal with Callaghan, the axe hanging over my head to save the airline, it's turned me into a fucking idiot.

She steps closer, shaking with rage. "You'd better do whatever the hell it takes to get this deal with Callaghan. Because I can't wait to get back to England and then never have to see you again."

"Makes two of us."

She glares fire at me, then exhales, spinning away from me.

"Ava?" I call after her. "You want to be useful?" I rub my throbbing jaw. "Go get some more fucking clothes on and come find Callaghan with me."

Satisfaction glitters in her eyes as she glances back. Then she turns and stalks off.

Chapter 19

Ava

JET'S A SOLID MASS of tension beside me as we sit in the bar area of the hotel's open air marble lobby.

I haven't said a word to the bastard since I slapped him. He deserved it and more. Yet a tiny fragment of empathy still glows in my heart for him. I know a broken person's outburst when I see one because I've had so many myself over the past ten years. Jet is grieving his mother's passing. He rarely talks about her. Magnus has chosen to let his grief out, bring it into the light with happy memories and gratitude for the time they had.

Jet wears his like a shadow, clouding everything he does.

I get the need for control, at least I think I do. It's similar to my reasons for not flying for so long. Because in a plane I have no control. Just like the day I lost my father. But it's the turning his back on love that confuses me the most. Especially when I've seen those old news images of him and Francesca. He can't seriously expect me to believe he's never felt anything for anyone. Not when he looked at her like that.

"Do you see him yet?" I take a sip of my pina colada, enjoying the fresh burst of pineapple on my tongue.

"No."

I sigh. I have a feeling it's going to be one syllable answers for the rest of this trip. I pray to god that Callaghan is ready to sign a deal, because the longer I have to be in the vicinity of Jet's foul mood, the more I'm in danger of slapping him again.

I slurp the remnants of my drink through the straw.

"Do you have to?" Jet scowls.

I hold his eyes and give my straw an extra-large suck, making the ice cubes rattle around the bottom of my glass. "Umm, yeah, I do actually." I do it again, reveling at the tightening in his jaw.

He rolls his lips, his nostrils flaring, before his attention is stolen across the lobby to a man approaching the check-in desk.

"Is that him?"

"It is. Stay here," Jet barks as he heads toward him like a missile on target.

I head toward the ladies' room. Callaghan and Jet are standing talking across the other side of the lobby. Callaghan looks amused while Jet, the asshole, looks surprisingly calm, despite his stiff posture.

My eyes rake over his cream pants and white shirt, rolled up at the sleeves, showing off tanned forearms. "Why do I have to find moody bastards hot?" I mutter.

"I used to ask myself the same question."

I look at the woman waiting with a suitcase.

"I'm sorry, I didn't mean to say that out loud." I give her an apologetic smile and she waves it off with a flick of her fingers.

"I think it's the passion they have when they want something. It's thrilling to be a part of it," she muses, looking at the exchange between Callaghan and Jet with interest. "Although, they're stubborn as old goats and need reminding you can't get everything you want by butting heads."

I laugh as Callaghan and Jet both shake their heads at the same time with matching hands-on-hips stances.

"I'm Ava. You're travelling with Mr. Callaghan?"

The older woman with soft blonde hair in a chic bob smiles, extending her hand. "Ophelia Callaghan. James is my husband."

I shake her hand. "Ava Roberts. Jet is my stubborn old goat of a boss."

She laughs. "I've met Mr. Grant a few times over the years. I can't say he's ever been anything other than charming."

My face must give away my surprise because her eyes light up as she looks at the two men again and then back at me.

"I don't think either of us are going to get to enjoy this beautiful resort until those two sort out whatever business they have to discuss. And I don't know about you, Ava. But I'd rather my husband doesn't talk about work the entire time. This is supposed to be our anniversary trip."

"I'm sorry."

She shakes her head. "Don't be, I'm used to it. One of us always brings work with us."

"Maybe we can lock them in your villa until they sort it out and you can stay with me. I've got writing to do. Between us, we'll be in calm, man-free heaven."

Jet scrubs a hand around his jaw and the traitorous part of me swallows at how he can make something so simple seem sexy.

Ophelia chuckles. "I'll tell you what. Let's all have dinner this evening. If we can't get this business sorted by the end of dessert, then I'll take you up on that."

"Deal." I grin as she walks over to the men. Jet shakes her hand, exchanging some words with her. She motions over her shoulder to me, and his eyes meet mine.

The intensity in his stare roots me to the spot. I lift a hand in a small wave. He says something that makes Ophelia laugh, then walks over to me.

"What did you say?" he murmurs in my ear as he places his hand on my lower back and leads me out of the lobby.

"Just chatting about goats."

"Goats?" His dark brows furrow, and the hint of a growl in his throat sends a shiver up my spine.

"Yeah." I shrug as he walks us along a wooden walkway toward our villa.

"Well, whatever it was, a few minutes with his wife and you've got us a meeting that I've been trying to get for days."

"Is that a thank you?" I tilt my head to look up at him, but the sun makes me squint. "Is it?" I press. "Because you'll have to warn me if you're about to start being civil. I might faint in shock."

"It's a thank you," he replies gruffly.

"Pardon? I didn't hear you."

His fingers flex on my lower back. "Yes, you did." His tone softens. "I said, thank you, Ava."

"Do you think it's working?" Ophelia asks as we walk down to the water's edge.

I glance back at the candlelit table we've dined at on the beach. This place would be ridiculously romantic with the right person.

Jet and Callaghan are deep in conversation. Jet looks calm, like always, but the way he cracked his neck before Ophelia and I excused ourselves to take a little walk tells me otherwise. She thinks giving them some time alone to talk business will help. But I don't share her optimism. Dining with James Callaghan taught me one thing: he's as much of a control freak as Jet. And he's incredibly proud of Skyline. He kept talking about its history, and how they started off after the second world war with just a few planes. He sounds like he was a total plane enthusiast from a young age, unlike Jet who had to learn to like flying. Callaghan talked about all sorts of vintage aircraft designs I've never heard of before.

"I hope it's working. I could really do with some peace to write."

"And I to read," she agrees.

"What are you reading?"

"Oh, some work things. Scripts—"

"Darling? Are you ready?"

James and Jet approach us. James smiles, reaching for Ophelia, and slides his arm around her waist.

"Done already? That was quick." She places her hand on his chest as I flick my eyes to Jet. His jaw is set, his lips in a grim line.

"Maybe we can do this again? It's been lovely," I offer.

I step forward and kiss Ophelia and then James on the cheek. Jet nods a curt good evening to them, and they walk away up the beach. I wait until they're out of earshot before I turn to him.

"It didn't go well, did it?"

He's already walking off over the sand, and I have to run to catch up with him.

"Jet?"

"Leave it, Ava," he spits. "I don't feel like talking right now."

I grab his bicep, making him stop. He whirls to face me, and the hardness in his eyes makes me flinch.

"What did he say?"

"I said leave it. Why the hell can't you just fucking listen?"

"Why the hell can't you just talk to me?" I fire back.

"Not now. Go back to the villa." He pulls our key card from his pocket and pushes it into my hand.

"Jet?" I call after him, but he ignores me, storming off toward the main hotel bar.

I rub the back of my neck as I pad barefoot into the kitchen to get a drink. It's 2AM and I spent a couple of hours writing when I got back from dinner before heading to bed. Jet never appeared during that time. Whatever Callaghan said to him can't have been good. I've seen him angry before. But this time, there was something else in his eyes. Something desperate.

The door to the deck is open and a familiar outline is slumped on the outdoor sofa. I grab a couple of bottles of water and walk out into the moonlight.

"Maybe it's time you switched refreshments."

Jet looks at my outstretched hand for a moment. Then he nods, placing a tumbler of amber-colored liquid onto the table and taking the bottle of water.

"Thanks," he murmurs.

I sit beside him on the sofa.

"What does it mean if you can't reach a deal?" I ask softly as I stare out over the calm surface of the ocean.

His hoarse whisper has my heart clenching. "*Everything.*"

He's already looking at me as I turn toward him, his eyes glassy.

"We could lose the whole airline, Ava."

"Jet," I breathe. This isn't him. The defeat in his eyes, the way his shoulders are sagged, conveying his hopelessness. I prefer asshole Jet to this version.

"Everything my great grandfather started and my family has built ever since, all lost because of me." He turns to stare out over the water.

"That can't be—"

"I'm the US CEO. It's all down to me. Thirty-one percent of our fleet's engines have a recently discovered design fault. They need replacing in the next two months, or we're screwed. The only engines manufactured that can replace them with minimal disruption to the flying schedule are the ones Callaghan has the supply contract for. He could spare enough to get us through until we take our first delivery from Logan Rich ourselves. It won't even affect his operation because he's introducing them in stages."

"Then why won't he—?"

"Because this is business. We're his biggest competitor. With Atlantic Airways gone, he'll have the monopoly of all North American routes."

"That's wrong, though? He'll be able to set his fares to whatever he likes."

"Regulations won't allow him to do that. But it'll be too late, anyway. We'll be finished."

Jet takes the lid off his bottle and tips his head back, drinking half of it in one go.

"There must be something you can do. Did he give you any idea what it would take for him to change his mind?"

Jet's eyes meet mine before he drops his gaze away. "Nothing that's mine to give."

I sink back into the cushion, my thigh brushing his as I look up at the starry sky.

"Don't give up. There'll be a way. You always win, remember?"

He exhales heavily. "I'll never give up, even if it kills me. If I give up, everyone who works for us will suffer. It has to survive." His voice drops to a hoarse mumble. "I'm nothing without it."

"Don't say that." I turn to face him, resting my head against the plush sofa cushion.

"It's true." He finishes the water and crunches the bottle up in his fist. "It's who I am."

"Maybe I can talk to Ophelia again, or to Callaghan myself. Maybe—"

"No." His voice is fierce. "He can be a bastard. I don't want you anywhere near him."

"What's he going to do? I'm no one to him."

"But you're someone to me, and that's what he'll care about."

He turns back to stare out over the ocean.

Someone to me.

"I thought I was just a cunt you have a short-lived addiction to."

His eyes shutter closed, and he draws in a measured breath, pinching the bridge of his nose. "I'm the cunt, Ava. You'll understand that the more time you spend with me."

I allow myself the indulgence of drinking him in. The sharp cut of his jaw, the days' worth of dark stubble dusting his chin. His soft lips, the way his brows give away his emotions when they pull low or hitch up. I doubt he even knows they do it.

"You just want people to think that because it's easier."

He snorts out a humorless laugh.

"It's easier than people knowing you fill hotel fridges with grapefruit juice and buy lingerie packing bags as gifts. You're only a cunt sometimes."

"Some?"

I want to smile at the way his eyes light up a little.

"Most of the time."

"What am I the rest of the time?" His eyes drop to my lips, and I shiver despite the air being warm.

"I'm not sure. I'm still finding out." I search his eyes.

He's silent for a beat.

"You won't like what you find, Ava, so stop looking." His expression clouds over again and my heart sinks.

"Do you think you're unlovable? Is that why you said what you did about hoping you never fall in love?"

"I didn't say I hope I don't... I said I won't."

"You said it's a game you refuse to play. You're scared."

His jaw clenches.

"You're scared because you can't control it."

"Enough, Ava."

"That's the whole point," I press, determined for him to listen for a change. "You're not supposed to control love. That's the beauty of it... the unknown. It's an adventure."

He turns, capturing me with his brilliant blue eyes. "My mother and father had love. Until they didn't. What's the point if it can be ripped from you like that?"

His tortured eyes hold mine. He can't see what he's doing to himself. What he's depriving himself of.

"What about Francesca? Didn't you have feelings for her?"

"Who?"

"Francesca Callaghan." I straighten in the seat, lifting my head off the cushion.

"Oh." He shakes his head. "No. That was nothing."

It didn't look like nothing to me.

I study him.

"I never got my question." He eyes me with growing interest.

"Huh?"

"I answered four of yours but never got to ask one."

I swallow the lump in my throat. "That's because you shouted and then told me that I was—"

"I should never have spoken to you like that." His eyes glisten with regret as his gaze roams over my face. "I'm sorry."

It's not, *'I didn't mean it. You aren't just a warm body for me to enjoy when I feel like it'*. But I guess it's all I'm going to get.

"Okay. What do you want to ask me?" I pull my legs up beneath me, twisting my torso to face him.

His thigh brushes my knee.

"Tell me about your father. What was he like?"

"You want to know about my father?" My heart clenches painfully as I think about my story. All the words that I've managed to get down. Each one harder to type than the last.

"He died when I was thirteen. The pilot re-routed to avoid a storm, but he flew too low and lost control. They crashed in a forest."

"Tell me *about* your father, Ava," Jet repeats gently. "Not the way he died. Tell me about who he was. What he loved. What you remember about him."

A lump forms in my throat, making my eyes burn.

"He was..." I wring my fingers. "He loved to fly. He loved exploring."

Jet's long fingers brush against mine, tracing across the back of my hand. I turn it without thinking and he slides his thumb over my palm, massaging it, before he runs it up to my wrist and places it over my racing pulse.

"What did you like to do together?"

I smile. "We used to go to the waterlily lake at the Silver Estate every time they had an open day. We'd sit and watch the fish, make up stories, skim stones. I'd splash him and he'd pick me up and run toward the edge of the water and pretend he was going to throw me in. Mum and Gramps would go sometimes too. The last time we were all together there was the day before he died."

"I'm sorry." Jet's soft tone makes me bite back tears.

"I miss him every day."

"I understand." His thumb strokes over my pulse in a way that has calmness washing over me.

I look into his eyes and smile sadly. "Do you think of her much?"

"Every day," he answers without missing a beat.

"What was she like?"

His lips curl into a ghost of a smile. "Fiery. Even up until her final day in hospital, she still glowed. She was amazing. So full of life, until she wasn't..." His lips flatten. "I fucking hate hospitals. She didn't belong in one."

"She sounds special."

"She was. She challenged my father. Pushed him to do more. Be more. She was everything to both of us, the strongest of all of us, fighting until the end."

"Was that her in the photo at the head office? Wing-walking on that plane?"

Jet's eyes soften. "That's her. Always pushing her own boundaries, chasing excitement... letting go."

"Giving up control," I whisper. My breath stalls as he exhales slowly and gazes at me.

"I feel my control being tested with you. You push me, Ava. All the fucking time. I hate it... And I love it too... I *crave* it."

His thumb moves in slow circles over my wrist, and warmth bursts up my spine like a shooting star, despite knowing this is just lust. We're two people who have sexual chemistry and have been spending time together, that's all.

"I mean, someone's got to push you. Imagine how big of an asshole you'd be if everyone let you get your own way all the time."

The rumble in his throat almost sounds like a laugh. "Imagine that."

We fall silent with only the sounds of the ocean drifting around beneath the deck.

"I am sorry for what I said earlier," he whispers, holding my eyes.

"I know. You told me."

"Forgive me. *Please.*" His breath stutters as he runs a hand around his jaw. "It's this deal with Callaghan, the airline, I... Fuck..."

"Don't." I take his hand as he teeters on the edge; a wild, ravaging despair growing in his eyes. "Don't."

He looks at me and my heart sinks into my stomach. I don't know what to do to bring the Jet I know back to the surface again.

I don't know what to do.

So I do the thing that I know we do well together.

I cup his face and pull his lips to mine.

Chapter 20

Jet

"Kiss me," she urges, threading her fingers through my hair.

"Ava," I breathe out her name, the sound sweet on my tongue as I pull her into my lap so that she straddles me. I grasp her hips and roll them, grinding her onto my aching dick.

"Keep doing it," I instruct as I lift my hands to her face and cup her cheeks so I can kiss her back properly.

She moans around my tongue, her hips circling in my lap as she keeps the motion going.

"Good girl," I rasp, pulling my lips from hers so I can lift the silk camisole pajama top over her head. I latch straight back onto her lips. She moans as I tilt her head and deepen our kiss.

"Feed them to me," I groan against her lips.

She looks at me with hooded lids. "What?"

I slide my lips to her neck, kissing beneath her ear. "Your breasts, Ava. Put them in my mouth before I bite." My teeth graze over her skin and she shivers.

I dip my head so my mouth can meet the perfect peak she's offering up to me. I suck on her nipple, relishing the way her hips buck against me.

"And the other," I groan.

She holds her other breast, meeting me halfway as I sink down onto it, cursing as I lap it with my tongue.

"Jet." She shudders as I suck hard and slide a hand straight into her sleep shorts. Her wetness coats my fingers, drawing a needy little whimper from her lips.

I look up into her face as I roll my tongue over her. Her cheeks are flushed, and her hair is falling out of her band, flowing over them. She leans down to kiss me, but I stop her, pressing my wet fingers to her lips and holding her eyes. She runs her tongue over them.

I watch her, desperately trying to hold on to some semblance of restraint as I picture flipping her over and burying myself inside her. I could crush her if I get carried away. Ruin her forever.

"What's wrong?" Her brows pinch and she moves back.

"Nothing." I reach for her, wrapping my palms around her face, pulling it to mine. "Nothing," I repeat, sliding my tongue past her lips again. My heart thunders at her tiny gasp as I devour her.

Her fingers go to the buttons on my shirt, and she starts undoing them one by one, working her hips over my dick with breathy little pants.

"Stop." I place my hands over hers and lift them away from the fabric. Confusion mars her face before I yank each side of my shirt.

The sound of ripping fabric pierces the night air.

"Don't you like that one?" Her lips twist into a smile.

"I don't like anything that gets in the way of being naked with you on my cock."

We become a tangle of hands as we kiss and moan our way out of my pants and her shorts. I grab onto her hips, pulling her back over me as I widen my thighs. I pause, holding her still as she tries to bring our bare skin together.

"What is it?"

"I just..." I reach up and tuck a strand of her hair behind her ear.

She frowns and shifts. Her inner thigh brushes against the head of my cock, and I swallow the flare of arousal that ignites in my veins.

"I'm so fucking sorry, Ava."

I don't give her time to soak in my words. I don't want her to change her mind. To take this all away. I grab her hips and thrust up into her, pulling her down forcefully onto my dick.

"Jet," she cries out, curling her fingers around the back of my neck and gripping it.

"Eyes on me."

She lifts her heavy lids and holds my eyes as I bring her up and back down on my cock.

"Ride me, Ava."

I cup her breasts and roll her nipples as they bounce in my hands with each movement of her hips.

"That's it. Take what you need," I groan.

She whimpers, grinding her hips each time I bottom out inside her, desperately chasing friction for her clit. Her hand drops to it as her pussy ripples around me.

"No." I lift it away, kissing the inside of her wrist. "I'm the one who makes you come now. That orgasm belongs to my cock."

"I can't, I've never—"

"But you will. I'll make sure of it. And when you do, you better chant my name."

I drive up inside her, making her shudder.

"How do you know?" she pants as I grip her hips and guide her down onto me harder.

"You told me on the flight to New York."

She frowns, pink staining her cheeks. "What else did I say?"

"Nothing." I bite my bottom lip with a hiss as she clenches around me. "Fuck, you feel good."

I tighten my grip on her hips, making her ride me faster. My gaze falls to where I'm disappearing inside her body. Our combined skin shines with arousal in the night air.

"Jesus, I need to come inside you, Ava. I need you... I need..." I grab her face and kiss her over and over. "You're mine. No one else can have you, you hear me? I won't allow it."

"I don't want anyone else," she says against my frenzied kisses as I drop one hand to her clit.

"Tell me."

"I want you," she gasps as I slap her clit lightly.

"Fuck yeah, you do. Tell me why."

"Because..." Her eyes roll in her head, and she struggles to kiss me back.

"Why, Ava?" I rasp.

"Because... because..."

"Look at me."

She brings her eyes to mine at the exact moment I feel her release. Her body falls into mine, her perfect lips parting on a moan as she squeezes my cock, coating it in a fresh slick of arousal.

"Jet," she cries.

I grab her chin, forcing her eyes to stay on mine as I rub her swollen clit into another orgasm.

"It's too much."

"It's not. You can take it."

She shakes around me, her body wringing the hell out of my cock. A third orgasm bursts quickly from her with a gasped cry.

"Good girl," I groan. "You're my good girl, Ava. Mine. I'll never leave you alone. This is mine." I pinch her clit, and she cries out against my lips.

"Say it."

"Y-yours."

"Mine," I grunt as I grip one of her hips and slide her up and down me, lifting her body easily. Her legs are spread wide, but I part my thighs more, loving the way it stretches her pussy further and I can see how well she takes me. "I'm going to come inside you. You ready for it?"

She nods.

"Say it."

"Please, Jet," she screams as I jerk my hips harder.

The sound of my name on her lips fills my ears as my vision blurs. I struggle to hold her gaze, trying to anchor myself to her blue eyes as she witnesses me be fucking ripped apart because of her.

I grab her neck and bring her to me by her throat.

"Stay with me," I choke as I spill deep inside her. "Ava, please," I beg.

"I will."

"Ava." I crush my lips to hers as I empty inside her so hard my abs clench to the point of pain. "Ava, please," I rasp. "Forgive me."

Chapter 21

Ava

JET HOLDS ME AROUND the waist, peppering kisses up and down my neck while placing me down onto my feet beside his bed.

"Don't move."

He strides into his bathroom, returning with a washcloth. He presses it between my thighs, his nostrils flaring as I flinch.

"Did I hurt you?"

"No."

"Ava?"

"I'm just tender. You made me come three times, And you're... big."

His brows lift, but the arrogant comment I'm expecting never comes. He throws the washcloth onto the nightstand and lifts me into his arms, before lowering me onto the bed. This is the third time we've had sex, and the third time he's insisted on carrying me afterward. Not that I'm complaining. My legs feel like jelly.

He crawls up, bracing himself over me on his arms. "I meant what I said. Stay with me. Sleep in here."

"I have my own room."

His brows flatten. "This giant fucking villa was a stupid idea. I want you here with me. Not alone in another room."

Alone.

I rub at my throat and the scratchy sensation there. "Okay."

"Good girl."

He presses a soft kiss to my lips, then lies behind me, pulling me into him.

"I want you here with me every night, Ava," he murmurs, sliding his arm around my waist and resting his hand on my stomach. "Every goddamn morning, noon, and night."

"Control freak," I whisper, sucking in a breath as his teeth nip my shoulder.

"I need control." His nip turns into a succession of slow, sleepy kisses that send warmth blooming over my skin. "So I can keep you safe," he murmurs. "It's all so you're safe with me."

I draw in a shaky breath as his breaths even out and he slips into a peaceful sleep. I haven't felt safe in ten years. But having Jet's warm body cocooning mine like I'm precious makes me feel close to it.

So close.

"Jet?" My voice strains through the darkness of the room.

I swipe away the tears on my cheeks as I sit up. The drapes to the balcony of Jet's upstairs bedroom are blowing in the breeze. I have no idea what time it is, only that it's still dark outside, and my dream woke me.

"What's wrong?" His hand finds my hip, his warm fingers caressing some calm back into the taut skin.

I stare out through the drapes, pulling in a shaky inhale. "I didn't tell you the truth earlier. Not all of it."

The warmth of his body fills the space beside me as he joins me, the thin white sheet pooling around his tanned waist.

"Tell me now."

The low, deep coaxing of his voice is like permission. A warm, safe permission, taking control and allowing me to open up and talk. Not worry about the consequences of how many pieces I will be broken into afterward.

I look into his dark eyes. They hold mine. Waiting.

"I was in the plane crash that killed my father and the pilot."

"I know."

"You know?" I blink, and he continues to hold my eyes, the perfect picture of control and calm that I so desperately need.

"I know you better than you think, Ava."

It must have been the way I acted on the flight to New York, being so anxious. Jet must have tuned into it, realized the reason.

His admission calms me, because sometimes I wonder if I even know myself. At least if someone knows me, then I won't ever get lost. Cease to exist. Forgotten.

"I saw it all. The blood, the..." I swallow, turning to look out through the blowing drapes at the night sky. "I was in the forest for three days before they found me. They were so close. I heard the helicopter. I screamed for them to see me. I screamed so hard I lost my voice. But they flew away. I thought I was going to be alone there forever."

His warm fingers flex on my hip before he continues stroking.

"I was unconscious when they found me. Gramps said I didn't talk for months after. I was too scared to remember it all."

I turn to him, tears racing down my cheeks as my breath turns into a sob.

"I'm sorry. I don't know why I'm telling you. I just... all the flights we've taken. It's bringing it back. And..."

He wraps me in his arms without saying anything. His lips dip into my hair and he kisses the crown of my head.

"It's what I've been writing about. My therapist suggested it years ago, but I could never bring myself to do it."

"That's what you've been working on," he says in understanding.

I sniff. "All the newspapers and TV shows kept calling for months afterward. They wanted my story. They even gave me a nickname... But I... I never wanted to tell it. I..." A sob escapes me, and Jet shushes me, turning my face inside his palm so I meet his eyes.

They bring an instant calm to me as I look into their unwavering depth.

"No one has to ever read it if that's what you want. It's for you, Ava, no one else."

I nod as he wipes my tears away with his thumbs. "I know. But I had this stupid idea that I might finally share it... If I feel ready once it's finished."

"I'm so fucking proud of you."

His words floor me.

"I am," he repeats, searching my eyes. "You're so strong."

"I'm not."

He moves slowly, pressing a kiss to my lips. "You are." He presses another kiss to my lips, then pauses. "Tell me what you want. We can stay up the rest of the night and talk. Or I can just be here beside you until you can get back to sleep. Whatever you want, Ava."

I swallow. "I want you to kiss me again. Keep kissing me."

"You sure?" His lips dust mine in the gentlest of kisses, and his hand skates up over my jaw.

"Yes," I breathe. "Do it again." I lean into his palm as he slants his mouth over mine.

He kisses me with a gentleness I've only seen fleeting glimpses of in him before. This time his kisses aren't urgent or infused with lust. He takes his time. Wanting nothing in return.

I pull him closer and whisper his name.

"Ava," he murmurs, sinking back onto the mattress and pulling me with him. His dark hair falls forward as he rolls us until he's hovering above me on strong arms.

His eyes blaze into mine before he kisses me again, making heat pool between my thighs.

"You can't fuck me better, Jet." I try and force a smile.

"No, I can't."

He holds my eyes as something unspoken passes between us. Then he dips his head and kisses me again. I wrap my arms around his neck, parting my thighs where I feel his growing hardness between us.

"Jet," I murmur.

He rests his forehead against mine. "I won't touch you, Ava. You can relax."

"I want you to." I wriggle, encouraging him to move closer. His eyes pinch at the corners as our skin slides together. "I want you to," I repeat as I trace a fingertip over his furrowed brows. "*Please, Jet.*"

His eyes search mine, and he must find whatever he's looking for, because his breath leaves his lungs in a slow exhale against my lips as he pushes himself inside me slowly.

"Goddamn, Ava," he groans.

My lips part on a quiet moan before he steals it straight from my lungs with another kiss. He moves inside me, threading his hands through my hair and stroking my cheeks with his thumbs.

"So beautiful," he rasps.

I lose track of how long our bodies move together, entwined in a beautiful heat that thrums through me, making me feel like I'm nowhere and everywhere at the same time. Like nothing exists outside of this moment.

Jet holds my eyes the entire time, pushing inside me again, a low groan caught in the back of his throat.

"Jet, that feels..."

He slides inside me again, bringing his body flush with mine.

"Let go," he breathes.

I stare into his eyes as tingling spreads through me.

"I'm... I'm..."

"I know, Ava."

His hold mine hostage as I unravel. It doesn't make me scream out his name like the others. It doesn't make me squeeze my eyes shut, unsure if I can take any more.

It makes me float.

It makes everything around me disappear except the light in his eyes as he watches me.

It makes me feel adored and treasured and blissful all at once.

Jet's lips curl, but before I can focus and see if it's a smile, he kisses me again, murmuring *"Ava"* against my lips as he comes inside me, spreading heat through every part of me that it reaches.

"So beautiful," he breathes, holding my face. *"So fucking beautiful."*

I stir sometime later, panicked as Jet's heavy arm pins me in place around the waist. I gaze at his calm face. It's lit up by the sunrise floating in through the open drapes.

He's so handsome. So devastatingly beautiful in a way that could break me if I let it. The aftercare and the sweet Jet who tells me I'm safe, is one I can't get used to. It's a dangerous hope to think that I could feel like this every day, and not have the fear of being alone clawing at me like it always has.

I've learned to live with it, like a constant companion. I can't place that weight onto him after one emotional night together. I'm sure he'll wake and act like nothing happened. Like I didn't cry in his arms and tell him how I screamed to be seen. How I felt terror grip me like an icy fist around my throat when I saw the helicopter move away.

Jet will wake up and gloss over the fact that our sex took on something tender and meaningful. Ignore that

I came by penetration alone, driven by eye contact and a connection that stole the air from my lungs.

Things will go back to whatever they were before. The way it's supposed to be.

I lift his hand, easing myself from under his arm. I shuffle to the edge of the bed, ready to slip out and back to my own room.

"Stop."

His husky voice makes me freeze.

"Ava?"

The edge in his tone sends my heart racing.

He pulls me back against him and rolls me beneath him, making my breath hitch.

"You need more convincing, don't you?" he asks softly, positioning himself between my thighs.

One hand encases my cheek as the other lifts my hip, placing my body where he wants it.

"You think I'm going to leave?" He lifts his chin as my thighs widen around his hips on instinct, inviting him closer. "You think you have to be scared of being alone?"

He looks into my eyes so deeply that I have to blink back the sting prickling at their corners.

"I'm here, Ava," he breathes, when I shake my head.

"I..." My lower lip shakes as he presses soft kisses along my jaw.

"I'm here," he rasps against my neck, sending goosebumps racing over my flesh. "You're not alone."

A whimper escapes my throat.

"I'm here," he whispers. "You're safe."

Chapter 22

Jet

> **James Callaghan: Let's talk.**

I PLACE MY PHONE on the table. It's 7AM. Callaghan's up to something. Last night, he told me he wasn't interested in a deal, yet now he suddenly wants to talk?

Turning my attention back to my laptop screen, large, trusting blue eyes shine back at me from the article.

"Jesus," I mutter, pushing my finger and thumb into my eye sockets.

Ava pads up behind me in just a silk robe before I have a chance to minimize the article. "Jet, what are you—?"

"Nothing."

She places a hand on my shoulder, stopping me from closing the laptop. "It's okay. I've seen it before."

Deep lines etch into her forehead as she stares at the headline of the news article.

"***Forest Girl*** – *The thirteen-year-old, assumed dead, was found barely alive three days after the fatal plane crash that killed her father and the pilot.*"

The picture accompanying it must be from before the crash. Ava's grinning, her auburn hair flowing around her shoulders as she stands between a man and woman with matching smiles.

"Mum and Dad," she explains as I close down the laptop.

"I'm sorry. You shouldn't have seen me looking at that. It was thoughtless of me."

"It's just facts in that article. I told you the worst parts."

I reach for her hand, but she slides it off my shoulder and walks over to the open glass doors.

"What's the plan for today then, Boss?" Her shoulders bunch up as she stands with her back to me.

"Callaghan's texted me. I'm meeting him."

"Do you want me to come?" She glances back over her shoulder.

"No. I need to do this one alone."

"Okay." She turns away, wrapping her arms around herself.

As I join her, her lips tip into a smile. "I didn't think they'd stock this brand here. Seeing as it's from a UK supermarket and all." She takes the bottle of grapefruit juice from me.

"Really?"

"Our fridge was full of it when we checked in. Funny, isn't it?" She knocks her shoulder against mine, her eyes lighting up.

"Hilarious," I murmur, looking at her as warmth blankets my chest.

We stare at each other for a few moments before I tilt her chin up. Her pupils dilate as I run the pad of my thumb over her lower lip.

"I'm going for a shower."

"You should. You're really sweaty from all that skipping." She screws up her nose, but her eyes glitter.

"Okay..." I run my thumb over her lip more, dipping it into her mouth to graze the underside of her top teeth before cupping her jaw.

"Okay," she repeats.

"Okay," I echo.

I press the lightest of kisses to her lips, energy racing to my dick as she sucks in a quick breath and leans into me.

"There's somewhere I want to take you tonight. You'll need your bikini... the white one."

That frilly little thing she calls swimwear is sexy as fuck on her. It barely covers her ass and makes me want to spank it and leave my mark.

"The white one?"

Nodding, I smirk, walking backward, enjoying the way her eyes narrow at me.

"Half of the engines you asked for. That's what I'm offering. You give me the extra slots and they're yours."

I keep my hands still against my legs as I lean back in the chair inside the hotel's open air cocktail lounge. The urge to smack Callaghan in the jaw is overwhelming. He's enjoying this. He knows full well that half the number of engines I asked for might as well be none. It won't help.

"Half?" I roll my lips, pretending to consider it.

"I think that's more than generous of me."

"Of course you would think that." I reach for the glass of brandy on the table and take a mouthful.

"If you want the full amount, you know what I want in return. You could stop this whole display of following me around."

My grip tightens around the glass before placing it down. "And you know that it will never be yours. It's non-negotiable." I lean back, steepling my fingers in front of my chest as I hold Callaghan's gaze.

He mirrors my posture, relaxing into his seat and letting his gaze roam across the open terrace of the cocktail lounge and out onto the beach.

"There are some positives to you turning up, though."

I follow his gaze and my entire body stiffens.

"My wife's enjoying getting to know your girlfriend. She's an interesting girl."

Ava's strolling along the shore in a blue bikini top and shorts, her head turned toward the water as she gazes out, lost in her own world.

"I recall the plane crash that killed her father. The press reported on it for weeks... Such a tragic story."

I jump forward in my seat, knocking our table and almost causing our glasses to crash to the floor. "She's got nothing to do with this. So let's keep it to business."

Callaghan pulls his eyes away from Ava, and I pin him with a glare, which he returns with a cold smile.

"You know what I want. Think about it," he says.

He stands and walks away. I force my ass to stay in the chair so I don't knock him out. My gaze tracks back to Ava, walking along with a serene smile. I inhale slowly, some tension leaving my shoulders as she stops and bends to retrieve something from the sand.

I pick up my brandy, a frisson of victory rumbling in my gut. Callaghan's negotiating. Which means I'm getting closer. He might think he's in control. But if he's already offering half, he'll give me the rest. He just doesn't know it yet.

I drink, warmth enveloping my throat as Ava studies the large shell she's picked up. Her eyes lift and she looks straight at me as if she can sense me. She waves, before holding the shell up.

I tip my chin in acknowledgment, and a smile lights up her face. My shoulders relax as she walks in my direction.

I'll get everything I need from Callaghan, even if it wrecks me to do it.

"This is incredible." Ava spins in the water, her eyes wide in wonder as she looks at the glow surrounding us. "Have you been here before?"

"No."

"How did you even know about this place?"

I swim through the chest-height water to get closer to her. The light from the bio-luminescent plankton surrounds us as I pull her into my arms.

"It's famous for it. Well, Ton Sai is. But this place..." I look around at the deserted area of the beach. "A friend told me about it."

"I can't believe it." She smiles as she wraps her arms around my neck and looks at the effervescent glow lighting up the water around us. "It's so bright. So beautiful."

She looks at me when I don't respond. The hint of vulnerability in her eyes has me pulling her lips to mine. "It is. *So fucking beautiful.*"

I kiss her, relishing the way she whimpers around my tongue and pushes her body into mine like she can't get close enough.

"You're glowing. Just like in New York."

Her eyes shine as she lifts her shoulders, then drops them with a grin.

"It's flying to new places and getting bitten by the adventure bug. I'm not Ava-stuck-in-England-Roberts anymore. You should call me—"

"Firefly."

"What?"

I stroke a strand of red hair back from her eyes. "You're a bright light. Radiant and captivating... and distracting me constantly."

She frowns, wrinkling her nose. "I thought you said Callaghan was opening up to agreeing on something. That you're getting somewhere?"

"I am."

She places her palm over my chest and eases back to study my face. "But if I'm distracting you, I shouldn't have come. This deal is huge."

"It is. It's everything."

Worry flashes in her eyes and I curse myself for making her feel any kind of responsibility to what's going on. For being the cause of anything other than pleasure to bloom in her eyes when she looks at me. Because physical pleasure is all that we'll ever have. There's no outcome where I won't cause her pain in the end. She deserves to be loved. Something she'll never get with me.

"Callaghan's shifting. I'll get what we need. It'll be over soon."

She looks at me skeptically. Heat flares through my chest as my attention drops to her mouth. I'm a selfish prick. An asshole, just like she's called me. Because I don't have the willpower to resist taking her in all the ways she'll let me for as long as I can. To make her mine and pretend the inevitable crash won't happen.

To accept that I *will* break her, and she'll hate me.

It's only a matter of time.

"Do you regret what's happened between us? Me being here? Last night got pretty heavy and..."

"Not for one second."

I lift her legs around my waist and hold her under the ass with one arm as I rest my forehead against hers.

"Not for one fucking second."

"But I'm distracting you—"

I cut her off with a kiss. "I never said that was a bad thing." I squeeze a handful of her ass. "I want your distractions. Every single one."

She sinks into me, running the tip of her tongue along the seam of my mouth.

"Especially the bratty ones," I murmur against her lips, taking the lower one beneath my teeth and gently nipping it until her nails scrape the back of my head.

"You're so rude," she tuts.

"You ever fucked in a glowing ocean before?"

She giggles, her pulse beating beneath my tongue as I lick down the side of her neck.

"No. Have you?"

"This one time. With a girl who's fiery as hell. One that likes to fuck in the ocean and then get eaten."

"What?" She smirks. "By a shark?"

I shrug. "Maybe. We're in their territory. I doubt we'd see them coming."

She whips her head side to side studying the surface of the ocean as her grip tightens on my neck. "You're joking?" Her eyes widen at my serious expression. "Put me down. I want to get out." She tries to remove her legs from my waist.

"Stop wriggling."

She squeals as movement of a fish beneath the surface causes a ripple to break nearby.

"Stop," I command as she struggles in my arms.

"Put me the fuck down, Jet!"

I want to spank her ass, but can't in the water, so I grab her chin instead and force her eyes to meet mine. She glares at me.

"Do as I say, Ava."

"You're being an asshole. Put me down." Her hands ball into fists against my chest.

"There are no sharks here. It's a cove."

She stops struggling, but her chest still rises and falls in anxious pants, so I carry her closer to the shore, stopping when the water reaches my groin.

"Now quit the attitude or I won't spend the rest of tonight with my head between your thighs *eating* you out."

Her brows shoot up her forehead. "You bastard. You made me think there were sharks on purpose."

I clasp her chin again and drag my thumb over her pouty lower lip.

"And why would I do that? Do you think I like you not listening to me? Like it when you do things that make me keep track of the number of times I need to spank your pretty, round ass?"

Her eyes narrow.

"You're right." She moves her hand down my chest, forcing it between our bodies and into my swimming trunks. She runs it over my rock-hard dick, moving lower, before digging her nails into my ball sack, enough to make me hiss.

"You wouldn't do something so mean." Her nails push deeper, and she smirks as my chest rumbles with a tortured groan. "But if there were sharks, I'm pretty sure they'd eat you first. Lying CEOs are probably their favorite. Extra salty."

I lean forward to kiss her, but she tugs my balls, making me curse.

"That's it, you fucking asked for it," I hiss.

I pull the white ties against her hips undone and rip her bikini panties off. "I've warned you before not to be a brat." I toss them away from us into the water.

"Jet! They'll float away."

"Let them fucking float."

She stares at the white fabric drifting out to sea. "I like them!" She tries to pry herself from my arms again.

"Stop being a brat," I growl.

She opens her mouth to protest but I clamp my hand over it, making her eyes snap to mine.

"I'm a fucking billionaire. I'll buy you more... I'll buy you whatever the hell you want, Ava. I'll spoil you every goddamn minute you're mine."

Her lids hood as she breathes through her nose, softening in my arms.

"That's better," I coo, dusting the tip of my nose over hers. "Now reach down and take my cock out. I've waited long enough to stuff your cunt full of it."

Her eyes flare in defiance as she refuses to move.

I raise a brow. "You know I'll play this game all night if I have to, Ava. It's nice and peaceful with your mouth shut."

She huffs against my palm, then frees my dick.

I hold her eyes as I position her, then pull her down onto it, savoring the way she stretches to take me.

"Fuck yeah," I groan, loving the way her whimper is muffled by my palm.

"This is mine." I hold myself deep and circle my hips. "You're mine."

She whimpers against my fingers.

"Take it," I grit. "You've got me fucking addicted, Ava. Now deal with the consequences."

She runs her hands through the hair at the back of my head as she looks at me.

"That's it." My voice softens as she loosens up and lets me fuck her, thrusting my hips up and making her ride my dick like she's my personal fuck toy. "You take my cock like such a good girl. *My* good girl."

Her eyes roll as I pull back and then drive up again, over and over. The water slaps against her ass each time I sink her down onto me.

"And you're going to come for me like this, aren't you?"

She tries to nod with my hand clamped over her mouth.

"Yeah, you fucking are," I groan, my balls aching to fill her as she clenches around me. "That's it... Let it go."

She holds my eyes, and I can pinpoint the exact moment her orgasm steals her from me, making her eyes glaze over and her breath stall. I bury myself inside her, enthralled. Ignoring the fact this will all end one day. It has to. But until then, I'll keep her distracting me. Because fuck, I crave being distracted by her. It's better than the high that comes with winning.

"Ava."

I rip my hand away from her mouth and replace it with my lips, kissing her with a guttural growl as I come hard inside her.

She cries out my name.

"That's it," I hiss as she squeezes me, milking every drop. "That's it, Firefly."

Better than winning.

Chapter 23

Ava

JET ZIPS HIS LAPTOP case shut and pulls his phone from his pocket. I rest one hip against the counter of the kitchen as I watch him. His face is serious. He's in a navy-blue suit and deep gold tie. It sets off his tan and makes him look like a bronzed god.

I press my thighs together, easing the happy ache. He was true to his word and kept me up most of the night coming on his tongue. I must have eventually passed out, because I woke this morning to the sound of him skipping on the deck.

"Home time already." I sigh and look around the luxurious villa as I unscrew the cap from my juice.

Jet frowns as he types on his phone.

"I'll be sad to leave," I say a little louder.

His attention stays on his phone as he says, "I'm sure you'll stay in other places you like now that you're flying again."

I open my mouth to confess that the idea of flying anywhere without him beside me is still terrifying. But his attention is glued to his phone. Callaghan and Ophelia joined some of their friends on a yacht this morning, so Jet's access to him has been removed. Not that he seems concerned. He told me to pack this morning because it's time to leave.

All his prior moodiness returned when he put his suit on this morning. Gone are the glimpses of the softer Jet I've been lucky enough to witness. The man in front of me isn't the same one who opened up and told me how he misses his mother every day, and admitted he believes love is a game that's not worth playing.

Jet Grant, emotionless, billionaire CEO is back.

I finish my juice and put the bottle in the recycling can.

"I'm looking forward to getting back to Rochwell. Do you think Margaret has missed us?" I walk over to the table and pack my laptop away into its case.

"You maybe. Not me. But she'll have to miss you a little longer. We aren't going back to England yet."

"Where are we going?"

"LA. I need to see Hayden and check in face-to-face."

"As in, California?"

"I own an airline. Don't sound so surprised."

He slides his phone into his pocket and finally looks at me. His brow furrows as I shift from foot to foot.

"Umm."

"Words, Ava," he clips.

"LA is where my mother lives."

His eyes soften a touch. "Then you'll be able to spend some time with her."

"I will." I nod, my heart fluttering as I soak in the magnitude of what this means. I haven't seen my mother in months. And I've never been to her place in LA. She's given me tours on video calls, but to actually be there in person with her will be incredible.

Jet strides over and packs away my laptop for me where my hands have ceased working.

"You ready to go?"

"I think so... I mean, yes. Yes!"

His eyes hold mine and something warm passes through the blue.

"Good. Then let's go."

"Are you getting out?" Jet arches a brow at me across the back seat.

I turn back to the door that his driver is holding open for me. "Um, yeah."

I take in the white two-story house with terracotta roof tiles. It's pretty, with a well-tended lawn out front and a path leading up from the sidewalk. I can't believe Mum is inside. That I'll be hugging her in a few minutes. I'm so excited, yet I'm struggling to make my legs move.

The sound of Jet's door opening and closing makes me jump, then he's standing at my door in his driver's place.

"Come on, Ava."

I climb out of the car, straightening my dress as Jet takes my suitcase and motions for me to go first up the path. He follows me up the path, wheeling my suitcase. The door flies open before I reach it and then she's there.

"Mum!" I run into her outstretched arms.

"My darling, darling girl." She squeezes me and strokes the back of my head. "Let me look at you."

She holds the top of my arms and moves back, her face lighting up into her movie-worthy smile as she takes me in.

"My darling, you look so well and happy. I can't believe you're here."

"I can't believe it, either." I grin. "You look amazing, Mum."

"It's the oxygen facials." She drops her hand and performs a twirl, the fabric of her white, embroidered kaftan dress swishing around her legs. "And a new dress."

Her gaze moves over my shoulder, and I follow it to Jet.

"Mum, this is Jet. Magnus's son. We've been traveling together. I was helping him work."

It's a lie. That might have been the reason this all began. But I've done nothing that resembles actual work.

I've just been a distraction.

Jet greets my mother with a newfound charm I've never noticed before. He even makes it look like he's smiling. But it's polite, practiced.

"So lovely to meet you, Zena," he says smoothly as my mother swoons.

He turns to me, holding my case out.

"Ava, I'm needed in the office. I'm sure you and your mother have lots you'd like to do together."

I beam at Mum. "We do."

She takes my case from Jet and smiles. "Thank you for looking after my daughter and bringing her to LA. I've been wanting her to come for years."

"She's a pleasure to take care of." His eyes meet mine and make my stomach flip.

"Come on." Mum takes my hand and leads me toward the open door.

I look back at Jet. "I'll call you, Ava. Have fun with your mum."

"I will." I grin. "Speak to you later."

"I'll call you," he repeats.

Chapter 24

Ava

Jet's version of 'I'll call' and mine are wildly different.

It's been three days and I've heard nothing from him, except a curt reply to a text I sent him yesterday checking if he was still alive. He replied at 2AM, so I imagine he's been pulling some late nights. Besides, I've been having too much fun with Mum to have much time to think about anything else.

I giggle as she spins in her kitchen, then dances her way over to me and takes my hands. I slide off the breakfast bar stool and the two of us spend the rest of "We are family" by Sister Sledge dancing around like a couple of lunatics before collapsing onto side-by-side stools as the song ends.

"Darling." Mum places a palm over her chest as she catches her breath. "Why haven't we done this sooner?" She looks at me, her eyes bright. "I'm so happy you're here."

"I know." I smile. "I wish I could have come years ago, but... getting on a plane after—"

She places her hand over mine, her eyes shining. "I know. I miss him, too."

"You do?"

She brushes a strand of hair from my cheek. "Your father was my first love, Ava. I'll always miss him and wonder what might have been." Her brow creases before she composes herself, forcing a bright smile. "Your grandfather has done a wonderful job. You've grown into such a special young woman. I'm so sorry I wasn't there to see it."

My heart seizes at the sight of water lining Mum's lower lashes before she blinks it away.

"You were grieving, too. You wanted me to move here with you. I'm the one who was too scared to do it after the crash. I've been..." I take a deep breath then blow it out. "I've been writing about it. It's silly, but—"

"It doesn't sound silly."

"I just..." I screw my eyes shut before opening them again. "It started as a way to process it. I should have done it years ago, but I was living in denial, I guess. Not wanting to remember it. But writing has felt good, it's felt..." I swallow, my voice coming out as a whisper. "I'm wondering if I'll be ready to tell it soon. Finally."

"Oh, Ava." Mum pulls me into a hug, stroking my back. "My darling girl, you've always been the strong one."

"I'm not strong, Mum."

"You are. So strong." She hugs me harder, then lets go, a pained smile on her face. "I knew you'd be okay without me. But I'm your mother, and I struggled everyday living so far away from you. Those early days here... I wouldn't have been able to support you, no matter how much I wished I could. I owe so much to William for making sure you had everything you needed. I remember how pleased he was when he got you into that school, despite how much it cost him in fees. He spent months fighting to get you a place there."

"School?"

Mum gets up and goes to the refrigerator, bringing back two glasses.

"You like mango juice, don't you?" She places the glass in front of me, and I curl my hands around its cool sides.

"Sure."

I stare at the vivid orange as a million thoughts run through my head. I always thought Mum had paid for my private school. Gramps couldn't have afforded it. After my father died, he sold his house and downsized. I assumed the memories were too much for him, living in the house where Dad grew up and Nana once lived with him. The two of us moved to a pretty two-bedroom cottage near my school instead. Close enough that he would walk to meet me at the end of the day, bringing ice creams in the summer, and a flask of hot chocolate in the winter.

"You okay? You look sick."

"Just thinking about Gramps." I force a smile. "I miss him. I might go and give him a call."

"Say hello from me," Mum says. "Then when you're done, I want to take you to lunch to meet Mitch."

"Your agent?"

Mum's cheeks tint with pink. "That's him. He's heard all about you. I'll be ready once you're done."

"The famous Ava." Mitch sweeps me into a double-cheeked kiss, his teeth so whitened that they glow as he flashes a smile.

"In the flesh," I say.

"I can see what you mean, Zena." His eyes roam over my hair. "Just beautiful."

My mother beams at him as he holds out my chair for me, and then one for her.

"Have you ever considered acting, Ava? You have the face for it. We could make you a huge star."

I smile as I sit. "No, thank you. I don't think that's for me."

He sits opposite me at the table, appraising me like a project. We've come to a fancy restaurant in Hollywood. Mum's head hasn't stopped swiveling since we arrived. She whispered to me about some big special effects director she spotted at another table as we walked in.

"That's a shame. I could get you a leading role. Maybe a romance. Do you fancy being paid to kiss Ryan Gosling?" Mitch lifts a hand, signaling a server.

I bite back a surprised laugh as the server fills our glasses with iced water and takes our drinks order before retreating.

"Mitch." Mum rolls her eyes affectionately. "My daughter has barely been here a week and already you're trying to cast her."

"I know a star when I see one." His eyes travel over to Mum, and she sighs happily.

"When did you two start dating?"

They both look at me in surprise.

"Come on." I laugh. "It's obvious."

Mum smooths a hand over her hair, her lips twisting into a smile as Mitch looks at her like a man obsessed.

"And here's me thinking I was a good actress." Mum laughs. "It's been a while, darling. All the working together turned into something more."

"I'm happy for you both," I say, meaning it.

"I'm a lucky man," Mitch says, making Mum giggle. "Your mother is a star, Ava. Knew it the moment I saw her." His gaze returns to Mum. "I've got you an audition for that movie with Tom Cruise."

Mum gasps and leans forward, almost toppling off the edge of her seat. "Really?"

"Told you, Zena. We've got this. The starring role… it'll be yours."

"Oh goodness." Mum sits back, her eyes dancing. "This is amazing."

"It's tomorrow afternoon. We'll run the lines together. You'll blow them away," Mitch says, chuckling as she fans herself with the menu.

"Don't mind your mother, Ava," she sings. "I'm just dying here. I can't believe it. First, you coming here to visit, and now this. I'm so happy."

Warmth bursts in my chest.

"So, Ava. What are you doing now? Your mom tells me you graduated recently. Any big plans?"

"I've been taking some time for myself… working on something." I glance at Mum. She nods at me encouragingly. I straighten and take a deep breath. "I've been writing my story. About the crash, the forest, not being found straight away… the whole thing."

Mitch's brows shoot up. "Really? That's something you've never spoken about publicly, isn't it?" His eyes dart to Mum, and she reaches for my hand.

I grip onto it for courage.

"I haven't. Not once. I've been asked so many times. TV companies still approach me now, but… I wasn't ready."

"And you are now?" The interest pitching Mitch's voice makes my heart hammer as self-doubt creeps in.

"I don't know. Maybe… I haven't decided. I'm almost finished writing it. Doing it has been a huge… relief."

Mum squeezes my hand, and I smile at her gratefully.

"I know people who would snap that up, Ava. It's an incredible story. We could make sure you retain all creative rights, be involved in the casting."

"It's a big decision," Mum says softly as the server returns with our drinks and places them down. "Not one to be made in haste."

"Of course," Mitch agrees. "Think about it, Ava. This could be huge for you, make a lot of money, make you famous. I have the connections to make it all happen."

I swallow down the unease that's manifested itself into a tight knot in my throat. Everything I've kept to myself for ten years could be shared with the world.

Be seen.

I'm not sure I'm ready for it. What if I never am?

I force a smile. "I'll think about it."

Mitch and my mother move into talking about her upcoming audition and I allow myself to be swept up in her excitement again as I sip my grapefruit juice. It's not my favorite brand, but the sharp tang makes me think of Jet.

I pull my phone out of my purse. A spark of energy shoots up my spine as I see his name on the screen.

> **Jet: What are you doing today?**

I toy with the idea of making him wait before I reply. But I've missed knowing what the moody bastard is up to. We've spent so much time together recently that him not being here is... weird.

> **Me:** Having lunch with Mum and her agent/boyfriend. You?

> **Jet:** Callaghan is coming back to the US in a few days. We're preparing contracts for him to sign.

> **Me:** For all the engines? He's agreed? That's amazing!

> **Jet:** Not yet. But he will.

> **Me:** Sounds like everyone's busy at your office.

> **Jet:** Like Tasmanian devils on speed.

I smile. I bet he's cracking the whip. Jet Grant in full suited control-mode.

> **Me:** Yet you have time to text me? You're getting distracted.

I add a smirking emoji before I click send. His response is instant.

> **Jet:** I wish my face was being distracted between your thighs right now.

I inhale my water, spluttering and spilling some. Mum and Mitch look at me but carry on talking when I signal I'm fine and grab a napkin to pat my lips.

> **Me: What will HR say if they read the dirty things you send to your employees on your company phone, Mr. Grant?**

> **Jet: Employees is plural.**

> **Me: You mean I'm the only special one allowed to distract the boss?**

> **Jet: Don't be a brat, Ava.**

> **Me: Why? I thought it made you hard.**

I sit back in my seat, satisfaction running through me. I've missed playing with him. No matter how heavy my chest gets talking about the crash, the banter with Jet makes me feel something else.

Free. Alive.

My phone buzzes with another message.

> **Jet: Tomorrow. All day. You're mine.**

My fingers dance over the keys.

> **Me: I might already have plans.**

I don't. Mum has her audition, but Jet doesn't know that.

> **Jet: Cancel them.**

> **Me: Maybe I don't want to.**

> **Jet: Push me and see where that gets you, Ava.**

Heat pools between my legs and I start to type back, but three more messages from him buzz through one after the other before I can.

> **Jet: Tomorrow.**

> **Jet: You're.**

> **Jet: Mine.**

Chapter 25

Jet

"Very convincing," I say, handing the script back to Ava's mother.

"Really? You think it was good?" Her face lights up as she fluffs her hair with one hand and reads the script with the other.

"The best one so far."

She beams. "You think so?"

"Number seven was strong." I clear my throat. "And number twelve was executed well. You'll be fine."

"I'll be fine," she repeats, clutching the script against her chest. "Maybe once more?"

"Oh my god, Mum! You were practicing when I went to bed. Have you even slept?"

Ava walks into the room, her eyes meeting mine with a smirk. I know she's kept me waiting on purpose. Brat.

"A few hours," her mother mumbles as she flicks through the script again.

"You'll be amazing, won't she, Jet?"

Ava turns to me, but I finish my appreciative sweep up her body before I answer. She's wearing a flowery sundress with thin little straps and a short skirt that barely covers her ass.

I run my tongue over my teeth. "Amazing," I reply as I reach her eyes.

"We should be going, Mum," she says, holding my eyes.

"Okay, darling. Have fun, whatever you have planned."

"I'm showing Ava my house," I say, my blood heating at the idea of sliding that tiny dress up over her full ass and grabbing a handful of it.

Work has been a shitshow since I got back to LA. The media team are fielding calls from the press, speculating over the security of the airline, following a leak about our situation. I'd bet my right nut Callaghan's behind it. Getting the press to do his dirty work is his style. My staff are tense. Hayden's tense. I'm fucking tense.

A day with Ava beneath me in my bed sounds like heaven.

"Actually, I've booked us something fun to do."

"You've done what?"

"A tour of all the best places." She bounces on her toes as I grunt.

"I can give you a tour. I live here."

"But I want the whole tourist experience on an open top bus."

She raises her chin in a smug challenge, then kisses her mum goodbye as I roll my neck side to side until it cracks.

"Bad for your bones," she sings as she slings her purse over her shoulder and waltzes over to me. "You ready?" She looks up at me through her lashes and my palm twitches.

"I'm always ready for you, Firefly."

Her lips part with a small, surprised inhale that makes my dick throb.

I place my hand on her lower back and she falls silent as I lead her to the front door. I slide it a fraction lower until my pinky grazes the top of her ass.

It's going to be so pretty and red when I've finished with her.

"Why have you never done this before? It's awesome!" Ava holds her phone up and snaps another photo of Malibu beach.

"It's hell."

My eyes wander to a kid in the front seat opposite ours. He pulls a giant booger from his nose, then eats it.

Gross. He twists his lips as he digs deep and produces another one. Then he reaches down and wipes it onto the seat. *Okay, that's grosser.*

My skin crawls as I shift in the cheap seat.

"Stand up," I bark at Ava.

"What? Why?"

"Do it."

She rolls her eyes and stands, holding onto the rail as she looks out of the open top bus at the street ahead.

I check her seat, then take my suit jacket off and place it down. Then I smooth both hands over the globes of her ass, running them over the fabric of her dress, checking for things that make me want to wretch.

"Jet," she hisses, swatting my hand.

I flick her away and finish my inspection, then grab her hips and pull her back to sit on my jacket. "You're safe."

"From what? Being reported for public indecency?"

"Can we get off now?" I grumble.

She sighs and side-eyes me. "Do you need to go back to work?"

"No."

"Then why are you wearing a suit?"

"I went into the office before I picked you up."

"Oh."

I yank my tie off and coil it around my fist before stuffing it into my pocket. Then I undo the top two buttons of my shirt and roll my sleeves up my forearms. "Happy now, Miss Tour guide? Do I look more like a guy who likes sitting on grimy buses and taking photos of shit?"

Ava ruffles my hair. "You do now."

She smirks and leans into my side, snapping a selfie of the two of us.

"I need proof that you can loosen up. Otherwise, Margaret won't believe me."

She checks her phone screen and giggles, then holds it up to show me. My head is turned toward her, eyes fixed on her face as she looks into the camera with a smile as bright as the fucking sun.

"You actually enjoy this, don't you?"

"What's not to enjoy?" She snaps another picture of the street below.

I look around the top level of the bus. It's a mix of families and couples who look like they're on vacation. Everyone's taking photos like Ava.

The tour guide's cheerful voice booms through the speakers. "Well, don't we have a treat for you all! We're just about to pass the entrance to award-winning actor, Jay Anderson's house."

An excited hum rumbles through the top deck, and a woman cries, "Lord have mercy, that man is fine."

"If we're super lucky, we might get a glimpse of the property through the security gate," the tour guide adds.

"Amazing!" Ava propels to her feet and leans over the rail, craning her neck to see down the street. "Did you hear that?"

I whip my jacket off the seat and grab her by the elbow.

"What are you doing?" she squeals.

"We're getting off."

I slam my palm over the emergency stop button and the bus jerks to a stop moments later. There's a collective gasp from the other passengers as I turn to Ava, who's still gripping the handrail.

"Off. Now," I grit.

She glances around, her cheeks flushing as everyone stares at us.

"Jet," she whispers. "You can't just get off where you want. This isn't one of the stops."

I hold her eyes, sucking in an agitated breath. "I said off, Ava... Now."

Her forehead creases, but she makes no attempt to move.

"Hold this." I tut, handing her my jacket.

She lets go of the rail to take it, and I seize my opportunity, hoisting her up over my shoulder.

"What the hell?" she gasps. "You're crazy."

"What's crazy is you spent a hundred bucks on something I can do better myself. Now be a good girl and stop squirming."

I plant one hand over her ass, holding her dress down so it covers her, and keep the other wrapped around the backs of her thighs as I stride along the aisle and carry her down the stairs.

"Sir, you can't get off here," the tour guide says as I get to the front of the bus.

I reach into my pocket and take out a money clip, pulling out a thick wad of hundreds.

"Thanks for the tour, but she's feeling sick."

I press the bills into the stunned guide's palm.

"This bus was cleaned this morning," she says, eyeing Ava suspiciously like she might throw up at any moment. I don't enlighten her to the booger boy upstairs.

"Best not take any chances, then."

She stands aside, looking relieved as we pass.

I step out onto the sidewalk, already more relaxed as the bus doors close behind us and it drives away.

"That was so embarrassing! You can't do that."

I set Ava down on her feet and she glares at me, prodding my chest. I catch her hand in mine.

"I just tipped enough to replace the whole bus with one that doesn't have roaches. I don't think they'll care."

She shoves my jacket back at me and rips her hand from mine. "I was enjoying myself."

"And you still will."

I take her hand in mine and walk up the sidewalk.

"Where are we going?" she huffs as she falls into step beside me. "It had better be somewhere worth losing our place for. We had the front row at the top. They're the gold seats."

"Yeah, luxury at its finest."

"You're such a jerk."

She frowns as we stop in front of a giant black gate and I push the intercom.

"What are you doing?"

"Using the intercom."

"I can see that," she snaps.

I turn, looking into her eyes as there's a click from the speaker.

"Hey, man!" the warm, instantly recognizable voice says. "What are you doing here?"

I smirk as Ava's eyes widen and she spots the security camera.

"Just thought we'd drop in and say hi. We were in the neighborhood."

"Absolutely. Come on up."

The intercom cuts out and the gate slides open smoothly.

"Jet?" Ava hisses.

"Ava," I reply, running my thumb over her knuckles as I lead her up the driveway to the front door.

"Why didn't you tell me you know Jay Anderson?"

"You never asked."

She yanks on my hand, so I look at her. "So what? You're like besties or something?"

"We're friends, yes."

Her mouth drops open. "You have friends? Sorry, I mean... Is he like, a passing friend, or a super close friend?"

"He's like *he came to my mother's funeral-we're that close* friend."

"Oh." Her eyes soften and the look she gives me makes my chest twinge.

The front door opens and Jay strides out, grabbing me into a back-slapping hug.

"Jet, man. It's been too long. How was England?"

"Challenging," I say.

He looks at Ava.

"Hi." She smiles, looking a little awkward.

"This is Ava. She's been working with me."

"Hey, Ava. Nice to meet you." Jay pulls her into a quick hug. "You guys are staying, right? We've just got brunch ready."

"We can't intrude." Ava's gaze flicks to me as he ushers us inside.

Jay laughs. "My wife's made enough for a small country. We need all the help we can get."

Ava's head swivels side to side as she takes in the impressive beach front house. I recall how excited Jay was to show me this place when he and his wife's offer was accepted. It's quite something.

He leads us through the giant kitchen and out the rear doors. There's a large pool to one side, but he takes us to a dining table on the giant deck, which runs along the width of the property. Malibu beach is behind it, and the ocean stretches out as far as you can see.

"Holy fuck," Ava murmurs under her breath.

I squeeze her hand before letting go to greet Holly, who spins away from where she's setting a bowl of blueberries down on the table.

"Jet!" She beams and pulls me into a hug. "Guys, look who it is."

I nod in greeting to the two guys sitting at the table. "Stefan, Matt. How are you guys? Ava and I thought we'd come say hi to Holly, Jay, and the kids. Didn't know we'd be getting you two as well."

They rise from the table, and Matt grabs me into a hug as Stefan pats my upper arm.

"Cheeky," Matt says. "You know I'm your favorite ex-employee."

"I heard that," Holly pipes up.

"You brought company." Matt's eyebrows wiggle as he pulls back. "Did he have to pay you to put up with him?"

Holly bats him on the chest.

"He did. But not nearly enough." Ava smiles.

"I like her," Matt declares, wrapping his arm around Ava and stealing her from me, leading her down the other end of the table where some drinks are set up. She's swept up into a conversation between him and his partner, Stefan, and Holly, so I put my jacket on the back of one of the chairs and hang back, watching her relax.

"Who is she?" Jay asks quietly, coming up beside me with his eldest daughter, Summer, in his arms.

"She's Ava," I reply.

Jay's grin turns shit-eating.

"Don't go getting ideas."

"I said nothing." His grin widens. "But you've never brought a woman here before."

"Hey, gorgeous girl. You got a cuddle for your favorite godfather?" I hold my arms out to Summer, ignoring Jay. He hands her over, and she wraps her little arms around my neck, planting a sloppy kiss on my cheek.

"Jet gone long time," she says.

I stroke her blonde hair and look into her wide, innocent eyes. "I went away on a plane to do some work."

"Like Mommy." Her face lights up.

"Yeah, like Mummy. She was one of our best flight attendants until your daddy stole her."

"Not sorry." Jay laughs.

"I heard that!" Matt yells from the other end of the table. "You mean second best flight attendant."

"I know what I meant," I reply.

My eyes move to Ava. She's got an easy smile on her face as she looks at me holding Summer in my arms.

"She's so sweet," she says to Holly.

"Don't let her cuteness fool you, she's a monkey."

Summer giggles as Holly walks over and swoops down on her, lifting her from my arms. "And her little sister is an even bigger handful."

"Sydney napping," Summer says seriously. "She a baby."

Holly puts Summer into her highchair and waves her hand around the table. "Sit. Eat."

I pull out a chair for Ava and she hovers. Matt drops into a seat beside Stefan, followed by Holly, then Jay.

"Sit," I say softly so only she can hear.

She glances at me and then sinks into the seat. I sit beside her and put my hand on her thigh under the table, feeling her leg relax as I give it a gentle squeeze.

We sit for hours, catching up. Jay's just been cast as the lead in a new action film. He's buzzing about working with director, Trent Forde, who's known as the king of special effects. And Matt gets me up to speed on how the events planning company he's set up since moving from London to LA is going.

"I know you're still mourning my loss." He winks at me as he rests his elbows on the table, mindlessly spinning his wedding band.

"Of course," I say without emotion, causing him to narrow his eyes as the rest of the table laugh.

He shakes his head with a smile.

"So how long have you worked at Atlantic Airways, Ava?" Jay asks.

"Oh, I don't work at the airline." Ava sips on her water. "I live in London. I've just been helping on a project. It's short-term."

"A project," Matt echoes, his brows rising in my direction. "So you'll be heading home soon, then?"

"I guess. Although I'm in no rush to leave. My mum lives here."

"Your mum?" Holly asks.

"Zena Hamilton." Ava's entire face lights up as she says her name. "She's an actress."

Holly and Matt look blank, but recognition flashes over Stefan and Jay's faces.

"I've never worked with your mom, but I look forward to meeting her one day," Jay says.

"She's amazing," Ava gushes. "It was always her dream to be an actress. She's played some brilliant roles over the past ten years since moving to LA."

"Did you go to school here, then?" Matt asks.

Ava tenses. "I—"

I pull my phone from my pocket and glance at the screen. "I'm so sorry guys. Ava, we need to go."

She turns to me, her eyes widening. "Oh... okay."

I stand and pull her chair out. "It was great to see you all."

Chapter 26

Jet

"What's happened? Is it Callaghan?"

"Nothing's happened." I relax back into the seat of the taxi.

Ava frowns. "But you got a message."

"No."

"On your phone," she presses. "At the table."

"I have a headache, that's all."

"What? You rushed us out of there like there was an emergency."

She studies me, giving up and looking out the window when I don't engage further. I glance at her, eating up every passing sight with a smile. Traveling looks good on her, exploring new places, seeing new things.

It's like she was born to explore.

"Beverly Hills?" She whips her head to me after we've been driving for thirty minutes.

"It's where I live."

Her mouth drops open as we pull up at a pair of security gates between two high hedgerows.

"Press this to the sensor." I hand a key fob to the driver and he uses it to open the gates.

Ava goes silent as we cruise up the long driveway to the house.

I pay the driver and climb out, coming around to open Ava's door for her. She looks at me in confusion.

"Isn't the driver dropping me at Mum's?"

"No."

"But you have a headache. Don't you need to lie down in a dark room or something?"

"I've had a miraculous recovery. Now, get out of the car."

She climbs out and stares up at the glass-fronted house.

"You live here alone? Oh my god, I'd get lost. Aren't you worried you'll die and no one will find you for months?"

"Why would that worry me? I'd be dead."

"You know what I mean." She rolls her eyes and follows me to the front door.

I use the retina pad and scan us both in.

Her reaction to my house is endearing. She looks like she walked into the cave of wonders in *Aladdin*.

"This is insane." She holds her arms out and does a 360 spin in the full height, glass entry foyer. "You could park a bus in here."

"As long as it's not a double-decker tour bus, feel free."

She laughs as we move through the ground floor, and I give her the tour she requests.

"Do you use that cinema room?" she asks as I take her upstairs to show her the first floor.

"Sometimes." I shrug.

"That's a no, then. I can't believe you have all these amazing rooms and you barely use any."

"I'm at work a lot. When I'm here, I'm sleeping," I reply, following her around as she strolls from room to room, inspecting them all with a grin.

"That's such a waste. You should have people around more. Now I know you've actually got friends."

She winks at me and I flex my fingers, my palm twitching.

"Is this your room?" She takes in the giant bed and airplane artwork on the walls. "The pictures are like the ones in your room at Rochwell."

"I know what I like." I lean against the doorframe.

She walks over to a bookshelf and picks up a frame. "This is the plane you have in the London office."

I move to stand behind her, gently taking the picture and placing it back onto the shelf. Her breath hitches as I sweep her hair back and over her shoulder.

"I've missed this," I murmur, inhaling her caramel and waterlily scent.

The tiny gasp that leaves her lips as I slide a finger beneath the strap of her dress and ease it off her shoulder makes blood rush to my dick.

I dip my head, pressing a kiss to her bare skin. She shudders as I pepper open-mouthed kisses up her neck, stopping at her ear.

"I'm trying to concentrate at work and all I can think about is how many days it's been since I was inside you," I whisper.

I splay my fingers against her lower stomach and pull her body back so it's flush against mine. Her ass cheeks press either side of my dick, enveloping it in soft heat.

"I've been distracting you again, have I?" she breathes, tilting her neck so I can suck it.

"Even when you're not there," I tsk, cupping both of her breasts roughly and making her gasp.

"Sounds like a *you* problem. You're in control of your own mind... Unless you've forgotten how to be in charge."

I pinch her nipples, and she yelps.

"Such a brat."

I spin her and kiss her hungrily without waiting for permission. She sinks into me, my name a soft whimper on her puffy lips as I catch the bottom one between my teeth.

"Lie on the bed."

My dick throbs when she obeys.

"Show me," I rasp.

"Show you what?"

"You know what."

"Tell me." She bites back a grin, enjoying toying with me.

"Your cunt, Ava," I clip, stuffing my hands into my suit pants like I have all the time in the world just to eat her up with my eyes, spread out on my bed for me, like an offering. "It's time it was reacquainted with me."

Her eyes flash with lust and she inches up the flowery hem of her dress until pale pink lace comes into view. The thin fabric is glistening, darkened by a wet line down the center.

I tut as I take off my shirt. "Have you been wet for me since we got to LA?" I walk closer to the bed, my chest expanding with a deep breath of anticipation as she watches me, her tongue darting out and leaving her lower lip glistening.

"Have you touched yourself?" I ask, running my palms up her inner thighs and eyeing the way her panties are outlining the folds of her. I slide my hands to her hips and tug the lace up. She gasps as it pulls tight between her lips, pushing her plump skin out either side, showing me exactly what's mine.

"It's not like you've been around to do anything about it."

She squeaks as I slap her clit with the back of my fingers. "Always such a mouthy brat. You don't deserve what I'm about to do. But it's for me, not you."

She lifts her head and shoulders from the bed, watching as I drop to my knees on the floor and place her legs over my shoulders.

I stick out my tongue and press it to the fabric where her asshole is, dragging it forward and licking toward her clit. I meet the area of wet lace, stuffed between her pussy lips, and groan as her taste seeps through and infuses my tastebuds.

"Goddamn, Ava."

I suck her clit through the fabric, and she bucks toward my face, her hands dropping to fist my hair.

"Jet."

The sound of her moaning my name sends heat racing to my dick. I lick her again, a deep, lust-filled groan leaving my chest.

"You didn't have a headache, did you? I know you didn't."

I suck the fabric, drawing her juices into my mouth with a gravelly groan.

"If you know I didn't, then why are you asking me?"

"You were saving me from answering questions about my past."

I dust my lips side to side, pressing gentler kisses to her. "I didn't want you to feel uncomfortable talking about it."

Her grip softens in my hair as she switches to stroking the strands.

"What if it's time I got uncomfortable? I'm not moving forward otherwise. I'm just... staying the same."

"What do you mean?"

"Mitch said he thinks producers would be interested in making a film of my story."

"I'm sure they would."

"I told him I'd think about it, but I—"

"Do it."

"What?"

She looks at me as I slide my mouth over her clit and suck before answering.

"If you're ready, then control it. Don't let it control you anymore."

"It doesn't control me."

"Really?"

Her face clouds. "Are you serious?"

I lick the soaked lace strip again, but she pulls me away from her by my hair, making my scalp sting.

"Jet?" She frowns, her cheeks flushed.

I growl at being denied her taste.

"You really think I should do it?" She searches my eyes.

"What do you want to do?"

She doesn't answer, so I shuck my hair from her grasp and pull her panties to one side, spitting on her clit. The second my mouth is back on her, she gasps, and her thighs tighten around my head. Her grip returns to my hair, fisting it tight as I eat her out until she's shuddering.

"Fuck, Ava. I could eat you all day. Best distraction ever."

"You think I should?" she breathes, still overthinking, when all I want is for her to give over her pleasure to me and come on my tongue.

I stand, undoing my belt and pulling my pants and boxers down. She can look into my eyes as she comes instead, then we can talk about this after I've made her nice and relaxed. I crawl over her, knocking her legs wide with my knee. I hook her panties to one side, giving the head of my cock free access to run through her lips, grunting at how wet she is.

"Jet? You think I should?" Her eyes search mine, her mouth popping into a pretty O as I push into her like I have every right to.

I groan, pulling back and sinking inside her again, my cock welcomed back with a tight squeeze.

"That's it," I encourage as she widens her thighs so I can push deeper. "Good girl."

I thrust again, but she frowns. "Jet?"

"After, Ava," I growl, pulling back and driving inside her again. "Let me make you feel good."

"Tell me."

I thrust harder, knocking a whimper from her.

"I don't think you should say no just because you're scared."

I lower my mouth to hers, but she pushes out of our kiss after a few seconds.

"Says the guy who's too scared to open himself up to the possibility of happiness."

"I am happy." I sink inside her again, my balls knocking against her skin. "And I'm about to be even happier when you come all over my cock."

I lift her hip with one hand, altering the angle so I can speed up. "Fuck I needed this. That's it." I look at the way she's stretched to take me. "Squeeze me, Ava. Fuck," I groan as she tightens around me. "I'm going to spend all night filling you with my cum. Have you drink it again."

"Jet," she moans as the head of my cock rubs the spot she likes deep inside her.

"You need more?"

"Yeah."

"That's right, you do. Because you love this, don't you?" I rasp as she squirms beneath me.

"I do," she whimpers. "And you need it, don't you?"

"Yeah, I need it." I look at my cock disappearing inside her wetness. "I need your tight little cunt squeezing me. Fuck."

"You need me," she pants. "Me. Admit it."

I fuck her harder, my balls ready to burst.

"What I need is to come inside you," I grit.

"Not until you admit that it's me that you want. And not just sex."

I increase my speed as she coats my cock with a fresh wave of arousal.

"Ava, all that matters right now is how hard I'm going to make you come for me."

"I'm not asking you to promise me anything," she pants, tugging on my hair. "But if you want me to be honest with myself, then you need to be, too."

I slide deep again with a groan at how good she feels.

"If this is just sex to you, then why aren't you having it with someone else right now?"

"Jesus." My hips stall, losing their rhythm. "Why are you being such a brat?"

"Why are you being an asshole?" She glares at me. "Where's Thailand-Jet? The one with a human side?"

I stare at her as she traces a finger along my jaw, her gaze softening.

"Tell me you need more than just sex. I don't mean with me. Just admit that you need someone to talk to and listen to you. I know you do."

"Stop," I growl, firing my hips again and thrusting into her so that her tits bounce. "I don't need a fucking therapy session from you, Ava, at how I'll be happier if I let love into my life or some shit like that."

"No?" She arches a brow. "You sure about that?"

"Shut up." I kiss her. She whimpers as I drive into her, forcing her into the mattress.

Her teeth slide along my lower lip, nipping it. "Admit it." Her eyes narrow. "You're not immune to wanting those things. You think you know me? Well, I know you, too. You can't hide from me."

"You'd be surprised what I can hide if I want to."

"Like what?"

"Stop. Talking," I grunt as I hold myself up on one arm and curl my other hand around her throat.

I fuck her so hard that the bed bangs against the wall. So hard that her eyes flutter, struggling to stay open as she utters my name in a pleasured moan. So hard that she'll be feeling me tomorrow. I'll make damn sure of it.

"Tell me," she croaks beneath my hand.

"Ava," I warn.

"Admit you need more. Admit you have a heart behind that asshole CEO persona."

I fuck her harder, my grip tightening on her neck.

"Come on my cock," I growl, perspiration collecting in the dip of my spine and coursing down my back, doing nothing to cool my rigid muscles, which are fired up by her persistent bullshit.

"When you say it." Fire burns behind her eyes.

"Come. On. My. Cock."

"Say it," she whimpers. But it's lost in her throat as I fuck her deeper, victory blooming in my chest as she fights it.

"Yes, good girl," I grunt, as her thighs quiver around my hips.

"Asshole," she cries, screwing her eyes shut, blocking me out as she comes hard, jerking beneath me.

"Fuck yes, Ava."

A few more thrusts, and white heat gathers in my balls as I look at her neck, at her pulse throbbing beneath my fingers.

"Jesus. I'm right there. I'm—"

"No!"

I freeze, my blood turning to ice as she snaps open her eyes. The look she gives me makes my stomach drop to my feet. Her makeup has smeared around her eyes and her cheeks are pink.

"Did I hurt you?" I rip my hand from her throat, ready to tear my own fingers off.

"I'm fine," she says, but the way her eyes have dimmed tell me she's anything but fine.

And it's my fault. I didn't keep her safe.

"Ava?" I breathe.

"Get off."

I pull out my rapidly deflating dick.

She straightens her clothes and rolls out from underneath me, stalking to the bedroom door.

"Ava?" I yell, racing after. "The fuck? Talk to me!"

She powers down the stairs, pulling her sandals on and grabbing her purse from near the front door, and then walks outside, leaving the door wide open.

"What did I say?" I run after her, one hand trying to cover my dick as we reach the main gates.

"Let me out."

"Like fuck I'm letting you leave without telling me what the hell that was all about." I advance toward her, but she throws her purse through the gap in the gates and hitches a foot up, beginning to climb toward the spiked top.

"Get the fuck down before you get hurt."

"Let me out or bear the risk of me dying and it being your fault."

I've never wanted to spank her so hard.

I drag in a burning breath as I walk to the control panel and press my thumb to the scanner. The gates open and Ava slips through the gap the moment there's enough space.

"Where are you going?" I stalk out behind her onto the sidewalk.

"Back to Mum's," she yells as she strides away.

"There's no one else. Is that what you want to hear?"

"Forget it," she snaps.

"What? You want me to drop to one knee and propose to you? Is that it?" I throw my arms wide, and a car blares its horn at me as it drives past. *Jesus.* I try to cover my dick back up with both hands.

"If this is some ploy to get me to admit that I can't give you up, then you'll be disappointed," I spit. More cars join in until the whole street fills with honking vehicle after honking vehicle. "I like you, Ava. But I don't *need* you. I'll never allow myself to need anyone."

Someone wolf-whistles out of a passing window, and I flip them off as they drive past.

Ava's stopped and is staring at me, a hopeless look in her eyes, like I'm a dog that's been hit by a car and can't be helped.

"I know this was just sex. You don't have to be such an ass about it. And please, don't ever drop to one knee for me. There isn't a chance in hell I'd marry someone like you."

"What's that supposed to mean?"

She shakes her head. "You're intelligent when you're not being a complete jerk. Work it out."

The she turns the corner and is gone.

Chapter 27

Ava

"Mum?" I rush into the house. *Please be home.*

My chest feels like it's on fire. This thing with Jet is physical attraction. I've never thought it was anything more. Even that night in Thailand when he was there when I needed someone to talk to, I knew it didn't change anything. I knew the moment he put his suit back on and that side of him disappeared again.

He has so much to give but refuses to allow himself the chance of feeling something. He's hiding behind grief, using it as an excuse. And I'm so mad at him for it. So mad and... so fucking miserable.

I can't watch him hurt himself anymore, even if he doesn't realize that's what he's doing.

"Mum?" I stride into the kitchen. Everything is as it was this morning, except for an empty bottle of wine on the counter.

A crash upstairs makes my heart pound, and I rush toward where it came from, taking the stairs two at a time.

"Mum?"

I run into her room just as she launches something through the air. It crashes into the wall, then falls onto the carpet.

"Useless," she sobs. "All useless."

"What's wrong?"

She falls to her knees, tears streaming down her face. Crouching, I put my arm around her.

"What's happened?"

"Too old." Her voice wavers, and she blinks at me with bleary eyes. Her face has been scrubbed free of makeup, and her hair is flat, stuck in wet clumps to her cheeks. "They said I was too old."

She picks up a jar, labeled anti-aging, and hurls it.

"Useless. All completely useless. I'll need more surgery. Then maybe they'll cast me instead of an ex-model in her twenties who hasn't worked her ass off for a whole damn decade!"

Another jar follows the previous one.

"You didn't get the role."

"No." Mum's voice wavers before she takes a deep breath.

"I'm so sorry. You were too good for them, anyway. They probably hired someone cheaper to save money."

She leans into my embrace and sniffs. "Thank you, darling."

"Why don't I run you a bath? Make you a coffee, too," I add, breathing in the scent of wine on her.

"You're an angel."

My fight with Jet is pushed to the back of my mind as I tend to her. She doesn't drink the coffee I make. Instead, she has a bath and then announces she needs a nap. I check on her, but the wine knocks her out and she's still sleeping hours later.

I pull out my phone and text Liv as I sit at the kitchen counter with a glass of mango juice, asking her to call me as soon as she can.

I scroll past the five missed calls from Jet and check my voicemail.

"Goddamn, Ava. Pick up the phone," his deep voice hisses, sounding increasingly pissed off with each word before it cuts out.

I delete it, before dialing another number.

"Gramps?" My voice cracks as he answers.

"Ava. How are you, love? Let me just turn down the radio."

His soothing, familiar voice makes my throat dry.

"I was just calling to see how you are. I miss you."

"I miss you, too. But you only called yesterday." He chuckles.

"I know." I smile, comfort wrapping around me like a warm duvet as I picture him in his house, sitting in his favorite chair as we talk.

"Not that this old man's complaining, but shouldn't you be out having fun with your mother?"

I wince. "She's... not feeling well, actually."

"Oh no. Nothing serious, I hope?"

My gaze wanders to the empty wine bottle.

"Nothing a nap won't fix."

"What about Jet?" Gramps asks. "Are you still working on this thing with him?"

My heart sinks. *Jet's beyond help.*

"No. He's doing fine without me. I've been doing some sightseeing, instead. I walked around Beverly Hills the other day. I saw a dog wearing shoes."

Gramps laughs and we fall into an easy conversation for the next twenty minutes. My phone beeps with a bunch of incoming calls. I lose count at number six.

After I say goodbye to Gramps, there's a knock at the door.

"Miss Roberts?" The courier guy reads my name from the tablet in his hand.

"Yes."

He hands me a large pink box with a champagne ribbon.

"Have a nice day."

I stare at the box. It looks expensive. I toy with the silk ribbon, running the fabric between my fingers as I carry it inside and place it onto the living room floor, dropping to my knees in front of it. A beautiful scent I can't place wafts from it as I open it. It even smells expensive.

Then it hits me.

It's from the same store that Mum sent my sixteenth birthday gift from. My heart pangs with nostalgia. I wish she were awake. Maybe I should wait so she can watch me open it.

I sit for approximately three seconds before impatience and excitement get the better of me and I throw the lid off, my fingers tingling.

"Oh my god!" I squeal as I take out the bodysuit. It's light as a feather, made from a sheer, fine mesh, with strands of pearls draped halfway down around the hips.

It's the most exquisite thing I've ever seen.

I lift the thick manila envelope beneath it and take out the card.

> ***This month's card statement wouldn't seem right without at least one line of yours on there.***

I drop the card back into the box and shove the lid on, covering up the beautiful lingerie before I get too attached to something I'll never keep now that I know it's from him.

The arrogant bastard didn't sign it. He knew I'd know it was from him at the mention of his credit card. Even the knowledge that I spent over a thousand dollars on lingerie in New York at his expense doesn't make me feel any better.

And the one he's sent me is so much nicer than any I own. It will have cost him a sickening amount, I'm sure.

I shove the box away just as there's another knock at the door.

"Miss Roberts?" A different delivery man holds out a small box.

"That's me."

I take it inside, a frustrated huff leaves my chest as I rip it open, taking none of the care that I did with the first package. I lift the lid off the smaller white box inside, a tidal wave of memories hitting me all at once as I take out the perfume bottle shaped like a tiny globe encased in a flower. It's the old design. The original bottle that's been discontinued. My father bought it for me for my twelfth birthday. The scent was too grown up for me then. But he said he knew I'd like the bottle. The perfume inside ran out years ago.

I take the lid off and inhale the waterlily and tonka bean scent that I fell in love with as I got older.

There's no card, but I know it's from him.

I run my thumb over the carved glass as I feel the weight of the full bottle in my palm. "And you still think you have nothing to give," I whisper. "Idiot."

There's a knock at the door again, and I rush to pull it open.

"Yes, I'm Miss Roberts," I say to the delivery woman on the other side.

"Okay, have a great day," she says as she hands me an envelope and a chilled glass bottle with beads of condensation running down the sides.

I scour the street for a delivery truck, but she hops back into a private car instead, then drives off.

I close the door and take the grapefruit juice into the kitchen, emptying out my mango juice from the glass to replace with the grapefruit. *What am I doing?* I abandon the glass and unscrew the bottle lid, drinking straight from the bottle instead.

I sigh as the fresh tang bursts across my tongue, invigorating and sharp.

I refuse to let Jet Grant ruin grapefruit juice for me. Asshole.

I rip open the envelope and spit out the mouthful of juice.

"What?"

I swipe the back of my hand over my lips as I scan the contents. The letter is addressed to the new majority shareholder of the juice company.

Me.

"What the hell did you do?" I gape, my eyes zoning in on words like, *unlimited supply* and *weekly deliveries*.

There's another knock at the door and I stomp to it, the letter in front of my face as I read the contents again.

"Yes, I'm Miss Roberts." I stuff the letter onto the hallway table so I can take whatever thing is coming next.

"And I'm the Asshole, here to deliver an apology."

I jerk back, my spine steeling itself as I look up into cool blue eyes.

Not *an* asshole, *the* asshole. He's got that right at least.

Jet stares at me, his gaze so intense that my goosebumps get goosebumps.

"Ava," he breathes.

I force my body to move, folding my arms as I stand firm in the doorway, blocking him from entering.

"What do you want? You got a unicorn out here in a box for me now?"

"Do you want one?" His eyes darken.

Sighing, I start to close the door.

Jet's hand flattens against it with a deep, authoritative thud.

"I'm sorry."

I say nothing and he curses, his eyes flashing with something. "I don't like you ignoring me."

I arch a brow.

"Please, Ava," he grits, his fingers clenching against the wood.

"You don't like me ignoring you because you aren't in control? Hmm?"

I wait for him to say something. For some give. Just a tiny bit. A smidge of a confession about what I've known for a while.

That he can't do it all alone.

A muscle ticks in his jaw and his nostrils flare with his deliberately slow breath.

"I don't like you ignoring me," he repeats.

"Tough shit. You'd better get used to it." I try to close the door again, but his foot joins his hand, holding it open.

"Tell me you'll forgive me. It doesn't have to be right away. But tell me that I haven't lost you," he rasps.

I stare at him, at the way his brow creases, at the wild gleam in his eyes as his pupils dilate, at the way his Adam's apple is bobbing in his throat like he's struggling to swallow.

"Lost me?"

My hold on the door eases, but he doesn't push it open. He just keeps his hand planted firmly on it. Watching me from beneath dark brows.

"I don't want to lose you, Ava," he whispers.

"You'd have to have me in the first place to lose me."

His eyes pinch and the vein in his temple pulses. "You're right. Excuse my error."

He takes his foot from the door, and my heart sinks. Is that it? He's going to give up?

He lets out a husky curse, his blue eyes capturing mine. "I shouldn't have taken stress over my work issues out on you… It's no excuse, but… it's a mess. I've got to make decisions I don't want to."

I lean against the doorframe, regarding him carefully. He looks like Jet Grant, all suited, oozing masculinity and power from every pore like a goddamn king. He sounds like Jet Grant, his deep voice thick and gravelly, ready to bark out orders to poor, unsuspecting victims.

But something about him is decidedly different.

"Keep going," I say, contemplating how long I should make him squirm.

"And I'm an asshole."

I twirl my fingers in a 'continue' motion.

"And I..." He clears his throat. "I've avoided getting close to anyone since my mother died. Even before that, if I'm honest. I've never... Until you, I..."

"Because?"

"Because..." He looks into the distance up the street and curses, his jaw clenching.

"I don't want anything from you," I say. The lines at the corners of his eyes deepen as he turns back to me, confusion marring his handsome face. "But you've helped me. I got on a plane again because of you. Okay, it was because I couldn't stand you and wanted to piss you off. But I did it. Because of you."

"Ava—"

"Shut up and listen."

He clamps his mouth shut with a grunt.

"I haven't helped you with work. So let me help you with this. Because I know you think you're happy with the world thinking you're this impenetrable bastard. But I've seen you. I saw you in Thailand and what you did for me when I needed someone. I saw the way your friends greeted you when we went to Jay's house. I saw the way his daughter looked at you like you hung the moon. I saw all of it, you stupid jerk. So if you think you're unlovable, or that you shouldn't share a piece of yourself with people because it could get taken from you one day, then you're a fool."

He runs his tongue over his teeth. "An asshole, a jerk, and a fool. Why would you want to help someone like that?"

"I've been asking myself the same question."

He opens his mouth.

"I haven't finished," I snap. "I'm doing it because there are worse things than losing someone who you've loved with every fiber of your being. Loved them so hard that their loss is like someone tearing your heart right out of your chest and then ripping it to shreds as you watch."

"Ava." He frowns and steps closer, but I hold a hand up to stop him.

"I watched my father die, Jet. Saw him suffer. Like you saw your mother be taken from you. When I was alone in that forest for days, do you know what gave me power? What gave me *control*?"

His body tenses like it's taking everything in him not to grab me and pull me into his arms.

"It was the love I had for Gramps, for Mum. I didn't give up, because I still had them. I had people who cared about me. I had people I loved." I look at him sadly. "You think being in control gives you the power not to get hurt. Not to feel loss again. But what's it all for if you're always doing it alone?"

He swallows, the sound of it cutting through the thick air between us.

I look at him and wait.

And wait.

Nothing.

It's like I feared, he's beyond help, too stubborn to admit he might be wrong about something for the first time in his life. The air seeps from between my lips in a hopeless sigh and I start to close the door.

"It's *you* I want."

His voice is so low, barely audible.

"What?"

"You." He steps closer until the heat from his body is spilling into mine across the tiny gap between us.

My heart races as his eyes roam over my face, pausing on my lips, then coming up to hold my eyes.

"Don't get me wrong. I still need control. I need to control you, to *worship* you, to function."

I shudder.

"But it's *you* I want, Ava. To talk to. To listen to. No one else."

"I didn't mean me, I just meant you shouldn't shut yourself off from—"

"I want you." His eyes pin me in place like a rabbit in front of a wolf. "No one else. Do you know how close I was to spanking you earlier for asking why I wasn't having sex with someone else? Your ass should wear my handprint for a week just for asking me that."

"I—"

"I can't fucking *control* the way I feel about you. And I hate it." He sucks in a deep breath, his chest expanding. "I'm not a guy who'll give you white picket fences and a cozy life, Ava. I'm a guy who'll threaten to liquidize a company if they don't sell me all their shares in a juice brand I don't even fucking like the taste of unless it's mixed with berry lipstick."

I choke on a laugh.

"I'm the kind of guy who's been in your room when you're out so I can smell your perfume. Who buys thousand-dollar lingerie for you, when all I'm picturing is ripping it off you so I can fuck you until the only name you know is mine. *Until the world knows that you're mine.*"

"You're deranged."

"I'm fucking obsessed."

His eyes drink me in like he's playing out every filthy desire of his in his head right now.

"But I'll ruin you, Firefly."

My heart skips a beat. *Firefly.*

A glimpse of Thailand-Jet seeps into his gaze as he twirls a strand of my hair around his finger, murmuring the word, *beautiful.*

"You think I can't handle you?" I whisper.

"I think you'll hate me one day when you realize what I've taken from you." He tucks the strand behind my ear and drops his hand to his side.

His voice carries a warning. He's telling me to keep away, but all it's doing is making my panties wet as I stare into his darkened gaze.

I want to hate him. I should tell him to take a long walk off a short jetty.

But I can't.

I can only be overcome by a buzzing energy heating the blood in my veins at how magnetic his eyes are when they're fixed on me like they are now. When they're locked onto mine, looking inside me so deeply, like he sees all of my weaknesses, and they only make him want me more.

"You only take what I willingly give."

His nostrils flare. "For now, maybe. But there'll come a day when you'll understand that being with me, means having things stolen from you that were never mine to take. I shouldn't even be here with you now. I should never have touched you. I'm a selfish asshole, Ava."

I shake my head, not understanding a word of his bullshit. Because that's what it is. *Bullshit.* Words he's hiding behind to try and make me keep my distance.

Like Jet Grant would ever ruin me. Like anyone ever could. I saw my father die in front of me while I was stuck in my seat, unable to move. He reached for me, but by the time I got to him, he was already gone. The light vanished from his eyes with his final breath, leaving them empty, staring into space.

"If that's what you think, then I want you to leave." My heart rate picks up, the back of my neck heating like it's on fire.

He makes no attempt to move, so I shove his chest. "You heard me. Fuck off."

Memories wash up over me like acid, assaulting me one by one. I'm unable to push them back down now that they've gathered momentum. They reach up and suffocate me.

The crunch of metal, breaking glass, screams, *agonizing screams.*

My fingers tingle, my palms getting clammy.

"Ava, what's wrong?"

I shake my head, trying to push him away. But my hand is useless, falling limply against his muscular chest like a fish that's been out of the water for too long.

"I'm fine."

Black and white spots dance across my vision as the rest of my skin tingles, prickling like it's being scratched at by all those passing branches again.

"Ava..."

Arms surround me as I drag in a splintered breath.

Empty eyes that haunt my dreams invade my consciousness.

"Stop," I murmur, pushing at the solid warmth in front of me.

A masculine scent envelops me as I'm lifted from my feet.

Then everything goes black.

Chapter 28

Jet

I LIFT MY GLASS, letting the whiskey burn a trail down my throat as I stare out of my office window.

My heart has never felt like it's about to drop out of my ass before. Not until I saw Ava's eyes roll back in her head as all the blood drained from her face. She came around after a cold towel on her forehead and her feet raised.

But my heart hasn't stopped feeling like I'm about to go into cardiac arrest since.

"Jesus," I utter as I pinch the bridge of my nose.

"That's the first time the media team has dealt with something like that." Hayden laughs as he walks into my office.

I turn away from the floor to ceiling windows and look at him. "Breathe a word and you're fired."

He stuffs his hands into his pants pockets as he strolls closer, his eyes dancing with mirth.

"Come on, you mean you don't want everyone knowing what a charitable member of the Beverly Hills community you are?"

I grumble.

"Fine," he concedes. "But next time you're going to get the cops called on you for having your dick out in public, can you do it in my neighborhood? A donation that size will get us the new library we want."

He sniggers, eyes lit up like the fourth of July. He's going to be cashing in on the fact I had to call him to help diffuse the situation at my house after Ava ran off for months, if not years.

Still, I'd have donated ten times what I did to the neighborhood community fund to have avoided a trip to jail. The fact it took me hours to make it to Ava's doorstep riles me.

What if she'd passed out with no one there to help her?

He studies my grave expression. "Everything okay?"

"Fine," I mutter.

He's known me long enough to know when to let something drop.

"So, how's the hiring going?" he asks instead.

"It's done. He starts tomorrow."

"He?" Hayden tips his head in interest. "You got a male PA? Is he hot?"

"Don't get ideas," I grit. "Patrick comes highly recommended; I don't want to have to replace him next week. Fuck your own PA if you must."

He smirks.

"Jesus Christ, I don't want to know. Just keep it out of office hours." I shake my head. How Hayden finds time to get as much action as he does, I've no idea.

"You ready for the final push?"

"I am. We've got him right where we need him."

I walk over to the display cabinet that holds some of the awards Atlantic Airways has won. I stare at the mixture of shiny plaques and laser-engraved glass before turning my back on it.

"Callaghan's getting what he wanted. And we're getting what we need."

He looks at me. "You saved the airline. Not even a smile?"

I grimace, and he walks over and grabs my shoulder, squeezing it in solidarity.

"You did what you had to. Everyone in the office will sleep easier. You're a great CEO, Jet."

My shoulders tighten at his rare compliment.

"I'm glad someone will," I say.

"What's Ava think about—?"

"She's no longer working for us."

"Oh. And she's okay about—?"

My jaw tightens. "She has her own life."

He stares at me.

"I'm taking her out tomorrow night," I grumble, regretting sharing the minute his brows shoot up his forehead.

"On a date?"

I press my lips together, my silence giving him all he needs.

"Never thought I'd see the day." He smiles, strolling toward the door.

"Sometimes you have to move forward, or you'll just keep standing still," I mutter as I walk over to my desk.

He turns back. "Good for you."

I sink into the deep leather chair as he leaves and pick up the framed photograph on my desk. I look at my mother's wide smile as she stands with her arm around a ten-year-old me. The bright blue plane behind us shines like a jewel.

Just memories now. Something to haunt me, like Ava's haunt her.

I push my finger and thumb into my eye sockets as the memory of her limp body in my arms surfaces again, making the hair on the back of my neck stand up.

"I'm fine, Jet," she murmurs as I climb onto the bed beside her and pull her into my arms.

"I'll be the judge of that." I slide my hand to her neck and check her pulse again as she closes her eyes. It's steady.

"Don't do that again, Ava," I soothe, my voice low. "Don't fucking scare me like that again."

Her gentle breathing as she slips into an exhausted sleep echoes around the room. I stroke her hair back from her face, watching the way her features relax as my fingertips dust her cheek.

I press a kiss to her forehead and just hold her while she sleeps.

I'm going to ruin her, just like I warned her I would.

She'll hate me.
But it has to be done.

"The view's better than the bus, I'll admit." Ava looks down at me through the limo sunroof.

"Good," I reply, one hand gripping onto her thigh beneath her dress. I know she can't fall out, but it doesn't stop me from being unable to let her go since she asked the driver to open it and then climbed up onto her seat and stuck the top half of her body out.

"Come and see." She reaches down and tugs the collar of my jacket.

I give in, squeezing myself out of the gap. Her hair is blowing in the evening air, her eyes glowing brightly with the magic of experiencing something new as she gazes at the sun setting over the ocean.

"See? It's fun." She grins, then throws her arms up in the air, hollering out a giant 'whoop' as the air blows past us.

She turns to me, and her grin settles into a soft smile.

"Forgive me," I rasp.

"Not yet."

She bites her lip, her eyes twinkling the same way they have every time she's said no since I picked her up hours ago. As soon as she woke after blacking out, and I'd satisfied myself that she was okay, I told her I wanted to bring her out tonight. I wanted to spend time with her. Show her I'm sorry and make it up to her.

Ask her for her forgiveness.

She told me 'no' three times before we left Zena's house. A further fifteen times over dinner. And we're up to number seven since we got into the limo I organized to take her on a tour of all the best places that booger-covered tour buses don't know about.

Only the 'no' has turned into a 'not yet'.

Soon it'll be a yes.

And it'll be the sweetest word I've heard.

"How do you get any work done living here?" She sighs dreamily. "I'd be too distracted."

I barely look at the sunset over the water. It's got nothing on the flame-haired woman beside me.

"Forgive me," I murmur, my eyes tracing over the curve of her cheek.

She laughs and shakes her head.

"You always want to win, don't you?" she tuts, playfully. Her blue eyes narrow. "What if I think you need to grovel harder first?"

"I'll get on my knees and stay there until they're just bone if that's what it takes."

She sighs, her shoulders softening.

"I don't need all the flashy gifts, Jet. I just want you to tell me that you're sorry, and to stop holding yourself back from what could be. To let yourself consider a future with something more."

I swallow, my throat thick as she turns back to the ocean.

"Are you happy?"

She frowns, like they're the last words she expected to hear from my lips. But then her brows smooth out and she smiles, her eyes locked on something in the distance.

"Yeah, I am. I've been to some amazing places. And now I'm here, seeing LA. Spending time with my mum. It's what I've dreamed about for years."

"You deserve to see the world, Ava."

She sighs wistfully.

"Forgive me," I breathe.

Her face creases as she laughs softly.

"I want to, just to stop hearing you ask over and over."

"Then do it."

"Fine."

The air in my lungs leaves all at once.

"Really?"

"I'll do it. On one condition."

"There'll be a unicorn in a box when we get back. A whole fucking herd of them."

She laughs as if I'm joking. "I don't want gifts. I want you to stop being an asshole who keeps people at arm's length all the time."

"I am an asshole."

She pops a brow at me, but I stand my ground until she rolls her eyes.

"Just the second part of that sentence, then. Be an asshole who lets people in sometimes."

"I'll consider it," I grit, knowing full well I've no intention of letting anyone closer to me than Ava has gotten.

I don't want anyone else.

I shouldn't even want her.

She snorts, shaking her head. "That's the best I'm going to get, huh?"

I grunt out a non-response that has her sighing.

"You know, I hope this business with Callaghan is over soon. You need a night out. A huge blow out once it's done. Get drunk and do something reckless. Lose control for a change."

"No," I clip, the collar on my shirt feeling tight against my windpipe.

"You do know how to do something reckless, don't you?" She sighs when I don't answer. "Okay... What do you do for fun? What do you enjoy? Apart from making multi-million-dollar business deals and skipping."

"I..." I run my tongue over my teeth as I think. "I don't have time for much outside of those two things. The airline is my life."

"Fine." She talks slowly like she's explaining something to a child. "Then just tell me one thing you enjoy doing that isn't work."

"I enjoy doing you."

Her eyes go wide. "O-kay. To the point, I guess."

"I mean, fucking you is amazing—"

"Romantic." She laughs.

"Fuck, what I mean is being with you... Anything that involves having you all to myself. Naked is a bonus. But..." I tip my head back and curse at how badly I'm screwing this up. "I like being around you, Ava. Even though you're a brat most of the time."

"Funny kind of apology." She smirks.

"Forgive me," I rasp.

"Do not start that again. I'm over hearing you apologize, even though you've got lots to be sorry for."

"Noted. No more apologies."

"And don't ever start a fight with me when we're in the middle of..." She side-eyes me. "That was probably the most awkward exit I've ever made from a guy's house."

My blood heats at the mention of her with any other men.

"Fine," I clip.

"I'm surprised you weren't arrested, coming out in the street like that."

The Beverly Hills neighborhood fund isn't surprised.

"I didn't want you to leave."

"You didn't want to lose me?"

"No, I didn't."

"So what now?" She searches my eyes. "What do we do now?"

I tuck a strand of hair behind her ear.

"Just enjoy the view before it gets dark."

Her gaze darts to the sunset over the ocean and back to me.

"Jet, I—"

I silence her with a kiss, and she whimpers.

"I'm sorry," I breathe. "For all of it."

"I forgive—"

I press my fingers to her lips. I've spent all day and evening aching to hear her say it. But now that she's about to, I can't let her. Because the truth is, I don't deserve her forgiveness. Not for what I've done, and for what I'm going to do if I don't get a handle on myself and take back control. I should never have taken her to Thailand with me. Let her trust me. Let her believe there is something good there when there isn't.

I'm the worst kind of asshole.

Clear blue irises, as bright as the reflection of the ocean beneath the fucking sun, dilate.

It's too late.

She was doomed the moment I lost control and touched her that first time. When I laid her out on my father's kitchen table and tasted every inch of her like it belonged to me.

This all has to end.

Just not tonight. I'm too damn selfish to let her go without one more night.

"Keep watching the view," I say against her lips, before giving her another kiss where my tongue entwines with hers with an urgency that races through my whole body. "The view," I grunt as I sink back inside the limousine, leaving Ava where she is, everything above her waist on full display to the outside world.

"What are you doing?"

I shush her, and she tuts.

Brat.

The privacy screen is up, shielding us from the driver. And the windows are tinted.

I push Ava's dress up and slide her silk panties down her thighs. No one sees me scrunch them against my face and inhale with trembling lungs, like a drowning man's life-saving breath. No one sees me stuff them into my pocket to treasure. To add to the ones she gave me in that alleyway before I spanked her. The ones I've wrapped around my cock. Fisting it to thoughts of her so hard it should be bleeding. And no one hears the guttural groan that leaves my throat as I bury my tongue inside her cunt and eat her out while she watches the sunset over Malibu beach with dreams in her eyes.

No one.

But I feel every twist of her fingers in my hair as she grabs it and grinds down against my mouth. I feel every pulse, ripple, and flutter she makes on my tongue as I press it against her clit and lick.

I feel every damn thing she does.

Including the moment she comes with my tongue buried in her. Comes so hard that her legs give way and I have to catch her around the underside of her ass and hold her up on my face so I can finish pushing her through her orgasm.

And I feel the emotion in her gaze as she looks down at me afterward, her cheeks flushed, her hands switching to a gentle stroke, fingers tracing over my eyebrows, lips parted as she sighs my name.

It's the final thing I focus on before I feel the excruciating tear right through the center of my heart knowing it's the last time.

She can't be mine.

Not anymore.

Chapter 29

Ava

"What was that paperwork Jet had you signing earlier when he dropped you off?" Mum asks as I sit in the kitchen, a bottle of grapefruit juice between my fingers.

I spent the night at his house with him after our sunset limo tour. Maybe there are some perks to him being an asshole who it's so easy to fight with, because making up sure is fun. I don't think I've ever been so exhausted from sex. I literally haven't slept for a single minute. Every time I thought Jet was finally worn out, he'd start kissing me again, and off we went. The final few times I could barely move. I just let him position me beneath him how he wanted as he sank inside me over and over, groaning my name like a mantra.

Maybe I'll pick another fight with him today.

I giggle, then wince as my pussy aches.

Tomorrow, maybe tomorrow.

"Oh, he said it was for HR. To revoke my pass or something now that I'm not working with him anymore."

"Didn't you read it?"

I take a gulp of juice. "No. I can barely see straight this morning."

"Hmm. Lack of sleep does that to you." Mum chuckles and finishes making her coffee, then joins me at the table.

"What would you like to do today?" I ask, yawning.

She laughs. "Oh, darling, I think you need to rest." She takes my hand and squeezes it. "We can have a wonderful day tomorrow. I'm meeting Mitch today, anyway. He wants to talk about some roles he's got in mind. He sounded excited; said they'll be huge."

"That's amazing."

We sit together and chat, until I'm yawning so hard the whole of LA is in danger of disappearing down my throat. Mum leaves to meet Mitch, and I drag myself upstairs to bed. I manage to fire off a text to Jet as my head hits the pillow.

> Me: How do you do that all night, then find the energy to skip this morning, and still go to work looking like a walking snack?

I giggle, picturing his grumpy face reading it. Maybe it'll get a small lip curl out of him. I type out another quick text, the screen blurring in front of my tired, stinging eyes.

> Me: I don't want a unicorn. I just want my own Jet.

Then I pass out.

When I wake, the house is dark.

"God," I mutter, checking my phone. The battery has run out, so I plug it in to charge and go downstairs.

Mum's in the living area, watching *After Hours*, a talk show presented by a man called Patrick Howard, who I recognize from billboards around the city.

"Darling, you must have needed that sleep."

She holds her arms out and I sink into them.

"I must have."

The two of us sit in silence, watching as a pretty young actress is introduced and Patrick interviews her.

Mum jabs the remote and the screen goes black.

"That's enough of that," she mutters, tossing it down onto the cushion beside her.

I rub the arm she has draped around me. "Is that the actress they gave the role to the other day?"

"So young and pretty." She sighs. "I'll never be able to compete."

"You don't need to. You don't want those roles if they can't see how amazing you are. You need big roles in hard-hitting stories. Ones people will talk about for years. Inspiring ones. Not just your regular movie that'll be forgotten about when another ten exactly the same are churned out within a few months."

"Thank you, darling." She rests her head against the back of the sofa and gives me a weak smile. "You're so like your father." She tucks a lock of my hair back over my shoulder. "He'd be so proud of you."

A lump forms in my throat.

"Do you want to order takeout and eat ice-cream in our pajamas?" Mum's eyes light up like she's just suggested egging the sports car of every casting director who's ever turned her down.

"I do want that, Mum. I really do."

I adjust the waistband of my jeans before the elevator dings. Then I walk out into the reception area of the skyrise's top floor.

The pearl strands feel cool against my skin. I can't wait to see Jet's pissed off face when I tell him I'm wearing the bodysuit he bought. It will be a tease. One I'll pay the price for later.

My pussy clenches at the thought.

"Good morning." I smile at the immaculate receptionist sitting behind the long shiny desk that's shaped like a wing and has Atlantic Airways' logo on it. "I'm Ava Roberts, here to see Mr. Grant."

"Mr. Grant doesn't take visitors without an appointment."

"Can you tell him Ava Roberts is here, please?"

"Does he know you?" She makes no effort to move.

"He should. I'm his girlfriend."

I bet he keeps his personal life completely separate from work. I'm not his girlfriend—I'm not sure what I'd label our relationship as—but this woman is starting to get on my last nerve, the way she's looking down her nose at me like I'm dirt.

"Girlfriend?" Her unimpressed gaze sweeps over my jeans and T-shirt. "Really?"

I rest my elbows on the desk, leaning forward.

"His bratty sugar baby. If we're going to be technical."

I hide my smirk at the way she gasps and grabs her desk phone. She taps the buttons, eyeing me with a terse frown. Then she holds up a finger, silencing me, and spins her chair so her back is to me.

I roll my eyes and pull my ringing phone from my purse. I don't recognize the number calling.

"Hello?"

"Ava. It's so lovely to speak to you again. Is now a good time?"

I struggle to place her voice, but then it comes to me.

"Ophelia?" I smile as I step away from the desk. Jet's catty receptionist looks over her shoulder at me, then turns away again and carries on talking.

"How was the rest of your trip?" I walk over to a water cooler in the waiting area and pull out a paper cup.

"It was great. Back to work now, though. And I'm glad. Because talking to you is exciting!"

"Oh, thank you... You too." I sip the water. Ophelia seemed lovely in Thailand, but I never expected her to call; we didn't exchange numbers.

"I'll be honest, Ava. I knew who you were the minute you told me your name. You never mentioned anything, though, so I didn't think it right to bring it up."

The cup of water slips from my grasp, spilling all over the carpet.

Like fresh blood on a cockpit floor.

"You knew who I was?" I grab the cup with a shaking hand, depositing it in the trash can.

"I did. And I was surprised at what landed on my desk yesterday. I'm so glad you want to do this. It will be incredible."

"Sorry? What will be—?"

"I've got a screenwriter working on the script already. There are some tweaks we'll need to make, but nothing major. And we'll go through them together."

The water sloshes around in my stomach, threatening to race back up my windpipe.

"Script?" I cough, trying to clear the lump from my throat as my head grows light.

"I'm so pleased you're choosing to move forward. I know it's been years."

"I'm sorry. What do—?"

"Jet's so proud of you for moving forward, not staying still. Sorry if that's a strange thing to say, but the way he sounded on the phone when he and James were talking about the movie was really very—"

"Movie?"

"I know there was a suggestion of a cable series in your proposal. But my gut says movie. Your story made headlines for weeks, Ava. People will be racing to the box office to see it on screen. I've got some ideas for castings. Can you come by my office? I'll send a car for you."

"I-I'm actually about to see Jet right now."

"Oh, okay. Well, I'll email them to you, and then we can meet to discuss when you get back from New York. Will you be coming back at the same time as Jet?"

Something cold and unpleasant binds its way around my lungs until taking a breath feels like razor blades scraping through my lungs.

"New York?"

"Ava, I'm so sorry, I have to go," Ophelia says as someone calls her name in the background. "I'll call you and we'll set up lunch the minute you get back. Maybe Jet and James can join us since they'll be working together now. It'll be less tense than dinner in Thailand when they couldn't stop butting heads." She laughs. "Speak soon."

The fast pulsing of my heart fills my ears as I stare at the dark, wet mark on the carpet.

My phone buzzes in my hand.

I click into the email, the name *Ophelia Callaghan, Producer*, in the sender's section, followed by the subject line.

The blood drains from my face, all of it crashing to my feet at once.

> ***Forest Girl – A screenplay based on true events: Casting Ideas.***

I choke on my own spit, as the cells in my body feel like they're all exploding.

"Mr. Grant isn't here," a condescending voice says from behind the sleek desk. "I'm surprised being his *bratty sugar baby*, you don't already know that."

I look up into her narrowed eyes. Maybe he's screwed her, and that's why she looks like she's about to call security to throw me out onto the street. Or maybe she's just a bitch. Either way, I'm not about to take her shit for a minute longer.

"I need to speak to him." I stomp toward the desk as my rage threatens to either explode into a wrath to rival the Big Bang, or dissolve into a nauseous puddle.

Either is possible.

"That's not—"

"I don't give a shit if he's in a meeting with the fucking president right now," I snap, pulling his number up on my phone and hitting call.

It goes straight to voicemail. "Bastard," I hiss, throwing my phone into my purse.

The receptionist tips her head, an amused glint in her eyes. "Like I said, you'll need an appointment to talk with Mr. Grant."

"Mr. Grant had me sign some documents a couple of days ago. I want to see them," I demand. "I'm not leaving until I do."

Some people exiting the elevator look over at my raised voice. The receptionist huffs and picks up the phone.

"Mr. Marks? There's a woman here making a scene. She says she knows Mr. Grant. She says she wants to see some papers he asked her to sign. I can call security?"

She looks at me from beneath her brows, nodding at whatever he says. "Name?"

"Ava Roberts," I repeat what I've already told her twice.

"Ava—" She snaps her mouth shut, listening, "...Yes, Mr. Marks." She places the phone down. "He's finishing up in his office, then he'll see you. Take a seat."

"Who's Mr. Marks?"

"Atlantic Airways' CFO."

"Thanks for your *help*." I give her a tight smile, then stride straight past the desk.

"You can't go back there!" She flies to her feet, but I'm already breaking into a jog down the hallway, rushing past curious faces as I read the signs on the doors.

I turn a corner, my heart clenching painfully as I rush past a giant office with the name *Jet Grant, CEO* on the door. I don't have time to take in the opulent office behind the glass as I run past. I bet it's full of arrogant wanky trophies and flashy art.

Fake bullshit. All fake.

Just like him.

The door ahead of me has a shiny name plaque with *Hayden Marks* on it. I burst through it, causing the man inside the room to rise to his feet behind the meeting table, his eyes widening in surprise.

"You must be Ava." He breaks into a grin, two rows of perfect white teeth flashing. "I'm Hayden." He advances, holding out his hand.

"Nice to meet you," I snap without shaking it. "Where is he?"

His brows rise. "Jet? He's in New York."

"I'm here, Ava." A familiar, deep voice cuts in, coming from the laptop on the table.

I stalk over to it.

"What the actual fuck? You're really in New York?" I cry, recognizing The Songbird hotel's décor behind him.

He runs a hand over his jaw. "I'm here for a meeting." His voice is devoid of emotion, his usually bright eyes dim.

"With James Callaghan?" I choke out.

"It was last minute. I called you before I left."

"My phone died." I stare at him, searching his face for innocence. For shock, for disbelief. For something that tells me he didn't do this to me.

He has the perfect poker face.

"I always win, Ava."

Well played, Asshole. Well fucking played.

"I'll be back tomorrow." His dark brows flatten as he studies me.

"You bastard," I whisper. "What the fuck did you do?"

"I did what I needed to, Ava," he rasps, his brows furrowing. "Tell me you understand that."

My legs buckle, and I grab onto the table, curling my hands around the smooth edges as he holds my eyes.

"Understand? How could you?"

He straightens his tie, his neck flexing. "I can see you're upset. We'll discuss it when I get back."

"We'll talk about it now!" I shriek. "That wasn't yours to give. This is a new low, even for you."

His gaze hardens as his nostrils flare. "Ava," he growls.

"Don't Ava me," I spit, slamming my palm onto the table and making the laptop shake. "Did you just fuck me to get close to me?"

He clears his throat. "Excuse me, please, everyone. We'll reconvene this meeting later."

I glance up at Hayden, who's watching in silence. Behind him, on the wall, is a giant TV screen filled with little windows. In each one, a face, listening raptly. I glimpse James Callaghan looking puzzled, and Magnus's shocked expression before the entire screen goes black.

"Ava." Jet's voice cuts through the deafening pounding in my head. "What—?"

"Tell me! Tell me what you did."

His punishing stare makes my blood turn to ice.

"I did what was needed to save the airline. Callaghan wasn't backing down; we were running out of time. People rely on me for their jobs, Ava. For their—"

"Fuck you!"

He glares at me. "It's the only thing he wanted. His wife—"

"Fuck you so fucking hard!" I scream, tears pricking at my burning eyes. I refuse to let them fall. I'm not giving him the satisfaction of seeing what he's done to me.

How much he's stolen from me.

"Do you have any idea what a bastard you are?"

He takes a deep breath. His eyes have never left mine.

"I know what I am."

The deep husk of his voice confirming it makes a sob catch in my throat.

"I never thought you'd do this."

"Ava, I had no other options." He sighs.

He looks exhausted. He sounds exhausted.

"You always have options," I say, managing to keep my voice level. "You chose this. You fucking chose to do this. This isn't some bargaining tool you get to use for yourself. This is my life! What the hell did you make me sign?"

"Ava."

The way he says my name, his voice softening, is too much.

"Shut up," I snap.

We stare at each other as my heart breaks. His blue eyes search mine like he never expected me to be so upset. Like he never thought about the magnitude of what he was doing.

He told me so many times he was an asshole, and that I'd realize it one day. I never listened.

Today is that day.

"I'll never forgive you," I whisper. "I hope you're proud of the man you've become. Because no one else will be." I slam the laptop lid down.

"Did you know he was going to do this?" My shoulders are heaving with uneven breaths as I lift my eyes to meet Hayden's. He looks stricken.

He swallows thickly, then nods once. "It's haunted him for months knowing it was a possibility."

"Months?" Ice slides up my spine, pinning me in place.

He's been planning this the whole time.

"He's not a bad guy, Ava." Hayden looks like he's about to throw up. If he wasn't an accomplice to this, I might feel sorry for him. "He's saved thousands of jobs. He searched for another way. There wasn't one. He... He's told me about you. He cares about..."

"He only cares about himself. He had no right," I whisper.

I walk past him toward the door. I need to get out of here. I need fresh air. I need water.

"Talk to him. I'll get you on a flight. You can be there by tonight."

I spin, ready to tell Hayden where to shove his suggestion. But then the pain in my chest drops lower, twisting inside my gut instead. And it's joined by a burning heat, like acid.

Rage.

"Will you tell him I'm coming?"

Hayden's brows lift, before relief washes over his face. "You'll go and speak to him?"

"If you don't tell him I'm coming."

He nods reluctantly.

"What time's my flight?"

Chapter 30

Ava

HE WALKS INTO THE marble lobby like nothing's wrong.

Like he didn't rip open the scar I've worn for the past ten years. The scar he helped to heal when he showed me the broken parts of himself in Thailand.

I trusted him. I told him things I've never told anyone.

I was so stupid.

He doesn't see me sitting inside one of The Songbird's bars, nursing the same glass of wine I've had for the past hour.

But I see him.

Everyone sees him.

People's heads turn, following him as he moves fluidly in his immaculate suit and Italian leather shoes. He commands attention effortlessly, exuding the grace and confidence of a man who has it all. And what he doesn't have, he gets.

"I always win, Ava."

I swallow down bile in my throat as a woman drops a book she's carrying as Jet approaches. He stops, picking it up and handing it to her. She gushes, flicking her hair over her shoulder as she tries and fails to draw him into conversation. She turns and watches him walk away, eyes drinking him in without shame.

I get it. I was falling for it too. The dark-haired, blue-eyed billionaire pilot who wears a suit like he was born in it. He couldn't look any better. But now I know it's all an act. A shiny façade to the self-preserving bastard beneath.

I shove my phone into my purse before slinging it over my shoulder.

"I need to check out early." Jet's deep baritone carries from where he's standing in his charcoal suit at the desk.

"Oh? Was everything to your satisfaction, Mr. Grant?" the male staff member asks.

"Everything was fine. But I need to get back to LA."

"Of course. I'll arrange someone to collect your luggage and bring it down for you."

"That's not necessary, I can manage."

They finish talking and he turns.

Piercing blue eyes, rimmed with red and shadowed by dark circles, meet mine with an intensity that makes me falter. Makes me question everything. Maybe I've got it wrong. He wouldn't do this to me. It's a mistake.

Tell me it's a mistake, Jet.

"Ava?"

That one word breathed out in his deep voice threatens to dissolve every barrier I've been putting up on the flight over here. Barriers to keep him out. To protect myself from further hurt, even if the catastrophic damage is already done.

"You're here." His eyes drop over my body like he's checking if I'm real. "When did you arrive?"

"My plane landed two hours ago."

His dark brows lift. "You flew here? Alone?"

"I don't need you to get on a plane anymore."

His face closes off, the hint of what I swear was admiration in his eyes, dying in a flash.

"You didn't need me the first time, either. You're strong all by yourself."

My heart squeezes as he places his hand on my lower back.

"Don't touch me," I hiss, before noticing the people behind me that I'm blocking from getting to the desk. Jet steers me to one side, positioning us in a quiet area against the wall. Then he removes his hand from me immediately.

"Ava, I'm—"

"If you tell me you're sorry, I swear to god, I'll kill you right here. Your apologies mean shit." My voice cracks, betraying my emotion.

It's written all over my face how much he's hurt me. I saw it in the airplane bathroom mirror before we landed. And again in the restrooms here while I've been waiting for him to appear.

It's obvious to the world.

Jet Grant has crashed into me, breaking everything I've spent years trying to fix.

"I don't care what your reasons were. I don't care if it was the last option you had. It wasn't yours to give."

"Ava." He steps closer, lowering his voice.

I take a step back. "Why?"

"It's just business," he replies, simply.

"Business?" I choke.

"The airline is everything to me. It's my future, it's all my employees' future. I chose them. I had to."

"You stole my story. It took me ten years to be able to write that, to be able to even think about it. And you took it after knowing me for two months. Like it belonged to you. Like you had the right. You didn't."

I drag in a splintered breath. I thought I needed to see him face to face. To confront him. To make him look me in the eyes as I ask him why he did it. But staring into the same light irises that have held mine so many times as I've poured out my heart to him, handed him myself, physically and mentally, over and over again, hurts so much that I'm scared I'll disappear with the pain. Implode silently.

Surrounded by people this time. But still alone.

"You forged my signature on those papers," I continue through a choked breath. "I was stupid. I didn't even read them. I've been so caught up being in LA with Mum. I've not felt happiness like this in years. I trusted you. I never... I never even read them..."

He's silent, watching me as I rub at my burning chest.

"I confided in you. I... We've been sleeping together for weeks," I hiss.

"Twenty-nine days."

"What?"

"It's been twenty-nine days since we..." His brows pinch. "This is the happiest you've been in years?"

I fold my arms, turning away with a tight nod. "The happiest since..." I can't finish the sentence.

"You were happy?" he repeats my words, inclining his head to make me meet his eyes again. They bore into mine, making my breath hitch.

"I *was*. I had everything I ever dreamed of. Being here with Mum. Traveling. Seeing the world. Then you ruined it, you selfish bastard. How could you?"

He runs his tongue over the edge of his perfect teeth, taking his time to study me, ignoring the curious glances we're attracting from passing guests.

"I never told you I was a good guy, Ava." Something passes over his face that I can't read.

Then again, even when I've thought I can read him, I can't.

I have no idea who he is. Not really.

"No, you didn't. And now you've proved it. What was it I signed, huh? A contract? Rights for my story to be made into a fucking movie? Ophelia said—"

Jet's nostrils flare. "You said you were ready. You said—"

"You mean when we were in the middle of fucking?" I screech, drawing more attention to us. "When you thought it was a good idea to tell me I was too scared, and that I should just do it. Was it then, huh?"

"I've apologized for that, I've—"

"All I'm hearing is you." I push him, but his solid body doesn't budge. "What you want. What you need. It was never your call to make. How long have you known she's a producer?"

His jaw tightens.

"How long?"

He clears his throat. "I've always known what Ophelia Callaghan does."

"Always..." The air rushes from my lungs. "Did you know this whole time who I was? The crash, the..." I swallow, my throat burning. "Did you know what the papers used to call me?" When he stays silent, it confirms my suspicions. "Oh my god. You told me you knew me better than I think. You knew who I was this whole time, didn't you? Did you plan this from the beginning? Was the whole me working with you just for fun? Something you'd laugh about when you went to bed at night?"

"Ava," he growls.

"Was the sex to gain my trust? Or an added bonus? A way to get your dick wet?"

"Stop," he snaps, stepping closer and towering over me. "Is that what you want it to be? Would it make it easier to hate me if I told you it was only sex?"

"It doesn't matter now. Either way you're a bastard that your friends and family should be ashamed of. *All* of them," I say cruelly, my chest heaving. It's a low blow, hinting that his mum would be ashamed, too. But it's the truth. My father would be if I'd done what Jet has.

He lowers his mouth to my ear. "In that case, if it was just sex, at least it was hot, dirty as fuck sex with you, Ava. Maybe it's worth everyone hating me for the memories I've got."

I shove him away.

"You're disgusting."

"Then you'll not miss me, will you?"

"Not for one second."

A coarse sound comes from the back of his throat before he squashes it and breaks eye contact with me for the first time since he saw me.

"Was any of it real?"

I hate myself the minute the words leave my mouth. For the hope inside them. For the power I'm handing over to him. But he's already taken everything. I've nothing left to lose.

"Did it feel real?" He brings his eyes back to mine. His expression doesn't soften. It stays the same, blue eyes penetrating my soul, reaching deep inside me, and taking what they want without asking permission.

Being Jet Grant.

"I thought it did," I breathe. "I thought a lot of things."

"Then it was real, Ava."

He moves closer, his hand reaching up and brushing my hair away from my cheek. His eyes still don't soften. But his jaw loosens as he runs his thumb over my wet cheek. The urge to lean into his palm overwhelms me, and I'm left frozen in place as I fight it.

"It was never meant to be like this. I never wanted to hurt you."

"Liar."

His eyes pinch at the corners as he drops his hand from my cheek.

"If you'd never wanted to hurt me, you wouldn't have played me. You've had one goal since we met. And it was for you to win. To hell with anyone else."

His eyes rake over my face like it's the last time he'll see it.

"Are you going to tell Ophelia?"

My heart falls to my feet and I stare at him as my chest burns in the hole it's left behind.

"That's all you care about? That your deal with Callaghan isn't ruined?"

His jaw ticks as he watches me. It takes everything I have in me to steady my voice.

"I don't know," I answer honestly.

It was one of my first thoughts. That I could retract the signed rights, prove it's not my signature. But I'd planned on possibly doing this one day. It's why I was writing it. My therapy. Time for me to finally take back the control that was stripped from me ten years ago.

But Jet took that control away.

It should have been me deciding when I was ready to share it. Not him. No one else but me. I'll never forgive him for that. Even if the outcome is the same, the route to get there was never his to navigate. It was mine.

He took away my control, so that he could keep his.

"Please don't," he rasps.

Air rushes into my lungs, the shot of oxygen making my head clearer. He's right. I need it to be easy to hate him. I need to take every feeling I ever had for him and turn them into hate.

It's the only way I'll survive again.

I need to take back control.

"Say it." I breathe in his scent without meaning to, then swallow down the pang of warmth it evokes in my memory. I don't want to remember anymore. I want to forget it all. Forget I ever met him.

"I need to hear you say it."

Deep lines appear along his brow as he reaches for me, sliding his hand around my ribs. The contact makes me shudder and I shove his hand away.

"Say it," I snap. "Admit what you did."

"I'm sorry."

"No," I sob as my eyes burn. "Don't fucking do that. I've forgiven you too many times for the shit you've pulled. There isn't any coming back this time. Just admit what you did. And then I'm going to walk out of here. And I never want to see you again. I never want to hear your name again. You understand? If you pass me in the street, keep walking. Don't look at me. Because I won't even notice you."

His Adam's apple rises in his throat as he swallows, then his eyes darken as he holds mine, unblinking.

"Say it," I urge in a hoarse whisper. "Don't make me beg. After all you've done, don't make me—"

"I took your story, Ava."

A strangled sound escapes my lips.

"I did it to save the airline. And, Firefly..." His whole body stiffens when I flinch at his nickname for me. "I am sorry. Because if I had to, I'd do it again."

I spin, unable to look at him anymore.

My vision blurs as I rush away and his final words follow me.

"I'd make the same choice every goddamn time, Ava."

Chapter 31

Ava

One month later

"You've been staring at your phone every day, darling. Are you hoping Jet will call?"

I click out of my banking app and look up into Mum's eyes as she walks into the kitchen. Each one of the million dollars that Jet deposited in my bank account are a painful reminder to his betrayal. It's a bribe for my silence. And so far, it's working. I'm too ashamed to admit to anyone what he's done. How I fell for his lies.

I told Mum we decided we weren't right together. Which is true. Everything about us was wrong. But I haven't been able to hide the way it's dragged me down every day since.

"I hate that I'm still thinking about him," I say, my voice weaker than the previous thousands of times I've said it.

He's drained me. Even all the trips I've taken with Mum since I got back from New York haven't helped the pain to lessen. And what I managed to turn into rage has eaten away at me just as much. It takes a lot of energy to wake up each day with so much hate in your heart.

"You need to keep busy. How about another trip? We had fun in San Diego last weekend, didn't we?"

I force a smile. "We did."

The effort to keep it there is too much, and it drops the minute Mum turns away to check her phone that's charging on the counter.

"How about San Francisco? We can tour Alcatraz? Ride a cable car?"

"Sure, sounds fun."

Guilt coils itself inside my chest. I'm getting exactly what I've always wanted. To be here with Mum. Seeing new places, exploring, just being mother and daughter again. She's taken so much time off work to keep me company and tried her best to distract me whenever we've seen an Atlantic Airways billboard when we're driving around the city.

"Great. I'll book something," she says, reading something on her phone.

"Okay." I inject a cheeriness into my voice. Maybe if I fake it, it'll start to feel real.

I've smiled in all of the photos we've taken on our trips. To anyone who didn't know, I'd look happy. Like I'm living my best life. I even convinced Gramps that I am. The happiness in his voice when I told him what a great time I'm having made me cry silently down the phone as he told me he loved me and hung up. Liv knows me better. She knows there's more to Jet's disappearance. She asked me if I found him with someone else. Because that's the worst thing she can think of him doing to me.

"Have you thought any more about the suggestions Ophelia had?" Mum asks, unplugging her phone and turning to me.

"Yeah, I like the British actress, Cora. I think I'd like the part to go to someone new who isn't well-known."

Mum nods. "Good. I liked her too. And she's a natural redhead. She looks a little like you did at that age."

I lift my bottle of grapefruit juice and take a sip. No one cares if I leave lipstick around the rim.

"It'll be good to get things moving. You don't want Ophelia to change her mind. She must get a pile of screenplays on her desk every day. You need to act quickly in this business, darling."

"I know. I'm ready to move forward with it now. I just needed a bit more time to get settled here, that's all." I lie so smoothly I almost believe myself.

Mum walks over and pulls me into a hug.

"I'm so proud of you. My daughter, the screenwriter," she hums happily as she holds me.

"Thanks, Mum."

She pulls back, her eyes glittering. "This is exciting. We'll be walking down that red carpet at your premiere, cameras going off everywhere, people calling our names." She pulls a dramatic pouty face, pretending to pose, which makes me smile a little.

"I need to work up to the idea of that not making me want to hurl."

"Nonsense. It's so fun, you'll love it. You can start practicing tonight."

"Tonight?"

She walks to her purse and pulls out a bow-wrapped card, presenting it to me with a beaming smile. "Open it."

The familiar caramel-colored bow slides through my fingers, making my skin tingle.

"Is this?"

Mum bites her lower lip, her eyes bright as I pull the ribbon and open up the card.

"No way." I look up at her, a jolt of excitement appearing from the depths of my stomach. The feeling is so alien, I almost don't recognize it. "You're going to this?"

"We both are." She taps the invitation to the couture lingerie house's new season runway show. "Girls' night out."

―∞◊∞―

"This is... Wow," I breathe, soaking up the atmosphere.

We're sitting in the second row near the end of the raised runway, surrounded by a whole bunch of people who look like they invented the word glamor. I smooth my hands over my emerald green, silk dress. It's got a high neckline, but there are cut-out sections along the torso, showing a glimpse of flesh. Mum and I spent the day shopping for new outfits and getting our hair styled. It's the most fun I've had in weeks, a real mother-daughter day.

I'm finally starting to feel like me again.

"That one's amazing," I whisper, as a dark-haired model struts down in a black thong and matching bustier adorned with crystals.

Mum takes my hand, a bright smile on her face as we sit together and watch each model showcasing stunning piece after stunning piece.

"That one's like the first set you sent me," I gasp as the face of the brand, a stunning model called Sinclair steps onto the runway. A hum of energy ripples through the room as she walks the runway in sky-high heels that make her legs look amazing. She reaches the end and turns, her blonde hair shining beneath the lights like ice before she struts back up again.

I smile as my gaze wanders, letting it track along the front row on the opposite side of the runway. There are two actresses I recognize, a male fashion designer, countless stylish women, and—

Fuck no.

Cool blue eyes burn into mine, making goosebumps scatter up my spine. He doesn't look surprised to see me. Not like I imagine I do—eyes wide, heart pounding, face on fire. He's sitting there with the calm arrogance he's known for. Like he's been watching me for a while.

"Shit," I mutter too quietly for Mum to hear above the music.

The familiar rage swirls in my gut as Jet stares at me. He's cut his hair, it's a little shorter on top, and he looks broader in his deep blue suit, his white shirt fitting snug over his chest, like he's been working out more.

He's probably skipping nine hundred times in a row now.

Bastard, I mouth, more to myself than anyone. But the way his eyes narrow and darken tells me he saw it.

I look away, forcing myself to concentrate on the show. But now that I've seen him, all I can see in my peripheral are intense blue eyes watching me. I straighten in my seat, lifting my chin, trying my best to look unaffected but my heart is hammering against my ribs, my blood heating at the relentless attention he's got fixed on me. I look back, checking the seats either side of him. Both are occupied by women talking to the people beside them. Neither appear to be with him, which means he's here on his own. But why would he come to a lingerie show alone?

"You have that one," Mum exclaims, drawing my attention back to the model on stage.

The nude lace bodysuit fits her perfectly. The pearl strands draping over her hips accentuate them in a way that's so sexy, everyone's eyes are on her. I look at her face, and my throat goes dry.

Francesca Callaghan.

She looked beautiful when I saw her in New York. But seeing her now... she's a literal goddess.

The back of my neck flares with heat as bile rises up my windpipe. I look at Jet, but his eyes are on Francesca, his usual scowl even deeper as he watches her do a spin.

"I feel sick," I mumble.

Mum squeezes my hand. "Let's go to the restroom. You look pale."

"I'm fine. You stay. I just need a minute."

I reassure her again, then apologize to the people in our row as I make my exit.

I push through the door at the rear of the room and march out into the cool corridor. The pearls that felt smooth against my skin now feel like barbed wire, each one tearing at my skin. What the hell was I thinking? I was so determined not to let Jet ruin the things for me that I love. Not to let him take anything else from me, that I've still been wearing the bodysuit he sent me.

"I'm such a fucking idiot," I hiss as I storm along, searching for a restroom where I can go and rip the stupid thing off. I don't even care that I'm about to throw a thousand dollars of silk and pearls into the trash. I'd pay ten times that amount to get the thing off me.

Maybe this is what he does. Sends all the women he fucks the same design, getting some weird perverse pleasure from knowing we all wear it for him.

"Asshole." I seethe as I rush around a corner. "Where are the fucking restrooms?" I yell in frustration as another deserted corridor greets me.

"You walked past them."

I spin so fast my brain rattles in my skull.

Jet's standing a few feet behind me, watching me with a grimace.

"I told you not to even look at me if we were in the same place again. What part of that didn't you understand?" I spit.

"I never agreed to that," he rasps, his deep voice bringing a flurry of memories with it. His eyes darken until he's glowering at me so hard it makes me swallow with unease.

"You always do what you want, don't you, Jet?"

"I do what I have to, Ava."

His eyes travel down my body, making me shiver. And I hate him even more for it. It might have been a month, but the betrayal is still there, burning bright.

"You expect me not to look at you when you wear that?"

I smooth my hands over the green fabric. "It's a dress, asshole. Never seen one before?"

His nostrils flare, his eyes holding mine as my hand skims over my hip, brushing over my bare skin... over smooth, round pearls.

"Fuck," I breathe.

His eyes darken as his gaze tracks back to where my dress is cut just that tiny bit low enough to see the delicate pearl strand against my hip.

"I'm on my way to tear the damn thing off and throw it in the trash."

His throat contracts as he lifts his eyes to mine. "You like it. Forget I sent it to you. Don't be a brat, Ava."

I choke out a muffled gasp.

"A brat?"

His jaw clenches as I storm closer, pointing my finger in his face.

"Excuse me if I don't want to wear the same thing that you buy every woman you fuck."

"I—"

"Shut up!"

He closes his sinfully perfect lips, his eyes narrowing.

"Don't tell me you being here is a coincidence. That Francesca Callaghan modeling today isn't the reason you're here."

"You don't like that I'm here with Fran?"

My stomach drops. *Fran.* So fucking cozy.

"What I don't like is being played." I grab the pearl strand and curl my fingers around it.

"Ava, stop," Jet growls, placing his hand over mine.

His skin burns against mine until I yank my arm so hard that his grasp is broken. Pearls fly onto the floor, rolling along until they come to a stop against his shoes. I grab the other side and break that too. All it takes is another couple of pulls in the right places and digging my nails through the sheer fabric before the entire thing falls away, disintegrating like I'd wish all the memories of him would. I pull the scrap of ruined fabric through the gap in my dress and shove it into his chest.

"Don't ever talk to me again."

"Ava," he snaps.

I turn, desperate to get away from him.

"Ava!"

He spins me back around, pressing me up against the wall so hard that the air is knocked from my lungs. The shredded bodysuit is scrunched inside his white knuckled fist beside my head. Just like in the alleyway when I let him spank me.

"You took that so well."

I'm never taking his bullshit again.

"Fuck off," I spit.

"I would never send you anything that I've bought for another woman. I've never bought a woman lingerie in my life."

"I don't care what you do. Now, let me go."

He crowds over me. We're not touching, but I'm caged between his arms, his fists planted against the wall on either side of me.

"I'm not stopping you," he grits, his eyes wild.

He's right. I could push his arms away or duck underneath them.

But I don't.

"I didn't know she'd be wearing that."

"I told you. I. Don't. Fucking. Care."

"Jesus." He slams a fist against the wall. "I'm telling you, Ava. I've never sent another woman lingerie. Or perfume. Or bought them half a juice company. Or been prepared to genetically engineer a fucking unicorn for them if they wanted one." He shakes his head with a curse. "Only you, Ava... It's only ever been you."

"What about stealing their work? Am I the special one there too?"

He pushes away from the wall, his chest expanding with an angry breath as he barks out another rough curse and turns away from me.

"Thought so." I sneer. "Aren't I lucky?"

I storm past him, ignoring his calls of my name as I find the restrooms and barge inside. I go into a stall and place the lid down, collapsing onto the seat as I suck in deep breaths to slow my heart down.

The main door opens, and the room fills with chatter as two women spill inside, gushing over how amazing the show is.

"Did you see Francesca?" one says.

"She looked hot," her friend agrees.

"You know her boyfriend's in the front row, Jet Grant?"

"Like I'd miss him." The friend giggles. "God, he's so good-looking. They're one hot couple. Imagine how beautiful their babies will be."

I flush the toilet and walk out, going to the sink to wash my hands.

"I've heard his dick's tiny."

The two women's eyes fly to mine as I dry my hands on a paper towel and fix my hair in the mirror.

"A man like that?"

"Yeah." I shrug. "He buys these herbal enlargement pills in the hope it'll grow. It's why he looks so moody all the time. The side effects of them are irritability." I turn and give them a sad smile.

"That's..." One of the woman's eyes widen.

"Such a shame," her friend says.

"Such a waste." The first one sighs.

I walk out with a smug smile and follow the signs until I find the open bar area where the after-show drinks are being served.

"Darling." My mother waves from across the room and I make my way over to her.

"Are you feeling okay? You look better."

I feel better, thanks." I smile at her before looking at the man beside her.

"Oh, Ava. This is Luca. He's an actor. We worked together on—"

"*The Hidden Paths*, I remember." I smile at the man in his late twenties and take his outstretched hand, shaking it as I take in his warm brown eyes and easy smile. "Nice to meet you."

"The pleasure is mine, Ava." He grins. "Zena was telling me you have a screenplay you've written in production. How exciting."

"She's extraordinary," Mum gushes. "And so brave. *Forest Girl* is all based on true events."

My smile turns brittle as Luca's eyes widen at the title.

"Oh, I see Jane." Mum waves to a woman across the room. "Back in a moment. I'll just go and say hello."

She walks off as Luca pins all of his attention on me.

"Oh, wow. That's... that's interesting. I've heard about it. I didn't realize that was you... Well, congratulations."

"Thanks." I take my hand back politely.

Luca moves a little closer, lowering his voice. "I can't imagine being in a plane crash and being the only survivor, to then be lost for, what was it? Two days?"

"Three," I croak.

"Three." He nods. "Wow. If you don't mind me asking—"

"She does mind."

Luca's eyes snap to the owner of the deep voice behind me, whose presence is like a burning inferno of flames licking up my spine.

"I can answer for myself, thank you, Jet." I incline my head over my shoulder, but not far enough to meet his eyes.

I turn back to Luca. "Sure. What did you want to—?"

"I fucking mind."

A hand curls around my hip, pulling my body into his side. I swallow at the way my stomach bounces up to my throat, then floats back down again as heat spreads in my core.

No matter how much I hate him, my body still reacts to him. Muscle memory. *Orgasm memory.*

"Well, you shouldn't. Go find your girlfriend."

I step away from him. Luca's eyes dart between the two of us like he doesn't want to get dragged into our spat.

"Nice to meet you, Ava. I'll catch you later."

Jet grumbles something as Luca escapes quickly.

"What part of 'don't talk to me' don't you understand?"

"I was talking to him, not you."

"Whatever." I turn to walk away.

"You're going ahead with the movie, then?"

I laugh, turning back to him in disgust. "Now I know what you really want. You're checking your precious deal isn't in jeopardy."

"Are you doing it?" His eyes bore into mine, and I swallow against the sudden lump in my throat.

How did I fall so easily for his lies?

"It's going ahead. So you can chill out. Or have a heart attack. I don't care. But you'd probably need a heart for that."

"Ava," he growls. His brows flatten, then furrow again immediately. "You're not happy."

It's a statement, not a question.

"Jet Grant said it, so it must be true." I snort and look around us, but everyone is having their own conversations, paying no attention to the tension radiating from our small space in the room.

"All these trips with your mum?"

"What?" I bring my eyes to meet his, ignoring the way my blood sparks like it's electrically charged as he looks deep into mine. "How do you know what I've been doing?"

His jaw tightens. "I know."

"Are you stalking me online or something?"

"You're still mine to keep safe, Ava."

"What? I was *never* yours! You made sure of that when you lied to me, over and over. When you betrayed me."

He leans closer, his voice taking on a dark edge, like gravel blackened from rain. "Tell me you're happy."

"I don't have to tell you anything. You're no one to me."

"But you're someone to me." His words from Thailand echo in my head. Lies. Lies. Lies.

"Ava," he rasps, his breath dusting the shell of my earlobe.

I stare at his tie, studying the emerald threads running through it as he stays so close that I can smell his aftershave.

"I want to talk to you," he whispers, "I..." His breath huffs over my skin, making me shudder. "I need to... Fuck..."

"There you are!"

He moves away quickly, his heated eyes catching mine for a split second before Francesca Callaghan wraps herself around his arm, leaning into his side.

"Fran," he acknowledges her, making no attempt to untangle himself. "This is Ava Roberts. She's the granddaughter of my father's friend."

"So nice to meet you. I'm Francesca." She smiles at me without a hint of recognition.

Granddaughter of his father's friend? Asshole.

I smile politely at Francesca, who's changed into a smart pant suit.

"Nice to meet you, too," I reply automatically.

"Baby, the press wants some photos," she tells Jet, giving me an apologetic shrug. "I'm sorry to steal him away. Why don't we all get dinner one night. I'd love to get to know one of Jet's friends. I've never met any."

I give her a tight smile as she leads him away. They move through some open double doors and into a large side room where some of the models are posing for photos in front of a branded backdrop. Francesca pulls Jet in front of it and then places her palm flat against his chest, while pushing her breasts against him. He stands there looking solemn, his hand wrapping around her waist, then slipping lower, resting on the spot where the pearls were sitting when she was on the runway.

I whip my eyes away and grab a champagne flute from a tray a passing server is carrying.

"Thank you."

I knock it back in one, then go in search of Mum.

I've seen enough.

Chapter 32

Jet

"Signed and sealed. Just to be delivered now."

"Yup," I grunt, swirling the deep amber brandy in my glass as Hayden's fucking cheery tone grates on my nerves as it carries down the phone.

"And the next batch of engines?"

"All ours, as I agreed with Rich."

I tip the rim of the glass and inhale the alcohol fumes before taking a throat burning swig.

"He okay?"

"Yeah, fine."

"Great," Hayden says.

I tip my chin at the bartender, motioning for the remainder of the bottle. He places what's left of it down on the bar beside me.

Yeah, fucking fantastic. Going back to the Silver Estate was just what I wanted to be doing today. But I pride myself on my business connections. Where possible, I prefer to meet face-to-face. What's it say about the CEO of an airline if he doesn't make the effort to travel?

"You getting the morning flight back?"

A woman wearing a tight-fitting dress slides onto the bar stool beside mine. Her eyes flick up to mine and she gives me a flirty smile.

"Yep," I reply, letting my eyes roam over her.

She bites her lower lip with a smile and pushes her black hair behind her ear.

"All right, I know when you don't want to talk. See you tomorrow, Boss."

I grunt in response and Hayden hangs up.

"What's the whiskey like here?" I ask the dark-haired woman.

"Isn't that what you're drinking?" She looks at the bottle beside me, the label facing away from her.

"No. This is brandy."

"Are you sure?" She narrows her eyes playfully and reaches over, past the bottle to pluck my glass from between my fingers. She takes a sip, her eyes holding mine over the rim as she lowers it and licks her lips. "So it is."

She hands the glass back with a wink and my eyes drop to the shiny pink lipstick mark on it.

"You used my glass."

"Who'd drink from the bottle when you have a glass?" She rolls her eyes with a giggle, tucking another loose strand of hair behind her ear. "You know what's better than the whiskey here?" she purrs.

"What's that?" I follow her hand with my eyes as she plays with her necklace, running the pendant side to side over the swell of her breasts.

"The whiskey at my place."

"Really?"

"I don't live far."

I slide off my stool, and she giggles as I hold her eyes and throw a wad of notes down onto the bar before tipping my head toward the door.

"Time to go."

"Fuck!" I lean down and rub my knee. *Since when did my father have a table there in the hallway?*

My shoulder bounces off the wall as I straighten up and continue my creep through the dark house.

"Fucking hell!" I yell as I stub my toe on something. "Enough of this bullshit." I move along the wall, hitting the first light switch I find. "Ugh." I squint as the glaring light fills the front hallway.

I spot the source of my throbbing toe.

A suitcase.

"Ava's things that she left here. William's coming by to collect them tomorrow."

I blink, making out my father's figure as he descends the stairs.

"Jesus, Son. How much have you had to drink?"

"One or two," I mumble, stepping toward him, then cursing as I bump into the suitcase again.

"What? Bottles?"

I grunt. "Of course... Never glasses. Always bottles... Or cartons."

My father lets out a tired sigh. "Let's get you to bed."

He walks over and throws my arm around his shoulder.

"Did you pack her things?" I turn to him and he screws his nose up as my breath hits his face.

"Margaret did. I didn't want to be looking at her... her female items."

I nod as we take our time going up the stairs.

"Margaret's not spoken to me since I came to visit."

"She will. She misses her, that's all."

"She's not coming back, and Margaret blames me." I puff out my cheeks, gripping the handrail with one hand so Dad doesn't have to support all my weight.

"I don't know what happened between you two. But Ava sure looked upset when she came into your office. You've not mentioned her once since then."

"She hates me," I slur.

"Hate's a big word, Son."

"Better this way," I mutter.

My father sighs again. "William sent her here where he thought she'd be looked after. He thought she'd be safe."

I wince as his words drip through me like acid.

"She should have been."

"You have company tonight?" My father frowns as we reach the top of the stairs and amble down the hallway toward my room.

"Why?"

His eyes zero in on something, and I slap a clumsy hand onto my cheek, wiping the spot he's looking at. Shiny pink lipstick coats my fingers as I pull them away.

"It was nothing."

He opens the door, flicking on the light and helping me into my room. It's just like it always was. All traces of her gone. Packed into a suitcase that's sitting in the hallway downstairs.

"Get some sleep." Dad sits me on the bed and pats my shoulder.

I watch him leave, then unbutton half of my shirt, getting annoyed when it's taking too long. I rip it over my head instead. I undo my pants, pulling them off and tossing them onto the floor. Then I collapse onto the bed, turning onto my side and burying my head into the pillow.

I inhale.

Nothing.

I toss it out of the way and try the one underneath instead.

Laundry detergent.

I toss that one too and pull the covers back, sniffing the sheet on the mattress.

Lavender.

"Fuck!"

I stagger to my feet, lurching across the room and into the dressing room. I yank open the top drawer so hard that it almost breaks away from the runner.

I stick my head inside and breathe in.

"Useless fucking—"

I slam it shut and stagger back into the bedroom, over to my suitcase I dropped off on my way to meet Logan Rich after landing from LA this morning. I throw out my neatly rolled clothes, hurling them all over the floor until I find what I'm looking for.

I clutch the cool glass to my chest as I sink to the floor, resting my head back against the bed behind me. My heart hammers, sweat breaking out across my hairline as I ease the cap off and lift it to my nose.

"Goddamn," I groan as I inhale waterlily and caramel.

I inhale again, my nostrils flaring wide as I fight to get enough. I curse. It's not enough. No matter how many times I suck hard through my nose, taking in enough air to make my head explode, *it's not fucking enough.*

I put my finger over the gold pump and squirt.

One. Two. Three....

I keep squirting until all the hair on my chest is doused in enough perfume that I'd go up like a cheap nylon suit on a barbecue. Then I slam a heavy palm against my skin, rubbing it in, her scent finally filling my nose, reaching my senses.

I tip my head back and stare at the ceiling as I inhale, remembering the way she smelled when her head was resting against my chest in bed. Remembering the way her perfume clung to her hair, scenting the strands that I'd run through my fingers as she slept in my arms. Back when sleeping with me kept her nightmares away.

Before I became one to her.

I let out a pained groan. The dark-haired woman with the pink lipstick smelled like wine and oranges when she whispered flirty things in my ear that most men would kill to hear, before trying to kiss me.

I threw another couple of fifties on the bar and told her it was my time to go. I could have taken up her offer. But I'm not sure I'd have even been able to get hard. The only way I've been able to since walking into my father's kitchen that day and finding a bratty guest barefoot at the fridge is if I picture *her*.

Only her.

No one else comes close.

If it's not flame-haired with a fiery attitude to match, I don't want it.

If it's not berry-flavored lipstick, I don't want it.

If it's not waterlilies and caramel, I don't want it.

If it's not Ava Roberts, I don't fucking want it.

What the hell have I done?

Chapter 33

Ava

"The location team have found the perfect place. We'll be ready to finalize castings as soon as you give the go-ahead."

Mum nods enthusiastically, hanging on to Ophelia's every word.

"That's wonderful news, isn't it, darling?" She squeezes my knee beneath the table as I lift my glass of water and take a sip.

"It is," I agree.

"Have you thought more about who you'd like to play your mum?" Ophelia asks as she walks over to a sideboard in her office, bringing back a fresh bottle of water and topping up my glass.

It's the last part we need to cast. I should feel grateful that Jet at least insisted the contract stipulated I had final say in everything. I've been able to sign off on all decisions.

I could even cancel the entire thing if I wanted to and walk away.

But I haven't.

"Um." I shake my head.

None of the actresses seemed right. I thought casting the actor to play Dad would be hardest, but actually, it was easy. I know that's not him on the screen. And the guy playing the part seems lovely. He's been really sensitive when we've met.

"What do you think?" I look at Mum.

She purses her lips. "I... could play the role myself."

"Really?"

Her brow pinches. "Mitch suggested it, but I wasn't sure how you'd feel—"

"Yes!" I sit straighter in my seat as I look at Ophelia. "Can she do that?"

Ophelia leans back in her chair, her hands steepled over her chest before she opens them, holding out her palms. "If that's what you want?"

Warmth fills my chest. She's been so accommodating. She's told me how much faith she has in this movie being a huge success. I think she'd agree to almost anything to make sure it goes ahead.

The warmth in my chest drops to my gut, turning into an uncomfortable burn instead.

James Callaghan knew how much this meant to his wife that she be the one to produce it. Something Jet must have known, too, when he decided to use my story as his bargaining tool.

I've not heard from him since the runway show two days ago. He's probably too busy with Fran or planning who he's going to betray next.

I look back at Mum, forcing him from my thoughts. Her eyes are bright with excitement.

"Do you want to?"

"Yes," she answers in a rush. "I mean, think how wonderful it will be. We'll be working together. We'll be on set every day, spend more time together."

I return her smile. We'll be doing something together, *really* together.

"Let's do it." I turn to Ophelia. "Let's start filming."

"You sound more like yourself today," Liv says, looking up from where she's painting her nails.

"I feel better. We're going to start filming in a week." I rest my chin on the back of my hands as I lie on my front on the bed, watching her on my laptop screen.

"Nothing more from Jet?"

"No, and I hope it stays that way." I ignore the tension radiating through my chest at his name.

"I can't believe he started dating her after all you two did together."

"Don't." I swallow down the taste of bile. "I don't want to think about the things we did."

"Sorry." She gives me a small smile.

The rage inside me takes over when I think about it. When I think that I told him things no one else knew. That I trusted him with my heart and my body. I've never let another man come inside me before. Yet I let Jet do that the *first* time, handing everything over to him so willingly. I even begged him for more, greedily taking it all, thinking that even if it was just sex, we at least respected each other.

I've never told a soul what he said to me about being scared to love someone. I've kept the things that scare him close to me. Protected them. *Kept him safe.*

He's shared mine with the world for his own gain.

"David's a lucky guy," I say.

Liv's face lights up. "You know he brought me a plant on our last date? Not flowers like a normal guy... A plant."

"Uh-huh." I smile as a dopey grin spreads over my best friend's face.

"It's because he's a landscaper. He likes helping things grow rather than cutting them off when they're at their most beautiful."

"That's almost poetic."

Liv scrunches her nose up. "What the hell's happening to me?"

"I think you like him." I laugh.

"I think I do, too," she groans like it's the last thing she wants. "Which sucks, because once I graduate, I don't want to be held back. I don't know what I want to do yet, but I want to be free to do it, you know? I mean, look at you! You're living in LA, making movies, and going to parties with celebrities."

"You can still do all those things."

She snorts. "We'll see. It's not easy, though. You've not been home in almost two months, you're so busy over there."

I let out a deep sigh. "I know. And I really miss you and Gramps. I'll come back for a visit as soon as I can."

"It's fine." She matches my sigh with a soft smile. "If you're happy, that's all that matters. Maybe I can come to you? I can pick up William and we'll fly over together. When was the last time he had a vacation?"

"He—" I frown as I wrack my brain. "We went away to Cornwall before I left for university."

"Caravan sites are not vacations." Liv scoffs.

"The site had a pool," I argue.

"If you say so." She rolls her eyes. "Listen, Bitch. I love you, but I have to go. David will be here in ten minutes."

"I love you, too. Have fun." I blow her a kiss and hang up.

I roll onto my back and stare at the ceiling. When did Gramps last go on a proper vacation? I don't think he's been on a plane since we lost Dad.

He was always there for me when I needed him.

Guilt pulls low in my stomach. I bring up his number and press call. We've spoken every day, sometimes twice since I went to stay with Magnus. But I haven't seen him in almost two months. I haven't hugged him.

His phone rings out, so I leave a message and hang up. It beeps as soon as I'm done. My heart plummets as I click into the text message.

> **Jet: You looked beautiful at the show.**

I rub at my eyes. Why can't he leave me alone? Hasn't he done enough?

> **Me: I'm going to block you.**

> **Jet: You should.**

My finger hovers over the screen but I can't bring myself to actually do it.

> **Jet: Why aren't you happy?**

> **Me: Why are you texting me? You have a girlfriend to listen to your shit now.**

It's petty, but Liv's right. He picked up with Francesca pretty fast after we ended. You don't move on that fast.

> **Jet: She's not my girlfriend.**

I snort as he sends another message.

> **Jet: It's good publicity now the deal with Callaghan has been announced. Fran and I are putting on a united**

> **front for appearance, the same as we have in the past when it's warranted it. That's all. It stops investors thinking they need to worry if we all appear to be getting along.**

I read his message over and over. It could be the truth. I can't tell with him anymore.

> **Jet: Ava, please. Tell me why you aren't happy.**

> **Me: Why the hell do you think? You betrayed me.**

> **Jet: You wanted to make that movie. Maybe you needed a push to do it.**

I scream, my grip on the phone tightening.

> **Me: Wasn't your job to push, Asshole!**

> **Jet: Cancel it.**

> **Me: What?**

> **Jet: If it's the one thing stopping you from being happy, cancel it.**

> **Me: I never said it was the one thing.**

> **Jet: Then what is?**

I choke back a sob. He knows me. Even after everything, the bastard still knows me better than I know myself. Just like he always told me he did. Because he's right, I'm not happy. I don't know why. I have everything I wanted.

I should be happy. But I don't feel it.

> **Me: You want me to cancel it? Make your deal evaporate. Make you lose the airline?**

Three dots bounce up as Jet types. Then they stop. Then start again.

I drag in a splintered breath and scrub at my eyes.

I type back before he does.

> **Me: Stop playing games with me, Asshole.**

Then I block his number.

Chapter 34

Ava

"Ava!" Mum's voice screeches up the stairs. She sounds out of breath.

"What is it?"

I rush out of the bathroom, my towel clutched around me. I was up late again last night. I haven't been able to sleep well since Jet texted me two days ago. It's like he stirred up all my emotions. Telling me to cancel the movie. *Playing with me. Again.*

"Ava." Her eyes are wide and glassy. "It's Gramps, darling. He—"

"No." I shake my head. "No."

He never called me back. It's the longest we haven't spoken. I was too busy hating Jet to notice.

"He collapsed and was taken to hospital. Pack a bag. I don't know how bad it is."

My heart falls to my feet as I sprint to my room. I throw some clothes on, dragging my wet hair into a knot on top of my head. I rip the closet doors open and pull out the silver suitcase Jet bought me, tossing my things in.

"We need to book a flight... We need to get a cab!"

I race downstairs with my suitcase. Mum's in the hallway, throwing things into her purse.

"It's all sorted, darling."

I glance toward the front window with bleary eyes, spotting a sleek black town car outside with the trunk open.

Mum stuffs her phone charger into her purse. "Mitch—"

"Tell him thank you," I cry as I pull my suitcase to the front door and wrench it open.

Mum rushes behind me and the driver takes our cases. We fall into the back seat as he gets in and starts to drive. My heart hammers as I pray we get to LAX airport fast. Get back to London fast. Get back to Gramps.

Please let him be okay.

"He was lucky," the female doctor says as we stand outside Gramps' private room. "His friend got him here in time. His insulin levels had dropped dangerously low."

"He said he hadn't been sleeping as well. I should have known something was wrong."

Mum wraps an arm around me and hugs me to her side. "You didn't know, Darling."

"I should have been here," I sniff.

"Now that we've diagnosed him, we'll be able to talk through management options going forward. Lots of people live very full, active lives with Type 2 Diabetes. I'll be back later to check on him."

"Thank you, Doctor." Mum gives her a watery smile.

"Wait," I call before she leaves. "You said his friend brought him in?"

"Yes. Mr. Grant. You just missed him. He's been here ever since."

"He's been here the whole time?"

"He has." The doctor smiles and leaves.

I look back at Gramps, peacefully sleeping in his bed. My heart clenches with gratitude for Magnus. For being here for Gramps when I wasn't.

"I need to go and see him later. To thank him."

"That sounds like a good idea, darling." Mum's gaze skitters around the immaculate hospital corridor. "He's done a lot."

She's right. Gramps has been brought to the best private hospital in the whole area. No way could we afford to have him brought here.

"He's waking up!"

I rush into the room as Gramps opens his eyes, blinking slowly. I go straight to the side of his bed and take his hand in mine.

"Gramps," I sob.

"Ava." His old eyes twinkle as they focus on me. "You're a sight for sore eyes."

I laugh through my tears and lean in to hug him. His whiskers graze my cheek as I soak in the familiar warmth of his embrace.

"You gave us a fright, Gramps. The doctor said Magnus found you collapsed in the kitchen."

"I can't remember, love." Gramps rubs my back, and his attention moves over my shoulder. "Zena?"

"Hi William," Mum says softly, coming over to the side of the bed. "It's good to see you."

Gramps' eyes widen and bounce between the two of us and he smiles. "Well, aren't I the lucky one? Two beautiful women rushing across the Atlantic for me."

"I should have come sooner. I've missed you." I perch on the side of his bed and clasp his hand in mine.

"You're living your life, Ava. I don't want you worrying about an old man like me."

"Stop." I shake my head with a smile, rubbing my thumb over the back of his palm as Mum sits in the seat beside his bed. "I'm always going to worry about you. And I'll be staying awhile. We've got a hotel nearby."

"We have," Mum confirms. "For as long as you need us, we'll be here."

"I'll be fine."

I'm about to argue with him when his next words make a lump form in my throat.

"I'm so proud of you, love. You wrote your story. Just like you said you were going to. And you've got a movie deal."

"I know," I whisper.

"Are you happy?" He places his warm, calloused hand over the back of mine, encasing it beneath both of his. "This is what you wanted, isn't it?"

I nod, unable to find any words.

Gramps smiles at me with pure, unbridled happiness. He looks content. I can't ruin that. Especially when he's healing. He's right. This is what I wanted. I planned I might share my story with the world when I began writing it. I was opening up to that possibility. Maybe I need to forget about how I got here and just accept that I am. Not that I'll ever thank Jet for taking my decision away from me.

The selfish bastard can still rot in hell for all I care.

"You've been wearing sunscreen, haven't you?"

I reassure Margaret for the third time that I've been taking care of myself in LA. This is her way of showing she cares. This and insisting when I arrived that I came straight inside with my shoes on even though she'd just mopped the front hallway.

Mum and I stayed with Gramps until he got tired, then I dropped her at the hotel so she could rest and call Mitch. I headed straight to Rochwell house. I gambled, assuming Magnus wouldn't be at work when the doctor told me we'd just missed him at the hospital.

"And how are *you*?" Margaret assesses me.

"I'm good."

She folds her arms, seeing right through my fake bright smile. "Did he think with his penis?"

"What?" I can't help but laugh at the way she says it so matter-of-factly.

"Jet." She sucks in a breath. "I didn't have him down as a cheater, and I'm usually a good judge of character. But I figured whatever it is, it's his fault."

"What makes you think the two of us even—?"

Margaret gives me a pointed look. "Nothing happens in this house without me knowing about it."

"Oh, right." I bite my lower lip. *God, I hope she never heard us.*

"Well, now that you're back here, you can—"

"Ava?" Magnus appears, walking across the entryway with his arms wide.

I give him a big hug.

"I thought I heard your voice. Have you come straight from the hospital?"

"Yeah. I dropped Mum at the hotel, she's checking us both in."

"Good. My driver is yours for as long as you need him. He'll take you from the hospital to the hotel, and anywhere else you need to go."

"Thank you. You don't have to. You've done so much already."

A phone starts ringing from the direction of Magnus's office.

"It'll be work. Come through, Ava. I'll only be a minute.

Margaret tells me she'll fix us a drink, so I follow Magnus into his office.

My gaze tracks outside, across the gardens, to the pool house. It seems strange seeing it again. I spent so many hours writing in there, hiding away. Alone. In some ways, it feels like a lifetime ago, not a few months.

I sink into a soft armchair beside his desk as I wait for him to finish his call. The frame on his desk has a picture of June inside it, and I look at him in question.

He nods encouragingly, so I lift it and study the photograph inside. She's beautiful, her eyes glimmering, her lips parted, like she's laughing at something the photographer is saying.

But it's the little blue-eyed boy with dark hair in her arms that grabs my attention.

A little boy with a smile so wide and radiant that it's almost splitting his face in two.

"Doesn't look like him, does it?" Magnus chuckles as he drops his phone onto the desk.

"I've never seen him smile," I murmur, looking from his face to the blue wing walker plane they're standing in front of.

"They're rare. But they exist." Magnus sinks into the seat at his desk and looks at the frame in my hands. "June was a spitfire. Kept me on my toes. Never a dull moment."

"She's beautiful. Is this the plane in your office? The one she wing-walked on?"

"That's the one." His eyes take on a mistiness. "She was pregnant with Jet the day she went up on it. We didn't know. Not that it would have stopped her. She thought flying was the safest thing in the world." He clears his throat, and I brush away the apology in his eyes.

Flying is safe most of the time. Unless you're my father or his pilot.

"She loved to watch birds. Said she wished she had wings and could fly like them at a second's notice. Her favorite were blue tits. Tiny little things. But she loved them. We had some nest in the gardens one summer. They have their young in June."

"You named the plane June's Blue." I grin at the photograph. "I get it now."

"Yep," Magnus chuckles. "Her favorite giant blue bird, that one. We named it that day, after we found out she was expecting. Seemed fitting."

"It's perfect." I place the frame back onto the desk carefully, angling it exactly the way I found it so that Magnus can see it as he works.

"Whatever my son did to hurt you, I'm sorry. I brought him up to be a good man... We both did."

His gaze tracks back to June's glowing image, and my heart aches.

"It wasn't his fault. We just weren't right for each other." The words come easily this time, eased along by the softening of Magnus's tense brow as I say them. "I think he's happier now. I saw him with Francesca, and they seemed... They looked good together."

"Perception, Ava," he says softly. "That's what he wants the world to think. He's always been a great businessman, putting the airline before all else."

"I don't know, I've seen the way he looks at her."

I hate that I sound pathetic, like a fool pining for something that wasn't real.

"I know all my son's faces," Magnus says, leaning back in his chair. "I've seen them for thirty-three years. Only one person has ever brought a new one to him. And that's you."

I try to hide the small, strangled sound in my throat as I blink rapidly and rise to my feet.

"Thank you for everything you've done for Gramps," I whisper. "I should get back to the hospital."

Chapter 35

Jet

"Again?" William throws his cards onto the hospital sheets with a deep rumble of a laugh. "At least I know you never let an old man win because you feel sorry for him almost dying and all."

"You just faked it so you could get some pretty doctors and nurses looking after you," I say as I scoop them up and add them back to the deck with mine and start to shuffle.

"Must be costing a bit." William fixes me with the same stern look that keeps sliding onto his face since he was brought into hospital. I ignore him, as I have been doing each time he's commented on the private hospital we're in.

"Ready to get beaten again?" I arch a brow at him as I split the card deck in two and riffle shuffle in my hands, ending it in a bridge finish.

William whistles, then chuckles. "Now you're just showing off."

I deal the cards, then lean back in the hospital chair beside his bed. He rolls his lips, eyeing me with a smile over the top of his cards.

"Careful, Gramps. Jet will cheat to make sure he wins."

"Ava!" William drops the cards onto the bed.

My shoulders tense, every muscle in my back coiling tight as the fury being aimed at my back takes on its own heat, like a laser searing through my clothes.

I turn and meet her eyes.

"Ava?"

She flinches when I say her name. I turn around, carefully gathering the cards up and putting them back into the case, willing the sudden ache in my throat to go away.

"Packing up because you know I was about to beat you this time?" William jests.

"I'll leave you two to have some time alone."

I rise from the seat, tucking the cards into my jacket pocket. The minute I turn, her eyes meet mine again, like she hasn't taken them off me since she walked into the room.

"What are you doing here? Shouldn't you be in LA?" The venom in her voice is harder than any slap around the face.

"I'm just leaving." I step toward her, and she tenses, the pain I've caused palpable in the fine lines around her tired eyes.

"Good." She sinks into the seat I've just vacated, taking William's hand in hers. Her face softens to the Ava I recognize as she gazes at him.

"How are you feeling?"

"I'm fine, love." William looks past her to me. "Where are you going? Sit down, you just got here."

"I can't stay." My gaze slides to Ava, her spine straight as she sits stiffly in the seat pretending I'm not here.

"He's busy working on a new business deal, aren't you?" she says, keeping her back to me.

William seems to register the sudden plummet of temperature in the room, and he looks back and forth between the two of us.

"Look, I know you two kissed and whatever."

"Gramps," Ava gasps.

"I was young once, love, I know how it is."

"Oh my god," she mutters.

"But whatever happened, you're both here now. And you've come to see me, not each other. So leave whatever this fall out is between you outside, you hear me? You can go back to ignoring each other after."

"Yes, Sir," I answer immediately.

Ava's eyes dart to my face, then she exhales, shaking her head in defeat. "Fine," she mutters, sounding anything but pleased.

"Sit down," William says to me. "Get that other chair." He points to one across the room.

I stay rooted to the spot until he jabs a finger toward it again. Then I slowly walk over and curl my hand around the back of it, twisting it to face the bed before

I sit, conscious of giving her as much distance as I can. It fucking wrecks me that she can barely stomach to be in the same room as me.

"Jet's been here since I was brought in," William says to Ava. Her eyes widen as she glances at me with a look of surprise. "And he's just got back after I kicked him out to take a rest. I'd like him to stay. At least until I beat him at cards. You know he's won five days straight?"

"Five days?" she croaks.

"Nearly had you on day three, though." William chuckles at me and I tip my chin in agreement.

"You did."

"You two have been meeting up for five days?"

"Jet brought your suitcase back from Magnus's house for you. Couldn't let him leave without beating him at a game first. We've had to have some re-matches, but I'll get there. Don't get complacent." He winks at me.

"Never." I nod.

"Were you the one who found him?"

It's the first time she's spoken to me in over a month with something other than contempt in her tone. And I want to fucking cling to it like a life buoy. Ask her to repeat it, just so I can record it and play it on a loop, hoping it'll allow me to get to sleep at night. Because the nights are the worst. When I'm alone with my thoughts. My regrets.

"I was."

An unreadable emotion passes across her face.

"Thank you," she whispers, then she turns back to William and starts talking quietly, acting like I'm not here again.

I wish I wasn't. I wish I hadn't seen the hate in her eyes the moment she saw me. Because all I want to remember is the way she looked at me that night in Thailand. When I promised her she was safe and would never be alone again. When she still trusted me.

I pull my phone from my pocket, seeing a missed call from Hayden.

"I really should go."

I stand at the exact moment the door opens and Zena walks through it carrying a cardboard tray with three cups inside.

"Jet." She smiles as she sees me. "I didn't know you were here. I'd have brought another coffee."

"He's leaving," Ava says, her back still to me.

"I am." I look at William. "I'll come back another time."

"That's a shame," Zena says. "Although I'm happy you two have made up. I knew it must have been a misunderstanding." She smiles in Ava's direction, missing the way her daughter's shoulders stiffen at her words. "The hotel's lovely, by the way. Thank you for arranging it all."

Ava spins, pinning an accusing glare on me. "What?"

"Jet dealt with everything," Zena chirps as she places the cup holder down onto the table beside William's bed and then shrugs out of her coat. "And the flight and cars. I didn't have to do a thing after he called."

I hold Ava's eyes in silence as Zena swans about, straightening up things on the table, then walking over to the window to open it wider.

"You were the one who called Mum?"

I clear my throat and nod. "I was."

"He tried to call you a million times, darling. Couldn't get through," Zena hums as she walks back across the room to get the coffees.

Ava lets out a small gasp, her lower lip trembling as something in her eyes makes my heart fall to my feet.

"I blocked your number," she whispers. "It's all my—"

"It's not your fault, Ava." My voice cuts through the room like a knife, making everyone fall silent and stare at me.

She blinks at me, her lower lids heavy with tears and I fucking hate myself more in this moment than I ever have in my life.

"Not your fault," I repeat more gently, holding her pained gaze.

She makes a choked sound and turns away, gripping onto the back of her chair so she can stand. "I need some air." She wobbles on her feet, and Zena reaches out, grabbing her before she falls.

"Darling, you're so pale."

"I feel a little sick."

"You okay, love?" William asks.

"I'm fine." Ava tries to brush her mother off, but Zena keeps ahold of her upper arms and studies her face with concern.

"You've not been sleeping well, and now this? This is exactly how I was when... Darling, are you pregnant?"

I move in a flash before I have time to comprehend what I'm doing, wrapping Ava in my arms, and holding her up as her legs wobble beneath her.

"Are you?" I look down at her pale face and into dim blue eyes.

"No." She scoffs. "So you can get off me."

She pushes at my chest, but I can't let her go.

"Leave me alone! You've done enough."

She wobbles again, her eyes losing focus, so I sweep her up into my arms, holding her close against my chest as I stride over to the door and kick it open.

"We need a doctor!"

Eyes snap up from the medical desk further down the hall, then two medical staff hurry toward us.

"I'm fine," Ava mumbles in a weak voice.

Zena rushes over and grabs her hand, but I hold her tighter to me as a nurse reaches us and starts talking to Ava.

"This is your fault!" Zena's brows shoot up her forehead. "She's not been herself since you left her for that model. You left her, and now she's pregnant."

"I'm not pregnant," Ava protests.

"You left my daughter. And now look what's happened."

"Listen to me," I hiss. "I would *never* leave Ava without a damn good reason. I wouldn't walk away from anyone I care about for my own goddamn selfish reasons. I protect the people I care about. I'd trade my happiness for theirs. Not that I'd expect you to understand that for one fucking minute."

Her eyes pop wide and the color drains from her skin. "I... I... That's not what it was like."

I grind my teeth so hard my head starts to pound. I've said too fucking much. My arms tighten around Ava as I drag in a splintered breath.

Zena shakes her head, the whites of her eyes popping. "Ava, tell him. That's not what it was like. You know it wasn't like that, don't you, darling?"

"I do, Mum," Ava mumbles, seeming to use a whole lot of energy to answer as she grows weaker in my arms.

I ignore Zena's frantic words tumbling out, focusing my attention on Ava as I place her down onto the hospital bed that's been wheeled in for her.

"I was grieving. I'd lost my husband," Zena babbles. "Losing someone you love means you need a fresh start sometimes. I had to move away. I was a mess; I couldn't be the mother she needed. I thought I was doing what was best for her, that she'd be better with her grandfather."

"Who are you trying to convince? Me? Or yourself?" I snap, losing all patience for the woman who let my girl down. The woman who left a scared child to grieve alone.

I turn away, using my body as a shield to block her out as I move closer to the bed. Ava looks at me with questioning eyes as Zena keeps blathering on behind me. I brace one hand on the metal frame and lean in.

"Best doctors and nurses in the world here, Ava. You'll be safe." I stroke her hair away from her face as the nurse straps a blood pressure cuff to her arm.

Her eyes track to the two medical staff before she looks back at me.

"You hate hospitals." Her forehead creases with a frown. "You told me in Thailand."

"That's right, I do."

"But you've been here since Gramps came in." She searches my eyes, and a flare of hope ignites in my dead heart that for the first time in over a month she's looking at me with something other than hatred in her eyes.

It's enough to make my breath stall in my throat.

Zena starts sobbing theatrically and tries to push around me to get closer. I stay rigid like a wall around a fortress, protecting what's inside. She scrambles to the other side of the bed instead, getting in the way of the nurse as she grabs ahold of Ava's hand.

"Darling, are you okay?"

"Fine," Ava croaks, her eyes never wandering from mine.

"You know I didn't want to be apart. I asked you to come to LA so many times." Zena keeps rambling, but Ava just looks at me, a barrage of questions building in her eyes. "And we're having a wonderful time together, aren't we? We're going to be working together, going to red carpet events, celebrating your movie, your success," she splutters. "It's what you wanted. You said so yourself."

I wish someone would slap her to shut her up.

"You're going to be famous, Ava. We'll be recognized everywhere we go. You and me. Mother and daughter. Your story will be talked about everywhere. It's the best thing that's ever happened. You'll see. Aren't you glad it's out there now? Being shared with the world? It was too big not to share, Darling. You know I'm right."

My stomach drops to my feet as the haunted look in Ava's eyes grows with each blink.

"Jet?" she whispers, her breath catching.

Zena sniffles. "Look at me, darling. Look at me. I can explain. Mitch thought it was a good idea. You wanted to say yes when he suggested it, I know you did."

My soul is torn from my body the second her pupils widen with realization. The second I see that stab of pain go right through her heart.

"What's going on? Tell me the truth, Jet. *Please*," she begs, searching my eyes.

Every cell in my body goes on high alert as I'm frozen in place, witnessing her crumple in front of my eyes.

"Jet?" she chokes.

I lean in, running the backs of my fingers down her cheek as caramel and waterlily wash over me in delicate waves. Ones I'd happily drown in for her. The touch of her skin against mine brings enough strength to me that I can get out the words I should have told her months ago.

"The truth is, I wish you all the happiness in the world. And I'd do absolutely anything to give it to you."

I kiss her on the forehead, screwing my eyes shut as my chest burns. *"Anything, Firefly."*

She reaches for me, but I catch her hand in mine and squeeze it gently, before placing it onto the bed.

"You need to talk with your mum."

"Ava?" Zena steals her attention, and she looks away from me for the briefest second, disbelief and heartbreak swimming in her eyes.

"Mum?" she sobs.

I turn away before I lose it and punch the wall.

"Look after her," I say to the nurse, unable to look at anyone else in the room as I stride out.

Chapter 36

Ava

"It was you all along." I stare at Mum as tears fall freely down her cheeks. She looks like a stranger to me. She grips my hand tight, like she's scared if she lets go, I'll run away.

The nurse eases her away, encouraging her to sit in the chair beside Gramps' bed as they continue checking me over. I answer their questions, my head heavy, like a fog has filled it. Once they're happy that my dizzy episode was nothing more than lack of food and all the traveling, they help me sit up, and I eat a sandwich and drink a juice that someone fetches for me.

The entire time Gramps and Mum sit in silence.

The second the door closes behind the nurses, Mum starts spluttering.

"I'm sorry, Ava. I..."

"Shut up!" I snap.

She flicks her gaze to Gramps as if looking for back-up. But he stays silent, his warm fingers wrapping around my hand in a show of support. He's always been the one there for me. I squeeze it back gratefully as my chest shakes.

"I thought it was Jet," I cry. "You let me think it was him!"

"I didn't know," Mum sobs. "You never told me that's why you two fell out. I would have said something if I'd known."

"Would you?" I pin my gaze on her, ignoring the pang in my heart as I study her, try to work out if I know her at all. Because I don't understand how she could do this. There's remorse in her eyes. But I don't know what the hell to do with it.

"Of course I would!" She sobs louder, pressing a tissue against her eyes and soaking up her smeared mascara. "You said you were thinking about it. I thought you wanted to do it, that you'd be excited once we got started. It's brought us closer. I've loved every minute. We're going to be working together, filming and—"

"Was it for me, or was it for you? For your career? Because you sure seemed quick to suggest you play the role yourself."

"I... It wasn't like that. Mitch sent it. He thought—"

"No one should have thought anything! Except me!" I jab my finger into my chest so hard I might bruise. "Me!" I choke. "That was no one's call to make but mine."

It doesn't matter if it was her idea or Mitch's. She went along with it. She's known this whole time.

"He forged my signature."

Mum gasps, and the way her eyes widen tells me she didn't know.

"Didn't you ever wonder how Ophelia got the rights to it?"

"You gave them to her."

I shake my head. "I didn't."

"B-but... I thought he sent the script so she'd read it and see how amazing it was. And that after when she called, you agreed to proceed on your own accord. I thought you were okay with it. I swear!"

"I never agreed to anything. She had the signed contracts before I ever knew she'd even seen it."

Mum squeezes her eyes shut, her shoulders trembling. The fact that I blamed Jet and never told her, means what she's saying could be true. That she thought I'd made the decision myself to go ahead. But she still knew Mitch was sending my story to Ophelia to read. Something I'd never consented to.

Something occurs to me as she's crying.

"The only copy of it is on my laptop."

She opens her eyes, guilt swimming in them.

Nausea threatens to spill up from my stomach. "The password is your name... I'm such an idiot."

"No, darling, you're—"

"I can't believe I never saw it. This is you all over. All these years your career has been more important to you. I made excuses for you. I told myself you were grieving, and that you had to leave. But really, I was holding you back from your selfish dreams of fame. I was never the child you wanted, was I? The love of your life has always been your career. It's always been about you!

"Mitch might have forged my signature. But he couldn't have done that if you hadn't given him the script in the first place." I press a hand to my mouth and swallow down the acid in my throat. "The sad thing is, I'd have given it to you if you'd just asked. If you'd explained how important it was to you. If you'd just told me, then I'd have let Ophelia read it. And I'd have signed production rights to her.

"Because as stupid as I feel admitting this now.... Being with you in LA has been like a dream come true. And working on it together has been incredible. But you've tainted every moment of our time together. Can't you see that? I'll never know if you did this for us, or for yourself. I've had you on a warped fucking pedestal for years. But enough of that shit, Mum. It's time I woke the hell up."

"Ava," she gasps and then crumples into more sobs, pressing her hands over her face.

"I'll never know, Mum. Can't you understand that? You did what was right for you all those years ago." My chest deflates and tears sting my eyes. "Maybe this was just you choosing yourself again," I whisper.

"I thought it would bring us closer after all these years apart. I thought we'd do it together." She hiccups, her whole body shaking as she cries. But I can't bring myself to comfort her. I can barely look at her.

Gramps squeezes my hand and I look up into his kind eyes. "This is a lot to take in, love. What do you need?"

"I..."

The look in his eyes is one of pity entwined with anger as they slide over to Mum. Maybe he sees the same broken woman she was after Dad died. One that chose herself over her daughter.

I've been so desperate not to lose her, too. Not to feel alone. I missed all the signs. Like Gramps downsizing his house so he could get me into the best school. Giving up traveling and staying home to be there for me whenever I needed him. The way he'd give me grace when I was sullen and moody for days after my mother returned to LA at the end of a visit. The times he'd sit up in the night with me because I'd had another nightmare.

He put me before himself.

My mother didn't.

"I need to speak to Jet. He told me he was the one who sent my story to Ophelia. Why would he do that?"

"Why does anyone do anything that doesn't make sense?" Mum says in a shaky voice.

Gramps squeezes my hand again as my chest tightens.

"We make our decisions out of love, darling. But sometimes, we get it all wrong."

Chapter 37

Ava

I BURST THROUGH THE rear door of Rochwell house, using the key Magnus gave me. The one I've forgotten to mail back. Maybe I was subconsciously holding on to it, unable to let go of this house and what it's brought to me. *The people it brought to me.*

"Jet?"

The heavy door swings closed behind me with an ominous thud. I stand still and listen.

Nothing.

I pull off my shoes and run barefoot across the cold stone floor, my heart in my throat. I'm so angry with him. So hurt and confused. But I'm determined to hear the truth from him.

I have to hear him say it.

I stop as I reach the bottom of the old staircase.

He's sitting in his usual spot in a pair of workout shorts, his skipping rope coiled on the step beside him, his chest shining with perspiration. His head is hung as he stares at something he's twirling between his fingers.

He looks exhausted.

"Jet?" I breathe.

He looks up, the hollowness in his eyes making me falter.

"You're supposed to be resting, Ava."

His deep voice sends a shiver through me. Even looking completely drained, the way he does, his voice always has that same steadiness about it. That same control.

"I'm fine. I just forgot to eat because I was worried about Gramps." I hover at the base of the stairs and study him. "But you know that already. The nurse said you wouldn't leave their desk until they told you how I was doing."

He says nothing.

"And I'm not pregnant. They checked."

His eyes pinch at the corners as his jaw tenses. I thought he'd look relieved, but torment clouds his features as he huffs out a heavy breath.

I force myself to sound calm, despite the banging inside my skull. "Tell me."

There's one swift shake of his head as he continues to spin the small object in his fingers, his attention fixed on it.

"I know it wasn't you. My mum…" My voice cracks, and I force a swallow. "You knew it was her, didn't you?"

He rolls his lips, still not meeting my eyes.

"Did you always know? That day I came to your office and you were on a video call? You acted like you knew something."

"I didn't." He lifts his eyes to mine. "I'd finalized the deal with Callaghan, and he mentioned how pleased Ophelia was to be working with you. I thought you'd made the decision yourself."

"I hadn't," I whisper.

His brows pull together. "I knew something was wrong the moment you mentioned your father."

"You let me scream at you. The way you were speaking... I thought you'd given it to her."

"I thought you were talking about something else. But the second I got off that call, I had my suspicions. I wanted to be wrong, Ava. I've never wanted to be so fucking wrong in my life. That son of a bitch, Mitch, told me it was just business when I figured it out," Jet hisses, his shoulders rippling with tension. "He spun me my own fucking line."

"But why did you tell me you did it? I flew all the way to New York, and you looked me in the eye and lied to my face."

"I was so damn proud of you when I saw you walk into the hotel that day. You got on that plane by yourself."

"Don't avoid the question," I say desperately holding a sob at bay. I knew he'd looked at me with pride in his eyes that day. And I hated him so much at that moment for what I thought he'd done.

Pain flashes over his face as he clenches his jaw.

"I lost my mother for good. You lost yours and got her back. I was given a choice.... For you to hate me but still have her. It's what you dreamed of. You told me."

"Jet—"

"It was only a matter of time before I had to let you go, anyway. I'd have stopped you spreading your wings. Stopped you from seeing the world. You'd have resented me for controlling you like that."

My throat feels like it's closing up, but I still manage to croak out the words, "But you love control."

His eyes hold mine and I feel every word of his seep into the cells of my body and heat them.

"Only when it keeps you safe, Ava. When it makes you happy. Not when it means caging you like a bird."

His gaze drops back to the tiny object in his hand.

"It's a replica of her plane, isn't it?"

He nods once before closing his fist around the tiny piece of blue metal, keeping it inside his palm.

"You need to see the world," he rasps. "You fucking *glow* when you travel. You crave adventure. But at that runway show, you'd lost it. It crushed me to see you like that. You weren't happy."

"How would you know? You were busy with Fran," I say, hating myself for being so childish. But it hurt to see him with her. To see him with *anyone* else.

His eyes flare with heat as he pins his blue gaze on me. "You know that's not what it was like."

I shiver at the way he looks at me, like he'd spank me given the chance for letting the flimsy accusation slip free. But I can't help the twist of jealousy in my gut that makes me say it anyway. I'm being petty when I came here for much bigger things.

For the truth.

"I know when you're happy, Ava. I could see it in New York. I could see it in Thailand. I could see it at Jay's house. You have this light in your eyes. The day you crashed my meeting, it was gone. Seeing you at the runway show, it was gone. You've gone from living in one box to living in another."

I want to tell him to go fuck himself because that stings.

But he's right. I knew something was missing, too. But it's not what he thinks.

"It's because I was with you."

His beautiful dark brows that I've learned give away so many of his emotions pull together, creating a crease down his forehead, marring his handsome face.

"No. You were being yourself. Who you're supposed to be. All those times we were traveling, you were this bright—"

"Distraction?" I breathe.

He drops his head again, uncurling his fist and looking into his palm.

"Guiding light," he murmurs so quietly I have to strain to hear him.

"What did you give Callaghan? If it wasn't my story, then what was it?"

Silence.

"Jet, what—"

"Something that wasn't mine to give."

I slowly ascend a couple of steps so that I can see the tiny blue wing walker plane in his hand.

"You gave him your mum's plane? June's Blue?"

He winces. "I gave away her pride and joy. Dad's memories of her with it. My memories. My fucking soul. I'm son of the year, just like you said."

"*You're* her pride and joy. Look at everything you've achieved."

He stares at the tiny plane, a grimace pulling on his lips.

"I'm an asshole."

"You're Jet Grant."

He looks up into my eyes, the weight in them pulling me up two more steps toward him, like a magnet bound to him.

"One and the same, isn't it?"

"Yesterday, I'd have said yes. But today..." I reply, stopping a few steps away from him. I want to run to him, wrap my arms around him. But the part of me that's still angry at him—angry, hurt, and confused, with a whole ton of questions—stops me.

"Today?"

"Today you're exactly who I've always known deep down you are." I climb another step. "Welcome back." I give him a small smile.

"Don't, Ava."

"Don't what?"

"Just fucking don't."

Something ignites in me. The anger of what he's put me through, what he's put *himself* through the past month reaches up and grips my windpipe, stealing my air.

"Is that too hard to hear? That you're not the asshole you like to play?"

His eyes snap to mine, a hardness in them that I ignore.

"If you want to be that, then go ahead. I'll walk out of here right now. You'll never have to speak to me again. But you'll not care, will you? Because you're an asshole devoid of feelings."

His nostrils flare as he takes in a measured breath.

"Yeah, didn't think so." I shake my head. "So let's cut the bullshit. You don't have this impenetrable stone heart."

He stares at me, his eyes darkening as I push him. He looks like a man on the edge, brow set firm, sweat clinging to his recently pounded muscles. I bet he skipped a thousand times in a row trying to disperse the tension that's commanding his body, holding him stiff and solid on the step.

Desperately trying to maintain a poker face, like it really is just a game.

"You've told me how you found out, before claiming it was you who took it. Now tell me *why* you did it."

"I have," he grits. "I wanted you to have that relationship with your mother you wanted, that—"

"That's not why, Jet! Tell me why you wanted me to have it. Why you did something so... so self-fucking destructive in order for me to have that?"

Silence.

"Why?" I say again, my voice rising.

More silence.

"Why?" I shout, blood rushing in my ears, setting all efforts to be calm flying out of the window. "Why did you do that?"

He looks at me from underneath dark brows.

"You know why."

I stomp higher, stopping two steps below him. "You need to do fucking better than that! I've spent weeks hating you! Questioning my judgment, my sanity... everything! I've hated myself for trusting you. Hated thinking of you every single day and asking myself why you would do this to me. And it wasn't even you. You even said in New York that you'd make the same decision again. The same decision to fucking lie to me. The least you can do is tell me the truth about why you'd do that."

"Ava, don't." He tips his head, making his neck crack. But he doesn't look at me. His eyes are fixed on the tiny model plane in his hand, his face taut, the vein in his temple bulging like it might explode.

"Don't what? Don't ask questions? Don't speak my own mind? Don't fucking what?"

"Just don't," he hisses.

"Don't keep pushing until you tell me the truth? Because guess what? That's exactly what I'm going to do."

"Ava," he growls.

"Don't growl at me, Jet! I'm not leaving until you tell me the truth."

He flies to his feet and launches the tiny model plane into the air with a booming, *"Fuck!"*

It smashes into the hallway wall and explodes, falling to the floor in pieces. He swipes up his skipping rope and spins, storming up the stairs.

I race after him. "Tell me why you did it!"

He continues striding away, and I grab his arm, curling my hand around it. His skin is on fire.

"Tell me!"

He grabs me so fast my head spins, and pushes me against the wall. One hand curls around my throat as the other slams against the wall in a fist, his skipping rope clenched between his fingers.

"You fucking know why!"

His eyes are like two blue flames, searing into mine. The sight makes energy dance in my veins. They aren't hollow anymore. They're bright and alive. He looks like Jet again. The Jet that I push to get a reaction from. The Jet whose heated looks make me weak at the knees. The Jet who held me when I stepped onto a plane again. The one who flew it home himself, so he could be in control and make me feel safe.

I inhale slowly, my windpipe meeting resistance against his palm. "Tell me."

He drags in splintered breaths, and for a crushing moment, I think he's going to stay silent again. But instead, he bangs his fist against the wall, his eyes wild like a man possessed as he roars, "Because of the way I feel about you, Ava. The way I fucking *feel*!"

He traces the pad of his thumb up my neck and along my jaw until he reaches my bottom lip. He pushes the tip inside my mouth, swiping it over my tongue. He's enthralled, his attention stolen by my mouth as he slides his thumb out and rubs my saliva over my lips.

"It's the one thing I vowed never to do… It's when I knew I had to let you go."

I part my lips to speak, but he presses his thumb over them, sealing them shut.

"I chose for you to hate me, to lose me. Not her. I didn't want you to lose your mother, Ava."

My breath escapes me in a sob as I look into the tortured blue eyes of the boy in the photograph in Magnus's office, still in so much pain over his grief, that he can't allow himself to admit what he needs to say.

Not for me, but for him.

The thought of him living his life like this makes my heart feel like it's being shredded.

I pull his hand away from my mouth. "You should have told me the truth when you knew it was her. Tell me why you didn't."

"And ruin your dream? Ruin the way your face lit up whenever you spoke about her? Wreck the one relationship you've been yearning after for the past ten years?"

Hope starts to fade in my chest as he curves my question.

"I had a right to know. That was my story. No one else's."

"It still is. It will always belong to you." He steps back from me in a rush. "You should go."

"What?" I step closer to him, removing the gap he's created. "That's it?"

"Ava," he hisses. "You. Should. Go."

"Or what?" I'm toe-to-toe with him, challenging him. Trying everything to get a reaction from him. To get something.

"You shouldn't be around me right now." His voice has a dangerous edge to it, a darkness that sends an unexpected thrill skating up my spine.

I stare at his mouth. At the way his lips are curled down, a muscle clenched tight in his cheek.

"You think you'll hurt me?" I push, flicking my eyes back up to his heated ones.

"No, but I might ruin you," he grits, his voice rough like sandpaper.

I drop my gaze to his hands. He's coiled his skipping rope around one hand, his fingers turning red with how tight he's pulling on it.

Maybe this is what he needs. A way to break through his barriers so he'll finally be honest with me. He's always communicated better with me when we're being physical. He opens up more when he feels in control. When he's giving me pleasure.

"Do it," I whisper, the same way I did in the alleyway the first time he ever touched me. The first time I made him snap.

"No." He grinds his teeth so hard I'm surprised he doesn't have to spit out dust. Then he curses and strides away.

"You don't get to walk away from this!"

I rush after him, following him into his bedroom. Everything logical tells me to leave, to do as he's asking and let him cool down. But pushing him feels like the most natural thing in the world to me. It's the language we both understand.

I want to tear the truth from him. But as he stops in front of the bed and turns, I see the wild, trapped gleam taking over his eyes, and everything stops.

The sight rips my heart out.

"You're scared? Scared telling the truth is a gamble that you can't control."

Beads of sweat gathered in his chest hair glint in the light as his entire body goes solid. His eyes burn into mine, heating every drop of blood in my body until they feel like they could combust. "You don't know what you're asking for."

He tightens the skipping rope around his palm. My eyes drop to it, and he curses as he sees me looking at it.

"You need to feel in control right now, I get it. You keep telling me you know me better than I know myself. Well, I know you, too," I breathe. "So take control."

"No," he hisses.

"Yes."

"No."

"Yes!"

"Don't be a brat, Ava."

"Don't be an asshole and I won't have to be!"

"Fuck!"

He roars as he closes the gap between us in a flash, another guttural curse leaving his chest as he lifts me and throws me down onto the bed on my back. He crawls up over me, his eyes darker than I've ever seen them as he grabs both of my wrists. My breasts tremble with my shaky breaths as he brings them together above my head.

"You want this?" he spits.

"I want the truth!"

Thick nylon drags against my skin as he binds my wrists together with the skipping rope. Every muscle in his body is tense, rippling with each move he makes.

"You want to be tied up for me, is that it?" He checks the knot, giving it a tug that makes me gasp as my body jerks beneath him. "You want to give up all your control to me? Why?"

"Because you need it."

His eyes blaze into mine. "You're telling me the what. Now tell me the why." He repeats my words back to me in a deep rasp.

"The same reason you lied to me. The same reason you can't say out loud."

His jaw tightens and he yanks the neckline of my top down roughly, rushing to cover my nipple with his hot mouth like he can't do it fast enough. He groans like an animal that's been starved as he sucks hard.

I writhe, my back arching off the bed as he switches to biting the side of my breast hard enough to leave marks.

"Admit it. Tell me why you did it," I plead.

He attacks my other breast in the same way.

"You know why." He shoves one hand up my skirt and grabs my panties, twisting the central scrap of material between my legs inside his palm and tearing them down my thighs in a rush.

I can't do anything with my hands tied. I'm completely at his mercy as he spears me with two fingers, screwing his face up like he's in pain.

"Fuck, you're soaking. You like fighting with me, huh? Is knowing you've fucking ruined me made you this wet?"

He spins me hard before I can answer, dragging me up to my knees, leaving my face pressing into the sheets. I turn to the side, crying out as his palm lands across my ass.

"You like the way I'm a wreck for you, don't you? The way I can't fucking think straight without you?"

There's a whoosh of air as he moves his hand fast and pulls his hard, angry-looking dick out of his pants. I shiver in anticipation, my face heating.

But nothing happens.

I crane to see better. He's staring between my legs, one hand fisting his cock so hard that the glistening ropes of pre-cum on the end fly off, landing across my stinging skin.

"Now you tell me something," he hisses. "Tell me why you're being a brat? Tell me why you're here when you should be living your life."

"I'm here because you lied to me. And I want to know why."

He strikes me again, making me cry out and fall forward. Then he flattens his palm over my burning skin and massages.

"Is that all?"

"Jet," I murmur as I push back against his palm.

The next strike steals my air, making my eyes water. I scrunch the sheets and whimper.

"Or maybe you're really here to finish the job? Make sure I never recover. Never get over you."

"You know that's bullshit. Now tell me," I bite back.

He grabs both of my hips at the same time as he pushes his cock into me. He works me back onto him with a rough curse. "You came here with your cunt dripping for me. Needing me to fill it in the way only I can. You knew I'd never be able to resist you, Ava. I've managed a whole month, letting you live your life. Doing the right thing. And you've turned up and got my cock inside you, putting us both back to square fucking one."

My moans are muffled against the sheets as he pounds into me, wet slapping sounds from our bodies ringing in my ears.

"You want to know why I did it?"

Thrust.

"Yes," I cry out, my core coiling tight as he circles inside me, stretching me wider so he's able to fuck me harder.

"You want the truth? That I've never met anyone like you who tests me every fucking day?"

Thrust.

I whimper as he leans over me, grabbing a fistful of my hair and pulling me up so my back is flush to his chest. He licks up the side of my neck, his voice a rough rasp against my ear.

"You want to know how ever since that day in the kitchen when I saw you drinking out of that carton, that I've not been able to get you off my mind? That I imagined how you'd taste and how you'd feel in my arms? That I imagined what you'd look like with my ring on your finger?"

I gasp as he pistons his hips, creating a delicious angle that hits a spot inside me that only he's ever found.

"That I'd fucking picture how beautiful you'd look when I put a baby inside you?"

I gasp and he buries his face against my neck.

"You want to know why?"

"Yes," I whimper.

He pumps his hips, fucking me hard. My breasts bounce where he's pulled my top down and he grabs them in his hands, tugging on my nipples. My bound hands press into my stomach.

"Because it's you, Ava. It'll only ever be you," he chokes out.

He drives up into me extra hard and then pulls out, throwing me onto my back. He grabs my wrists, pushing them above my head, then thrusts back inside me.

"Only fucking you."

He kisses me for the first time, and I lift up, desperately chasing more. Needing to taste him, to remember the way his kisses always took control of me and left my head spinning. He groans, his hips thrusting into me at a determined pace. I start to shake, and he pauses to look into my eyes.

Wild, glittering blue assaults me, swimming with moisture.

"You, Ava," he rasps.

He thrusts deep and I come hard around him, my body clamping down onto him like it's scared to let go.

"Fuck, the way you look coming on my cock."

His words and deep thrusts pull another orgasm from me, and my vision blurs as I stare up at him.

"Tell me," I choke.

He thrusts harder, his body tensing, sweat dripping off him and onto me.

"Ava," he warns.

"Tell me!" I clench around him, feeling the way his cock swells inside me. "This isn't just fucking, is it?"

"It's never been just anything with you."

"So tell me the truth," I cry as he thrusts deep.

"Goddamn, Ava." He holds my eyes as he starts coming. His chin jerks up and he groans as liquid heat fills me. Every muscle in his body tightens as he thrusts every drop inside me, pushing it deep.

"Jet," I breathe.

He pushes and curses until he's given me everything. I wrap my legs around his waist and grip him tight. Jet stops and holds himself wedged deep inside me, his chest shaking.

"I love you, Ava," he chokes, the tears brimming in his eyes finally spilling free and falling onto my parted lips. "*I fell in fucking love with you.*" He drops his forehead to mine as he whispers, "Game over."

Chapter 38

Jet

"Don't," I soothe. "Don't cry. Fuck, Ava. Please don't cry."

"Why not? You are?" she sobs.

I press my face to hers, screwing up my stinging eyes as I kiss her. She whimpers and kisses me back, tilting her chin up to get closer.

I pull back and rush to undo the rope as quickly as I can. I bring both of her wrists to my mouth and kiss them over and over.

"I'm so sorry," I breathe, cursing myself for the heat in her skin. For the red angry marks I put there.

"You didn't hurt me," she whispers. "What you just said—"

"I love you." I grab her face and kiss her again. "I'm so fucking in love with you that I might lose my mind."

She cradles my face. We stare at each other, only the sound of our heavy breaths between us. She's never been this quiet before. Maybe I did hurt her and she doesn't realize it yet. I was so rough.

Fuck.

I pull out of her, scanning her face for a wince of pain. Relief washes through me when there's nothing except the same stunned gaze on her face.

"Hold my neck," I instruct, scooping her up into my arms.

"What? Why?"

"Do it."

She wraps her arms around me as I carry her into the bathroom. I whip a towel from the rack and place it down onto the counter, before placing her on top of it.

"I've got you," I soothe as I grab a robe and wrap it around her shoulders, then step away to set the bath running. I throw in extra bath oil, then turn back to her.

"What are you doing?" She frowns at the scented steam rising from the tub.

"Taking care of you, Ava. You're mine to—"

She slides off the counter and picks up the bottle of oil I've just used. "This is the same as my perfume." She looks up at me, then her gaze darts across the marble counter and comes to rest on a half empty bottle of the same perfume.

I tuck my fingers under her chin and turn her face back to me. "I needed something," I confess.

Understanding blooms in her eyes, and she blinks, more tears falling. My chest burns at the sight.

"Don't speak. Just let me do this."

I push the robe off her shoulders and lift her, lowering her into the water. She sighs as it rises up over her body like a fragrant tide.

"I'm going to wash you, okay? Tell me if anywhere hurts."

She nods and her eyes follow the soft sponge as I work it slowly from her hands up to her neck. I move around her collarbone and down the other side. The redness on her wrists is already fading.

"Jet? Look at me," she urges.

I take a deep breath and lift my chin. Her eyes study mine like she's seeing them for the first time.

"Tell me," she whispers.

And this time, the words come. Jesus, do they fucking come. One after another, over and over as I look into her eyes and bare my soul. Doing everything I swore I'd never do.

"I did it because I love you... I make difficult decisions all the time. And I always get it right. I make them because I have to, no matter how hard they are... But this one felt like ripping my soul out, Ava. And then I saw you at that show and I knew I'd gotten it so fucking wrong. I wanted to tell you the truth then, even if it meant you'd hate me even more."

She places her hand over mine, the soapy sponge stopping on her chest. "I never hated you. I wanted to. I said I did. But I just hated what you'd done... What you said you'd done." Her expression clouds.

"I wanted you to be happy."

"I was... Until you let me believe you'd betrayed me."

I drop my head, scrubbing my free hand down it.

"Why did you start visiting Gramps?"

"Dad had a case of your things to return. I offered to take it. I wanted to talk to someone who understands."

"Understands what it's like to make sacrifices for me?" She looks at me, sadness swirling in her eyes.

I shake my head. "Understands what it's like to love you so much that it feels like their entire existence makes sense now. Because your happiness means more to them than anything else."

"Jet... You can't put me before yourself, you need to—"

"Why can't I?"

Her eyes widen. "Seriously? Look what it's done to you. Look what it's done to us. Do you know what it was like thinking you hurt me in the worst way you could?"

I swallow down the shame.

"It was horrendous," she whispers.

"I'm so fucking sorry."

She exhales shakily. "And knowing Mum..." She blinks up at the ceiling as she fights to remain composed. "Knowing it was Mum who took it floored me; I'm not going to lie. She said she did it to bring us closer, but I..."

I keep the deep growl locked away in my chest. It isn't for me to tell Ava how to feel about her mother's actions. But I'll be here for her to work through it in whatever way she needs.

"I don't know what the truth is." She brings her eyes back to mine, and they're clear, like she's gained clarity. "But I know that it hurt more thinking you did it. You think I've wrecked you? You've wrecked me, too. This past month, I've felt so... *alone*." Her breath catches in her throat as a pained whimper.

"Jesus." I pull her to me, pushing wet strands of hair away from her face as I kiss her until she's breathless. "I never want you to feel alone," I choke, my lips still over hers, our foreheads pressed together. "And I fucking hate myself for making you feel that way. I would give up everything I have to stop you feeling that way. To make sure you're safe."

Her hands slide down my body as she strokes her fingers through my chest hair. The feel of her fingertips dancing over my thundering heart brings a calmness over me. I hold her chin in place so her eyes hold on mine.

"I love you, Ava. I've never said that to anyone. Never come close to feeling it. I've given everything to the airline, it's been my purpose. Given me control. My life was planned, and I liked it that way."

She parts her lips to speak.

"Listen to me."

She closes her mouth and gazes at me, bright blue capturing my fucking soul.

"I had everything I wanted. Then you showed up, throwing me into the biggest reroute of my life. For the first time, it wasn't about winning. Everything became about you. I could have told you the truth. Kept you to myself. But I cared more about you being happy, even if that meant losing you."

"Jet." Her hands slide up to my face. I turn and kiss her wrist.

"I didn't think you'd suffer like this. I didn't think you'd miss me."

She shakes her head. "You're—"

"An asshole, I know."

"No... You're wrong. I missed you. I missed you so much."

"Ava, I—"

"I love you, too."

Her fingers trace over my brows as they shoot up my face.

"You can't."

"Don't you dare tell me I can't. That you don't deserve it. You don't get to control the way I feel."

"I hurt you."

"Yes, you did. But it's what made me realize how I felt. It wouldn't have hurt so much otherwise. I would have been angry, and shocked. But I wouldn't have felt lost again. I wouldn't have felt alone, like I did after losing..."

I pull her to me for another kiss. It's soft and gentle, weighted with emotion.

"I never meant to hurt you."

"I know," she whispers against my mouth. "Because you never thought I'd feel the same. And that's my fault for not telling you. If you knew how I—"

I silence her with another kiss, practically climbing into the tub with her. Water sloshes over the side as I kiss her over and over.

"It's not your fault. I never want to hear you say that again," I growl.

I lift her into my arms and carry her to the counter. I rest her on the edge, and she immediately wraps her legs around my hips.

"I'm uncontrollably in love with you," I say as she pulls me to her, kissing me and sliding her fingers through my hair.

I kiss her, unable to stop, never wanting to let her go. She widens her thighs and pulls me to her. I shudder as I slide back inside her wet heat.

"Jet," she cries.

We become a tangle of gripping hands, holding each other as close as possible, mouths glued together, shared air, shared confessions, shared declarations of love repeated until the moment she whimpers my name and I choke out hers.

It's not until we're lying in bed together afterward, watching the sun setting through the balcony drapes that I deliver the words that kill me to say.

"You need to go," I whisper.

Ava hums contentedly, snuggling into my side, her face resting on my chest. "Gramps knows where I am. I told him I'd be back in the morning."

"That's not what I mean."

The seriousness in my voice must be palpable because she lifts her head, her brow furrowing as she looks at me. I reach up and dust my thumb over her lower lip.

"When I told you I would steal things from you that were never mine to take, I was telling the truth."

"Jet..." Her smile slides from her face as she stares at me. "I don't understand."

"You trusted me to tie you up earlier. Now trust me with this. Because this time, I know I'm right." I fight to keep my voice even. If I let it break for one second, I'll not be able to go through with it. And I'll ruin my girl forever with my selfishness.

There'll be no coming back from it.

"You need to leave. Travel. See the world. You can't be tethered to me."

"I won't be. You own an airline. We can take trips."

Her eyes search mine and the confusion in them is like a grenade going off in my chest.

"We could. But with the new engines coming, things are going to be nonstop for a while."

"I can wait."

I stroke my thumb up, following the curve of her cheekbone. "I can't hold you back a second longer to do the things you've already waited years for. You know I'm right."

Her eyes turn glassy. "But what about—?"

"I'll be waiting for you." I press a kiss to her forehead.

"Jet..."

"Tell me you understand, Ava."

She throws her arms around my neck and pulls me close.

"I don't," she breathes. "Not for one second..."

"But do you trust me?"

"Don't make me," she sobs. "Don't make me leave."

"Ava," I soothe, kissing her hair as she buries her face into my neck. "Tell me you—"

"I trust you," she whispers through her tears. "I t-trust you."

Her words piece back together my pulverized heart.

"Good girl," I breathe.

I stroke her back as she moves to meet my eyes.

"In the bathroom... that was goodbye sex, wasn't it?"

"No, Firefly." I stroke away her tears.

"It was *don't forget me* sex."

Chapter 39

Ava

Two weeks later

"What have you got in there? A body?" Gramps chuckles at the sight of Liv's overstuffed backpack.

"Bikinis mostly." Liv grins. "We're headed to Bondi Beach as soon as we land."

She throws herself into David's arms, hanging off him like a baby monkey as she kisses him goodbye next.

"You excited, love?" Gramps asks.

"I am," I answer truthfully.

I am excited. And nervous. And nauseous. And a whole host of emotions that I can't put into words. The day we're leaving is finally here.

Jet's 'don't forget me' sex turned into two whole weeks of 'my body has now been re-molded into your shape internally' sex. Magnus went to stay in his city apartment, saying Margaret was on vacation, so he might as well stay there where he can meet up with friends. But I suspect he wanted to give us some time alone before today came.

Jet barely let me come up for air. Only if it was so he could feed me. I'd wake up every morning and he'd be finishing up with work, still sweaty and in his shorts after skipping. I tried to get him to tell me how much sleep he was missing to be able to do everything he needed to before I woke up, but he refused to tell me. Just said that it was worth it. Then he'd take me back to bed all day.

Maybe my body needs this break before he kills me through physical exhaustion.

"I'll call you as soon as we land." I give Gramps another hug as Liv untangles herself from David, giving him a final kiss.

"Don't worry about me. You girls have fun. And look after each other."

"We'll be fine." Liv winks and waves something in the air.

"What's that?"

"Nothing." She grins at me.

"Jet gave you his credit card, didn't he?" I deadpan as we approach airport security.

She hums like she hasn't heard me, throwing me a smirk as we're processed and then allowed through to the departure gates.

"Liv?" I press as we carry our giant backpacks toward our gate number.

"Your boyfriend's a billionaire." She snorts, rolling her eyes.

"A billionaire who kept returning the million dollars he paid me for working with him each time I tried to send it back to his bank account... And adding another million each time!"

"You should have kept sending it back and seen how high you could have gotten him to go." She laughs.

Even now I know that was Jet's idea of 'payment' for me working with him, and not his guilt money, like I first thought, I still can't accept it. I mean, it's millions! He's being completely ridiculous if he thinks I deserve that much.

"We don't need his credit card," I tut.

"He told me you'd said that. That's why he entrusted it to me."

"Unbelievable," I mutter.

"Oh, come on, we'll only use it if we have to. But you'll need to get used to it. That man is going to spoil you whether you like it or not."

We walk up to the boarding gate and hand our passports and tickets over.

"Miss Roberts?" The gate agent smiles as she reads the name in my passport. "The captain's expecting you."

"I thought he might be," I reply drily.

Liv pokes me in the side, and I smile at her. I can't be pissed at Jet for giving her his card when I wouldn't take it. This is Jet, Mr. Must have Control.

"She means, we know," Liv squeals. "And we're excited to be the first to fly with the new fancy-pants engine, aren't we?"

"What?"

The gate attendant smiles. "This is the inaugural flight of our first one hundred percent eco-fuel engine. The plane even got renamed when it went in for the refit."

Jet never said anything about that to me. I snap my head to the window, looking out at the plane parked on stand. The boarding bridge has been connected to it, and the front half of it is visible from the boarding gate.

Each plane in the fleet has its own name displayed on the side beneath the cockpit windows. I search for it, then my heart stalls.

There it is, in scripted text. All shiny and new.

Firefly.

"You've got to be kidding me," I gasp.

I slide my eyes up to the left-hand window, zeroing in on the four gold stripes on his epaulets.

He's looking straight at me, expecting me.

Asshole. I shake my head with a grin.

I swear his lips twitch. He rises from his seat and disappears. A few moments later he strides up the boarding bridge looking like a walking wet dream in his pilot's uniform that fits snugly to his toned torso.

"Ava," he breathes.

"Jet."

The scent of him, warm and masculine, and everything that makes my core heat, flows over me as he looks at me with a piercing blue gaze. It doesn't matter that I was pinned beneath him only hours ago. The way he looks at me makes me want to strip my clothes off and beg him to take me again, right here on the floor.

His eyes darken, one brow arching like he can read my thoughts.

"You called the plane Firefly."

"You said you wanted your own jet." He shrugs one broad shoulder, a tiny curve gracing the corner of his mouth.

"You know this isn't what I meant." I fail to hide my smile.

Liv giggles behind us. "So flipping romantic. I'm swooning."

I turn to give her a friendly glare, but she just grins back without shame.

Warm fingers hook around my jaw, bringing my eyes back to his.

"You ready to board?"

I let out a small exhale, my body zinging with anticipation.

"Yes."

"Good girl," he rasps, his eyes glittering.

He takes my bag from my shoulder. Then he holds out his hand for me to take.

"Time to fly, Firefly."

Chapter 40

Jet

I LAND BACK FROM Australia, exhausted. The crew spent two days there on a layover. Two more days of saying goodbye to my girl. Two more days of devouring her body, desperately trying to make her taste last as long as possible in my memory.

I left her and Liv excited and buzzing for their adventure. Liv's already started a travel blog for the two of them and called it, "Sugar Adventures." She thought the sugar baby reference was hilarious. I told her I'm not thirty-four yet and that's hardly old enough to be a sugar daddy. But Ava smirked as I said it, which she paid for later with my palm against her ass.

It's going to feel like forever. I scrub a hand around my jaw as I wait for the automatic gates to open. Then I drive straight through, up to the house.

My phone rings as I'm parking. "Are you okay? Do you need money?" I ask the second the call connects.

"We're fine. Liv and I are at the beach."

"Have you eaten?"

She laughs, and my hand twitches because I know she's rolling her eyes at me.

"Yes, I finished a burger twenty-one minutes and fourteen seconds ago."

"Ava," I growl.

Her voice softens. "Relax. We're okay... And I love you... And I miss you already."

Every shred of tension in my body dissolves and I sink into my seat.

"And... I got you a gift so you don't forget me," she adds.

"You know that's impossible," I grumble.

"Just go inside and find it."

"Is it your panties?" I groan. "Fuck if it is, I hope you made yourself come wearing them first. I could happily spend the rest of the day in bed with those keeping me company."

"It's not panties," she hums.

"Damn."

"But I think you'll like it just as much."

I exit the car and open the front door hastily. "I don't think there's anything you could get me that I'd like more than your—"

My breath leaves my body in a whoosh.

"Surprise?" Her voice has turned wary. "Do you like it? Please say something."

"I..." I stand rooted to the spot as I take in the brilliant blue wing walker in my hallway.

"You said as long as it wasn't a bus?" she whispers.

"Goddamn, Ava," I rasp, walking over to it and running my hand along the smooth wingtip.

"It was always meant to stay in your family. I figured you'd like it back, but—"

"I love you. I love you so damn much."

She sighs. "Thank god. For a minute, I thought I'd screwed up."

"Never." I walk around the plane, inspecting it. It looks even better than last time I saw it. Brighter, more alive. "Thank you," I say, still processing the fact that the thing my mother loved so much is here in my house. Not gone anymore. Back where it belongs.

"How did you get it back?"

"I told Ophelia I was going to pull the movie. But that I'd agree to sign all rights and royalties over to her if she persuaded James."

"You did what?"

"She said I didn't need to surrender my royalties, that she'd persuade him. All she wanted was for the movie to go ahead. She thinks it's a story that has to be told. But I wanted Callaghan to think they were getting something in return. You know what he's like."

I grunt. "Unfortunately, I do. But that's your story. Your royalties. Why would you do that?"

"Because I don't need it anymore," she replies easily, a lightness in her voice I've never heard before now. "I needed to write it, to share it. And I've done that. The movie, it's... Maybe Mum needs it. But I don't."

"Jesus." I rub a hand over my jaw as I sink to the floor and rest against the wall, my eyes fixed on the plane in front of me. "You amaze me."

"I know," she teases.

We fall into a comfortable silence.

"Tell me when you're ready to come home to me," I whisper.

I hear the way she sucks in a small breath and picture the way her plump lower lip will be lifting into the smile that's evident in her voice.

"I could come home to you right now."

I screw my eyes shut, pressing my thumb and finger into them. "You know I'd come and get you if you asked."

"I know you would. But I trust you when you say I need to do this." Her voice is soft, and hearing her faith in me again makes my heart swell to twice its size, forcing a lump to my throat.

"You *do* need to do this. As much as I'm already missing you, you have to do this."

I listen to her breathe, just happy to be connected to her, to know she's miles away, and I'm the one she's thinking of. Just like I'm always thinking of her.

"I'll call you the second I can come back to you," she says, her breath catching in a small sob.

"Good girl." I gaze at my mother's plane.

"I'll be waiting."

Chapter 41

Jet

Six months later

"Your phone's ringing, Son," Dad shouts.

I hit the controls on the shower, not bothering to check if I've washed all the shampoo out. I grab a towel from the rack and sling it around my waist as I stalk out of the bathroom, through my dressing area, and over to the bedside table where I left my cell charging.

"You could call them back if you miss it," Dad says from my bedroom doorway.

"It's Ava's ringtone," I bark.

I look up into his eyes as I hit answer. They're twinkling in amusement. He knows it's Ava calling. He also knows I've paused meetings, held up traffic, and generally inconvenienced everyone around me without giving a shit, all so I never miss a single call of hers.

He winks and walks away.

"Hi." Bright blue eyes fill the screen, the light behind her haloing her hair like a ring of rose gold around her. She's got a wide grin.

"You're beautiful."

She laughs, her eyes raking over me. "And you're naked and wet."

"You could join me?" I arch a brow as I whip the towel from my waist and use it to rub my chest dry. I drop it onto the bed when I've finished.

She lowers her voice. "No phone sex right now. This is a serious call."

"We can have serious sex," I growl.

She snorts. The light is back in her eyes. We've spoken every day since she left, and each time she's glowed brighter and brighter.

I'm so fucking proud of her.

"I was just calling to tell you something."

My heart flies into my throat, but she continues speaking, not saying the words I've been longing to hear come from her lips for months. *I'm ready to come home.*

"I left you something."

I drop onto the edge of the bed. "Here?"

She nods. "Yeah, at Rochwell. I knew you'd be there this weekend for your dad's birthday. Did he have a good time?"

"You know he did. You and Liv called and sang to him from that river boat you were on. Now, where is it?"

She laughs as I huff impatiently. "Go look under the step."

I throw my workout shorts on, then stride from my room, making the journey to the old rear staircase as quickly as I can.

"You put this here before you left?" I ask as I jog down them and sit in my usual spot.

"I did," she hums.

I curl my hand around the edge of the step below and yank it loose. The space beneath should be empty now that the toy plane is gone.

"I thought you'd appreciate it." She bites her lower lip.

"Fuck, it's your panties, isn't it?"

"Just look inside."

I lift the step. There's a small box inside. I reach in and take it out, then prop my phone up so Ava can see me. I glance at her. The only person who has ever left me gifts, who ever knew about this hiding place before I showed it to Ava, was my mother.

"Open it," she coaxes in a gentle voice, understanding flashing in her eyes.

I ease the lid off.

The tiny replica plane is inside. Fixed back together.

"Ava," I rasp, my chest pulling tight.

"It needed fixing."

I turn the plane between my fingers, overcome with nostalgia from the day I found it as a boy.

"Thank you," I murmur.

"There's more in there," she says. I place the toy plane onto the step beside me and remove a layer of tissue paper.

The groan of appreciation in my chest is rich and full bodied as I lift out a glass filled with silk.

My dick twitches as I stare at the pink and gold encased inside. *Waterlilies.*

"Ava, have your lucky panties been underneath my father's staircase since you left?" I growl.

She giggles as I hook the delicate fabric out with one finger; another deep rumble of approval vibrating my chest as a faint leftover scent of her perfume and arousal on the fabric reaches me.

"We're using this glass the minute you come home," I groan, lowering the panties back into it.

Her cheeks flush pink. "If you say so."

"I say so."

"There's one more thing," she breathes.

I peel back another layer of tissue paper at her instruction.

I grip the piece of card between my fingers. "Ava, why do I have an IOU for three million dollars?" I snap.

"I've not spent any of what you paid me." She pouts. "You're taking it back, even if I have to shove it down your throat."

"Don't be a—"

"Why? I thought you liked it."

Her eyes are twinkling as I curse and shake my head, my palm throbbing with the need to assert control over her for her brattiness. Daily calls and phone sex have done little to take the edge off. She's asked me so many times to fly over and see her. But we both know that she needed to do this alone.

Because once she comes home, I'm never letting her out of my sight again.

"Turn it over." She smiles.

I twist the card and look at the words on the back.

Everything stops as I let out a sound between a growl and a groan.

I'm ready to recommence my brat duties. Bring me home, Jet. I love you, Ava x

Fuck yes.

Chapter 42

Ava

Twenty-four hours later

WE'RE IN THE ARRIVALS hall at the airport when his private plane lands. Liv's told me the way I'm dancing around on my tiptoes looking for him makes me look like I have a bladder infection. But she's doing the exact same thing as she looks for David.

"Do you think he'll have missed me as much as I've missed him?" Liv gnaws her bottom lip, unusually nervous for her.

"You really like him." I laugh, glancing at her.

She breaks into a smile. "Okay, I do. But don't tell him. I want to maintain some element of playing hard to get so he doesn't get lazy."

"I don't think you'll ever let him get slack."

She tilts her head, her lips twisting into a coy smile. "True."

I start to laugh again but then my breath hitches as I spot a dark head of hair exiting from a private doorway nearby.

"They're here!" I squeak.

He moves so fluidly, taller than anyone else around him. Power, control, and brilliance ooze from every pore as he wears his navy-blue suit pants and white shirt unbuttoned at the neck.

My gaze rakes over the parts of him I can see before the crowd parts, giving him a clear pathway to me.

They know. The whole world knows.

One look at Jet Grant and it's obvious he's someone special.

It feels like every cell in my body freezes, and I'm rooted to the spot as my eyes meet his. Nothing could have prepared me for the way my heart feels like it's about to explode. Daily video calls are nothing compared to the real thing.

Clear blue pierces me, like a shot of oxygen when your brain is just about to close down.

He's here.

Liv curses gently under her breath as she sees David. But all I can focus on is the man walking toward me with purpose, closing the distance that six months of traveling through fourteen countries has created.

I break into a run, no longer controlling my body consciously. Every second of the time we've been apart is carrying me. Powering me to end that distance once and for all.

"Jet!"

The tears streaming down my face and blurring my vision are happy ones as I launch myself into the air. He drops the bag he's carrying and catches me underneath the ass, immediately pulling my body against his tight enough to make me dizzy.

But I don't care.

Nothing matters except that he's here.

"Goddamn, Ava." His words send a shiver running through my body as he buries his face into my neck, inhaling with a pantie-melting groan. "Fuck, you smell amazing."

I grab his face between my hands and our eyes meet. His are shining with a new brightness in them I haven't seen before.

But god does it suit him.

We continue staring at each other, drinking the other in. My heart pounds as his breath fans over my lips.

So much emotion. So much time.

But it's what I needed. He knew it. And I trusted him. I trust him with my life. After everything, it's the thing I'm most sure of.

Jet Grant. The serious, ruthless grump... with a heart of pure gold hidden beneath that solid chest.

"Ava," he breathes, leaning close.

"What's this?" I bite my lower lip as I trace my fingers over his sinful lips, halting his advance.

They're soft, a hint of five o'clock shadow above them.

"A man about to lose it if you don't fucking kiss him."

I laugh at his deep groan. But I hold back, despite being so desperate to kiss him I might lose my mind.

I just want to look at him a little longer. I want to remember this moment forever.

"I mean this." I press the lightest of touches to the corner of his mouth.

The place where his lips curl up a tiny fraction.

I dust my lips over the spot in a whisper of a kiss, and he groans in response as he squeezes two handfuls of my ass, pulling me closer.

"What's it look like?" he rasps.

I look into dazzling blue.

"It looks like a smile. A Jet Grant version," I whisper.

His dark brows hitch. "Then that's what it is."

"Then that's what it is," I repeat in a hushed voice.

"Ava," he growls.

"Jet," I murmur."

"Just fucking kiss me."

I surge forward, smashing my mouth against his. The second our skin connects, Jet takes control, kissing me, devouring me, breathing life back into my body in a way I haven't felt in six long months.

"I love you," I gasp into his mouth.

He slides my body down his so he can angle my head back. His kisses grow slower, but they deepen as he takes his time reacquainting himself with my lips, my taste. I can feel the energy flowing through his every breath as it falls against my lips in the small moments that he pulls back to look at me like he's checking that I'm real, before he dives back in and kisses me again.

His thumbs swipe up the happy tears that are still falling, then he rests his forehead against mine.

"You're never leaving me again."

"I never want to."

The hint of a curl is back on his lips.

"I love you, Firefly."

"It's beautiful. But watch out for sharks," I say.

Liv's lips curl into a smirk as David looks at Jet for reassurance. Jet shrugs, and I bite back my laugh at David's audible gulp.

We say goodbye as the two of them head out for the evening. Jet whisked us away from the airport in a private car and brought us back to the resort in Krabi where we came together all those months ago. He booked us side by side villas, and we've only just checked in. Our suitcases are sitting inside the doorway, untouched.

Liv insisted to David that they go to the bioluminescent beach tonight. She didn't want to wait any longer to see it.

"I'm happy we came back here. It seems kind of fitting to reunite in the spot where I first saw the man beneath the suit," I say, running my fingers along the edge of the kitchen counter in the exact same villa we stayed in when we were following Callaghan around.

The one that changed the way I saw Jet.

I open the built-in refrigerator and grin as I pull out a bottle of grapefruit juice.

"Where have my shareholder deliveries been going?" I ask as I turn.

Jet wraps his arms around my waist and pulls me close.

"I rerouted the delivery from your mum's place to mine."

"Have you been drinking it?"

An amused huff of air escapes from his lips. "Can't stand the stuff."

"Unless it comes with berry flavor, huh?" I press a light kiss to his mouth.

"Ava," he growls.

"Jet," I tease.

His eyes darken and take on a heat like he's about to devour me whole.

"Put the bottle down."

I place it on the counter behind me with a clunk, my eyes glued to his.

"Done," I breathe.

"Now," he rasps, pulling me against him so his erection presses into my stomach. "We need to talk."

I swallow at the gravel in his voice. And at the delicious ache in my core as his dick strains between us, giving off enough heat to power this whole luxury resort we're in. It's been months since I saw it, touched it, tasted it... felt it inside me.

"Let's talk after." I lift up on my toes to kiss him. He doesn't reciprocate as my lips meet his soft, warm ones. Instead, he arches a dark brow, his voice taking on an authority that has slickness pooling between my legs.

"A plane in my hallway?"

"Uh-huh." I bite my lower lip, looking up at him through my lashes.

"A glass beneath the step?"

My lips curl into a flirty smile. "You're welcome."

"These?" he rasps, producing a scrap of pink and gold silk from his pocket and holding it up.

"Oh, yeah. Thought you'd appreciate those."

He groans, and the sound sends goosebumps scattering up my spine in the most addictive way. I'll never tire of hearing him groan, growl, moan, curse... do anything for me that tells me I'm testing his control.

He scrunches my panties in his fist and brings them to his nose. "You made yourself come wearing them, I could smell you on them." He inhales deeply, his eyes fixed on mine. "It's faded now."

"That's what happens when you jerk off with them too much."

"Hmm." He smirks, pocketing them again. "Still leaves one question, though..." He pushes a strand of my hair away from my face, letting his thumb linger over my cheekbone. I lean into him with a lust-filled sigh.

"What question?"

His eyes flash with something dark. We both know it's only a matter of minutes before we'll both be naked and he'll be inside me, fucking me deep, the way only he ever has. It's been six long months since the last time, and the fact we've held back this long surprises me.

But Jet likes playing games, so I should indulge him a little if that's what he wants.

"How a brat like you should be punished for being such a fucking tease."

A thrill shoots through me as he grabs my hand and places it over the front of his suit pants, curling my fingers beneath his own until we're gripping his throbbing erection tightly.

Fuck, I think it's grown in six months.

I gasp when he flexes it beneath my palm.

"Is that sweet pussy dripping for me?" he rasps, pushing my hand harder against him.

"Yes," I moan. "Fuck me, Jet. Please."

"Needy girl," he tsks.

Then he hoists me over his shoulder, spanking me, as he strides to the bedroom and drops me onto the cool white sheets.

He stands between my legs at the side of the bed and unbuttons his shirt. The sight of the short, dark hair dusting his solid pecs has my clit pulsing, aching for friction.

"Faster," I beg.

He arches a brow as he undoes his belt and then drags down his zipper.

"You aren't the one controlling how this goes, Ava."

Fuck.

The blood in my veins heats to the point of spontaneous combustion. I'm practically salivating as he pushes his clothes down over his hips and frees his thick cock.

There's a hint of a smirk on his face as he catches my reaction.

"You missed this cock?" he asks, pumping it slowly. Pre-cum drips off the end, landing on my cotton sundress. His eyes fall to the fabric, and he skates a thumb over the drops, pushing the moisture through the thin fabric so I feel it against my burning skin underneath.

"God, yes."

"Then take your dress off before I rip it off."

I know he will, so I pull each strap off my shoulder before easing it down over my breasts, past my waist, and down my legs, revealing my lack of bra and panties.

"Ava," Jet scolds. "You came to the airport without panties?"

I bit my lip innocently. "I was too hot wearing them."

He glowers, watching every move with a precision gaze, like a hunter. The hunger in his eyes makes me more and more turned on as I imagine that first thrust inside me, and how good it's going to feel as he stretches me to take him again.

"Uh-uh." He grasps my chin and tilts my head up. "Bad girls don't get fucked when they want it. They have to wait."

I pout and he shakes his head with a curse like he's so close to giving in and fucking me hard. I wriggle, trying to press my thighs together. Jet reaches down, clamping each thigh and pinning them apart on the mattress.

"No one gives your clit attention, except me, understood?"

I nod, my breath quickening as I wait to see what he's going to do, because surely, he has to fuck me now. He can't make us wait any longer. This is torture.

He holds my eyes until he's happy I'm going to obey. Then he slides them down over my body, assessing every inch, like he needs to make sure I've been taking care of what's his while we've been apart.

His hands bracket my ribs and slide upward, pushing my breasts together. A satisfied grunt leaves his lips as he leans down and sucks one nipple. "I can't wait to watch these pretty tits bounce when you ride my cock later." He sucks the other one, ignoring the fact that I'm squirming beneath him, panting with desire.

He's going to take his time despite how badly I need him to just let loose and fuck me.

Bastard.

"What have we here?" He smooths his thumb over the short hair that's grown. He dusts over my clit, and

I jerk with a whimper. Amusement glints in his eyes. "I like it... It'll look good coated in cum."

"Please." I shudder as he curls his hand, cupping my pussy and dipping the tip of one finger inside me a tiny fraction.

"Soaking," he tuts like he's disappointed with me, but his grip tightens on his cock as he pumps it harder. "A fucking IOU," he grunts as he pushes two fingers inside me without warning.

"Yes!" I arch off the bed, pleasure firing through my body at having him touch me again. His fingers feel better than I remember, thicker, longer.

"You left me an IOU. And just for that, you'll find another ten million in your account."

"What?"

His brows flatten like he's daring me to argue with him. "I look after what's mine, Ava. And you're going to let me, aren't you?"

His entire forearm moves back and forth, the veins popping beneath his skin as he finger-fucks me arrogantly, knowing a single stroke at the correct angle will have me combusting in seconds.

"Jet," I cry, my body hugging him tight with needy wet sounds.

"Tell me," he asks with a sinister calmness.

"Tell you what?" My eyes roll in my head as I struggle to concentrate.

"Tell me you're never going to stop me from spoiling you ever again. If I want to buy you lingerie covered in diamonds and fuck you in it, if I want to buy a new yacht just to watch you sunbathe naked on the deck, if I want to name a whole fucking plane after you so I can fly it and feel like you're sitting beside me, then you're going to let me, aren't you?"

"Yes," I cry, delirious with the need to come.

He keeps his movements going, watching me intently, but makes sure never to hit that exact spot. Not in the way he knows will make me crumble.

I pant and stare into his eyes. "I promise," I moan. "Please, Jet. I fucking promise."

All he does is tilt his chin up, evidence that my reply was satisfactory. Then he slides his fingers out and pushes them down my throat.

"Suck."

I do as he says, watching the way his eyes narrow as my cheeks hollow out around his fingers. I expected him to have less restraint. I thought I'd have his cum running down my thighs by now. But the fact he's dragging it out, only makes it hotter. He wants to be inside me as much as I need to feel him there. I can see it in the dark heat of his eyes, in the tenseness of his rigid muscles and his sharp jaw.

But he's in control.

Even the need to fuck his girlfriend he hasn't seen in six months isn't enough to make him snap. He's getting off on this. He's in his element. Exercising complete self-control.

But he never said I can't push him.

"I touched myself in the airport bathroom before you landed. I was just so hot, knowing you were close,"

I confess, a frisson of energy twirling in my gut as his nostrils flare.

"You made yourself come in public when I wasn't there?" he grits, his features set in a mock look of disappointment.

"Yeah. Shall I show you how?" I slide my hand between my legs, but he knocks it away with a growl.

"Never touch yourself unless you're videoing it for me. Better still, phone me and show me exactly how hard you can make yourself come." He sucks in air past his teeth with a hiss. "Then I know you'll be warmed up for me. Because I'll be there in a fucking shot, Ava, filling this perfect damn pussy until you beg me to stop."

"Do it," I murmur.

He lifts me like I weigh nothing, positioning me so that I'm straddling him.

"Fuck," he groans, his hands gripping my hips hard where they're spread around his waist.

I take my opportunity, arching my back and moving down so I can grind onto his cock, my wetness coating it as I whimper at how good it feels rubbing my swollen clit.

"You want this cock?" He lifts his shoulders off the bed so he can look at me shamelessly trying to get myself off using him.

"Yes," I answer in a rush, reaching for the base of him and positioning myself over him.

His hands tighten on my hips, holding me in place. I huff in frustration as I struggle to push down and get him inside me. It's no use; he's too strong.

"First, you need to take your punishment."

He digs his fingers into my flesh, jerking me forward. I cry out as he tuts.

"So fucking greedy."

I know what's coming. And I've craved having his mark on me again.

"Make my ass red. Leave your handprint on it."

I swear the bastard almost chuckles before he pins me with a burning gaze.

"No."

One single word and I'm staring back at him in confusion.

"Spank me," I whisper.

He holds my eyes.

"Bite me," I breathe.

His jaw hardens.

"Please?"

His nostrils flare and then he curses, grabbing handfuls of my ass as he pushes his cock into the groove between my ass cheeks.

"Fuck. You begging me for it makes me want to blow all over your sweet little asshole."

I gasp as he flexes his cock.

"And I will... later. When you take my cock there." He swipes his tongue over his teeth with a rough breath. "Your pretty ass will be full of my cock tomorrow."

I whimper needily at the promise of something new we haven't done together yet and his dark eyes glint in approval.

"But first. Brats have to sit on the naughty step," he growls.

"The what?"

He lifts me, bringing me down roughly against his mouth. I'm thrown forward with a deep moan as he grips my hips and pulls me down hard.

"Hold the fucking headboard, Ava."

It's the only warning I get before he lunges. I grip the headboard tightly as he eats me out like a man starved. Every month, day, hour... fraction of a second that he's missed me is communicated in the merciless way he sucks, kisses, licks and curses me into a fast, deep orgasm.

"Jet!" I keep one hand on the headboard for support, the other dropping to his hair and grabbing a handful of it. I yank, feeling his hissed curse against my skin. But the pain only spurs him on, and he dives into me again, working me up into another soul-shattering orgasm on his face.

"Too much."

But he doesn't ease off. My wetness drips over his chin, coats his cheeks, and slides down my inner thighs. I feel every hot drop as he curses and growls, holding my hips tighter as he pulls me down even harder.

"Come for me," he demands.

"I have," I choke, spots dancing in my vision.

My ass stings as he slaps it hard.

"Six fucking months. You can give me more than two."

"It's too much." I shake above him, every inch of my skin tingling.

"Six months, six orgasms, Ava."

I screw my eyes closed as he sucks my clit, sending me spiraling into another.

Fuck.

"Good girl." His voice is rough with deep praise as I surrender all control of my body and hand it over to him.

I whimper as he lifts me, flicking his tongue over my ass.

"Mine," he groans, sliding his tongue around it in teasing spirals. "All fucking mine."

I'm a whimpering, sweaty mess by the time he pulls my fifth orgasm from me. My mascara is probably smeared, and I bet my hair is wild.

I must look like a hot wreck.

But all the exertion has made Jet look better. His face is glowing, his eyes glittering with the vigor of a man who's been training for physical exertion like this his entire life. Maybe this is why he admitted to me he'd started doubling his skipping time in the mornings since I left.

He was training to ruin me with sex.

"Wow," I breathe as he kneels between my thighs. They fall open automatically, allowing him access even though I feel like my soul has left my body.

"Did you count?" He arches a brow as he circles the head of his cock against me.

"Five," I gasp as he slides the first inch inside me.

"Five," he repeats.

Then he thrusts inside, giving me the rest, knocking what little air I've managed to gasp back from my lungs once again. My eyes roll in my head and we groan as his body meets mine with a solid slap.

"Eyes," he grunts.

I blink, staring up into the vibrant blue.

"Tell me you love me," he whispers. And the heat of vulnerability tinging his voice has me pulling his lips to mine in a desperate kiss.

"I love you," I gasp as he starts to rock his hips, fucking me in slow, deep strokes.

He runs his nose along my jaw and up the side of my face.

"Tell me you'll always need me," he utters in my ear.

"Always." I pull him closer, lifting my hips to meet each controlled thrust.

"Tell me you're mine and no one else's."

"I've only ever been yours."

I press a kiss to his temple as he buries his face into my neck.

"I love you, too," he rasps, kissing my neck. "I love you so goddamn much."

He takes a deep breath, his chest expanding. Then he pulls back and his eyes blaze into mine as he picks up his pace and does what we've both needed for the past six months.

He fucks me hard.

The bed bangs against the wall, the sound is so loud, but it's nothing compared to my moans of his name, and his curses of mine.

It's the filthiest thing I've ever heard, and it only makes me wetter, allowing him to drive harder, deeper, faster.

I cling to him, my nails biting into the flesh of his muscular buttocks as they flex and ripple, pistoning his cock into me at an angle that has me shaking with need from each pump.

"Jet, oh fuck, yes."

"Tell me you love me again," he grits.

"I love you."

He fucks me the way he did that first time at Rochwell; holding my eyes as his body drives into mine with punishing hits. His eyes were dark with lust then, glittering with danger. Now they're softer, still intense enough to burn me, but different somehow. They're like they were in Thailand when he opened up to me. When he told me I was safe and wasn't alone. The night I started really falling for him.

But there's something else, too.

They're shining. Shining with carefully controlled emotion. Shining with a future full of promises.

Shining with love.

"Fuck, Ava." He jerks his chin, driving deeper and making me moan louder than should be physically possible. "I need you to come."

Maybe it's the angle, or the way he's looking at me. Or maybe it's because sometimes I like him telling me what to do, even though I'll never admit it.

But I do as he says.

I come hard.

I come so hard that wetness squirts from me, flooding his cock.

"Jesus. Milk me, fucking milk me." His eyes pinch as my body squeezes his cock with each wave of my orgasm. It tears through me, clamping down on him with force.

"Goddamn." He hisses, then holds my throat, pinning me in place beneath him as his eyes blaze into mine. "I'm going to come, Ava."

His jaw slackens and his eyelids hood. He keeps watching me. Watching me take the liquid fire that he's filling me with.

"Wider," he grunts.

I stretch my legs, letting his hips get closer, letting him push even deeper.

I moan as his cock swells inside me with each new wave of his release.

"Goddamn, Firefly." He lets out a low husky groan, his eyes dropping to where our bodies meet. "I've so much cum for you," he rasps.

I feel it. I feel it filling me, heating me inside. And I feel it running out down the sides of him as he pulls back and then slams back inside. It's coating my inner thighs, drenching them. Covering me, branding me, owning me inside and out.

Jet groans, thrusting his hips a few more times to empty out the final drops, then he stills inside me.

"Jesus," he rasps.

I pull him to me, kissing him over and over, wrapping my arms around his neck and gluing our bodies together so we're one sticky, slick, sweaty mass.

"I love you," I breathe.

He grips my chin, kissing me again. "Good."

His dark hair falls into his eyes, so I sweep it back.

"Stay there," he says before pressing a kiss to my lips.

"What? Where are you going?"

"Stay," he barks, leaving the room.

I don't think I can even sit, let alone get my legs to work. I lie stunned. I can't believe he's just walked off. No cuddles after reuniting. No being held in his arms, resting my head on his chest and listening to his deep, steady heartbeat. The one I find so soothing.

I fly to my feet, ignoring the shake in my legs as I wobble over to the bedroom door.

"I swear you better not be checking your phone for work calls."

He flies through the bedroom door, scooping me up underneath my knees.

"You think I'd do that?" His dark eyes burn into mine ruthlessly as he carries me back over to the bed and places me down onto it. "I told you to stay. Why don't you ever listen?"

"Get a dog if you want to train someone," I huff. "Tell me what you were doing?" I gaze up at him as he dusts the back of his knuckles over my cheek.

"Just getting this."

He lifts his other hand. It's curled around the base of a glass.

My breath hitches and I snap my eyes back to his.

"You know what to do," he rasps.

I bite my lower lip and part my thighs so he can place the cool glass against my skin. His pupils dilate as his gaze drops between my legs. I can feel him dripping out of me.

"Ava." He licks his lips, but his hand holding the glass never moves.

"Jet?"

His eyes are glued to my pussy. Slowly, he runs the fingers of his free hand up my inner thigh, collecting up our mixed cum. He brings it to the soft patch of hair I have and then coats it. "Knew it would look good," he growls.

I drop my eyes back to the glass, and he tilts it toward me. It's not empty. His fingers were covering the sides so I couldn't see before. But now the small piece of white paper inside is visible.

"Take it out."

I pull it out and unfold it.

"I don't understand."

I stare at his handwriting. *"IOU everything?"*

He moves the glass closer, tipping it toward me. The deep clink inside it makes me dip my eyes back past the rim.

"Take it out," he says again, his eyes taking on an even deeper intensity.

My breath stalls as I reach in and curl my fingers around the object. I lift it out and he eases it from my shaking fingers.

"I owe you everything, Ava," he breathes. "A life of adventures, arms to keep you safe, a heart that beats for you, so you'll never be alone. I'm a man who's so fucking wrecked because of you that an existence without you would be pointless. These six months apart have been hell."

He places the ring against the tip of my finger on my left hand.

"Marry me."

I'm too shocked to speak.

"You're so close to saying yes. I can see it in your eyes."

His words float over to me, seeping through my skin and settling inside the hole that I've carried inside my chest for over ten years.

So close.

"I found you, Ava." His blue eyes search mine. "And you found me."

I gulp back a sob, but another replaces it immediately, bubbling from my lips. Jet's hold on my left hand is gentle, the ring still poised in place.

"Say it," he breathes.

I nod.

"Say it," he repeats, waiting patiently, like he'd wait forever for me if I needed him to.

But I don't need forever.

I just need my own Jet.

"Yes."

The breath leaves his lungs, his chest softening as he slides the ring onto my finger.

I stare at the giant yellow diamond as he pulls my forehead to his.

"I love you," he breathes.

A smile finally breaks onto my face.

"I love you, too."

His eyes follow mine to the huge rock that's weighing my finger down.

"Looks good on you."

I bite my lip. It does. And it feels good.

"I know where I want to get married," I blurt. "I know exactly where."

Jet clears his throat, his posture stiffening.

"What?"

He's silent.

"Jet?" I gasp, studying the deep line between his brows. "You've booked it already, haven't you?"

He rolls his lips, a muscle in his jaw tensing. "I always win, Ava," he rasps, looking into my eyes.

"Oh my god! What if I'd said no?"

His eyes heat. "I'd have kept asking."

"You're insane." I scoff. But I can't help the grin on my face growing wider as I recall the words he once said to me. "You're fucking obsessed," I repeat them, expecting him to agree.

"No." His voice is more serious than I've ever heard it. "I'm just in love with you."

My heart dances. I don't think I'll ever tire of hearing those words.

"Where is it?" I ask, scanning his face for a clue.

"You'll see." He pulls me into his arms, wrapping my legs either side of him.

"I'll see?"

The subtle curl of his lips is back. "You'll see," he repeats.

"That's all I'm getting?"

He lifts me, pulling me back down onto his hard cock with a deep groan, his fingers digging into my hips. "Fuck, you're so beautiful."

"Jet," I argue, even though the pleasure he's sending through my body is threatening to take over my senses. "I want to know."

He ignores me as he starts moving my body how he wants it, working me up and down his cock.

"This conversation isn't over," I gasp as the head of him rubs the special spot deep inside me.

He groans, looking at where he's disappearing inside me.

"If I don't like it, we're changing it."

He lies back onto the bed, looking up at me with heated desire burning in his eyes. "You'll like it."

"So damn sure of yourself," I mutter as his fingers flex on my hips and he picks up the pace, pulling me down onto him harder.

"You trust me, don't you?" he grits, thrusting his hips up, urging me to work with him.

I bite my lower lip, my eyes dropping to my hand, spread out over his chest as I sink down onto him with more force. He grunts as I curl my fingers into his dark chest hair, the yellow diamond like a bright burning light shining out between the strands.

"Yeah, I trust you," I breathe, squeezing him until he lets out a rasped curse.

"Fuck... Good girl."

"You're still going to tell me." I squeeze him again and the tendons in his neck flex as he lets out a deep groan.

"We'll see."

"Yeah, we'll see," I say, squeezing him again.

He looks up at me, his dark brows pulling low as I smirk.

"Shut up and ride my cock, Fiancée."

Chapter 43

Ava

I STARE AT THE giant yellow diamond, spinning the ring side to side, letting it catch the light.

"You like it?"

I glance at Jet sitting beside me in Atlantic Airways' airport lounge as we wait for our flight to LA.

"You know I love it," I answer.

He tips his chin with a small grunt, which is his way of saying he'll get me another one if I want him to. He'll get me anything I want. Even a unicorn.

I look back at the jewel. But nothing could be as perfect as this, knowing that he picked it himself, that he pictured me wearing it as he chose it. I don't care that it's a special commission made by some bigshot jewelry firm based in New York who make crowns and things for royal families. I wouldn't even have known if Mum hadn't gushed about how perfect Beaufort Diamonds are when I video called her to share our news.

To me, it's a symbol of our future. A new adventure.

"It's perfect," I hum. Jet watches me over the rim of his glass as I admire it again. "You did good."

"I did good?" He arches a brow.

"You did... Good boy," I coo like I'm praising a puppy.

His eyes heat and his fingers twitch around his glass. "Ava," he rumbles.

I smirk at his warning tone. Then he shakes his head.

"Brat," he murmurs, having another drink.

"Your life would be boring without me," I tease.

"My life wouldn't be a life without you," he says easily, placing his glass down and checking his watch. "Almost time to board," he adds, like his words didn't just open a whole box full of butterflies in my stomach.

"Almost time," I repeat, twirling my ring again.

We stayed at Rochwell for a couple of weeks after Thailand, spending time with Magnus and Margaret. Liv stayed for the first week, then had to go back home for a job interview she managed to snag for some big media company. David drove her to it. She was so excited when they offered her the job the day after. It's based in London. I knew moving to LA with Jet would mean leaving her and Gramps behind. It still makes my stomach knot knowing I'll be so far away. But Jet said we can fly them over whenever they like and vice versa.

But living in LA means seeing Mum again. We've spoken since everything happened, but it's been strained. It kills me that after all these years, we still don't have the relationship I dreamed about. She's adamant she wants to repair it and has arranged joint therapy sessions for us. I'll go. She's still my mother, no matter what. But I'm not sure it'll ever be the way it could have been.

"Stop worrying."

"I'm not."

"Ava," he clips.

I smile and take his hand, wrapping my fingers through his.

"Maybe a little," I admit.

I asked Mum not to talk about the movie when we speak. I need to bury it, leave it behind me now, or it'll just stop me from moving on. Ophelia said she'll send me an advance copy of it when it's ready. I'll watch it. But once will be enough. I saw my father and the pilot die for real. I don't need to keep reliving it again.

I don't need to see that lost girl anymore.

I look up and catch Jet watching me.

"Nothing better than looking at a guy and finding him already staring at you." Liv's words ring in my head and I smile.

"You're okay, Ava," he says softly.

A statement, not a question. Because he knows me. I am okay. I'm not screaming to be seen anymore. I'm not alone.

He pulls me to my feet, grabbing our matching carry-ons that he's stacked on top of each other with his other hand.

"Ready?" He arches a dark brow.

"Not quite."

Before he can say anything, I grab his tie and pull him to me, kissing him hard.

"Now I am." I smile and kiss him again. "I love you," I whisper against his lips. "I can't wait to marry you."

Bright, dazzling blue pins me in place as I move back.

Then his lips curl up a fraction.

The Jet Grant smile.

Rare.

Unique.

Mine.

He takes my hand, his thumb dusting over the diamond. "It can't come soon enough," he rasps.

"You know we're serving grapefruit cocktails in bottles at the wedding, right? No glasses."

I smirk as he growls, his fingers twitching against mine.

"Don't think I won't pull your dress up and yank your panties off so I can spank your bare ass on a plane full of people if I have to."

I laugh and press another kiss to his lips. His eyes darken as I bat my eyelashes, playing with him.

"I thought you might say that, so I made it easier for you. Check your pocket."

He narrows his eyes at me as he puts his hand into his pants pocket. His jaw ticks, his brows pulling low as he finds his present.

I reach up and whisper in his ear, "They're the ones you got messy before we left."

I move back, enjoying the way the vein in his temple throbs as he casts his eyes around the airline lounge. A muscle in his cheek tightens as he lowers his voice, barely above a growled whisper.

"Goddamn, Ava."

"You're welcome," I breathe, kissing him on the cheek, right over the twitching muscle.

He grumbles something, but I miss it as an announcement plays over the speakers. He looks at me, tightening his grip on my hand. I squeeze it back in response.

"Come on. Time to go."

I nod, emotion suddenly bubbling in my throat.

Happiness, safety, adventure.

They aren't *so close* anymore.

They're here.

They're him.

He looks at me in understanding, taking hold of my chin and tilting it up so he can kiss me gently.

"If you're not happy in LA, we'll move. Or William can move over. I'll build him a house. Liv too."

I smile at how serious his handsome face is. My beautiful, complicated, grumpy man. Ready to do anything for me.

"I am happy. And I'll be happy living in LA with you, listening to you skip like a lunatic at 6AM. What's your record now?"

"Nine fifty."

"Nine hundred and fifty," I muse, running my fingers down his tie as he watches me. "You're insane."

He places his hand over mine and holds it against his chest.

"I'm obsessed." His lips curl up a fraction.

"I love you," I say again. I tell him so much, but he only seems to want to hear it more. It's like he's finally given himself permission to accept it. To embrace it.

"I love you, too, Firefly." He kisses my forehead. "Now let's go."

"Is it time?"

"It is."

His eyes meet mine as the announcement repeats; the female voice signaling a new adventure.

"Final call for Atlantic Airways flight 77 to Los Angeles, boarding at Gate 22."

Epilogue - Jet

"Nervous?"

I keep my attention fixed on the other end of the petal-covered aisle.

"No."

Jay chuckles and slaps a hand onto my shoulder. "Could have fooled me. Listen, getting married is the best thing you'll ever do."

"I know that," I grunt in response.

I'm not nervous about marrying Ava. I can't fucking wait to add a second ring to the one of mine she's already wearing and show the whole world that she's mine forever.

But she should be nervous after what I found out this morning.

The string quartet continue to play as we all wait for the bride to arrive. I catch my father's eye, and he raises his brows at the ice sculptures shaped like waterlilies that I had specially flown in. I shake my head at him as he smirks.

No, she didn't ask for them. Ava never asks for a thing. But it doesn't mean I'm not going to try and give her the world.

Give her everything.

Because Goddamn, it makes me a sap, but I love that woman with every drop of blood in my body. And I'd bleed them all out onto the floor if it meant seeing her smile.

"Where is she?" I hiss at Jay.

"Relax. Wait until you have kids, then you'll get used to waiting on other people all the time." He laughs, easily falling into his role as a supportive friend and best man.

I stiffen at his words, my palm twitching.

I force myself to take a slow, deep breath as I wait.

Holly and their two daughters, Summer and Sydney, are sitting with Matt and Stefan. The group of them are in deep conversation with Hayden and his boyfriend and girlfriend. He catches me looking and throws me a cocky wink. How the bastard has time to work and keep two people happy in their relationship, I don't know. But he's been doing a great job. Atlantic Airways have now taken delivery of all of our new engines; Callaghan's, and the second batch direct from Logan Rich. Business is thriving.

I should be able to step back, breathe a little.

But I can't.

Not knowing what I know now.

Jay pats my shoulder in support again as the string quartet move into another song.

Still no sign of her.

My gaze tracks over the other guests, settling on Zena. If I wasn't already wound tight as a spring, then the sight of her would do it. She looks remorseful, her shoulders curling down as she meets my eyes. I clench my jaw and offer her a nod. She returns it. I should at least be grateful she's trying for Ava. Mitch was no longer on the scene when we returned to LA. And Zena's kept to her word, never mentioning the movie, and being there for all of her and Ava's therapy sessions. Ava comes home a little brighter after each one, but it still tears my heart out to see the pain in her eyes whenever her mother is mentioned.

Jay leans closer to me, his voice lowering in seriousness. "You sure you want to do this? You look like you're about to blow an artery."

"Of course I fucking want to. She's my life."

He leans back, holding his palms up.

"I'm sorry," I grumble.

"It's okay."

He gives me a reassuring smile. The last time we were together in London was for my mother's funeral. I don't have many friends, but he's always been there for me.

"It's not. I'm sorry." I sigh. "I just can't wait any longer to see her."

"She's coming," he says. "Don't worry."

"I'm not worried," I reply, my eyes tracking back to the end of the aisle.

I can feel Jay studying the grimace on my face, but he's a good friend and says nothing more as I continue to wait for my fiancée to appear.

My fiancée, who I'm going to spank until her ass is red later for what she left me as a gift this morning.

This time, it wasn't panties with a plane and a fucking IOU.

It was something I never dared dream I'd have.

Epilogue - Ava

"You look stunning."

I stand on the gravel driveway of the Silver Estate after stepping out of the car and twirling in front of Liv and Gramps. The long train on my dress kicks up, encircling me in a spinning mass of white as each of the hundreds of silk waterlilies sewn onto the fabric ruffle with the movement.

"Gorgeous, isn't it?" I grin down at my dress. The dress that Jet paid for with his black AMEX.

I find it hard accepting his money, even though he keeps telling me he's a billionaire and growling when I don't let him buy me things. Except lingerie and bespoke wedding dresses covered in waterlilies, because well, a girl has some things she can't resist.

But when I can, I like to pay for things myself. And the job I got working for a casting company means I can sometimes afford to surprise him. I love seeing the look on his face when I do. The lowering of those brows as he tells me not to spend my money on him. The deep grit of his voice, like I've been a bad girl.

The inevitable spankings that follow.

He claims he doesn't want my surprises. But judging by how hard they make him, and what he does to me after, I disagree.

Jet Grant loves my playful surprises.

Just like I'm hoping he'll love the one I left for him this morning.

I take a deep breath, smoothing my hands down my dress.

"You ready, love?" Gramps asks, holding out his hand.

I bite my lower lip and nod. I've never felt more ready.

I slide my hand into his, the heat of his palm against mine bringing a sense of calm to my hammering heart. The same way it did when Ophelia sent me the advanced copy of the movie she promised. I sat between Gramps and Jet when I watched it. One hand held by each of them.

And I cried.

I cried as I watched it all play out, Hollywood style.

And I sobbed hardest as I watched the young actress nail her part. *Her* part. Because it didn't feel like I was watching myself on that screen. I'd already left that girl in the past the moment I wrote 'The End' on my story. It's no longer mine. It's no longer the one I'm stuck in, reliving day after day, night after night.

The two men either side of me as I sobbed have made sure of that. I lost my father that day. But I didn't lose myself. At least, not forever.

Getting ready this morning in my old bedroom, I stared at the picture on the wall. The picture I willed myself to remember when I was lost in the forest, to pretend I was home. And safe.

It was of a glowing beach.

I'm not sure how much I believe in fate. But looking at it this morning as I stepped into my wedding dress made my breath catch. I always meant to visit it one day. I know it. I just didn't know I'd be falling in love with a man who claimed love was a game he'd never play when I did go there.

"Your father would be so proud of you," Gramps says as he leads me around the large stately home and to the rear lawn to where everyone is waiting.

Liv looks back from in front of us, holding her bridesmaid's bouquet in her hand.

"He would, Bitch."

I laugh as she grins at me, effectively halting potential make-up wrecking tears in their wake with her words.

"I love you both."

"We love you, too," she replies.

We reach the bottom of the aisle and heat hits me like a force, making the air whoosh from my lungs.

"I hope he's going to at least try and smile for the photos," Gramps mutters.

I meet Jet's dark, burning gaze. I can't help but smile. He's glowering at me like he's mad.

My core buzzes to life in response. I'm guessing he found my gift.

We walk up the aisle behind Liv. Even some of the guests are starting to look puzzled at the intensity on Jet's face.

But I can't keep the smile off mine.

He shakes Gramps's hand as we reach the top of the aisle, nodding at him, before his eyes immediately return to me. The heat in them makes goosebumps dance up my spine as I kiss Gramps and hand my flowers to Liv to hold.

"Ava," he clips under his breath the moment we're left standing facing one another.

"Jet."

One dark brow hitches in question and I nod.

"Goddamn." He exhales, pinching the bridge of his nose. "Let's make this quick," he says to the minister.

I bite back my laugh as there is a confused rumble from the guests.

"The shortest version you've got," he snaps, glancing at the minister, a man who now looks positively petrified.

Jay leans forward and says something in Jet's ear, but he shakes his head, muttering back, *"She knows why."*

His eyes return to mine, pinning me in place as we repeat our vows to one another. Jet delivers them perfectly, the intensity in his gaze racking higher and higher with each word. Until they've all been spoken.

"You may now kiss your—"

Jet's mouth is on mine before the minister finishes, causing a ripple of laughter through our guests. He holds my face in his hands kissing me the way he did when I ran to him in the airport after six months apart.

Then he pulls away and grabs my hand, turning and pulling me back down the aisle.

I smile at our guests as he strides along, taking me with him. Some of them look puzzled, but the ones that know him well don't seem fazed. Hayden even gives me a knowing smile.

"Ava," Jet barks, willing me to hurry up.

"I have five-inch heels on," I retort.

Grunting, he lifts me, gathering me up into his arms, my dress spilling out like a cloud around us.

Then he storms off with me like a caveman as amused cheers echo behind us.

"This is so romantic. You did all this?"

I look around in awe at the candlelit pathway that's been set up beside the waterlily lake. It leads to a patch of grass covered in blankets and cushions, protected overhead by a sheer draped awning strung with fairy lights.

"Fuck the romance." Jet lowers to his knees and places me down on to the blankets, his movements soft, even though his voice is rough. "Are you...?"

His blue eyes round onto me, his dark brows lifting in hope. I know exactly what he's asking.

I gaze back, mesmerized.

"Yes," I whisper.

"Goddamn." He screws his face up and crushes his lips against mine, making me fall back onto the cushions as he kisses me. He fights to push the layers of my dress out of the way, his hands urgent as they search for my skin beneath silk.

"Feeling eager for something, *husband*?" I tease.

He pauses his ravaging kiss long enough to look into my eyes. His pupils dilate as he pants against my mouth, tension rolling off him in waves.

"My *wife*," he growls hoarsely, "thinks it's acceptable to leave a pregnancy test wrapped up in her panties in the pocket of my wedding suit. I'm not eager... I'm fucking fuming."

His hands find my ass beneath my dress, and he squeezes it with both hands as a deep, skin-tingling groan leaves his lips.

"You're pregnant, Ava. And you told me when you knew I'd have to wait hours to see you."

He sucks on the swell of my breast above the tight bodice as his hard dick strains in his suit pants against my thigh.

"You made me wait when you knew telling me would mean I've never needed to be inside you so badly."

"Even more than when we were apart?" I ask.

He slides one hand between my thighs. I arch my back as he palms my pussy possessively, wetness seeping through my panties and onto his skin.

"Even then," he grits, shoving my dress up around my waist so he can see me.

He tuts as he moves his hand away and looks at my soaked panties.

"These are ridiculous." He trails a finger down the center, making me writhe for more friction. "So tiny and thin. You can see your greedy cunt right through them."

"You bought them for me," I whimper as he circles my clit through the sheer fabric.

"I bought them for my fiancée to wear when she married me. But only so I could do this."

He hooks a finger beneath the fabric, tearing through it with one easy flick of his wrist. Cool air hits my clit and I moan.

But it's quickly replaced by the heat of his body as he pushes my knees up to my chest and leans over me. He holds my eyes as he undoes his pants with one hand and frees his cock.

The second the thick head swipes through my wetness, I whimper.

"So fucking needy," he tsks. "Putting a baby inside you wasn't enough, huh? You're a greedy girl who wants to be fucked more, aren't you?"

"God, yes," I moan, not even trying to deny it. I love how filthy Jet is. And it's only gotten better since I moved in with him. He has constant access to me now, and it's like it's unlocked even more dirty desires from him. The only break he's given me is when I was sick for a day last month. The day I couldn't keep anything down, including my birth control pill. I knew this could happen, but the chance was so small that I never said anything to him when I was late.

I waited until this morning to take that test.

If it had been negative, he'd have still gotten the panties inside his jacket pocket. But something about the dark primal look in his eyes tells me he's glad it wasn't just those he found.

"Tell me," he urges, tipping his chin.

"Spit on me," I moan.

His eyes flash and he pulls back, spitting on my clit. The shock of it hitting me makes me jerk, before sending my clit into a deep, desperate throb.

"Please," I beg.

He leans back over me, one hand grasping the base of his cock. He taps the broad head against my clit, before moving it in circles, rubbing his spit all over me.

"How badly do you want to get fucked, Mrs. Grant?"

I shiver at the way my new name sounds coming from his mouth.

"Until you're running down my thighs." I bite my lip, blinking up at him, relief blooming in my chest as I see the moment he snaps behind his eyes.

I don't think I could have waited a second longer.

He pushes inside me with a rough curse, and I exhale with a satisfied moan as I stretch around him. We stare at each other, our chests rising, skimming each other with each breath.

"I love you," Jet murmurs, softness passing through his eyes briefly.

"I love you, too."

"We're having a baby," he chokes.

"I know."

"A baby," he repeats in awe. "When did you find out?"

"Only this morning."

He nods and drops his gaze to the swell of my breasts as he pulls back and thrusts inside me. They bounce with his movement, and he does it again, his eyes fixated on them.

"Fuck, I wish I could suck on your tits, Ava," he groans.

"Me, too," I moan, arching them up toward his mouth even though my dress is fastened too tight to be able to get it off easily and allow him access.

He dips his head, sucking on the swell of my other breast not quite hard enough to leave any evidence.

"You know if we didn't have to go back into our wedding after this, that you'd be wearing my mark all over you," he rasps into my neck as he moves his mouth up it in nipping kisses.

"I know." I lean to the side, allowing him easier access to where my pulse is thundering in my neck. He sucks on it, making me whimper.

"Tell me you love me."

"I love you."

He lifts his head, resting his forehead against mine.

"Good." He thrusts inside me again. "Girl." *Thrust.* "Good." *Thrust.* "Fucking." *Thrust.* "Wife."

He moves up onto arms and slams into me, building up a pace that has us both panting and gasping for air.

"You're going to go back out there to our guests with your husband's cum running down your thighs. What do you think about that?"

"Do it," I urge.

"You'd like that, wouldn't you?" He tsks, thrusting so deep that his balls hit my skin each time with a solid thud. "Cutting the cake while you feel me dripping from your cunt. Full of my cum... Full of our baby."

His words are my undoing and I come hard, arching up beneath him. He slams my body back to the ground as he bears down onto me, his hand curled around my throat so he can kiss me through my orgasm. I cry out against his mouth as he hits the angle that always sends me spinning, and I tumble into another deep orgasm, my body squeezing him in desperate pulses.

"Fuck, Ava."

He grunts as he comes long and hard, spilling inside me. His thrusts slow but stay hard and deep as he empties himself inside me, his thumb stroking the column of my neck.

He leans down and captures my lips in a lingering kiss. "My wife."

He lets go of my neck and places it between our bodies and onto my stomach. "Our baby," he rasps. "You're both my fucking world."

I look up at him, the breath returning to my body as every inch of my skin tingles with energy.

"They're going to have the most amazing daddy," I whisper with a smile.

He shakes his head and pulls out, before moving down my body and pressing a kiss to my stomach.

"The strongest mummy," he murmurs against my skin, his eyes fixed on mine.

He slides lower and lifts my legs, placing them over his shoulders one by one. Then he drags his tongue over me, his eyelids hooding with an appreciative groan as he drinks up our combined taste.

"We should get back," I say, stroking my fingers through his hair.

"In a minute."

"Jet," I murmur.

My protest only spurs him on, and he starts to lick, suck, and tease me with his mouth.

"I've got all I need here, Firefly."

He flattens his palm over my stomach and holds my eyes as he slides his tongue up inside me. He circles it around, dragging it out and swallowing with a curse.

"You sure? You don't need time to think about it?" I hum, watching the way his eyes darken as he swallows his own cum mixed with mine. I've never seen anything hotter.

"Don't fucking play with me, Ava," he warns, sliding two fingers inside me as his hand strokes my stomach protectively.

I moan at how good both feel.

Our guests won't miss us for a little longer.

"Husband?" I whisper.

"Wife?"

I grip his hair and pull him into me more.

"I'll never get tired of playing with you."

I feel his sharp intake of air against me before he slowly releases it over my clit, making me shudder.

"And I won't ever let you," he says in a low gravelly husk.

"Now either come on my tongue, or I'll spank you so hard you'll spend the first year of our marriage unable to sit."

Laughing, I part my thighs wider.

"Sounds like my kind of game. Let's play, Mr. Grant."

The (Almost) End.

Bonus Epilogue - Ava

Five Years Later

"Don't fidget," Jet clips, his fingers flexing around mine as he leads me toward the ballroom.

"I'm not," I argue.

He halts abruptly, turning a heated gaze on me from beneath his dark brows.

"Is it the new..." His tongue rolls over his lower lip, his eyes dropping over my champagne-colored silk dress. "...lingerie I bought for you? Is it uncomfortable?"

"No, it's perfect. I'm just concerned you can see the back of it," I say, twisting my exposed skin in the plunging back of my dress toward him.

"You can't, Ava."

"Are you sure?" I ask, feigning concern and smoothing the silk over my ass, making sure to pull it low enough for Jet to see the giant diamond at the top of my G-string.

My skin heats at the animalistic glint in his eyes.

"I'm sure," he replies, his voice strained.

"It seems a shame to cover up something so beautiful," I hum.

"I know what you're doing, Firefly."

"What?"

I smile as he cups my ass. Groaning, he squeezes it, brushing his thumb over the five-carat Beaufort diamond he had added as a surprise for our wedding anniversary yesterday. I'd very innocently reminded him that the traditional gift for five years is wood, to which he'd chuckled and called me a brat.

God, I love my husband.

"When you've quite finished making me want to take you somewhere so I can spank your ass, can we go back inside? I need to show my face a little longer before I take you to our suite and rip this dress off."

I giggle and spin inside his arms, reaching up around his neck to toy with the hair at the nape of his neck. "Okay, seeing as you asked so nicely. It is your party, after all."

His eyes twinkle when I press a kiss to his lips.

"It's everyone's party. Everyone who's played a part in making the airline what it is." His voice softens. "I couldn't have done it without them. And I couldn't do anything without you, Leah, and Ace."

"You getting sappy on me, *Daddy?*" I smile softly.

"Mm," he grunts, smiling.

I love these moments with Jet. He's more likely to buy me diamond encrusted gifts and act fiercely protective over me and the kids to show his love for us.

But every now and then, I get this.

Whispered words that make my heart skip a beat.

And his smile.

He leads us into the ballroom and my breath hitches. The space has been transformed. Everything has been decorated in Atlantic Airways' signature red and white. Thousands of glittering paper stars hang from the ceiling, and in their center is a paper replica of Jet's mother's plane. The real one still sits in our hallway in LA. The kids love it, and no matter how many times I see Jet hoisting them up to sit inside it, my heart always swells so much it feels like it could burst.

I squeeze his hand and he squeezes mine back.

Jet chose The Songbird hotel in New York to host the airline's fiftieth birthday party. It coincides with the year they also won the prestigious 'Best Airline of the Year' award for the tenth year running. People from all over the globe who work for Atlantic Airways are here. Along with customers who are members of their loyalty program.

I suggested to Jet that he run a competition open to the public, to win an all-expenses paid vacation to New York, as well as be guests to the party. A family from France with four children won it and were ecstatic because they've never won anything before.

That also led to my second suggestion; that we hire children's entertainers and make the party a family event. So many industry dinners and events that I accompany Jet to are formal and stuffy. Atlantic Airways is a family business, founded by Jet's great grandfather.

It felt right that we include children on all of the invitations.

Jet takes two flutes of champagne from a passing server and hands one to me. His other hand moves to my lower back, resting over the diamond beneath my dress.

"Are you trying to work out how he's doing it?" I ask as we approach the area that's been designated as the children's zone.

My grandfather shakes his head as we walk over to join him.

"He had me with the pigeon inside his hat. Must have been in there the whole time." He chuckles as a magician continues his set at the front of an enthralled group of kids sitting on the floor.

He's turned down multiple offers to move to LA to live near us. He loves his house, says it's where his fondest memories are; the ones of me growing up there with him. Plus, he argues that Magnus needs him around. The two spend a lot of time together. But I miss not living close enough to see Gramps every day.

My mother, on the other hand, lives close by. Despite going to therapy sessions together, our relationship is still tarnished by what she did. I can tell she's trying to make up for it by being the best grandmother she can be, and I love that the children are able to have that from her. Jet tolerates her for me. But our relationship will never be a close one.

It makes me even more determined to be a good mum.

"Where's Leah?" I ask Gramps.

Her little brother, Ace, is sitting cross-legged in the front row, eyes wide as he watches the magician. But Leah isn't with the other children.

Gramps smiles and jerks his head to one side where some children are playing.

"That's too noisy! The guests are sleeping!" a little boy yells.

Leah ignores him, making exaggerated take-off noises as she flies her toy plane over the boy's giant building he's constructed in intricate detail from Lego.

He jumps to his feet, standing more than a few inches taller than her. "Fly your plane somewhere else," he complains.

"You built your hotel near the airport." Leah shrugs.

His eyes volley between the plane and his building, his brow furrowed in thought. "How much to change your route?" he asks seriously.

"You can't afford it," our daughter replies breezily.

"That's my girl," Jet murmurs, watching their exchange.

I elbow him gently in the side, biting back my smile.

"Try me," the little boy replies, folding his arms and arching a brow at her.

Our daughter purses her lips, assessing him in his small navy suit. They face one another in a silent stand-off of wills.

"Is he causing trouble?" a female voice asks.

I glance over to the couple who've appeared beside us—the hotel owner, Griffin Parker, and his wife, Maria.

"He's negotiating, Sweetheart. Leave him to it," Griffin says, his eyes sliding to Jet's. The two smirk at one another in understanding.

A small girl races through the space, narrowly missing taking out both Leah and the boy.

"Daddy!" she squeals, jumping into Griffin's arms.

"Hello, Darling," he says, pressing a kiss to her cheek.

"Uncle Reed said I can ride in his car with him, Auntie Harley, Ryder, and Hope, before they go back home. And that we can put the sirens on."

"Pidge," Maria says. "I'm not sure Uncle Reed will have time to do that."

Griffin grumbles something about the use of bird nicknames, shooting a look at Maria that makes her smile.

"*Malin*," he says, emphasizing her name, "you can tell Uncle Reed that's fine. The White House can wait while my son and daughter take a ride around the city."

"Yes!' The little girl grins.

Maria shakes her head. "I guess it would be rude to say no when you're invited by the President himself."

Malin wrinkles her nose. "It's just Uncle Reed."

I catch Jet's eye. Who would have known that the President would be at Atlantic Airways' party? Apparently he and Griffin have been friends for years, and his family were regular flyers with the airline, visiting his wife's sister in England, before he was elected and started using Air Force One.

A squeal of laughter comes from the kids watching the magic show, where the magician has pulled an adult from the audience. The man, a handsome older guy with salt and pepper hair, is asked to hand over his wedding ring, but he shakes his head and takes off his watch instead, handing it to the magician.

"Jaxon King," Jet whispers.

"The head of the publishing company?"

He nods and my stomach does a little leap of excitement.

"I'll introduce you once he's free."

"Please," I breathe as the magician makes his watch disappear, to the delight of the kids and a woman with amazing red curls, and a girl with matching ones, who are standing to one side, watching.

"His wife, Megan, and their daughter, Nevaeh," Jet adds.

My husband's memory for names and details astounds me. A lot of people in the room he might have only met once, years ago, but he remembers them all.

I've heard of Jaxon King because his publishing company has expressed an interest in the story I'm working on as head of casting. We've got Trent Forde directing the movie and I can't wait. He's renowned for his company's special effects, and we're definitely going to need the pyrotechnics to accurately depict the tragic events that occur.

It's about the Beauforts. One of New York's wealthiest families, known for Beaufort Diamonds, a luxury jewelry brand that's coveted worldwide, and has been commissioned by royal families to design unique pieces. But they've been a constant source of press attention since what happened a few years ago. Sterling Beaufort, the father of the family, finally decided to share their story with the world. Jet thinks it was to be free from speculation and to get the truth out. But I think it's to give hope. To show that no matter what happens, your family is always your family. Maybe it's also a tool to aid healing from their past. I understand that more than anyone.

None of the Beauforts are here, but I did meet a woman named Sophie earlier, a friend of Sterling's wife. She's a lawyer from London and is pregnant. We chatted while her husband stood with his business partner, whose wife works for Atlantic Airways as a flight attendant, and they kept an eye on their collective brood of eight kids. Both men wore equally exhausted, proud, father smiles.

"I need to go and speak to some people," Jet says discreetly in my ear.

"I'll come with you."

"Go. I'll keep an eye on them," Gramps says, his eyes creasing at the corners as he watches his great granddaughter, still *negotiating* with Griffin and Maria's son.

We spend the next forty minutes chatting to Logan Rich and his wife, Maddy. Logan's the engineer who designed the eco engines that saved Atlantic Airways.

He's here with his friend, Dax, and his wife, Rose, who run the British distillery that provides the UK part of the airline with Aunt Iris's gin. The US supplier and owner of the recipe is also here; a woman named Daisy. I've met her and her husband, Blake, plenty of times because Blake is Jay Anderson's brother, and he, Daisy, and their four kids are often at Jay and Holly's house when we go over. The entire neighborhood knows when we're all there. The noise the kids make is quite something.

"You're fidgeting again," Jet clips.

"I'm not," I protest. But I subtly sway my hips so that Jet's hand presses more firmly against my lower back, flattening the diamond against my skin. I love the feel of it there. It's the most exquisite lingerie I've ever owned.

"Then why are you grinding your ass into my palm like you want me to spank it?"

"I just like reminding myself of what a beautiful piece I'm wearing." I blink up at him and his jaw tightens.

I drain the remainder of my latest flute of champagne.

"Would you look at that?" I hum, tilting the empty glass so the crystal catches the light. "It's empty. I should get a refill."

His nostrils flare and his fingers entwine with my free hand, before he strides across the room. I rush in my heels to keep up.

"Where are we going?"

"You'll see," he grits, tugging me into the hotel's main reception area.

He pauses briefly with his head in the direction of the elevators before he pulls me along in the other direction.

"And here's me thinking you were going to take me up to our suite for something." I giggle.

He shoots a blistering look over his shoulder at me. "There isn't time for that, Ava. But believe me, as soon as the kids are in bed tonight, I'll be marking that ass of yours bright red while I do with you as I please."

I wet my lips in anticipation. "Can't wait."

"Such a needy wife," Jet tsks.

He stalks down an opulently decorated hallway and stops in front of a closed door. He reaches for the handle when a muffled whimper comes from inside.

"Griff..."

"Fuck, Sweetheart, you like that?"

"I think this one's taken." I bite back my laugh as Jet's nostrils flare and he pulls me further down the hallway, then tries a door on the opposite wall.

It opens to reveal a small storage closet.

"In," he growls.

I peer inside. There's barely room to move around a large table in the middle of the space. The walls are lined with shelving filled with hotel brochures and stationery supplies.

"I said in, Ava," he repeats.

He yanks on our joined hands when I don't move and places mine over his erection.

"Unless you want me to make you come out here, *Wife*, then I suggest you do as I tell you."

I scrabble to get into the closet and Jet pushes in behind me, closing the door with a thud. His piercing blue eyes lock onto mine and for a few seconds we just stare at one another.

"Are you just going to stand there?" I tease, twirling my empty glass by the stem.

Jet steps forward so I'm trapped between him and the table.

"No. But you are." He extracts the glass from my hand and calmly places it onto a shelf. "Turn around."

"Why?" I bite my lower lip, knowing I'll be getting to him by not doing as he says.

He arches a brow at me, his look hot enough to burn. "Ava," he warns.

I slowly do as he says. His tongue clicks against the roof of his mouth in disapproval.

"I married a brat," he murmurs, stepping closer until his breath skates down the back of my neck. "You've always needed me to take care of you in a certain way, haven't you? I shouldn't let you get away with testing my patience the way you insist upon doing."

"If you say so," I breathe, a shiver of anticipation coursing through me as he drags the tip of one finger down the dip of my spine. He grunts as he pulls my dress lower, so the diamond encrusted G-string is exposed.

"I do say so," he clips, taking his time to admire my lingerie, running his finger between the lace and my skin like he's contemplating what to do with me.

It's a slow torture as he slowly inches the silk of my dress up my thighs, inch by inch, until it's gathered just beneath my ass.

"Bend over, hands on the table," he growls.

I don't argue this time. I lean forward, presenting myself how he wants.

"Good girl," he croons, pushing the fabric all the way up over the curve of my ass cheeks until it pools beneath my ribs.

He steps closer and his hard cock presses against my ass.

"Fuck, you look good like this." One palm kneads my ass, while the sound of his zipper being pulled down fills the tiny space.

"Jet," I whine.

He gives my ass a soft slap that makes me cry out. "Greedy girl. You'll get this cock, but when I'm ready."

"Fine," I huff, and I swear I feel his smirk burn into my back.

"I want to watch you come in these sexy little panties you've got me addicted to buying you first."

"*Needing* to buy me because you keep tearing them all," I say as he hooks a skilled finger beneath the fabric.

"They're flimsy. It's not my fault that they can't withstand the way we fuck."

I whimper as he swipes through my wetness, gathering some on his fingertip before working it inside me slowly.

"Yes," I moan, rocking back against his hand as he draws his finger out, then pushes back in with two.

He finger-fucks me leisurely, massaging my ass cheek and pulling it open so he can watch his fingers disappear inside me.

"Fuck," he hisses; his dick leaking pre-cum over my skin.

He replaces his hand with the head of his cock and uses it to rub the wetness over me. But he's purposely keeping a distance from where I ache to feel him.

"Touch my clit," I plead.

He stops moving, making me do all the work as I circle over his hand. Making me beg for it. My cheeks heat with frustration as I try unsuccessfully to take his fingers deeper.

"Jet... Please."

"I'll make you come, Ava, you know I will. But I'll do it my way. And on my timescale. And right now, I want to watch your pretty wet cunt as it sucks in my fingers."

"Asshole," I mutter, as he jerks himself off behind me.

I'm not mad, not really. Our hottest sex always starts like this. With him establishing control and me pretending to be outraged. The truth is, I get off on it as much as he does, and he knows it.

He groans, moving his fingers again, and fucking me with them in time to his strokes of his dick. "See, not so hard doing as you're told, is it?"

I pant, desperately chasing the growing high that's building inside me.

Then he stops, and his fingers disappear.

I squeal in frustration.

Seconds later, his hot tongue swipes through my flesh from behind as he pulls my panties out of the way. I almost collapse in relief as he kneels behind me and eats me out like he's ravenous.

"Fuck..." he grits, between fevered sucks and kisses. "Mine. So fucking sweet and mine."

He grips both of my ass cheeks, pulling them apart, then laps at my asshole. I moan as he teases it, before returning his attention forward again.

"Bend lower," he barks.

I drop my upper body against the table, the metal like a shot of cold water as I rest my cheek on it.

"Better," he rasps, pushing deeper as the angle allows me to open more for him.

His tongue seeks out my swollen clit and flattens against it.

"Jet," I pant, tension building in my core.

"Come on my tongue so I can fuck these panties in you," he growls.

"Yes," I whimper, not correcting him in case it gives him reason to withhold my orgasm as punishment.

A few more confident strokes of his tongue, and I come hard against his mouth, my legs shaking in my heels. He keeps lavishing attention on my clit, easily pulling another orgasm from me until I'm writhing against the metal table and whimpering his name.

I catch my breath as he eases my panties down.

"I thought you wanted to fuck me in those," I breathe.

His palm flattens over my ass cheek, and he massages it, grunting appreciatively. "No, I said I was going to fuck them in you."

I frown in confusion.

Buttery-soft material is pushed inside me with strong, determined fingers, and I gasp.

"Of course, we need to find another place for this while I do. It's a good job that you've got my cock leaking so hard for you, my darling wife. Because it'll make this easier."

I turn to look over my shoulder, just in time to see him squeeze the head of his cock, then smear drops of pre-cum over something out of view.

He looks up, jerking his chin arrogantly as something smooth and hard is eased inside my ass.

"You did not just put a five-carat diamond there," I gasp.

"Five carats is nothing... Wait until our ten-year anniversary." His eyes darken dangerously.

He pushes inside me, stuffing his cock in beside the lace that's already there.

"Jesus," he hisses.

His eyes drop to where he's bottoming out inside me. There's no time for slow and gentle.

"Ava," he growls, his eyes snapping up to mine. He grips my hips hard, his fingertips tight enough to leave bruises.

"Jet," I mewl.

He fucks me like an animal with rough, deep thrusts. The tendons in his neck pop as his torso strains with the effort of holding back.

"You can let go, I want it," I cry, my body getting pushed against the table with each hard rut into me.

"You know what you need to do first," he forces out between gritted teeth.

I hold his eyes as I hand myself over to the arousal flooding my body and give him what he wants. I cry out his name as I come with the lace G-string stuffed inside me, and a diamond worth over one hundred and fifty thousand dollars nestled in my ass.

My muscles clench in unison around the gem and his cock as I shake beneath him.

"Fuck yes," he groans as he explodes.

His balls push against me, and his thrusts slow, but he pushes deeper, insistent on emptying every drop. "I love you," he groans, holding himself deep with a final thrust. "God, do I love you."

His chest heaves and his eyes fix onto mine. The love that's entwined with desire makes my heart pang, and the moment he caresses the side of my face I almost lose it.

"I love you, too," I whisper, leaning into his touch.

His lips curl at the corners as we stare at one another.

He takes his time, gently removing the diamond first, then pulling out and easing the soaking lace from inside me.

I move to stand, but Jet commands me to stay with a deep growl as he pulls his zipper back up.

Cool glass grazes my inner thighs.

"You know what to do," he says.

I squeeze my inner muscles, releasing and contracting around where he was stretching me moments ago. Warm liquid runs from inside me.

Jet sucks in a sharp breath. "Good girl."

He places the flute on the table, and I eye the fluid inside it. Helping me up, he smooths the silk of my dress down, fixing it into place.

I turn to face him, but he's so close I'm wedged between him and the table. His eyes drop to my lips as he picks the glass up.

"Happy anniversary, Firefly."

My lips part on instinct.

"Cheers," he says, before tilting his head back and draining the contents of the glass.

His blue eyes glitter as he swallows, the strong muscles in his neck contracting.

"Now open wide," he instructs.

I do as he says, and he cups my face and kisses me, filling my mouth with his tongue, swirling it around mine until I have to break away to breathe.

"You taste that?" he rasps.

"Yes. It tastes like us."

He runs his thumb over my lower lip. "Us," he repeats.

Standing at the front of the crowd, I watch with pride as Jet speaks. He's a vision. All dark hair, dark tuxedo, penetrating blue eyes that scan the crowd as he delivers each word with charm and precision.

"I want to thank you all for coming here today to celebrate fifty years of Atlantic Airways with us. My great grandfather, Cedric, founded this airline after serving in the British Royal Air Force during World War Two. Those years fueled his love of flying, and so, with little more than a dream, the money in his pocket, and a stubbornness that was bordering on deranged..."

A laugh rumbles through the audience.

"... he started working as a pilot while learning more about the business side of running an airline. Because, as he realized, there was no greater motivation than being told by his five siblings that he couldn't, to which my great grandfather simply replied, 'Watch me.'

"And so Atlantic Airways was born, with its first ever trans-Atlantic flight taking place between London and

Los Angeles, piloted by my great grandfather. My father, Magnus, then joined the business, eventually taking over as CEO." He turns his head to Magnus, who's standing beside him on stage. "And then ten years ago..."

Jet pauses, looking at his feet and taking a breath. My heart goes out to him. No matter how many years pass, he still struggles some days with the weight of his grief after losing his mother.

Magnus claps a hand on his shoulder and gives it the reassuring pat of a father who couldn't be prouder of his son.

Jet clears his throat. "Ten years ago, I moved to LA in order to invest in, and expand, the airline in the US. This airline is what it is today because of the people who have given themselves to it. Not only my family, but all of you, and everyone who places their trust in us when they choose to fly with Atlantic Airways. So thank you. Each and every one of you... thank you for making it what it is today."

A ripple of applause breaks out in the crowd. He holds a hand up to halt the clapping.

"Over the past fifty years, our crew have delivered seventeen babies onboard, assisted in two hundred and thirty-nine marriage proposals, and transported millions of people to see their loved ones around the world. And we've also had our own share of love stories."

Jet looks straight up into the crowd, his face deadly serious.

"Jay Anderson," he barks, "I still haven't forgotten that you stole one of our kindest flight attendants so you could marry her."

The crowd's heads whip toward the rear of the room where Jay and Holly are standing. Jay throws a hand up with a chuckle. "She isn't coming back, Grant, so you'd better get over it."

Holly rolls her eyes as Jay presses a kiss to her temple, and I look back just in time to see the smirk on Jet's face before he schools his expression.

"Application forms for flight attendants can be picked up by the door," he mumbles, causing another rumble of laughter through the room.

He's always been serious, but over the years I've seen a lighter side emerge. Becoming a father was a huge turning point. I don't think I'll ever get over how it feels to see your grumpy, uptight husband melt over chubby little cheeks and wriggly toes as he plays.

"To each and every one of you who have made all of this possible," he says, wrapping up, "you have mine and my family's eternal gratitude. Thank you for choosing Atlantic Airways... and we hope to see you onboard again soon."

The applause is deafening and filled with whistles and cheers. Jet walks off stage, making a beeline for me.

"Good job." I beam as he reaches me and slides his arm around my waist.

"I had a little help with my speech from my wife," he says, kissing my hair.

"Really?"

"Yep. You know she wrote an award-winning screenplay once?"

"Mm, did she?" I muse.

I've still only watched the film of what happened to me once. That was enough. But I was incredibly proud of the actors who played the part of me, my father, and the pilot who lost his life. The English actress who performed my role was so young when the movie was filmed, but she won an Oscar for her performance. And I'm so happy for her.

"So did she help you with your speech? Or did she write one and you stole it?"

Jet's eyes darken as I tilt my head back and gaze up at him, pressing my lips together so I don't laugh.

"Five years and you're ready to joke about it?" he growls.

"I'm just teasing," I say, letting my smile spread.

His hand slides lower on my back and his fingers twitch against my ass like he's fighting the need to spank me.

"I love you," I say, dusting my fingers along the set line of his jaw. It softens under my touch.

"I love you, too." His eyes warm as he gazes down at me. "Marry me."

"What?" I search his eyes in confusion. "We are married."

He shakes his head, looking at me with the intensity he has when he's focused on an exciting new business deal.

"Marry me again, Ava. Renew our vows. This ballroom is licensed for ceremonies, as are multiple other areas of the hotel, and I know there are people in this room with the necessary experience who can oversee it."

I gape at him before a laugh bubbles up from my throat. "You're serious?"

"Deadly."

"You want me to marry you again when I'm not wearing any panties, and my thighs are still wet with your—"

"I do." His eyes flash darkly as they drop to my lower stomach.

I exhale, glancing around the room at all the people.

"We can go to a quieter area. Just family and friends," he says.

I turn back to him, butterflies fluttering in my stomach. "Okay."

The corners of his lips curl up, stealing my breath. "Okay?"

I beam at him. "Let's do it."

The (Actual) End.
Want to keep reading?
Keep turning to see the other titles in The Men series.
Read them all?
Keep an eye out for Elle's new series – Beaufort Billionaires
Book 1 – The Matchmaker (Sterling's story)
Coming Soon!

PLAYING WITH MR. GRANT

Elle's Books

Playing with Mr. Grant is Book 10 in 'The Men Series', a collection of interconnected standalone stories. They can be read in any order, however, for full enjoyment, the suggested reading order is:
Meeting Mr. Anderson – Holly and Jay
Discovering Mr. X – Rachel and Tanner
Drawn to Mr. King – Megan and Jaxon
Captured by Mr. Wild – Daisy and Blake
Pleasing Mr. Parker – Maria and Griffin
Trapped with Mr. Walker – Harley and Reed
Time with Mr. Silver – Rose and Dax
Resisting Mr. Rich – Maddy and Logan
Handling Mr. Harper – Sophie and Drew
Playing with Mr. Grant – Ava and Jet
(Also available by Elle, Forget-me-nots and Fireworks, Shona and Trent's story, a novella length prequel to The Men Series)
Coming Soon
Beaufort Billionaires Series

Book 1 – The Matchmaker (Sterling's story)
Get all of Elle's books here: http://author.to/elle nicoll

About Elle

Elle Nicoll is an ex long-haul flight attendant and mum of two from the UK.
After fourteen years of having her head in the clouds whilst working at 38,000ft, she is now usually found with her head between the pages of a book reading or furiously typing and making notes on another new idea for a book boyfriend who is sweet-talking her.
Elle finds it funny that she's frequently told she looks too sweet and innocent to write a steamy book, but she never wants to stop. Writing stories about people, passion, and love, what better thing is there?
Because,
Love Always Wins
xxx
To keep up to date with the latest news and releases, find Elle in the following places, and sign up for her newsletter below;
https://landing.mailerlite.com/webforms/landing/m7a1n0

Facebook Reader Group – Love always Wins – https://www.facebook.com/groups/686742179258218
Website – https://www.ellenicollauthor.com

http://author.to/ellenicoll

facebook.com/ellenicollauthor

instagram.com/ellenicollauthor

bookbub.com/authors/elle-nicoll

pinterest.com/ellenicollauthor

tiktok.com/@authorellenicoll

goodreads.com/author/show/21415735.Elle_Nicoll

Acknowledgements

This is it! The final book in The Men Series.
Can you believe it? Here we are, eleven stories later.
Never did I imagine where this journey would take me when I wrote that first word back in September 2020 after being encouraged by the wonderful TL Swan and the rest of her supportive cygnets.
I've met so many amazing people, and made incredible memories.
There are so many people to thank for their support and help; Sara, Zee, Kelly, Rita, Taylor, Casey, Lilibet, Abi, Sherri, my amazing street and ARC team, and everyone who helps share each new release.
And a huge thanks to YOU for making all of this possible, by stepping into The Men Universe and letting these characters into your hearts.
These would just be words on a page without you.
Thank you for bringing these stories to life by reading them.
May reading continue to bring you the magic and joy of escaping between the pages when you need it most.

If you enjoyed Playing with Mr. Grant then please leave a review on Amazon and tell your friends about Ava and Jet. It helps indie authors so much.
Thank you, thank you, thank you.
xxxxx
And... because the amount of messages I have received about Sterling Beaufort, he HAD to have his story told.
This is one silver fox who does not like to be kept waiting.
So....see you for the new series(!)... Beaufort Billionaires...
Until then...
Elle x

Printed in Great Britain
by Amazon